WUTHERING HEIGHTS

EMILY BRONTË

NELSON

The Brontë sisters were born at Thornton, Yorkshire, Charlotte on 21 April 1816, Emily on 30 July 1818, and Anne on 17 January 1820. They spent a great part of their lives at Haworth, Yorkshire, of which their father was perpetual curate. Their earlier poems and novels were published under the pseudonyms of Currer, Ellis, and Acton Bell. Emily died at Haworth on 19 December 1848, Anne at Scarborough on 28 May 1849, and Charlotte (who married Rev. A. Nicholls in 1854) at Haworth on 31 March 1855. Charlotte Brontë's novels are Jane Eyre (1847), Shirley (1849), Villette (1853), and The Professor (1857). Emily Brontë's one novel is Wuthering Heights (1847). Anne Brontë's novels are Agnes Grey (1847) and The Tenant of Wildfell Hall (1848). Poems by Currer, Ellis, and Acton Bell appeared in 1846. A number of stories, poems, etc., were published posthumously.

Printed in Great Britain by
Thomas Nelson (Printers) Ltd, London and Edinburgh

Published by Thomas Nelson and Sons Ltd
36 Park Street London W1

WUTHERING HEIGHTS.

CHAPTER I.

1801.—I HAVE just returned from a visit to my landlord
—the solitary neighbour that I shall be troubled with.
This is certainly a beautiful country. In all England
I do not believe that I could have fixed on a situation
so completely removed from the stir of society—a perfect misanthropist's heaven; and Mr. Heathcliff and I
are such a suitable pair to divide the desolation between
us. A capital fellow! He little imagined how my
heart warmed towards him when I beheld his black
eyes withdraw so suspiciously under their brows, as I
rode up, and when his fingers sheltered themselves, with
a jealous resolution, still further in his waistcoat, as I
announced my name.

"Mr. Heathcliff?" I said.

A nod was the answer.

"Mr. Lockwood, your new tenant, sir. I do myself
the honour of calling as soon as possible after my arrival,
to express the hope that I have not inconvenienced you
by my perseverance in soliciting the occupation of
Thrushcross Grange. I heard yesterday you had had
some thoughts——"

"Thrushcross Grange is my own, sir," he interrupted,
wincing. "I should not allow any one to inconvenience
me, if I could hinder it. Walk in!"

The "walk in" was uttered with closed teeth, and
expressed the sentiment, "Go to the deuce." Even the

gate over which he leant manifested no sympathizing movement to the words; and I think that circumstance determined me to accept the invitation. I felt interested in a man who seemed more exaggeratedly reserved than myself.

When he saw my horse's breast fairly pushing the barrier, he did put out his hand to unchain it, and then sullenly preceded me up the causeway, calling, as we entered the court, " Joseph, take Mr. Lockwood's horse, and bring up some wine."

" Here we have the whole establishment of domestics, I suppose," was the reflection suggested by this compound order. " No wonder the grass grows up between the flags, and cattle are the only hedge-cutters."

Joseph was an elderly, nay, an old man—very old, perhaps, though hale and sinewy. " The Lord help us ! " he soliloquized in an undertone of peevish displeasure, while relieving me of my horse, looking, meantime, in my face so sourly that I charitably conjectured he must have need of divine aid to digest his dinner, and his pious ejaculation had no reference to my unexpected advent.

Wuthering Heights is the name of Mr. Heathcliff's dwelling. " wuthering " being a significant provincial adjective, descriptive of the atmospheric tumult to which its station is exposed in stormy weather. Pure, bracing ventilation they must have up there at all times, indeed. One may guess the power of the north wind blowing over the edge by the excessive slant of a few stunted firs at the end of the house, and by a range of gaunt thorns all stretching their limbs one way, as if craving alms of the sun. Happily the architect had foresight to build it strong. The narrow windows are deeply set in the wall, and the corners defended with large jutting stones.

Before passing the threshold, I paused to admire a quantity of grotesque carving lavished over the front, and especially about the principal door; above which, among a wilderness of crumbling griffins and shameless little boys, I detected the date " 1500," and the name

" Hareton Earnshaw." I would have made a few comments, and requested a short history of the place from the surly owner ; but his attitude at the door appeared to demand my speedy entrance or complete departure, and I had no desire to aggravate his impatience previous to inspecting the penetralium.

One step brought us into the family sitting-room, without any introductory lobby or passage. They call it here " the house " pre-eminently. It includes kitchen and parlour generally. But, I believe, at Wuthering Heights the kitchen is forced to retreat altogether into another quarter — at least I distinguished a chatter of tongues and a clatter of culinary utensils deep within ; and I observed no signs of roasting, boiling, or baking about the huge fireplace, nor any glitter of copper saucepans and tin cullenders on the walls. One end, indeed, reflected splendidly both light and heat from ranks of immense pewter dishes, interspersed with silver jugs and tankards, towering row after row, on a vast oak dresser, to the very roof. The latter had never been underdrawn ; its entire anatomy lay bare to an inquiring eye, except where a frame of wood laden with oatcakes and clusters of legs of beef, mutton, and ham concealed it. Above the chimney were sundry villainous old guns and a couple of horse-pistols, and, by way of ornament, three gaudily painted canisters disposed along its ledge. The floor was of smooth, white stone ; the chairs, high-backed, primitive structures painted green, one or two heavy black ones lurking in the shade. In an arch under the dresser reposed a huge liver-coloured bitch pointer surrounded by a swarm of squealing puppies, and other dogs haunted other recesses.

The apartment and furniture would have been nothing extraordinary as belonging to a homely, northern farmer, with a stubborn countenance and stalwart limbs set out to advantage in knee-breeches and gaiters. Such an individual seated in his armchair, his mug of ale frothing on the round table before him, is to be seen in any circuit of five or six miles among these hills, if you go at the

right time after dinner. But Mr. Heathcliff forms a
singular contrast to his abode and style of living. He
is a dark-skinned gipsy in aspect, in dress and manners
a gentleman—that is, as much a gentleman as many a
country squire; rather slovenly, perhaps, yet not looking amiss with his negligence, because he has an erect
and handsome figure, and rather morose. Possibly,
some people might suspect him of a degree of under-
bred pride; I have a sympathetic chord within that
tells me it is nothing of the sort. I know, by instinct,
his reserve springs from an aversion to showy displays
of feeling, to manifestations of mutual kindliness. He'll
love and hate equally under cover, and esteem it a
species of impertinence to be loved or hated again. No,
I'm running on too fast. I bestow my own attributes
over liberally on him. Mr. Heathcliff may have entirely
dissimilar reasons for keeping his hand out of the way
when he meets a would-be acquaintance to those which
actuate me. Let me hope my constitution is almost
peculiar. My dear mother used to say I should never
have a comfortable home, and only last summer I proved
myself perfectly unworthy of one.

While enjoying a month of fine weather at the sea
coast, I was thrown into the company of a most fasci-
nating creature—a real goddess in my eyes, as long as
she took no notice of me. I "never told my love"
vocally; still, if looks have language, the merest idiot
might have guessed I was over head and ears. She
understood me at last, and looked a return—the sweetest
of all imaginable looks. And what did I do? I confess
it with shame—shrank icily into myself, like a snail;
at every glance retired colder and farther, till finally the
poor innocent was led to doubt her own senses, and,
overwhelmed with confusion at her supposed mistake,
persuaded her mamma to decamp. By this curious turn
of disposition I have gained the reputation of deliberate
heartlessness; how undeserved I alone can appreciate.

I took a seat at the end of the hearthstone opposite
that towards which my landlord advanced, and filled

up an interval of silence by attempting to caress the canine mother, who had left her nursery, and was sneaking wolfishly to the back of my legs, her lip curled up, and her white teeth watering for a snatch. My caress provoked a long, guttural gnarl.

"You'd better let the dog alone," growled Mr. Heathcliff, in unison, checking fiercer demonstrations with a punch of his foot. "She's not accustomed to be spoiled —not kept for a pet." Then, striding to a side door, he shouted again, "Joseph!"

Joseph mumbled indistinctly in the depths of the cellar, but gave no intimation of ascending; so his master dived down to him, leaving me *vis-à-vis* the ruffianly bitch and a pair of grim shaggy sheep-dogs, who shared with her a jealous guardianship over all my movements. Not anxious to come in contact with their fangs, I sat still; but, imagining they would scarcely understand tacit insults, I unfortunately indulged in winking and making faces at the trio, and some turn of my physiognomy so irritated madam that she suddenly broke into a fury and leapt on my knees. I flung her back, and hastened to interpose the table between us. This proceeding roused the whole hive. Half a dozen four-footed fiends, of various sizes and ages, issued from hidden dens to the common centre. I felt my heels and coat-laps peculiar subjects of assault; and parrying off the larger combatants as effectually as I could with the poker, I was constrained to demand, aloud, assistance from some of the household in re-establishing peace.

Mr. Heathcliff and his man climbed the cellar steps with vexatious phlegm. I don't think they moved one second faster than usual, though the hearth was an absolute tempest of worrying and yelping. Happily, an inhabitant of the kitchen made more dispatch. A lusty dame, with tucked-up gown, bare arms, and fire-flushed cheeks, rushed into the midst of us flourishing a frying-pan, and used that weapon and her tongue to such purpose that the storm subsided magically, and she only remained, heaving like a sea after a high wind, when her master entered on the scene.

"What the devil is the matter?" he asked, eyeing me in a manner that I could ill endure after this inhospitable treatment.

"What the devil, indeed!" I muttered. "The herd of possessed swine could have had no worse spirits in them than those animals of yours, sir. You might as well leave a stranger with a brood of tigers!"

"They won't meddle with persons who touch nothing," he remarked, putting the bottle before me, and restoring the displaced table. "The dogs do right to be vigilant. Take a glass of wine."

"No, thank you."

"Not bitten, are you?"

"If I had been, I would have set my signet on the biter."

Heathcliff's countenance relaxed into a grin.

"Come, come," he said; "you are flurried, Mr. Lockwood. Here, take a little wine. Guests are so exceedingly rare in this house that I and my dogs, I am willing to own, hardly know how to receive them. Your health, sir!"

I bowed and returned the pledge, beginning to perceive that it would be foolish to sit sulking for the misbehaviour of a pack of curs; besides, I felt loath to yield the fellow further amusement at my expense, since his humour took that turn. He—probably swayed by prudential consideration of the folly of offending a good tenant—relaxed a little in the laconic style of chipping off his pronouns and auxiliary verbs, and introduced what he supposed would be a subject of interest to me— a discourse on the advantages and disadvantages of my present place of retirement. I found him very intelligent on the topics we touched; and before I went home I was encouraged so far as to volunteer another visit to-morrow. He evidently wished no repetition of my intrusion. I shall go, notwithstanding. It is astonishing how sociable I feel myself, compared with him.

CHAPTER II.

YESTERDAY afternoon set in misty and cold. I had half a mind to spend it by my study fire, instead of wading through heath and mud to Wuthering Heights. On coming up from dinner, however (*N.B.*—I dine between twelve and one o'clock. The housekeeper, a matronly lady, taken as a fixture along with the house, could not, or would not, comprehend my request that I might be served at five), on mounting the stairs with this lazy intention, and stepping into the room, I saw a servant girl on her knees surrounded by brushes and coal-scuttles, and raising an infernal dust as she extinguished the flames with heaps of cinders. This spectacle drove me back immediately. I took my hat, and after a four miles' walk, arrived at Heathcliff's garden gate just in time to escape the first feathery flakes of a snow-shower.

On that bleak hill-top the earth was hard with a black frost, and the air made me shiver through every limb. Being unable to remove the chain, I jumped over, and running up the flagged causeway bordered with straggling gooseberry bushes, knocked vainly for admittance, till my knuckles tingled and the dogs howled.

"Wretched inmates!" I ejaculated mentally, "you deserve perpetual isolation from your species for your churlish inhospitality. At least, I would not keep my doors barred in the daytime. I don't care; I will get in!" So resolved, I grasped the latch and shook it vehemently. Vinegar-faced Joseph projected his head from a round window of the barn.

"What are ye for?" he shouted. "T' maister's down i' t' fowld. Go round by th' end ot' laith, if ye went to spake to him."

"Is there nobody inside to open the door?" I hallooed responsively.

"There's nobbut t' missis, and shoo'll not oppen't an ye mak yer flaysome dins till neeght."

"Why? Cannot you tell her who I am, eh, Joseph?"

"Nor-ne me! I'll hae no hend wi't," muttered the head, vanishing.

The snow began to drive thickly. I seized the handle to essay another trial, when a young man without coat, and shouldering a pitchfork, appeared in the yard behind. He hailed me to follow him; and, after marching through a wash-house, and a paved area containing a coal-shed, pump, and pigeon-cot, we at length arrived in the huge, warm, cheerful apartment where I was formerly received. It glowed delightfully in the radiance of an immense fire, compounded of coal, peat, and wood; and near the table, laid for a plentiful evening meal, I was pleased to observe the "missis," an individual whose existence I had never previously suspected. I bowed and waited, thinking she would bid me take a seat. She looked at me, leaning back in her chair, and remained motionless and mute.

"Rough weather!" I remarked. "I'm afraid, Mrs. Heathcliff, the door must bear the consequence of your servants' leisure attendance. I had hard work to make them hear me."

She never opened her mouth. I stared—she stared also. At any rate, she kept her eyes on me in a cool, regardless manner, exceedingly embarrassing and disagreeable.

"Sit down," said the young man gruffly. "He'll be in soon."

I obeyed, and hemmed, and called the villain Juno, who deigned, at this second interview, to move the extreme tip of her tail, in token of owning my acquaintance.

"A beautiful animal!" I commenced again. "Do you intend parting with the little ones, madam?"

"They are not mine," said the amiable hostess, more repellingly than Heathcliff himself could have replied.

"Ah, your favourites are among these?" I continued, turning to an obscure cushion full of something like cats.

"A strange choice of favourites!" she observed scornfully.

Unluckily it was a heap of dead rabbits. I hemmed

once more, and drew closer to the hearth, repeating my comment on the wildness of the evening.

"You should not have come out," she said, rising and reaching from the chimney-piece two of the painted canisters.

Her position before was sheltered from the light; now, I had a distinct view of her whole figure and countenance. She was slender, and apparently scarcely past girlhood; an admirable form, and the most exquisite little face that I have ever had the pleasure of beholding; small features, very fair; flaxen ringlets, or rather golden, hanging loose on her delicate neck; and eyes, had they been agreeable in expression, that would have been irresistible. Fortunately for my susceptible heart, the only sentiment they evinced hovered between scorn and a kind of desperation, singularly unnatural to be detected there. The canisters were almost out of her reach. I made a motion to aid her. She turned upon me as a miser might turn if any one attempted to assist him in counting his gold.

"I don't want your help," she snapped. "I can get them for myself."

"I beg your pardon," I hastened to reply.

"Were you asked to tea?" she demanded, tying an apron over her neat black frock, and standing with a spoonful of the leaf poised over the pot.

"I shall be glad to have a cup," I answered.

"Were you asked?" she repeated.

"No," I said, half smiling. "You are the proper person to ask me."

She flung the tea back, spoon and all, and resumed her chair in a pet. Her forehead corrugated, and her red under-lip pushed out, like a child's ready to cry.

Meanwhile, the young man had slung on to his person a decidedly shabby upper garment, and, erecting himself before the blaze, looked down on me from the corner of his eyes, for all the world as if there were some mortal feud unavenged between us. I began to doubt whether he were a servant or not. His dress and speech were both rude, entirely devoid of the superiority observable in Mr. and Mrs. Heathcliff. His thick brown curls were rough and uncultivated, his whiskers encroached bearishly over his cheeks, and his hands were embrowned like those of a common labourer. Still his bearing was free, almost haughty, and he showed none of a domestic's assiduity in attending on the lady of the house. In the absence of clear proofs of his condition, I deemed it best to abstain from noticing his curious conduct; and, five minutes afterwards, the entrance of Heathcliff relieved me, in some measure, from my uncomfortable state.

"You see, sir, I am come, according to promise," I exclaimed, assuming the cheerful; "and I fear I shall be weather-bound for half an hour, if you can afford me shelter during that space."

"Half an hour?" he said, shaking the white flakes from his clothes. "I wonder you should select the thick of a snowstorm to ramble about in. Do you know that you run a risk of being lost in the marshes? People familiar with these moors often miss their road on such evenings; and I can tell you there is no chance of a change at present."

"Perhaps I can get a guide among your lads, and he might stay at the Grange till morning. Could you spare me one?"

"No, I could not."

"Oh, indeed! Well, then, I must trust to my own sagacity."

"Umph!"

"Are you going to mak' th' tea?" demanded he of the shabby coat, shifting his ferocious gaze from me to the young lady.

"Is he to have any?" she asked, appealing to Heathcliff.

"Get it ready, will you?" was the answer, uttered so savagely that I started. The tone in which the words were said revealed a genuine bad nature. I no longer felt inclined to call Heathcliff a capital fellow. When the preparations were finished, he invited me with—

" Now, sir, bring forward your chair." And we all, including the rustic youth, drew round the table, an austere silence prevailing while we discussed our meal.

I thought, if I had caused the cloud, it was my duty to make an effort to dispel it. They could not every day sit so grim and taciturn ; and it was impossible, however ill-tempered they might be, that the universal scowl they wore was their everyday countenance.

" It is strange," I began, in the interval of swallowing one cup of tea and receiving another—" it is strange how custom can mould our tastes and ideas. Many could not imagine the existence of happiness in a life of such complete exile from the world as you spend, Mr. Heathcliff ; yet I'll venture to say that, surrounded by your family, and with your amiable lady as the presiding genius over your home and heart——"

" My amiable lady ! " he interrupted, with an almost diabolical sneer on his face. " Where is she—my amiable lady ? "

" Mrs. Heathcliff, your wife, I mean."

" Well, yes—— Oh, you would intimate that her spirit has taken the post of ministering angel, and guards the fortunes of Wuthering Heights even when her body is gone. Is that it ? "

Perceiving myself in a blunder, I attempted to correct it. I might have seen there was too great a disparity between the ages of the parties to make it likely that they were man and wife. One was about forty—a period of mental vigour at which men seldom cherish the delusion of being married for love by girls. That dream is reserved for the solace of our declining years. The other did not look seventeen.

Then it flashed upon me—" The clown at my elbow, who is drinking his tea out of a basin and eating his bread with unwashed hands, may be her husband— Heathcliff, junior, of course. Here is the consequence of being buried alive. She has thrown herself away upon that boor from sheer ignorance that better individuals existed ! A sad pity. I must beware how I cause her to regret her choice." The last reflection may seem conceited. It was not. My neighbour struck me as bordering on repulsive. I knew, through experience, that I was tolerably attractive.

"Mrs. Heathcliff is my daughter-in-law," said Heathcliff, corroborating my surmise. He turned, as he spoke, a peculiar look in her direction—a look of hatred, unless he has a most perverse set of facial muscles that will not, like those of other people, interpret the language of his soul.

"Ah, certainly; I see now. You are the favoured possessor of the beneficent fairy," I remarked, turning to my neighbour.

This was worse than before. The youth grew crimson, and clenched his fist, with every appearance of a meditated assault. But he seemed to recollect himself presently, and smothered the storm in a brutal curse, muttered on my behalf, which, however, I took care not to notice.

"Unhappy in your conjectures, sir," observed my host. "We neither of us have the privilege of owning your good fairy. Her mate is dead. I said she was my daughter-in-law; therefore she must have married my son."

"And this young man is——"

"Not my son, assuredly."

Heathcliff smiled again, as if it were rather too bold a jest to attribute the paternity of that bear to him.

"My name is Hareton Earnshaw," growled the other; "and I'd counsel you to respect it!"

"I've shown no disrespect," was my reply, laughing internally at the dignity with which he announced himself.

He fixed his eye on me longer than I cared to return the stare, for fear I might be tempted either to box his ears or render my hilarity audible. I began to feel unmistakably out of place in that pleasant family circle. The dismal spiritual atmosphere overcame, and more than neutralized, the glowing physical comforts round me; and I resolved to be cautious how I ventured under those rafters a third time.

The business of eating being concluded, and no one uttering a word of sociable conversation, I approached a window to examine the weather. A sorrowful sight I saw—dark night coming down prematurely, and sky and hills mingled in one bitter whirl of wind and suffocating snow.

"I don't think it possible for me to get home now without a guide," I could not help exclaiming. "The roads will be buried already; and, if they were bare, I could scarcely distinguish a foot in advance."

"Hareton, drive those dozen sheep into the barn porch. They'll be covered if left in the fold all night. And put a plank before them," said Heathcliff.

"How must I do?" I continued, with rising irritation.

There was no reply to my question; and on looking round I saw only Joseph bringing in a pail of porridge for the dogs, and Mrs. Heathcliff leaning over the fire, diverting herself with burning a bundle of matches which had fallen from the chimney-piece as she restored the tea-canister to its place. The former, when he had deposited his burden, took a critical survey of the room, and in cracked tones grated out,—

"Aw wonder how yah can faishion to stand thear i' idleness un war, when all on 'em's goan out! Bud yah're a nowt, and it's no use talking; yah'll niver mend o' yer ill ways, but goa raight to t' divil, like yer mother afore ye!"

I imagined for a moment that this piece of eloquence was addressed to me; and, sufficiently enraged, stepped towards the aged rascal with an intention of kicking him out of the door. Mrs. Heathcliff, however, checked me by her answer.

"You scandalous old hypocrite!" she replied. "Are you not afraid of being carried away bodily, whenever you mention the devil's name? I warn you to refrain from provoking me, or I'll ask your abduction as a special favour. Stop! Look here, Joseph," she continued, taking a long, dark book from a shelf; "I'll show you how far I've progressed in the black art. I shall

soon be competent to make a clear house of it. The
red cow didn't die by chance, and your rheumatism can
hardly be reckoned among providential visitations!"

"Oh, wicked, wicked!" gasped the elder; "may the
Lord deliver us from evil!"

"No, reprobate; you are a castaway. Be off, or I'll
hurt you seriously. I'll have you all modelled in wax
and clay; and the first who passes the limits I fix shall
—I'll not say what he shall be done to, but you'll see!
Go! I'm looking at you."

The little witch put a mock malignity into her beautiful eyes, and Joseph, trembling with sincere horror,
hurried out, praying and ejaculating "wicked" as he
went. I thought her conduct must be prompted by a
species of dreary fun; and, now that we were alone, I
endeavoured to interest her in my distress.

"Mrs. Heathcliff," I said earnestly, "you must excuse
me for troubling you. I presume, because, with that
face, I'm sure you cannot help being good-hearted. Do
point out some landmarks by which I may know my
way home. I have no more idea how to get there than
you would have how to get to London."

"Take the road you came," she answered, ensconcing
herself in a chair, with a candle, and the long book open
before her. "It is brief advice, but as sound as I can give."

"Then, if you hear of me being discovered dead in a
bog or a pit full of snow, your conscience won't whisper
that it is partly your fault?"

"How so? I cannot escort you. They wouldn't let
me go to the end of the garden wall."

"You! I should be sorry to ask you to cross the
threshold for my convenience on such a night," I cried.
"I want you to tell me my way, not to show it; or else
to persuade Mr. Heathcliff to give me a guide."

"Who? There is himself, Earnshaw, Zillah, Joseph,
and I. Which would you have?"

"Are there no boys at the farm?"

"No; those are all."

"Then, it follows that I am compelled to stay."

"That you may settle with your host. I have nothing to do with it."

"I hope it will be a lesson to you to make no more rash journeys on these hills," cried Heathcliff's stern voice from the kitchen entrance. "As to staying here, I don't keep accommodations for visitors. You must share a bed with Hareton or Joseph, if you do."

"I can sleep on a chair in this room," I replied.

"No, no! A stranger is a stranger, be he rich or poor. It will not suit me to permit any one the range of the place while I am off guard!" said the unmannerly wretch.

With this insult, my patience was at an end. I uttered an expression of disgust, and pushed past him into the yard, running against Earnshaw in my haste. It was so dark that I could not see the means of exit; and, as I wandered round, I heard another specimen of their civil behaviour amongst each other. At first the young man appeared about to befriend me.

"I'll go with him as far as the park," he said.

"You'll go with him to hell!" exclaimed his master, or whatever relation he bore. "And who is to look after the horses, eh?"

"A man's life is of more consequence than one evening's neglect of the horses. Somebody must go," murmured Mrs. Heathcliff, more kindly than I expected.

"Not at your command!" retorted Hareton. "If you set store on him, you'd better be quiet."

"Then I hope his ghost will haunt you; and I hope Mr. Heathcliff will never get another tenant till the Grange is a ruin!" she answered sharply.

"Hearken, hearken; shoo's cursing on 'em!" muttered Joseph, towards whom I had been steering.

He sat within earshot, milking the cows by the light of a lantern, which I seized unceremoniously, and calling out that I would send it back on the morrow, rushed to the nearest postern.

"Maister, maister, he's staling t' lanthern!" shouted the ancient, pursuing my retreat. "Hey, Gnasher! Hey, dog! Hey, Wolf, holld him, holld him!"

On opening the little door, two hairy monsters flew at my throat, bearing me down and extinguishing the light; while a mingled guffaw from Heathcliff and Hareton put the copestone on my rage and humiliation. Fortunately, the beasts seemed more bent on stretching their paws and yawning, and flourishing their tails, than devouring me alive; but they would suffer no resurrection, and I was forced to lie till their malignant masters pleased to deliver me. Then, hatless and trembling with wrath, I ordered the miscreants to let me out—on their peril to keep me one minute longer—with several incoherent threats of retaliation that, in their indefinite depth of virulency, smacked of King Lear.

The vehemence of my agitation brought on a copious bleeding at the nose; and still Heathcliff laughed, and still I scolded. I don't know what would have concluded the scene had there not been one person at hand rather more rational than myself and more benevolent than my entertainer. This was Zillah, the stout housewife, who at length issued forth to inquire into the nature of the uproar. She thought that some of them had been laying violent hands on me; and, not daring to attack her master, she turned her vocal artillery against the younger scoundrel.

"Well, Mr. Earnshaw," she cried, "I wonder what you'll have agait next! Are we going to murder folk on our very door-stones? I see this house will never do for me. Look at t' poor lad; he's fair choking!—Wisht, wisht! you munn't go on so. Come in, and I'll cure that. There now, hold ye still."

With these words she suddenly splashed a pint of icy water down my neck, and pulled me into the kitchen. Mr. Heathcliff followed, his accidental merriment expiring quickly in his habitual moroseness.

I was sick exceedingly, and dizzy and faint, and thus compelled perforce to accept lodgings under his roof. He told Zillah to give me a glass of brandy, and then passed on to the inner room; while she condoled with me on my sorry predicament, and having obeyed his orders, whereby I was somewhat revived, ushered me to bed.

CHAPTER III.

WHILE leading the way upstairs, she recommended that I should hide the candle, and not make a noise, for her master had an odd notion about the chamber she would put me in, and never let anybody lodge there willingly. I asked the reason. She did not know, she answered. She had only lived there a year or two; and they had so many queer goings on, she could not begin to be curious.

Too stupefied to be curious myself, I fastened my door and glanced round for the bed. The whole furniture consisted of a chair, a clothes-press, and a large oak case, with squares cut out near the top resembling coach windows. Having approached this structure, I looked inside, and perceived it to be a singular sort of old-fashioned couch, very conveniently designed to obviate the necessity for every member of the family having a room to himself. In fact, it formed a little closet; and the ledge of a window, which it enclosed, served as a table. I slid back the panelled sides, got in with my light, pulled them together again, and felt secure against the vigilance of Heathcliff and every one else.

The ledge where I placed my candle had a few mildewed books piled up in one corner, and it was covered with writing scratched on the paint. This writing, however, was nothing but a name repeated in all kinds of characters, large and small—*Catherine Earnshaw*, here and there varied to *Catherine Heathcliff*, and then again to *Catherine Linton*.

In vapid listlessness I leant my head against the window, and continued spelling over Catherine Earnshaw—Heathcliff—Linton, till my eyes closed. But they had not rested five minutes when a glare of white letters started from the dark as vivid as spectres—the air swarmed with Catherines; and rousing myself to dispel the obtrusive name, I discovered my candle-wick reclining on one of the antique volumes, and perfuming the place with an odour of roasted calf-skin. I snuffed it off, and, very ill at ease under the influence of cold and lingering nausea, sat up and spread open the injured tome on my knee. It was a Testament, in lean type, and smelling dreadfully musty. A fly-leaf bore the inscription, "Catherine Earnshaw, her book," and a date some quarter of a century back. I shut it, and took up another, and another, till I had examined all. Catherine's library was select, and its state of dilapidation proved it to have been well used, though not altogether for a legitimate purpose. Scarcely one chapter had escaped a pen-and-ink commentary — at least, the appearance of one — covering every morsel of blank that the printer had left. Some were detached sentences; other parts took the form of a regular diary, scrawled in an unformed, childish hand. At the top of an extra page (quite a treasure, probably, when first lighted on) I was greatly amused to behold an excellent caricature of my friend Joseph, rudely yet powerfully sketched. An immediate interest kindled within me for the unknown Catherine, and I began forthwith to decipher her faded hieroglyphics.

"An awful Sunday!" commenced the paragraph beneath. "I wish my father were back again. Hindley is a detestable substitute—his conduct to Heathcliff is atrocious—H. and I are going to rebel—we took our initiatory step this evening.

"All day had been flooding with rain. We could not go to church, so Joseph must needs get up a congregation in the garret; and while Hindley and his wife basked downstairs before a comfortable fire—doing anything but reading their Bibles, I'll answer for it—Heathcliff, myself, and the unhappy plough-boy were commanded to take our prayer-books and mount. We were ranged in a row on a sack of corn, groaning and shivering, and hoping that Joseph would shiver too, so that he might give us a short homily for his own sake.

A vain idea! The service lasted precisely three hours; and yet my brother had the face to exclaim, when he saw us descending, 'What! done already?' On Sunday evenings we used to be permitted to play, if we did not make much noise; now a mere titter is sufficient to send us into corners!

"'You forget you have a master here,' says the tyrant. 'I'll demolish the first who puts me out of temper! I insist on perfect sobriety and silence. O boy! was that you?—Frances darling, pull his hair as you go by. I heard him snap his fingers.' Frances pulled his hair heartily, and then went and seated herself on her husband's knee; and there they were, like two babies, kissing and talking nonsense by the hour— foolish palaver that we should be ashamed of. We made ourselves as snug as our means allowed in the arch of the dresser. I had just fastened our pinafores together, and hung them up for a curtain, when in comes Joseph on an errand from the stables. He tears down my handiwork, boxes my ears, and croaks,—

"'T' maister nobbut just buried, and Sabbath no o'ered, und t' sound o' t' gospel still i' yer lugs, and ye darr be laiking! Shame on ye! Sit ye down, ill childer; there's good books eneugh if ye'll read 'em. Sit ye down, and think o' yer sowls!'

"Saying this, he compelled us so to square our positions that we might receive from the far-off fire a dull ray to show us the text of the lumber he thrust upon us. I could not bear the employment. I took my dingy volume by the scroop, and hurled it into the dog-kennel, vowing I hated a good book. Heathcliff kicked his to the same place. Then there was a hubbub!

"'Maister Hindley!' shouted our chaplain. 'Maister, coom hither! Miss Cathy's riven th' back off "Th' Helmet o' Salvation," un Heathcliff's pawsed his fit into t' first part o' "T' Brooad Way to Destruction!" It's fair flaysome that ye let 'em go on this gait. Ech! th' owd man wad ha' laced 'em properly; but he's goan!'

"Hindley hurried up from his paradise on the hearth,

and seizing one of us by the collar, and the other by the arm, hurled both into the back kitchen, where, Joseph asseverated, ' owd Nick ' would fetch us as sure as we were living ; and, so comforted, we each sought a separate nook to await his advent. I reached this book, and a pot of ink from a shelf, and pushed the house door ajar to give me light, and I have got the time on with writing for twenty minutes ; but my companion is impatient, and proposes that we should appropriate the dairy-woman's cloak, and have a scamper on the moors, under its shelter. A pleasant suggestion ; and then, if the surly old man come in, he may believe his prophecy verified. We cannot be damper or colder in the rain than we are here.''

*   *   *   *   *   *

I suppose Catherine fulfilled her project, for the next sentence took up another subject. She waxed lachry-mose.

" How little did I dream that Hindley would ever make me cry so ! " she wrote. " My head aches, till I cannot keep it on the pillow ; and still I can't give over. Poor Heathcliff ! Hindley calls him a vagabond, and won't let him sit with us, nor eat with us any more ; and he says he and I must not play together, and threatens to turn him out of the house if we break his orders. He has been blaming our father (how dared he ?) for treating H. too liberally, and swears he will reduce him to his right place——''

*   *   *   *   *   *

I began to nod drowsily over the dim page. My eye wandered from manuscript to print. I saw a red orna-mented title—" Seventy Times Seven, and the First of the Seventy-First. A Pious Discourse delivered by the Reverend Jabes Branderham, in the Chapel of Gimmer-den Sough.'' And while I was half consciously worrying my brain to guess what Jabes Branderham would make of his subject, I sank back in bed and fell asleep. Alas for the effects of bad tea and bad temper ! What else could it be that made me pass such a terrible night ? I don't remember another that I can at all compare with it since I was capable of suffering.

I began to dream, almost before I ceased to be sensible of my locality. I thought it was morning, and I had set out on my way home, with Joseph for a guide. The snow lay yards deep in our road; and as we floundered on, my companion wearied me with constant reproaches that I had not brought a pilgrim's staff, telling me that I could never get into the house without one, and boastfully flourishing a heavy-headed cudgel, which I understood to be so denominated. For a moment I considered it absurd that I should need such a weapon to gain admittance into my own residence. Then a new idea flashed across me. I was not going there. We were journeying to hear the famous Jabes Branderham preach from the text, "Seventy Times Seven," and either Joseph the preacher or I had committed the "First of the Seventy-First," and were to be publicly exposed and excommunicated.

We came to the chapel. I have passed it really in my walks twice or thrice. It lies in a hollow between two hills—an elevated hollow, near a swamp, whose peaty moisture is said to answer all the purposes of embalming on the few corpses deposited there. The roof has been kept whole hitherto; but as the clergyman's stipend is only twenty pounds per annum, and a house with two rooms, threatening speedily to determine into one, no clergyman will undertake the duties of pastor, especially as it is currently reported that his flock would rather let him starve than increase the living by one penny from their own pockets. However, in my dream, Jabes had a full and attentive congregation, and he preached — good God! what a sermon, divided into *four hundred and ninety* parts, each fully equal to an ordinary address from the pulpit, and each discussing a separate sin! Where he searched for them, I cannot tell. He had his private manner of interpreting the phrase, and it seemed necessary the brother should sin different sins on every occasion. They were of the most curious character—odd transgressions that I never imagined previously.

Oh, how weary I grew! How I writhed, and yawned, and nodded, and revived! How I pinched, and pricked myself, and rubbed my eyes, and stood up, and sat down again, and nudged Joseph to inform me if he would *ever* have done! I was condemned to hear all out. Finally, he reached the "First of the Seventy-First." At that crisis, a sudden inspiration descended on me. I was moved to rise and denounce Jabes Branderham as the sinner of the sin that no Christian need pardon.

"Sir," I exclaimed, "sitting here within these four walls, at one stretch, I have endured and forgiven the four hundred and ninety heads of your discourse. Seventy times seven times have I plucked up my hat and been about to depart; seventy times seven times have you preposterously forced me to resume my seat. The four hundred and ninety-first is too much.—Fellow-martyrs, have at him! Drag him down, and crush him to atoms, that the place which knows him may know him no more!"

"*Thou art the man!*" cried Jabes, after a solemn pause, leaning over his cushion. "Seventy times seven times didst thou gapingly contort thy visage; seventy times seven did I take counsel with my soul. Lo, this is human weakness; this also may be absolved! The 'First of the Seventy-First' is come. Brethren, execute upon him the judgment written. Such honour have all His saints!"

With that concluding word, the whole assembly, exalting their pilgrim's staves, rushed round me in a body; and I, having no weapon to raise in self-defence, commenced grappling with Joseph, my nearest and most ferocious assailant, for his. In the confluence of the multitude several clubs crossed; blows aimed at me fell on other sconces. Presently the whole chapel resounded with rappings and counter-rappings. Every man's hand was against his neighbour; and Branderham, unwilling to remain idle, poured forth his zeal in a shower of loud taps on the boards of the pulpit, which responded so smartly that at last, to my unspeakable relief, they woke me. And what was it that had suggested the tremendous tumult? What had played Jabes's part in the row? Merely the branch of a fir-tree that touched my lattice, as the blast wailed by, and rattled its dry cones against the panes! I listened doubtingly an instant, detected the disturber, then turned and dozed, and dreamt again — if possible, still more disagreeably than before.

This time I remembered I was lying in the oak closet, and I heard distinctly the gusty wind and the driving of the snow. I heard also the fir-bough repeat its teasing sound, and ascribed it to the right cause. But it annoyed me so much that I resolved to silence it, if possible; and I thought I rose and endeavoured to unhasp the casement. The hook was soldered into the staple—a circumstance observed by me when awake, but forgotten. "I must stop it, nevertheless!" I muttered, knocking my knuckles through the glass, and stretching an arm out to seize the importunate branch; instead of which, my fingers closed on the fingers of a little, ice-cold hand! The intense horror of nightmare came over me. I tried to draw back my arm, but the hand clung to it, and a most melancholy voice sobbed, "Let me in —let me in!" "Who are you?" I asked, struggling, meanwhile, to disengage myself. "Catherine Linton," it replied shiveringly. (Why did I think of *Linton*? I had read *Earnshaw* twenty times for Linton.) "I'm come home. I'd lost my way on the moor." As it spoke, I discerned, obscurely, a child's face looking through the window. Terror made me cruel; and finding it useless to attempt shaking the creature off, I pulled its wrist on to the broken pane, and rubbed it to and fro till the blood ran down and soaked the bedclothes. Still it wailed, "Let me in!" and maintained its tenacious gripe, almost maddening me with fear. "How can I?" I said at length. "Let *me* go, if you want me to let you in!" The fingers relaxed; I

snatched mine through the hole, hurriedly piled the
books up in a pyramid against it, and stopped my ears
to exclude the lamentable prayer. I seemed to keep
them closed above a quarter of an hour; yet the instant
I listened again, there was the doleful cry moaning on!
"Begone!" I shouted; "I'll never let you in—not if
you beg for twenty years." "It is twenty years,"
mourned the voice—"twenty years. I've been a waif
for twenty years!" Thereat began a feeble scratching
outside, and the pile of books moved as if thrust forward.
I tried to jump up, but could not stir a limb, and so
yelled aloud in a frenzy of fright. To my confusion, I
discovered the yell was not ideal. Hasty footsteps
approached my chamber door; somebody pushed it
open with a vigorous hand, and a light glimmered
through the squares at the top of the bed. I sat shuddering yet, and wiping the perspiration from my forehead.
The intruder appeared to hesitate, and muttered to
himself. At last he said in a half-whisper, plainly not
expecting an answer, "Is any one here?" I considered it best to confess my presence, for I knew Heathcliff's accents, and feared he might search further if I
kept quiet. With this intention I turned and opened
the panels. I shall not soon forget the effect my action
produced.

Heathcliff stood near the entrance, in his shirt and
trousers, with a candle dripping over his fingers, and
his face as white as the wall behind him. The first
creak of the oak startled him like an electric shock.
The light leaped from his hold to a distance of some
feet, and his agitation was so extreme that he could
hardly pick it up.

"It is only your guest, sir," I called out, desirous to
spare him the humiliation of exposing his cowardice
further. "I had the misfortune to scream in my sleep,
owing to a frightful nightmare. I'm sorry I disturbed
you."

"Oh, God confound you, Mr. Lockwood! I wish you
were at the——" commenced my host, setting the candle

on a chair, because he found it impossible to hold it steady. "And who showed you up into this room?" he continued, crushing his nails into his palms and grinding his teeth to subdue the maxillary convulsions. "Who was it? I've a good mind to turn them out of the house this moment."

"It was your servant Zillah," I replied, flinging myself on to the floor, and rapidly resuming my garments. "I should not care if you did, Mr. Heathcliff; she richly deserves it. I suppose that she wanted to get another proof that the place was haunted, at my expense. Well, it is—swarming with ghosts and goblins! You have reason in shutting it up, I assure you. No one will thank you for a doze in such a den!"

"What do you mean?" asked Heathcliff, "and what are you doing? Lie down and finish out the night, since you *are* here; but, for Heaven's sake, don't repeat that horrid noise. Nothing could excuse it, unless you were having your throat cut!"

"If the little fiend had got in at the window, she probably would have strangled me!" I returned. "I'm not going to endure the persecutions of your hospitable ancestors again. Was not the Reverend Jabes Branderham akin to you on the mother's side? And that minx, Catherine Linton, or Earnshaw, or however she was called, she must have been a changeling—wicked little soul! She told me she had been walking the earth those twenty years—a just punishment for her mortal transgressions, I've no doubt."

Scarcely were these words uttered, when I recollected the association of Heathcliff's with Catherine's name in the book, which had completely slipped from my memory, till thus awakened. I blushed at my inconsideration; but without showing further consciousness of the offence, I hastened to add, "The truth is, sir, I passed the first part of the night in——" Here I stopped afresh. I was about to say "perusing those old volumes"—then it would have revealed my knowledge of their written as well as their printed contents; so, correcting myself,

I went on, " In spelling over the name scratched on that window-ledge — a monotonous occupation, calculated to set me asleep, like counting, or——"

" What *can* you mean by talking in this way to *me ?* " thundered Heathcliff, with savage vehemence. " How —how *dare* you, under my roof ?—God, he's mad to speak so ! " And he struck his forehead with rage.

I did not know whether to resent this language or pursue my explanation ; but he seemed so powerfully affected that I took pity and proceeded with my dreams, affirming I had never heard the appellation of " Catherine Linton " before, but reading it often over produced an impression which personified itself when I had no longer my imagination under control. Heathcliff gradually fell back into the shelter of the bed as I spoke, finally sitting down almost concealed behind it. I guessed, however, by his irregular and intercepted breathing, that he struggled to vanquish an excess of violent emotion. Not liking to show him that I had heard the conflict, I continued my toilet rather noisily, looked at my watch, and soliloquized on the length of the night. Not three o'clock yet ! I could have taken oath it had been six. Time stagnates here. We must surely have retired to rest at eight !

" Always at nine in winter, and rise at four," said my host, suppressing a groan, and, as I fancied, by the motion of his arm's shadow, dashing a tear from his eyes. " Mr. Lockwood," he added, " you may go into my room. You'll only be in the way, coming downstairs so early ; and your childish outcry has sent sleep to the devil for me."

" And for me too," I replied. " I'll walk in the yard till daylight, and then I'll be off ; and you need not dread a repetition of my intrusion. I'm now quite cured of seeking pleasure in society, be it country or town. A sensible man ought to find sufficient company in himself."

" Delightful company ! " muttered Heathcliff. " Take the candle, and go where you please. I shall join yon directly. Keep out of the yard, though—the dogs are unchained; and the house—Juno mounts sentinel there, and—nay, you can only ramble about the steps and passages. But away with you! I'll come in two minutes!"

I obeyed, so far as to quit the chamber; when, ignorant where the narrow lobbies led, I stood still, and was witness, involuntarily, to a piece of superstition on the part of my landlord which belied oddly his apparent sense. He got on to the bed and wrenched open the lattice, bursting, as he pulled at it, into an uncontrollable passion of tears. "Come in! come in!" he sobbed. "Cathy, do come! Oh, do—*once* more! Oh, my heart's darling! hear me *this* time, Catherine, at last!" The spectre showed a spectre's ordinary caprice. It gave no sign of being; but the snow and wind whirled wildly through, even reaching my station, and blowing out the light.

There was such anguish in the gush of grief that accompanied this raving that my compassion made me overlook its folly, and I drew off, half angry to have listened at all, and vexed at having related my ridiculous nightmare, since it produced that agony; though *why* was beyond my comprehension. I descended cautiously to the lower regions, and landed in the back kitchen, where a gleam of fire, raked compactly together, enabled me to rekindle my candle. Nothing was stirring except a brindled, gray cat, which crept from the ashes, and saluted me with a querulous mew.

Two benches, shaped in sections of a circle, nearly enclosed the hearth. On one of these I stretched myself, and Grimalkin mounted the other. We were both of us nodding ere any one invaded our retreat, and then it was Joseph, shuffling down a wooden ladder that vanished in the roof, through a trap—the ascent to his garret, I suppose. He cast a sinister look at the little flame which I had enticed to play between the ribs, swept the cat from its elevation, and bestowing himself in the vacancy, commenced the operation of stuffing a

three-inch pipe with tobacco. My presence in his sanc-
tum was evidently esteemed a piece of impudence too
shameful for remark. He silently applied the tube to
his lips, folded his arms, and puffed away. I let him
enjoy the luxury unannoyed ; and after sucking out his
last wreath, and heaving a profound sigh, he got up,
and departed as solemnly as he came.

A more elastic footstep entered next ; and now I
opened my mouth for a " good-morning," but closed it
again, the salutation unachieved, for Hareton Earnshaw
was performing his orisons, *sotto voce*, in a series of curses
directed against every object he touched, while he
rummaged a corner for a spade or shovel to dig through
the drifts. He glanced over the back of the bench,
dilating his nostrils, and thought as little of exchanging
civilities with me as with my companion the cat. I
guessed by his preparations that egress was allowed,
and leaving my hard couch, made a movement to follow
him. He noticed this, and thrust at an inner door with
the end of his spade, intimating by an inarticulate sound
that there was the place where I must go if I changed
my locality.

It opened into the house, where the females were
already astir — Zillah urging flakes of flame up the
chimney with a colossal bellows ; and Mrs. Heathcliff,
kneeling on the hearth, reading a book by the aid of the
blaze. She held her hand interposed between the fur-
nace-heat and her eyes, and seemed absorbed in her
occupation, desisting from it only to chide the servant
for covering her with sparks, or to push away a dog,
now and then, that snoozled its nose over-forwardly into
her face. I was surprised to see Heathcliff there also.
He stood by the fire, his back towards me, just finishing
a stormy scene to poor Zillah, who ever and anon interrupted her labour to pluck up the corner of her apron
and heave an indignant groan.

" And you, you worthless—" he broke out as I entered,
turning to his daughter-in-law, and employing an epithet
as harmless as duck or sheep, but generally represented

by a dash ——. "There you are at your idle tricks again! The rest of them do earn their bread: you live on my charity! Put your trash away, and find something to do. You shall pay me for the plague of having you eternally in my sight. Do you hear, damnable jade?"

"I'll put my trash away, because you can make me if I refuse," answered the young lady, closing her book and throwing it on a chair. "But I'll not do anything, though you should swear your tongue out, except what I please!"

Heathcliff lifted his hand, and the speaker sprang to a safer distance, obviously acquainted with its weight. Having no desire to be entertained by a cat-and-dog combat, I stepped forward briskly, as if eager to partake the warmth of the hearth, and innocent of any knowledge of the interrupted dispute. Each had enough decorum to suspend further hostilities. Heathcliff placed his fists, out of temptation, in his pockets; Mrs. Heathcliff curled her lip, and walked to a seat far off, where she kept her word by playing the part of a statue during the remainder of my stay. That was not long. I declined joining their breakfast, and at the first gleam of dawn took an opportunity of escaping into the free air, now clear, and still, and cold as impalpable ice.

My landlord hallooed for me to stop ere I reached the bottom of the garden, and offered to accompany me across the moor. It was well he did, for the whole hill-back was one billowy, white ocean, the swells and falls not indicating corresponding rises and depressions in the ground. Many pits, at least, were filled to a level, and entire ranges of mounds, the refuse of the quarries, blotted from the chart which my yesterday's walk left pictured in my mind. I had remarked on one side of the road, at intervals of six or seven yards, a line of upright stones, continued through the whole length of the barren. These were erected and daubed with lime on purpose to serve as guides in the dark, and also when a fall, like the present, confounded the deep swamps on either hand with the firmer path ; but, excepting a dirty dot pointing up here and there, all traces of their existence had vanished, and my companion found it necessary to warn me frequently to steer to the right or left, when I imagined I was following correctly the windings of the road.

We exchanged little conversation, and he halted at the entrance of Thrushcross Park, saying I could make no error there. Our adieus were limited to a hasty bow, and then I pushed forward, trusting to my own resources, for the porter's lodge is untenanted as yet. The distance from the gate to the Grange is two miles : I believe I managed to make it four, what with losing myself among the trees, and sinking up to the neck in snow—a predicament which only those who have experienced it can appreciate. At any rate, whatever were my wanderings, the clock chimed twelve as I entered the house, and that gave exactly an hour for every mile of the usual way from Wuthering Heights.

My human fixture and her satellites rushed to welcome me, exclaiming tumultuously they had completely given me up. Everybody conjectured that I perished last night, and they were wondering how they must set about the search for my remains. I bid them be quiet, now that they saw me returned, and, benumbed to my very heart, I dragged upstairs ; whence, after putting on dry clothes, and pacing to and fro thirty or forty minutes, to restore the animal heat, I am adjourned to my study, feeble as a kitten—almost too much so to enjoy the cheerful fire and smoking coffee which the servant has prepared for my refreshment.

CHAPTER IV.

WHAT vain weather-cocks we are ! I, who had determined to hold myself independent of all social intercourse, and thanked my stars that at length I had lighted on a spot where it was next to impracticable—I, weak wretch, after maintaining till dusk a struggle with low spirits and solitude, was finally compelled to strike my colours; and under pretence of gaining information concerning the necessities of my establishment, I desired Mrs. Dean, when she brought in supper, to sit down while I ate it, hoping sincerely she would prove a regular gossip, and either rouse me to animation or lull me to sleep by her talk.

"You have lived here a considerable time," I commenced—"did you not say sixteen years?"

"Eighteen, sir. I came, when the mistress was married, to wait on her; after she died, the master retained me for his housekeeper."

"Indeed."

There ensued a pause. She was not a gossip, I feared —unless about her own affairs, and those could hardly interest me. However, having studied for an interval, with a fist on either knee, and a cloud of meditation over her ruddy countenance, she ejaculated,—

"Ah, times are greatly changed since then!"

"Yes," I remarked; "you've seen a good many alterations, I suppose?"

"I have; and troubles too," she said.

"Oh, I'll turn the talk on my landlord's family!" I thought to myself. "A good subject to start! And that pretty girl-widow, I should like to know her history —whether she be a native of the country, or, as is more probable, an exotic that the surly *indigenæ* will not recognize for kin." With this intention I asked Mrs. Dean why Heathcliff let Thrushcross Grange, and preferred living in a situation and residence so much inferior. "Is he not rich enough to keep the estate in good order?" I inquired.

"Rich, sir!" she returned. "He has nobody knows what money, and every year it increases. Yes, yes; he's rich enough to live in a finer house than this. But he's very near—close-handed; and if he had meant to flit to Thrushcross Grange, as soon as he heard of a good tenant he could not have borne to miss the chance of getting a few hundreds more. It is strange people should be so greedy when they are alone in the world ! ''

" He had a son, it seems ? "

" Yes, he had one. He is dead."

" And that young lady, Mrs. Heathcliff, is his widow ? "

" Yes."

" Where did she come from originally ? "

" Why, sir, she is my late master's daughter. Catherine Linton was her maiden name. I nursed her, poor thing ! I did wish Mr. Heathcliff would remove here, and then we might have been together again."

" What ! Catherine Linton ? " I exclaimed, astonished. But a minute's reflection convinced me it was not my ghostly Catherine. " Then," I continued, " my predecessor's name was Linton ? "

" It was."

" And who is that Earnshaw—Hareton Earnshaw—who lives with Mr. Heathcliff ? Are they relations ? "

" No ; he is the late Mrs. Linton's nephew."

" The young lady's cousin, then ? "

" Yes ; and her husband was her cousin also—one on the mother's side, the other on the father's side. Heathcliff married Mr. Linton's sister."

" I see the house at Wuthering Heights has ' Earnshaw ' carved over the front door. Are they an old family ? "

" Very old, sir ; and Hareton is the last of them, as our Miss Cathy is of us—I mean of the Lintons. Have you been to Wuthering Heights ? I beg pardon for asking ; but I should like to hear how she is."

" Mrs. Heathcliff ? She looked very well, and very handsome ; yet, I think, not very happy."

" Oh dear, I don't wonder ! And how did you like the master ? "

" A rough fellow, rather, Mrs. Dean. Is not that his character ? "

" Rough as a saw-edge, and hard as whinstone. The less you meddle with him the better."

" He must have had some ups and downs in life to

make him such a churl. Do you know anything of his history ? "

" It's a cuckoo's, sir. I know all about it—except where he was born, and who were his parents, and how he got his money at first. And Hareton has been cast out like an unfledged dunnock ! The unfortunate lad is the only one in all this parish that does not guess how he has been cheated."

" Well, Mrs. Dean, it will be a charitable deed to tell me something of my neighbours. I feel I shall not rest if I go to bed, so be good enough to sit and chat an hour."

" Oh, certainly, sir ! I'll just fetch a little sewing, and then I'll sit as long as you please. But you've caught cold—I saw you shivering ; and you must have some gruel to drive it out."

The worthy woman bustled off, and I crouched nearer the fire. My head felt hot, and the rest of me chill ; moreover, I was excited, almost to a pitch of foolishness, through my nerves and brain. This caused me to feel, not uncomfortable, but rather fearful (as I am still) of serious effects from the incidents of to-day and yesterday. She returned presently, bringing a smoking basin and a basket of work ; and having placed the former on the hob, drew in her seat, evidently pleased to find me so companionable.

*   *   *   *   *

Before I came to live here, she commenced—waiting no further invitation to her story—I was almost always at Wuthering Heights, because my mother had nursed Mr. Hindley Earnshaw (that was Hareton's father), and I got used to playing with the children. I ran errands, too, and helped to make hay, and hung about the farm, ready for anything that anybody would set me to. One fine summer morning—it was the beginning of harvest, I remember—Mr. Earnshaw, the old master, came downstairs, dressed for a journey ; and after he had told Joseph what was to be done during the day, he turned to Hindley, and Cathy, and me—for I sat eating my porridge with them—and he said, speaking to his son, " Now, my bonny man, I'm going to Liverpool to-day; what shall I bring you ? You may choose what you like. Only let it be little, for I shall walk there and back. Sixty miles each way—that is a long spell ! " Hindley named a fiddle, and then he asked Miss Cathy. She was hardly six years old, but she could ride any horse in the stable, and she chose a whip. He did not forget me, for he had a kind heart, though he was rather severe sometimes. He promised to bring me a pocketful of apples and pears; and then he kissed his children, said good-bye, and set off.

It seemed a long while to us all—the three days of his absence—and often did little Cathy ask when he would be home. Mrs. Earnshaw expected him by supper-time on the third evening, and she put the meal off hour after hour. There were no signs of his coming, however, and at last the children got tired of running down to the gate to look. Then it grew dark. She would have had them to bed, but they begged sadly to be allowed to stay up; and just about eleven o'clock the door-latch was raised quietly, and in stepped the master. He threw himself into a chair, laughing and groaning, and bid them all stand off, for he was nearly killed. He would not have such another walk for the three kingdoms.

" And at the end of it, to be flighted to death ! " he said, opening his greatcoat, which he held bundled up in his arms. " See here, wife ! I was never so beaten with anything in my life ; but you must e'en take it as a gift of God, though it's as dark almost as if it came from the devil."

We crowded round, and over Miss Cathy's head I had a peep at a dirty, ragged, black-haired child, big enough both to walk and talk. Indeed, its face looked older than Catherine's ; yet when it was set on its feet it only stared round, and repeated over and over again some gibberish that nobody could understand. I was frightened, and Mrs. Earnshaw was ready to fling it out of doors. She did fly up, asking how he could fashion to bring that gipsy brat into the house, when they had their own bairns to feed and fend for; what he meant to do with it, and whether he were mad. The master tried to explain the matter; but he was really half dead with fatigue, and all that I could make out, amongst her scolding, was a tale of his seeing it starving, and houseless, and as good as dumb, in the streets of Liverpool, where he picked it up and inquired for its owner. Not a soul knew to whom it belonged, he said; and his money and time being both limited, he thought it better to take it home with him at once, than run into vain expenses there, because he was determined he would not leave it as he found it. Well, the conclusion was that my mistress grumbled herself calm; and Mr. Earnshaw told me to wash it, and give it clean things, and let it sleep with the children.

Hindley and Cathy contented themselves with looking and listening till peace was restored; then both began searching their father's pockets for the presents he had promised them. The former was a boy of fourteen, but when he drew out what had been a fiddle, crushed to morsels in the greatcoat, he blubbered aloud; and Cathy, when she learned the master had lost her whip in attending on the stranger, showed her humour by grinning and spitting at the stupid little thing, earning for her pains a sound blow from her father to teach her cleaner manners. They entirely refused to have it in bed with them, or even in their room; and I had no more sense, so I put it on the landing of the stairs, hoping it might be gone on the morrow. By chance, or else attracted by hearing his voice, it crept to Mr. Earnshaw's door, and there he found it on quitting his chamber. Inquiries were made as to how it got there. I was obliged to confess, and in recompense for my cowardice and inhumanity was sent out of the house.

This was Heathcliff's first introduction to the family. On coming back a few days afterwards (for I did not consider my banishment perpetual) I found they had christened him "Heathcliff." It was the name of a son who died in childhood, and it has served him ever since, both for Christian and surname. Miss Cathy and he were now very thick; but Hindley hated him, and, to say the truth, I did the same; and we plagued and went on with him shamefully, for I wasn't reasonable enough to feel my injustice, and the mistress never put in a word on his behalf when she saw him wronged.

He seemed a sullen, patient child, hardened, perhaps, to ill-treatment. He would stand Hindley's blows without winking or shedding a tear, and my pinches moved him only to draw in a breath and open his eyes, as if he had hurt himself by accident and nobody was to blame. This endurance made old Earnshaw furious when he discovered his son persecuting the poor, fatherless child, as he called him. He took to Heathcliff strangely, believing all he said (for that matter, he said precious little, and generally the truth), and petting him up far above Cathy, who was too mischievous and wayward for a favourite.

So from the very beginning he bred bad feeling in the house; and at Mrs. Earnshaw's death, which happened in less than two years after, the young master had learned to regard his father as an oppressor rather than a friend, and Heathcliff as a usurper of his parent's affections and his privileges, and he grew bitter with brooding over these injuries. I sympathized a while; but when the children fell ill of the measles, and I had to tend them, and take on me the cares of a woman at once, I changed my ideas. Heathcliff was dangerously sick; and while he lay at the worst he would have me constantly by his pillow. I suppose he felt I did a good deal for him, and he hadn't wit to guess that I was compelled to do it. However, I will say this—he was the quietest child that ever nurse watched over. The difference between him and the others forced me to be less partial. Cathy and her brother harassed me terribly; *he* was as uncomplaining as a lamb, though hardness, not gentleness, made him give little trouble.

He got through, and the doctor affirmed it was in a

great measure owing to me, and praised me for my care. I was vain of his commendations, and softened towards the being by whose means I earned them; and thus Hindley lost his last ally. Still I couldn't dote on Heathcliff, and I wondered often what my master saw to admire so much in the sullen boy, who never, to my recollection, repaid his indulgence by any sign of gratitude. He was not insolent to his benefactor, he was simply insensible, though knowing perfectly the hold he had on his heart, and conscious he had only to speak and all the house would be obliged to bend to his wishes. As an instance, I remember Mr. Earnshaw once bought a couple of colts at the parish fair, and gave the lads each one. Heathcliff took the handsomest, but it soon fell lame, and when he discovered it, he said to Hindley,—

"You must exchange horses with me—I don't like mine; and if you won't, I shall tell your father of the three thrashings you've given me this week, and show him my arm, which is black to the shoulder." Hindley put out his tongue and cuffed him over the ears. "You'd better do it at once," he persisted, escaping to the porch (they were in the stable). "You will have to; and if I speak of these blows, you'll get them again with interest." "Off, dog!" cried Hindley, threatening him with an iron weight used for weighing potatoes and hay. "Throw it," he replied, standing still, "and then I'll tell how you boasted that you would turn me out of doors as soon as he died, and see whether he will not turn you out directly." Hindley threw it, hitting him on the breast, and down he fell, but staggered up immediately, breathless and white; and had I not prevented it, he would have gone just so to the master, and got full revenge by letting his condition plead for him, intimating who had caused it. "Take my colt, gipsy, then!" said young Earnshaw. "And I pray that he may break your neck. Take him, and be damned, you beggarly interloper; and wheedle my father out of all he has. Only afterwards show him what you are, imp of Satan. And take that! I hope he'll kick out your brains!"

Heathcliff had gone to loose the beast and shift it to his own stall. He was passing behind it, when Hindley finished his speech by knocking him under its feet, and without stopping to examine whether his hopes were fulfilled, ran away as fast as he could. I was surprised to witness how coolly the child gathered himself up, and went on with his intention—exchanging saddles and all, and then sitting down on a bundle of hay to overcome the qualm which the violent blow occasioned, before he entered the house. I persuaded him easily to let me lay the blame of his bruises on the horse. He minded little what tale was told, since he had what he wanted. He complained so seldom, indeed, of such stirs as these, that I really thought him not vindictive. I was deceived completely, as you will hear.

CHAPTER V.

In the course of time Mr. Earnshaw began to fail. He had been active and healthy, yet his strength left him suddenly; and when he was confined to the chimney-corner he grew grievously irritable. A nothing vexed him, and suspected slights of his authority nearly threw him into fits. This was especially to be remarked if any one attempted to impose upon or domineer over his favourite. He was painfully jealous lest a word should be spoken amiss to him, seeming to have got into his head the notion that, because he liked Heathcliff, all hated and longed to do him an ill turn. It was a disadvantage to the lad, for the kinder among us did not wish to fret the master, so we humoured his partiality; and that humouring was rich nourishment to the child's pride and black tempers. Still it became in a manner necessary. Twice or thrice Hindley's manifestation of scorn, while his father was near, roused the old man to a fury. He seized his stick to strike him, and shook with rage that he could not do it.

At last our curate (we had a curate then, who made

the living answer by teaching the little Lintons and Earnshaws and farming his bit of land himself) advised that the young man should be sent to college ; and Mr. Earnshaw agreed, though with a heavy spirit, for he said, "Hindley was nought, and would never thrive as where he wandered."

I hoped heartily we should have peace now. It hurt me to think the master should be made uncomfortable by his own good deed. I fancied the discontent of age and disease arose from his family disagreements, as he would have it that it did. Really, you know, sir, it was in his sinking frame. We might have got on tolerably, notwithstanding, but for two people—Miss Cathy and Joseph the servant. You saw him, I dare say, up yonder. He was, and is yet most likely, the wearisomest self-righteous Pharisee that ever ransacked a Bible to rake the promises to himself and fling the curses to his neighbours. By his knack of sermonizing and pious discoursing he contrived to make a great impression on Mr. Earnshaw ; and the more feeble the master became, the more influence he gained. He was relentless in worrying him about his soul's concerns, and about ruling his children rigidly. He encouraged him to regard Hindley as a reprobate ; and night after night he regularly grumbled out a long string of tales against Heathcliff and Catherine, alway minding to flatter Earnshaw's weakness by heaping the heaviest blame on the latter.

Certainly she had ways with her such as I never saw a child take up before ; and she put all of us past our patience fifty times and oftener in a day. From the hour she came downstairs till the hour she went to bed we had not a minute's security that she wouldn't be in mischief. Her spirits were always at high-water mark, her tongue always going—singing, laughing, and plaguing everybody who would not do the same. A wild, wicked slip she was ; but she had the bonniest eye, the sweetest smile, and lightest foot in the parish. And, after all, I believe she meant no harm ; for when once she made you cry in good earnest, it seldom happened that she would not keep you company, and oblige you to be quiet, that you might comfort her. She was much too fond of Heathcliff. The greatest punishment we could invent for her was to keep her separate from him; yet she got chided more than any of us on his account. In play she liked exceedingly to act the little mistress, using her hands freely, and commanding her companions. She did so to me, but I would not bear shopping and ordering, and so I let her know.

Now, Mr. Earnshaw did not understand jokes from his children. He had always been strict and grave with them; and Catherine, on her part, had no idea why her father should be crosser and less patient in his ailing condition than he was in his prime. His peevish reproofs wakened in her a naughty delight to provoke him. She was never so happy as when we were all scolding her at once, and she defying us with her bold, saucy look and her ready words, turning Joseph's religious curses into ridicule, baiting me, and doing just what her father hated most—showing how her pretended insolence, which he thought real, had more power over Heathcliff than his kindness; how the boy would do *her* bidding in anything, and *his* only when it suited his own inclination. After behaving as badly as possible all day, she sometimes came fondling to make it up at night. "Nay, Cathy," the old man would say, "I cannot love thee; thou'rt worse than thy brother. Go say thy prayers, child, and ask God's pardon. I doubt thy mother and I must rue that we ever reared thee!" That made her cry at first; and then being repulsed continually hardened her, and she laughed if I told her to say she was sorry for her faults, and beg to be forgiven.

But the hour came at last that ended Mr. Earnshaw's troubles on earth. He died quietly in his chair one October evening, seated by the fireside. A high wind blustered round the house and roared in the chimney. It sounded wild and stormy, yet it was not cold, and we were all together—I, a little removed from the hearth, busy at my knitting, and Joseph reading his Bible near the table (for the servants generally sat in the house then, after their work was done). Miss Cathy had been sick, and that made her still. She leant against her father's knee, and Heathcliff was lying on the floor with his head in her lap. I remember the master, before he fell into a doze, stroking her bonny hair—it pleased him rarely to see her gentle—and saying, "Why canst thou not always be a good lass, Cathy?" And she turned her face up to his, and laughed, and answered, "Why cannot you always be a good man, father?" But as soon as she saw him vexed again, she kissed his hand, and said she would sing him to sleep. She began singing very low, till his fingers dropped from hers, and his head sank on his breast. Then I told her to hush, and not stir, for fear she should wake him. We all kept as mute as mice a full half-hour, and should have done so longer, only Joseph, having finished his chapter, got up and said that he must rouse the master for prayers and bed. He stepped forward, and called him by name, and touched his shoulder; but he would not move, so he took the candle and looked at him. I thought there was something wrong as he set down the light, and seizing the children each by an arm, whispered them to "frame upstairs, and make little din; they might pray alone that evening—he had summut to do."

"I shall bid father good-night first," said Catherine, putting her arms round his neck before we could hinder her. The poor thing discovered her loss directly. She screamed out, "Oh, he's dead, Heathcliff—he's dead!" And they both set up a heartbreaking cry.

I joined my wail to theirs, loud and bitter; but Joseph asked what we could be thinking of to roar in that way over a saint in heaven. He told me to put on my cloak and run to Gimmerton for the doctor and the parson. I could not guess the use that either would be of then. However, I went through wind and rain, and brought one, the doctor, back with me; the other said he would come in the morning. Leaving Joseph to explain matters, I ran to the children's room. Their door was ajar. I saw they had never laid down, though it was past midnight; but they were calmer, and did not need me to console them. The little souls were comforting each other with better thoughts than I could have hit on. No parson in the world ever pictured heaven so beautifully as they did in their innocent talk; and, while I sobbed and listened, I could not help wishing we were all there safe together.

CHAPTER VI.

MR. HINDLEY came home to the funeral; and—a thing that amazed us, and set the neighbours gossiping right and left—he brought a wife with him. What she was, and where she was born, he never informed us. Probably she had neither money nor name to recommend her, or he would scarcely have kept the union from his father.

She was not one that would have disturbed the house much on her own account. Every object she saw, the moment she crossed the threshold, appeared to delight her, and every circumstance that took place about her, except the preparing for the burial, and the presence of the mourners. I thought she was half silly, from her behaviour while that went on. She ran into her chamber, and made me come with her, though I should have been dressing the children; and there she sat shivering and clasping her hands, and asking repeatedly, "Are they gone yet?" Then she began describing with hysterical emotion the effect it produced on her to see black, and started, and trembled, and at last fell a-weeping; and when I asked what was the matter, answered she didn't know, but she felt so afraid of dying. I imagined her as little likely to die as myself. She was rather thin, but young and fresh-complexioned, and her eyes sparkled as bright as diamonds. I did remark, to be sure, that mounting the stairs made her breathe very quick; that the least sudden noise set her all in a quiver, and that she coughed troublesomely sometimes; but I knew nothing of what these symptoms portended, and had no impulse to sympathize with her. We don't in general take to foreigners here, Mr. Lockwood, unless they take to us first.

Young Earnshaw was altered considerably in the three years of his absence. He had grown sparer, and lost his colour, and spoke and dressed quite differently; and on the very day of his return he told Joseph and me we must thenceforth quarter ourselves in the back kitchen, and leave the house for him. Indeed, he would have carpeted and papered a small spare room for a parlour; but his wife expressed such pleasure at the white floor and huge glowing fireplace, at the pewter dishes and delf-case, and dog-kennel, and the wide space there was to move about in where they usually sat, that he thought it unnecessary to her comfort, and so dropped the intention.

She expressed pleasure, too, at finding a sister among her new acquaintance; and she prattled to Catherine, and kissed her, and ran about with her, and gave her quantities of presents, at the beginning. Her affection tired very soon, however; and when she grew peevish Hindley became tyrannical. A few words from her, evincing a dislike to Heathcliff, were enough to rouse in him all his old hatred of the boy. He drove him from their company to the servants, deprived him of the instructions of the curate, and insisted that he should labour out of doors instead, compelling him to do so as hard as any other lad on the farm.

Heathcliff bore his degradation pretty well at first, because Cathy taught him what she learned, and worked or played with him in the fields. They both promised fair to grow up as rude as savages, the young master being entirely negligent how they behaved, and what they did, so they kept clear of him. He would not even have seen after their going to church on Sundays, only

Joseph and the curate reprimanded his carelessness when they absented themselves; and that reminded him to order Heathcliff a flogging, and Catherine a fast from dinner or supper. But it was one of their chief amusements to run away to the moors in the morning and remain there all day, and the after punishment grew a mere thing to laugh at. The curate might set as many chapters as he pleased for Catherine to get by heart, and Joseph might thrash Heathcliff till his arm ached; they forgot everything the minute they were together again—at least, the minute they had contrived some naughty plan of revenge. And many a time I've cried to myself to watch them growing more reckless daily, and I not daring to speak a syllable, for fear of losing the small power I still retained over the unfriended creatures. One Sunday evening it chanced that they were banished from the sitting-room for making a noise, or a light offence of the kind, and when I went to call them to supper I could discover them nowhere. We searched the house, above and below, and the yard and stables. They were invisible; and at last Hindley in a passion told us to bolt the doors, and swore nobody should let them in that night. The household went to bed; and I, too anxious to lie down, opened my lattice and put my head out to hearken, though it rained, determined to admit them in spite of the prohibition, should they return. In a while I distinguished steps coming up the road, and the light of a lantern glimmered through the gate. I threw a shawl over my head, and ran to prevent them from waking Mr. Earnshaw by knocking. There was Heathcliff, by himself. It gave me a start to see him alone.

"Where is Miss Catherine?" I cried hurriedly. "No accident, I hope?" "At Thrushcross Grange," he answered; "and I would have been there too, but they had not the manners to ask me to stay." "Well, you will catch it!" I said; "you'll never be content till you're sent about your business. What in the world led you wandering to Thrushcross Grange?" "Let

me get off my wet clothes, and I'll tell you all about
it, Nelly," he replied. I bid him beware of rousing the
master; and while he undressed, and I waited to put out
the candle, he continued, "Cathy and I escaped from
the wash-house to have a ramble at liberty, and getting
a glimpse of the Grange lights, we thought we would
just go and see whether the Lintons passed their Sunday
evenings standing shivering in corners, while their father
and mother sat eating and drinking, and singing and
laughing, and burning their eyes out before the fire. Do
you think they do? Or reading sermons, and being cate-
chized by their man-servant, and set to learn a column
of Scripture names, if they don't answer properly?"
"Probably not," I responded. "They are good children, no doubt, and don't deserve the treatment you
receive for your bad conduct." "Don't cant, Nelly,"
he said; "nonsense! We ran from the top of the
Heights to the park without stopping, Catherine completely beaten in the race, because she was barefoot.
You'll have to seek for her shoes in the bog to-morrow.
We crept through a broken hedge, groped our way up
the path, and planted ourselves on a flower-plot under
the drawing-room window. The light came from thence.
They had not put up the shutters, and the curtains were
only half closed. Both of us were able to look in by
standing on the basement and clinging to the ledge,
and we saw—ah! it was beautiful—a splendid place
carpeted with crimson, and crimson-covered chairs and
tables, and a pure white ceiling bordered by gold, a
shower of glass-drops hanging in silver chains from the
centre, and shimmering with little soft tapers. Old Mr.
and Mrs. Linton were not there; Edgar and his sister
had it entirely to themselves. Shouldn't they have been
happy? We should have thought ourselves in heaven!
And now, guess what your good children were doing.
Isabella—I believe she is eleven, a year younger than
Cathy—lay screaming at the farther end of the room,
shrieking as if witches were running red-hot needles into
her. Edgar stood on the hearth weeping silently, and

in the middle of the table sat a little dog, shaking its
paw and yelping; which, from their mutual accusations,
we understood they had nearly pulled in two between
them. The idiots! That was their pleasure—to quarrel
who should hold a heap of warm hair, and each begin to
cry because both, after struggling to get it, refused to
take it. We laughed outright at the petted things. We
did despise them. When would you catch me wishing
to have what Catherine wanted, or find us by ourselves
seeking entertainment in yelling, and sobbing, and rolling
on the ground, divided by the whole room? I'd not
exchange for a thousand lives my condition here for
Edgar Linton's at Thrushcross Grange—not if I might
have the privilege of flinging Joseph off the highest gable,
and painting the house-front with Hindley's blood!"

"Hush, hush!" I interrupted. "Still you have not
told me, Heathcliff, how Catherine is left behind."

"I told you we laughed," he answered. "The Lintons
heard us, and with one accord they shot like arrows
to the door. There was silence, and then a cry, 'O
mamma, mamma! O papa! O mamma, come here.
O papa, oh!' They really did howl out something in
that way. We made frightful noises to terrify them still
more, and then we dropped off the ledge because somebody was drawing the bars, and we felt we had better
flee. I had Cathy by the hand, and was urging her on,
when all at once she fell down. 'Run, Heathcliff, run!'
she whispered. 'They have let the bull-dog loose, and
he holds me!' The devil had seized her ankle, Nelly;
I heard his abominable snorting. She did not yell out—
no! she would have scorned to do it if she had been
spitted on the horns of a mad cow. I did, though. I
vociferated curses enough to annihilate any fiend in
Christendom; and I got a stone and thrust it between
his jaws, and tried with all my might to cram it down his
throat. A beast of a servant came up with a lantern
at last, shouting, 'Keep fast, Skulker, keep fast!' He
changed his note, however, when he saw Skulker's game.
The dog was throttled off, his huge purple tongue

hanging half a foot out of his mouth, and his pendent lips streaming with bloody slaver. The man took Cathy up. She was sick—not from fear, I'm certain, but from pain. He carried her in. I followed, grumbling execrations and vengeance. 'What prey, Robert?' hallooed Linton from the entrance. 'Skulker has caught a little girl, sir,' he replied; 'and there's a lad here,' he added, making a clutch at me, 'who looks an out-and-outer. Very like, the robbers were for putting them through the window to open the doors to the gang after all were asleep, that they might murder us at their ease.—Hold your tongue, you foul-mouthed thief, you! You shall go to the gallows for this.—Mr. Linton, sir, don't lay by your gun.' 'No, no, Robert,' said the old fool. 'The rascals knew that yesterday was my rent-day. They thought to have me cleverly. Come in; I'll furnish them a reception.—There, John, fasten the chain.—Give Skulker some water, Jenny. To beard a magistrate in his stronghold, and on the Sabbath, too! Where will their insolence stop?—Oh, my dear Mary, look here! Don't be afraid; it is but a boy, yet the villain scowls so plainly in his face; would it not be a kindness to the country to hang him at once, before he shows his nature in acts as well as features?' He pulled me under the chandelier, and Mrs. Linton placed her spectacles on her nose and raised her hands in horror. The cowardly children crept nearer also, Isabella lisping, 'Frightful thing! Put him in the cellar, papa. He's exactly like the son of the fortune-teller that stole my tame pheasant. —Isn't he, Edgar?'

"While they examined me Cathy came round. She heard the last speech, and laughed. Edgar Linton, after an inquisitive stare, collected sufficient wit to recognize her. They see us at church, you know, though we seldom meet them elsewhere. 'That's Miss Earnshaw!' he whispered to his mother; 'and look how Skulker has bitten her—how her foot bleeds!'

"' Miss Earnshaw! Nonsense!' cried the dame; 'Miss Earnshaw scouring the country with a gipsy!

And yet, my dear, the child is in mourning. Surely it is. And she may be lamed for life.'

" ' What culpable carelessness in her brother!' exclaimed Mr. Linton, turning from me to Catherine. ' I've understood from Shielders ' " (that was the curate, sir) " ' that he lets her grow up in absolute heathenism. But who is this ? Where did she pick up this companion ? Oho ! I declare he is that strange acquisition my late neighbour made in his journey to Liverpool —a little Lascar, or an American or Spanish castaway.'

" ' A wicked boy, at all events,' remarked the old lady, ' and quite unfit for a decent house ! Did you notice his language, Linton ? I'm shocked that my children should have heard it.'

" I recommended cursing—don't be angry, Nelly— and so Robert was ordered to take me off. I refused to go without Cathy. He dragged me into the garden, pushed the lantern into my hand, assured me that Mr. Earnshaw should be informed of my behaviour, and bidding me march directly, secured the door again. The curtains were still looped up at one corner, and I resumed my station as spy ; because, if Catherine had wished to return, I intended shattering their great glass panes to a million of fragments, unless they let her out. She sat on the sofa quietly. Mrs. Linton took off the gray cloak of the dairymaid which we had borrowed for our excursion, shaking her head and expostulating with her, I suppose. She was a young lady, and they made a distinction between her treatment and mine. Then the woman-servant brought a basin of warm water, and washed her feet ; and Mr. Linton mixed a tumbler of negus, and Isabella emptied a plateful of cakes into her lap, and Edgar stood gaping at a distance. Afterwards they dried and combed her beautiful hair, and gave her a pair of enormous slippers, and wheeled her to the fire ; and I left her, as merry as she could be, dividing her food between the little dog and Skulker, whose nose she pinched as he ate, and kindling a spark of spirit in the vacant blue eyes of the Lintons—a dim reflection from her own enchanting face. I saw they were full of stupid admiration; she is so immeasurably superior to them—to everybody on earth, is she not, Nelly?"

"There will more come of this business than you reckon on," I answered, covering him up and extinguishing the light. "You are incurable, Heathcliff; and Mr. Hindley will have to proceed to extremities—see if he won't." My words came truer than I desired. The luckless adventure made Earnshaw furious. And then Mr. Linton, to mend manners, paid us a visit himself on the morrow, and read the young master such a lecture on the road he guided his family that he was stirred to look about him in earnest. Heathcliff received no flogging, but he was told that the first word he spoke to Miss Catherine should ensure a dismissal; and Mrs. Earnshaw undertook to keep her sister-in-law in due restraint when she returned home, employing art, not force. With force she would have found it impossible.

CHAPTER VII.

CATHY stayed at Thrushcross Grange five weeks—till Christmas. By that time her ankle was thoroughly cured, and her manners much improved. The mistress visited her often in the interval, and commenced her plan of reform by trying to raise her self-respect with fine clothes and flattery, which she took readily; so that, instead of a wild, hatless little savage jumping into the house, and rushing to squeeze us all breathless, there lighted from a handsome black pony a very dignified person, with brown ringlets falling from the cover of a feathered beaver, and a long cloth habit, which she was obliged to hold up with both hands, that she might sail in. Hindley lifted her from her horse, exclaiming delightedly, "Why, Cathy, you are quite a beauty! I should scarcely have known you. You look like a lady now.—Isabella Linton is not to be compared with her, is she, Frances?"

"Isabella has not her natural advantages," replied his wife; "but she must mind and not grow wild again here.—Ellen, help Miss Catherine off with her things.— Stay, dear; you will disarrange your curls. Let me untie your hat."

I removed the habit, and there shone forth beneath a grand plaid silk frock, white trousers, and burnished shoes; and while her eyes sparkled joyfully when the dogs came bounding up to welcome her, she dare hardly touch them lest they should fawn upon her splendid garments. She kissed me gently. I was all flour making the Christmas cake, and it would not have done to give me a hug; and then she looked round for Heathcliff. Mr. and Mrs. Earnshaw watched anxiously their meeting, thinking it would enable them to judge, in some measure, what grounds they had for hoping to succeed in separating the two friends.

Heathcliff was hard to discover at first. If he were careless and uncared for before Catherine's absence, he had been ten times more so since. Nobody but I even did him the kindness to call him a dirty boy, and bid him wash himself, once a week; and children of his age seldom have a natural pleasure in soap and water. Therefore, not to mention his clothes, which had seen three months' service in mire and dust, and his thick uncombed hair, the surface of his face and hands was dismally beclouded. He might well skulk behind the settle, on beholding such a bright, graceful damsel enter the house, instead of a rough-headed counterpart of himself, as he expected. "Is Heathcliff not here?" she demanded, pulling off her gloves, and displaying fingers wonderfully whitened with doing nothing and staying indoors.

"Heathcliff, you may come forward," cried Mr. Hindley, enjoying his discomfiture, and gratified to see what a forbidding young blackguard he would be compelled to present himself. "You may come and wish Miss Catherine welcome, like the other servants."

Cathy, catching a glimpse of her friend in his concealment, flew to embrace him. She bestowed seven or eight kisses on his cheek within the second, and then stopped, and drawing back, burst into a laugh, exclaiming, " Why, how very black and cross you look ! and how—how funny and grim ! But that's because I'm used to Edgar and Isabella Linton. Well, Heathcliff, have you forgotten me ? "

She had some reason to put the question, for shame and pride threw double gloom over his countenance, and kept him immovable.

" Shake hands, Heathcliff," said Mr. Earnshaw, condescendingly ; " once in a way that is permitted."

" I shall not," replied the boy, finding his tongue at last ; " I shall not stand to be laughed at. I shall not bear it."

And he would have broken from the circle, but Miss Cathy seized him again.

" I did not mean to laugh at you," she said ; " I could not hinder myself. Heathcliff, shake hands at least. What are you sulky for ? It was only that you looked odd. If you wash your face and brush your hair it will be all right ; but you are so dirty ! "

She gazed concernedly at the dusky fingers she held in her own, and also at her dress, which she feared had gained no embellishment from its contact with his.

" You needn't have touched me," he answered, following her eye and snatching away his hand. " I shall be as dirty as I please ; and I like to be dirty, and I will be dirty."

With that he dashed head foremost out of the room, amid the merriment of the master and mistress, and to the serious disturbance of Catherine, who could not comprehend how her remarks should have produced such an exhibition of bad temper.

After playing lady's-maid to the newcomer, and putting my cakes in the oven, and making the house and kitchen cheerful with great fires, befitting Christmas Eve, I prepared to sit down and amuse myself by singing carols all alone, regardless of Joseph's affirmations that he

considered the merry tunes I chose as next door to
songs. He had retired to private prayer in his chamber,
and Mr. and Mrs. Earnshaw were engaging Missy's attention by sundry gay trifles bought for her to present to
the little Lintons, as an acknowledgment of their kindness. They had invited them to spend the morrow at
Wuthering Heights, and the invitation had been accepted,
on one condition. Mrs. Linton begged that her darlings
might be kept carefully apart from that " naughty, swearing boy."

Under these circumstances I remained solitary. I
smelt the rich scent of the heating spices, and admired
the shining kitchen utensils, the polished clock, decked
in holly, the silver mugs ranged on a tray ready to be
filled with mulled ale for supper, and, above all, the
speckless purity of my particular care—the scoured and
well-swept floor. I gave due inward applause to every
object, and then I remembered how old Earnshaw used
to come in when all was tidied, and call me a cant lass,
and slip a shilling into my hand as a Christmas-box ; and
from that I went on to think of his fondness for Heathcliff, and his dread lest he should suffer neglect after
death had removed him ; and that naturally led me
to consider the poor lad's situation now, and from singing I changed my mind to crying. It struck me soon,
however, there would be more sense in endeavouring
to repair some of his wrongs than shedding tears over
them. I got up and walked into the court to seek him.
He was not far. I found him smoothing the glossy
coat of the new pony in the stable, and feeding the other
beasts, according to custom.

" Make haste, Heathcliff ! " I said ; " the kitchen is so
comfortable, and Joseph is upstairs. Make haste, and
let me dress you smart before Miss Cathy comes out,
and then you can sit together, with the whole hearth
to yourselves, and have a long chatter till bedtime."

He proceeded with his task, and never turned his head
towards me.

" Come ; are you coming ? " I continued. " There's

a little cake for each of you, nearly enough ; and you'll need half an hour's donning."

I waited five minutes, but getting no answer left him. Catherine supped with her brother and sister-in-law. Joseph and I joined at an unsociable meal, seasoned with reproofs on one side and sauciness on the other. His cake and cheese remained on the table all night for the fairies. He managed to continue work till nine o'clock, and then marched dumb and dour to his chamber. Cathy sat up late, having a world of things to order for the reception of her new friends. She came into the kitchen once to speak to her old one ; but he was gone, and she only stayed to ask what was the matter with him, and then went back. In the morning he rose early ; and as it was a holiday carried his ill-humour on to the moors, not reappearing till the family were departed for church. Fasting and reflection seemed to have brought him to a better spirit. He hung about me for a while, and having screwed up his courage, exclaimed abruptly,—

" Nelly, make me decent ; I'm going to be good."

" High time, Heathcliff," I said ; " you *have* grieved Catherine. She's sorry she ever came home, I dare say. It looks as if you envied her because she is more thought of than you."

The notion of *envying* Catherine was incomprehensible to him, but the notion of grieving her he understood clearly enough.

" Did she say she was grieved ? " he inquired, looking very serious.

" She cried when I told her you were off again this morning."

" Well, *I* cried last night," he returned, " and I had more reason to cry than she."

" Yes. You had the reason of going to bed with a proud heart and an empty stomach," said I. " Proud people breed sad sorrows for themselves. But, if you be ashamed of your touchiness, you must ask pardon, mind, when she comes in. You must go up and offer to kiss her, and say—you know best what to say; only do it heartily, and not as if you thought her converted into a stranger by her grand dress. And now, though I have dinner to get ready, I'll steal time to arrange you so that Edgar Linton shall look quite a doll beside you; and that he does. You are younger, and yet, I'll be bound, you are taller and twice as broad across the shoulders. You could knock him down in a twinkling. Don't you feel that you could?"

Heathcliff's face brightened a moment; then it was overcast afresh, and he sighed.

"But, Nelly, if I knocked him down twenty times, that wouldn't make him less handsome or me more so. I wish I had light hair and a fair skin, and was dressed and behaved as well, and had a chance of being as rich as he will be."

"And cried for mamma at every turn," I added, "and trembled if a country lad heaved his fist against you, and sat at home all day for a shower of rain. Oh, Heathcliff, you are showing a poor spirit! Come to the glass, and I'll let you see what you should wish. Do you mark those two lines between your eyes; and those thick brows that, instead of rising arched, sink in the middle; and that couple of black fiends, so deeply buried, who never open their windows boldly, but lurk glinting under them, like devil's spies? Wish and learn to smooth away the surly wrinkles, to raise your lids frankly, and change the fiends to confident, innocent angels, suspecting and doubting nothing, and always seeing friends where they are not sure of foes. Don't get the expression of a vicious cur that appears to know the kicks it gets are its desert, and yet hates all the world as well as the kicker for what it suffers."

"In other words, I must wish for Edgar Linton's great blue eyes and even forehead," he replied. "I do, and that won't help me to them."

"A good heart will help you to a bonny face, my lad," I continued, "if you were a regular black; and a bad one will turn the bonniest into something worse than ugly. And now that we've done washing, and combing, and sulking, tell me whether you don't think yourself rather handsome? I'll tell you I do. You're fit for a prince in disguise. Who knows but your father was Emperor of China, and your mother an Indian queen, each of them able to buy up, with one week's income, Wuthering Heights and Thrushcross Grange together? And you were kidnapped by wicked sailors and brought to England. Were I in your place, I would frame high notions of my birth; and the thoughts of what I was should give me courage and dignity to support the oppressions of a little farmer."

So I chattered on; and Heathcliff gradually lost his frown and began to look quite pleasant, when all at once our conversation was interrupted by a rumbling sound moving up the road and entering the court. He ran to the window and I to the door, just in time to behold the two Lintons descend from the family carriage, smothered in cloaks and furs, and the Earnshaws dismount from their horses. They often rode to church in winter. Catherine took a hand of each of the children, and brought them into the house and set them before the fire, which quickly put colour into their white faces.

I urged my companion to hasten now and show his amiable humour, and he willingly obeyed; but ill luck would have it that, as he opened the door leading from the kitchen on one side, Hindley opened it on the other. They met, and the master, irritated at seeing him clean and cheerful, or, perhaps, eager to keep his promise to Mrs. Linton, shoved him back with a sudden thrust, and angrily bade Joseph "keep the fellow out of the room; send him into the garret till dinner is over. He'll be cramming his fingers in the tarts and stealing the fruit, if left alone with them a minute."

"Nay, sir," I could not avoid answering; "he'll touch nothing—not he; and I suppose he must have his share of the dainties as well as we."

"He shall have his share of my hand if I catch him

downstairs till dark," cried Hindley.—" Begone, you vagabond! What! you are attempting the coxcomb, are you? Wait till I get hold of those elegant locks; see if I won't pull them a bit longer."

"They are long enough already," observed Master Linton, peeping from the doorway; "I wonder they don't make his head ache. It's like a colt's mane over his eyes."

He ventured this remark without any intention to insult; but Heathcliff's violent nature was not prepared to endure the appearance of impertinence from one whom he seemed to hate, even then, as a rival. He seized a tureen of hot apple sauce—the first thing that came under his gripe—and dashed it full against the speaker's face and neck, who instantly commenced a lament that brought Isabella and Catherine hurrying to the place. Mr. Earnshaw snatched up the culprit directly, and conveyed him to his chamber, where, doubtless, he administered a rough remedy to cool the fit of passion, for he appeared red and breathless. I got the dish-cloth, and rather spitefully scrubbed Edgar's nose and mouth, affirming it served him right for meddling. His sister began weeping to go home, and Cathy stood by confounded, blushing for all.

"You should not have spoken to him!" she expostulated with Master Linton. "He was in a bad temper; and now you've spoilt your visit, and he'll be flogged. I hate him to be flogged. I can't eat my dinner. Why did you speak to him, Edgar?"

"I didn't," sobbed the youth, escaping from my hands and finishing the remainder of the purification with his cambric pocket-handkerchief. "I promised mamma that I wouldn't say one word to him, and I didn't."

"Well, don't cry," replied Catherine contemptuously; "you're not killed. Don't make more mischief. My brother is coming; be quiet!—Hush, Isabella! Has anybody hurt you?"

"There, there, children; to your seats," cried Hindley, bustling in. "That brute of a lad has warmed me nicely. Next time, Master Edgar, take the law into your own fists; it will give you an appetite."

The little party recovered its equanimity at sight of the fragrant feast. They were hungry after their ride, and easily consoled, since no real harm had befallen them. Mr. Earnshaw carved bountiful platefuls, and the mistress made them merry with lively talk. I waited behind her chair, and was pained to behold Catherine, with dry eyes and an indifferent air, commence cutting up the wing of a goose before her. "An unfeeling child," I thought to myself; "how lightly she dismisses her old playmate's troubles! I could not have imagined her to be so selfish." She lifted a mouthful to her lips, then she set it down again; her cheeks flushed, and the tears gushed over them. She slipped her fork to the floor, and hastily dived under the cloth to conceal her emotion. I did not call her unfeeling long, for I perceived she was in purgatory throughout the day, and wearying to find an opportunity of getting by herself, or paying a visit to Heathcliff, who had been locked up by the master, as I discovered, on endeavouring to introduce to him a private mess of victuals.

In the evening we had a dance. Cathy begged that he might be liberated then, as Isabella Linton had no partner. Her entreaties were vain, and I was appointed to supply the deficiency. We got rid of all gloom in the excitement of the exercise, and our pleasure was increased by the arrival of the Gimmerton band, mustering fifteen strong—a trumpet, a trombone, clarionets, bassoons, French horns, and a bass viol, besides singers. They go the rounds of all the respectable houses, and receive contributions every Christmas, and we esteemed it a first-rate treat to hear them. After the usual carols had been sung, we set them to songs and glees. Mrs. Earnshaw loved the music, and so they gave us plenty.

Catherine loved it too, but she said it sounded sweetest at the top of the steps, and she went up in the dark; I followed. They shut the house door below, never noting our absence, it was so full of people. She made no stay at the stairs' head, but mounted farther to the garret where Heathcliff was confined, and called him. He stubbornly declined answering for a while; she persevered, and finally persuaded him to hold communion with her through the boards. I let the poor things converse unmolested, till I supposed the songs were going to cease, and the singers to get some refreshment; then I clambered up the ladder to warn her. Instead of finding her outside, I heard her voice within. The little monkey had crept by the skylight of one garret, along the roof, into the skylight of the other, and it was with the utmost difficulty I could coax her out again. When she did come, Heathcliff came with her, and she insisted that I should take him into the kitchen, as my fellow-servant had gone to a neighbour's to be removed from the sound of our " devil's psalmody," as it pleased him to call it. I told them I intended by no means to encourage their tricks, but as the prisoner had never broken his fast since yesterday's dinner, I would wink at his cheating Mr. Hindley that once. He went down. I set him a stool by the fire, and offered him a quantity of good things; but he was sick, and could eat little, and my attempts to entertain him were thrown away. He leant his two elbows on his knees, and his chin on his hands, and remained wrapt in dumb meditation. On my inquiring the subject of his thoughts he answered gravely,—

" I'm trying to settle how I shall pay Hindley back. I don't care how long I wait, if I can only do it at last. I hope he will not die before I do ! "

" For shame, Heathcliff ! " said I. " It is for God to punish wicked people ; we should learn to forgive."

" No ; God won't have the satisfaction that I shall," he returned. " I only wish I knew the best way. Let me alone, and I'll plan it out ; while I'm thinking of that I don't feel pain."

But, Mr. Lockwood, I forget these tales cannot divert you. I'm annoyed how I should dream of chattering on at such a rate, and your gruel cold, and you nodding for bed! I could have told Heathcliff's history—all that you need hear—in half a dozen words.

Thus interrupting herself, the housekeeper rose and proceeded to lay aside her sewing; but I felt incapable of moving from the hearth, and I was very far from nodding. " Sit still, Mrs. Dean," I cried, " do sit still another half-hour! You've done just right to tell the story leisurely—that is the method I like; and you must finish it in the same style. I am interested in every character you have mentioned, more or less."

" The clock is on the stroke of eleven, sir."

" No matter. I'm not accustomed to go to bed in the long hours. One or two is early enough for a person who lies till ten."

" You shouldn't lie till ten. There's the very prime of the morning gone long before that time. A person who has not done one half his day's work by ten o'clock runs a chance of leaving the other half undone."

" Nevertheless, Mrs. Dean, resume your chair, because to-morrow I intend lengthening the night till afternoon. I prognosticate for myself an obstinate cold, at least."

" I hope not, sir. Well, you must allow me to leap over some three years. During that space Mrs. Earnshaw—"

" No, no; I'll allow nothing of the sort. Are you acquainted with the mood of mind in which, if you were seated alone, and the cat licking its kitten on the rug before you, you would watch the operation so intently that puss's neglect of one ear would put you seriously out of temper?"

" A terribly lazy mood, I should say."

" On the contrary, a tiresomely active one. It is mine at present; and, therefore, continue minutely. I perceive that people in these regions acquire over people in towns the value that a spider in a dungeon does over a spider in a cottage, to their various occupants; and yet the deepened attraction is not entirely owing to the situation of the looker-on. They *do* live more in earnest, more in themselves, and less in surface, change, and frivolous external things. I could fancy a love for life here almost possible ; and I was a fixed unbeliever in any love of a year's standing. One state resembles setting a hungry man down to a single dish, on which he may concentrate his entire appetite and do it justice ; the other, introducing him to a table laid out by French cooks. He can perhaps extract as much enjoyment from the whole, but each part is a mere atom in his regard and remembrance."

"Oh, here we are the same as anywhere else, when you get to know us," observed Mrs. Dean, somewhat puzzled at my speech.

"Excuse me," I responded. "You, my good friend, are a striking evidence against that assertion. Excepting a few provincialisms of slight consequence, you have no marks of the manners which I am habituated to consider as peculiar to your class. I am sure you have thought a great deal more than the generality of servants think. You have been compelled to cultivate your reflective faculties, for want of occasions for frittering your life away in silly trifles."

Mrs. Dean laughed.

"I certainly esteem myself a steady, reasonable kind of body," she said—"not exactly from living among the hills and seeing one set of faces and one series of actions from year's end to year's end, but I have undergone sharp discipline, which has taught me wisdom ; and then, I have read more than you would fancy, Mr. Lockwood. You could not open a book in this library that I have not looked into, and got something out of also—unless it be that range of Greek and Latin, and that of French ; and those I know one from another. It is as much as you can expect of a poor man's daughter. However, if I am to follow my story in true gossip's fashion, I had better go on ; and instead of leaping three years, I will be content to pass to the next summer—the summer of 1778 ; that is nearly twenty-three years ago."

CHAPTER VIII.

ON the morning of a fine June day my first bonny little nursling, and the last of the ancient Earnshaw stock, was born. We were busy with the hay in a far-away field when the girl that usually brought our breakfasts came running an hour too soon, across the meadow and up the lane, calling me as she ran.

"Oh, such a grand bairn!" she panted out. "The finest lad that ever breathed! But the doctor says missis must go. He says she's been in a consumption these many months. I heard him tell Mr. Hindley; and now she has nothing to keep her, and she'll be dead before winter. You must come home directly. You're to nurse it, Nelly—to feed it with sugar and milk, and take care of it day and night. I wish I were you, because it will be all yours when there is no missis!"

"But is she very ill?" I asked, flinging down my rake and tying my bonnet.

"I guess she is; yet she looks bravely," replied the girl, "and she talks as if she thought of living to see it grow a man. She's out of her head for joy, it's such a beauty! If I were her, I'm certain I should not die; I should get better at the bare sight of it, in spite of Kenneth. I was fairly mad at him. Dame Archer brought the cherub down to master, in the house, and his face just began to light up, when the old croaker steps forward, and says he, 'Earnshaw, it's a blessing your wife has been spared to leave you this son. When she came, I felt convinced we shouldn't keep her long; and now, I must tell you, the winter will probably finish her. Don't take on and fret about it too much. It can't be helped. And besides, you should have known better than to choose such a rush of a lass!'"

"And what did the master answer?" I inquired.

"I think he swore; but I didn't mind him—I was straining to see the bairn." And she began again to describe it rapturously. I, as zealous as herself, hurried

eagerly home to admire, on my part, though I was very
sad for Hindley's sake. He had room in his heart only
for two idols—his wife and himself. He doted on both,
and adored one, and I couldn't conceive how he would
bear the loss.

When we got to Wuthering Heights, there he stood
at the front door; and, as I passed in, I asked, " How
was the baby?"

" Nearly ready to run about, Nell!" he replied,
putting on a cheerful smile.

" And the mistress?" I ventured to inquire; " the
doctor says she's——"

" Damn the doctor!" he interrupted, reddening.
" Frances is quite right; she'll be perfectly well by
this time next week. Are you going upstairs? Will
you tell her that I'll come, if she'll promise not to talk.
I left her because she would not hold her tongue; and
she must. Tell her Mr. Kenneth says she must be quiet."

I delivered this message to Mrs. Earnshaw. She
seemed in flighty spirits, and replied merrily,—

" I hardly spoke a word, Ellen, and there he has gone
out twice, crying. Well, say I promise I won't speak;
but that does not bind me not to laugh at him."

Poor soul! Till within a week of her death that gay
heart never failed her, and her husband persisted doggedly
—nay, furiously—in affirming her health improved every
day. When Kenneth warned him that his medicines
were useless at that stage of the malady, and he needn't
put him to further expense by attending her, he retorted,—

" I know you need not; she's well—she does not
want any more attendance from you! She never was
in a consumption. It was a fever, and it is gone; her
pulse is as slow as mine now, and her cheek as cool."

He told his wife the same story, and she seemed to
believe him; but one night, while leaning on his shoulder
in the act of saying she thought she should be able to
get up to-morrow, a fit of coughing took her—a very
slight one. He raised her in his arms; she put her two

hands about his neck, her face changed, and she was dead.

As the girl had anticipated, the child Hareton fell wholly into my hands. Mr. Earnshaw, provided he saw him healthy, and never heard him cry, was contented, as far as regarded him. For himself, he grew desperate; his sorrow was of that kind that will not lament. He neither wept nor prayed; he cursed and defied—execrated God and man, and gave himself up to reckless dissipation. The servants could not bear his tyrannical and evil conduct long. Joseph and I were the only two that would stay. I had not the heart to leave my charge; and besides, you know I had been his foster-sister, and excused his behaviour more readily than a stranger would. Joseph remained to hector over tenants and labourers, and because it was his vocation to be where he had plenty of wickedness to reprove.

The master's bad ways and bad companions formed a pretty example for Catherine and Heathcliff. His treatment of the latter was enough to make a fiend of a saint. And, truly, it appeared as if the lad *were* possessed of something diabolical at that period. He delighted to witness Hindley degrading himself past redemption, and became daily more notable for savage sullenness and ferocity. I could not half tell what an infernal house we had. The curate dropped calling, and nobody decent came near us at last, unless Edgar Linton's visits to Miss Cathy might be an exception. At fifteen she was the queen of the countryside; she had no peer, and she did turn out a haughty, headstrong creature! I own I did not like her after her infancy was past, and I vexed her frequently by trying to bring down her arrogance; she never took an aversion to me, though. She had a wondrous constancy to old attachments—even Heathcliff kept his hold on her affections unalterably; and young Linton, with all his superiority, found it difficult to make an equally deep impression. He was my late master; that is his portrait over the fireplace. It used to hang on one side, and his wife's on the other; but hers has been removed, or else you might see something of what she was. Can you make that out?

Mrs. Dean raised the candle, and I discerned a soft-featured face, exceedingly resembling the young lady at the Heights, but more pensive and amiable in expression. It formed a sweet picture. The long light hair curled slightly on the temples; the eyes were large and serious, the figure almost too graceful. I did not marvel how Catherine Earnshaw could forget her first friend for such an individual. I marvelled much how he, with a mind to correspond with his person, could fancy my idea of Catherine Earnshaw.

"A very agreeable portrait," I observed to the housekeeper. "Is it like?"

"Yes," she answered. "but he looked better when he was animated. That is his everyday countenance. He wanted spirit in general."

Catherine had kept up her acquaintance with the Lintons since her five weeks' residence among them; and as she had no temptation to show her rough side in their company, and had the sense to be ashamed of being rude where she experienced such invariable courtesy, she imposed unwittingly on the old lady and gentleman by her ingenious cordiality, gained the admiration of Isabella, and the heart and soul of her brother—acquisitions that flattered her from the first, for she was full of ambition, and led her to adopt a double character without exactly intending to deceive any one. In the place where she heard Heathcliff termed a "vulgar young ruffian," and "worse than a brute," she took care not to act like him; but at home she had small inclination to practise politeness that would only be laughed at, and restrain an unruly nature when it would bring her neither credit nor praise.

Mr. Edgar seldom mustered courage to visit Wuthering Heights openly. He had a terror of Earnshaw's reputation, and shrank from encountering him; and yet he was always received with our best attempts at civility.

The master himself avoided offending him, knowing why he came; and if he could not be gracious, kept out of the way. I rather think his appearance there was distasteful to Catherine. She was not artful, never played the coquette, and had evidently an objection to her two friends meeting at all; for when Heathcliff expressed contempt of Linton in his presence, she could not half coincide as she did in his absence; and when Linton evinced disgust and antipathy to Heathcliff, she dared not treat his sentiments with indifference, as if depreciation of her playmate were of scarcely any consequence to her. I've had many a laugh at her perplexities and untold troubles, which she vainly strove to hide from my mockery. That sounds ill-natured, but she was so proud it became really impossible to pity her distresses, till she should be chastened into more humility. She did bring herself, finally, to confess, and to confide in me. There was not a soul else that she might fashion into an adviser.

Mr. Hindley had gone from home one afternoon, and Heathcliff presumed to give himself a holiday on the strength of it. He had reached the age of sixteen then, I think, and without having bad features or being deficient in intellect, he contrived to convey an impression of inward and outward repulsiveness that his present aspect retains no traces of. In the first place, he had by that time lost the benefit of his early education. Continual hard work, begun soon and concluded late, had extinguished any curiosity he once possessed in pursuit of knowledge, and any love for books or learning. His childhood's sense of superiority instilled into him by the favours of old Mr. Earnshaw was faded away. He struggled long to keep up an equality with Catherine in her studies, and yielded with poignant though silent regret; but he yielded completely, and there was no prevailing on him to take a step in the way of moving upward, when he found he must necessarily sink beneath his former level. Then personal appearance sympathized with mental deterioration. He acquired a slouching gait and ignoble look; his naturally reserved disposition was exaggerated into an almost idiotic excess of unsociable moroseness, and he took a grim pleasure, apparently, in exciting the aversion rather than the esteem of his few acquaintance.

Catherine and he were constant companions still at his seasons of respite from labour, but he had ceased to express his fondness for her in words, and recoiled with angry suspicion from her girlish caresses, as if conscious there could be no gratification in lavishing such marks of affection on him. On the before-named occasion he came into the house to announce his intention of doing nothing, while I was assisting Miss Cathy to arrange her dress. She had not reckoned on his taking it into his head to be idle, and imagining she would have the whole place to herself, she managed, by some means, to inform Mr. Edgar of her brother's absence, and was then preparing to receive him.

"Cathy, are you busy this afternoon?" asked Heathcliff. "Are you going anywhere?"

"No; it is raining," she answered.

"Why have you that silk frock on, then?" he said. "Nobody coming here, I hope?"

"Not that I know of," stammered miss; "but you should be in the field now, Heathcliff. It is an hour past dinner-time. I thought you were gone."

"Hindley does not often free us from his accursed presence," observed the boy. "I'll not work any more to-day; I'll stay with you."

"Oh, but Joseph will tell," she suggested. "You'd better go."

"Joseph is loading lime on the further side of Peniston Crag; it will take him till dark, and he'll never know."

So saying, he lounged to the fire and sat down. Catherine reflected an instant with knitted brows; she found it needful to smooth the way for an intrusion. "Isabella and Edgar Linton talked of calling this afternoon," she said, at the conclusion of a minute's silence. "As it rains, I hardly expect them; but they may come, and if they do you run the risk of being scolded for no good."

"Order Ellen to say you are engaged, Cathy," he persisted. "Don't turn me out for those pitiful, silly friends of yours! I'm on the point, sometimes, of complaining that they—but I'll not."

"That they what?" cried Catherine, gazing at him with a troubled countenance.—"Oh, Nelly!" she added petulantly, jerking her head away from my hands, "you've combed my hair quite out of curl. That's enough; let me alone.—What are you on the point of complaining about, Heathcliff?"

"Nothing—only look at the almanac on that wall." He pointed to a framed sheet hanging near the window, and continued, "The crosses are for the evenings you have spent with the Lintons, the dots for those spent with me. Do you see? I've marked every day."

"Yes; very foolish—as if I took notice!" replied Catherine, in a peevish tone. "And where is the sense of that?"

"To show that I *do* take notice," said Heathcliff.

"And should I always be sitting with you?" she demanded, growing more irritated. "What good do I get? What do you talk about? You might be dumb, or a baby, for anything you say to amuse me, or for anything you do either."

"You never told me before that I talked too little, or that you disliked my company, Cathy," exclaimed Heathcliff in much agitation.

"It's no company at all, when people know nothing and say nothing," she muttered.

Her companion rose up; but he hadn't time to express his feelings further, for a horse's feet were heard on the flags; and, having knocked gently, young Linton entered, his face brilliant with delight at the unexpected summons he had received. Doubtless Catherine marked the difference between her friends, as one came in and the other went out. The contrast resembled what you see in exchanging a bleak, hilly, coal country for a beautiful fertile valley; and his voice and greeting were as opposite as his aspect. He had a sweet, low manner of speaking, and pronounced his words as you do— that's less gruff than we talk here, and softer.

"I'm not come too soon, am I?" he said, casting a look at me. I had begun to wipe the plate and tidy some drawers at the far end in the dresser.

"No," answered Catherine.—"What are you doing there, Nelly?"

"My work, miss," I replied. (Mr. Hindley had given me directions to make a third party in any private visits Linton chose to pay.)

She stepped behind me and whispered crossly, "Take yourself and your dusters off. When company are in the house, servants don't commence scouring and cleaning in the room where they are."

"It's a good opportunity, now that master is away," I answered aloud. "He hates me to be fidgeting over these things in his presence. I'm sure Mr. Edgar will excuse me."

"I hate you to be fidgeting in my presence," exclaimed the young lady imperiously, not allowing her guest time to speak. She had failed to recover her equanimity since the little dispute with Heathcliff.

"I'm sorry for it, Miss Catherine," was my response; and I proceeded assiduously with my occupation.

She, supposing Edgar could not see her, snatched the cloth from my hand, and pinched me, with a prolonged wrench, very spitefully on the arm. I've said I did not love her, and rather relished mortifying her vanity now and then—besides, she hurt me extremely; so I started up from my knees, and screamed out, "O miss, that's a nasty trick! You have no right to nip me, and I'm not going to bear it."

"I didn't touch you, you lying creature!" cried she, her fingers tingling to repeat the act, and her ears red with rage. She never had power to conceal her passion; it always set her whole complexion in a blaze.

"What's that, then?" I retorted, showing a decided purple witness to refute her.

She stamped her foot, wavered a moment, and then, irresistibly impelled by the naughty spirit within her, slapped me on the cheek—a stinging blow that filled both eyes with water.

"Catherine, love! Catherine!" interposed Linton, greatly shocked at the double fault of falsehood and violence which his idol had committed.

"Leave the room, Ellen!" she repeated, trembling all over.

Little Hareton, who followed me everywhere, and was sitting near me on the floor, at seeing my tears commenced crying himself, and sobbed out complaints against "wicked Aunt Cathy," which drew her fury on to his unlucky head. She seized his shoulders, and shook him till the poor child waxed livid, and Edgar thoughtlessly laid hold of her hands to deliver him. In an instant one was wrung free, and the astonished young man felt it applied over his own ear in a way that could not be mistaken for jest. He drew back in consternation. I lifted Hareton in my arms, and walked off to the kitchen with him, leaving the door of communication open, for I was curious to watch how they would settle their disagreement. The insulted visitor moved to the spot where he had laid his hat, pale and with a quivering lip.

"That's right!" I said to myself. "Take warning and begone! It's a kindness to let you have a glimpse of her genuine disposition."

"Where are you going?" demanded Catherine, advancing to the door.

He swerved aside, and attempted to pass.

"You must not go!" she exclaimed energetically.

"I must and shall!" he replied in a subdued voice.

"No," she persisted, grasping the handle; "not yet, Edgar Linton. Sit down. You shall not leave me in that temper. I should be miserable all night, and I won't be miserable for you!"

"Can I stay, after you have struck me?" asked Linton.

Catherine was mute.

"You've made me afraid and ashamed of you," he continued. "I'll not come here again."

Her eyes began to glisten, and her lids to twinkle.

"And you told a deliberate untruth," he said.

"I didn't," she cried, recovering her speech. "I did nothing deliberately. Well, go, if you please—get away. And now I'll cry—I'll cry myself sick."

She dropped down on her knees by a chair, and set to weeping in serious earnest. Edgar persevered in his resolution as far as the court; there he lingered. I resolved to encourage him.

"Miss is dreadfully wayward, sir," I called out. "As bad as any marred child. You'd better be riding home, or else she will be sick only to grieve us."

The soft thing looked askance through the window. He possessed the power to depart as much as a cat possesses the power to leave a mouse half killed or a bird half eaten. Ah, I thought, there will be no saving him; he's doomed, and flies to his fate! And so it was. He turned abruptly, hastened into the house again, shut the door behind him; and when I went in a while after to inform them that Earnshaw had come home rabid drunk, ready to pull the whole place about our ears (his ordinary frame of mind in that condition), I saw the quarrel had merely effected a closer intimacy —had broken the outworks of youthful timidity, and enabled them to forsake the disguise of friendship, and confess themselves lovers.

Intelligence of Mr. Hindley's arrival drove Linton speedily to his horse, and Catherine to her chamber. I went to hide little Hareton, and to take the shot out of the master's fowling-piece, which he was fond of playing with in his insane excitement, to the hazard of the lives of any who provoked or even attracted his notice too much; and I had hit upon the plan of removing it, that he might do less mischief if he did go the length of firing the gun.

CHAPTER IX.

HE entered, vociferating oaths dreadful to hear, and caught me in the act of stowing his son away in the kitchen cupboard. Hareton was impressed with a wholesome terror of encountering either his wild beast's fondness or his madman's rage; for in one he ran a chance of being squeezed and kissed to death, and in the other of being flung into the fire or dashed against the wall; and the poor thing remained perfectly quiet wherever I chose to put him.

"There, I've found it out at last," cried Hindley, pulling me back by the skin of my neck, like a dog. "By heaven and hell, you've sworn between you to murder that child! I know how it is, now, that he is always out of my way. But, with the help of Satan, I shall make you swallow the carving-knife, Nelly! You needn't laugh, for I've just crammed Kenneth, head-downmost, in the Blackhorse marsh; and two is the same as one—and I want to kill some of you. I shall have no rest till I do."

"But I don't like the carving-knife, Mr. Hindley," I answered; "it has been cutting red herrings. I'd rather be shot, if you please."

"You'd rather be damned!" he said; "and so you shall. No law in England can hinder a man from keeping his house decent, and mine's abominable. Open your mouth."

He held the knife in his hand, and pushed its point between my teeth; but, for my part, I was never much afraid of his vagaries. I spat out, and affirmed it tasted detestably; I would not take it on any account.

"Oh!" said he, releasing me, "I see that hideous little villain is not Hareton. I beg your pardon, Nell. If it be, he deserves flaying alive for not running to welcome me, and for screaming as if I were a goblin. Unnatural cub, come hither. I'll teach thee to impose on a good-hearted, deluded father. Now, don't you

think the lad would be handsomer cropped? It makes
a dog fiercer, and I love something fierce—get me a
scissors—something fierce and trim! Besides, it's infernal affectation—devilish conceit it is to cherish our
ears—we're asses enough without them. Hush, child,
hush! Well, then, it is my darling! Wisht, dry thy eyes
—there's a joy; kiss me. What! it won't? Kiss me,
Hareton! Damn thee, kiss me! By God, as if I
would rear such a monster! As sure as I'm living, I'll
break the brat's neck."

Poor Hareton was squalling and kicking in his father's
arms with all his might, and redoubled his yells when he
carried him upstairs and lifted him over the banister. I
cried out that he would frighten the child into fits,
and ran to rescue him. As I reached them, Hindley
leant forward on the rails to listen to a noise below,
almost forgetting what he had in his hands. "Who is
that?" he asked, hearing some one approaching the
stair's foot. I leant forward also, for the purpose of
signing to Heathcliff, whose step I recognized, not to
come farther; and at the instant when my eye quitted
Hareton, he gave a sudden spring, delivered himself
from the careless grasp that held him, and fell.

There was scarcely time to experience a thrill of
horror before we saw that the little wretch was safe.
Heathcliff arrived underneath just at the critical moment; by a natural impulse he arrested his descent,
and setting him on his feet, looked up to discover the
author of the accident. A miser who has parted with
a lucky lottery ticket for five shillings, and finds next
day he has lost in the bargain five thousand pounds,
could not show a blanker countenance than he did on
beholding the figure of Mr. Earnshaw above. It expressed, plainer than words could do, the intensest anguish
at having made himself the instrument of thwarting his
own revenge. Had it been dark, I dare say he would
have tried to remedy the mistake by smashing Hareton's
skull on the steps; but we witnessed his salvation,
and I was presently below with my precious charge

pressed to my heart. Hindley descended more leisurely, sobered and abashed.

"It is your fault, Ellen," he said; "you should have kept him out of sight. You should have taken him from me. Is he injured anywhere?"

"Injured!" I cried angrily; "if he's not killed, he'll be an idiot! Oh, I wonder his mother does not rise from her grave to see how you use him! You're worse than a heathen—treating your own flesh and blood in that manner!"

He attempted to touch the child, who, on finding himself with me, sobbed off his terror directly. At the first finger his father laid on him, however, he shrieked again louder than before, and struggled as if he would go into convulsions.

"You shall not meddle with him," I continued. "He hates you; they all hate you—that's the truth! A happy family you have, and a pretty state you're come to!"

"I shall come to a prettier yet, Nelly," laughed the misguided man, recovering his hardness. "At present, convey yourself and him away.—And hark you, Heathcliff; clear you too quite from my reach and hearing. I wouldn't murder you to-night, unless, perhaps, I set the house on fire; but that's as my fancy goes."

While saying this he took a pint bottle of brandy from the dresser and poured some into a tumbler.

"Nay, don't!" I entreated. "Mr. Hindley, do take warning. Have mercy on this unfortunate boy, if you care nothing for yourself!"

"Any one will do better for him than I shall," he answered.

"Have mercy on your own soul!" I said, endeavouring to snatch the glass from his hand.

"Not I! On the contrary I shall have great pleasure in sending it to perdition to punish its Maker," exclaimed the blasphemer. "Here's to its hearty damnation!"

He drank the spirits and impatiently bade us go,

terminating his command with a sequel of horrid imprecations too bad to repeat or remember.

"It's a pity he cannot kill himself with drink," observed Heathcliff, muttering an echo of curses back when the door was shut. "He's doing his very utmost, but his constitution defies him. Mr. Kenneth says he would wager his mare that he'll outlive any man on this side Gimmerton, and go to the grave a hoary sinner, unless some happy chance out of the common course befall him."

I went into the kitchen and sat down to lull my little lamb to sleep. Heathcliff, as I thought, walked through to the barn. It turned out afterwards that he only got as far as the other side the settle, when he flung himself on a bench by the wall, removed from the fire, and remained silent.

I was rocking Hareton on my knee, and humming a song that began—

> " It was far in the night, and the bairnies grat,
> The mither beneath the mools heard that "—

when Miss Cathy, who had listened to the hubbub from her room, put her head in and whispered,—

"Are you alone, Nelly?"

"Yes, miss," I replied.

She entered and approached the hearth. I, supposing she was going to say something, looked up. The expression of her face seemed disturbed and anxious. Her lips were half asunder, as if she meant to speak, and she drew a breath; but it escaped in a sigh instead of a sentence. I resumed my song, not having forgotten her recent behaviour.

"Where's Heathcliff?" she said, interrupting me.

"About his work in the stable," was my answer.

He did not contradict me; perhaps he had fallen into a doze. There followed another long pause, during which I perceived a drop or two trickle from Catherine's cheek to the flags. Is she sorry for her shameful conduct? I asked myself. That will be a novelty. But she may come to the point as she will; I shan't help her. No; she felt small trouble regarding any subject save her own concerns.

"Oh dear!" she cried at last, "I'm very unhappy!"

"A pity," observed I. "You're hard to please. So many friends, and so few cares, and can't make yourself content!"

"Nelly, will you keep a secret for me?" she pursued, kneeling down by me and lifting her winsome eyes to my face with that sort of look which turns off bad temper even when one has all the right in the world to indulge it.

"Is it worth keeping?" I inquired less sulkily.

"Yes, and it worries me, and I must let it out. I want to know what I should do. To-day Edgar Linton has asked me to marry him, and I've given him an answer. Now, before I tell you whether it was a consent or denial, you tell me which it ought to have been."

"Really, Miss Catherine, how can I know?" I replied. "To be sure, considering the exhibition you performed in his presence this afternoon, I might say it would be wise to refuse him; since he asked you after that, he must either be hopelessly stupid or a venturesome fool."

"If you talk so, I won't tell you any more," she returned peevishly, rising to her feet. "I accepted him, Nelly. Be quick, and say whether I was wrong."

"You accepted him! Then what good is it discussing the matter? You have pledged your word, and cannot retract."

"But say whether I should have done so—do!" she exclaimed in an irritated tone, chafing her hands together and frowning.

"There are many things to be considered before that question can be answered properly," I said sententiously. "First and foremost, do you love Mr. Edgar?"

"Who can help it? Of course I do," she answered.

Then I put her through the following catechism; for a girl of twenty-two it was not injudicious.

"Why do you love him, Miss Cathy?"

"Nonsense; I do—that's sufficient."

" By no means ; you must say why."

" Well, because he is handsome and pleasant to be with."

" Bad ! " was my commentary.

" And because he is young and cheerful."

" Bad still."

" And because he loves me."

" Indifferent, coming there."

" And he will be rich, and I shall like to be the greatest woman of the neighbourhood, and I shall be proud of having such a husband."

" Worst of all. And now, say how you love him."

" As everybody loves. You're silly, Nelly."

" Not at all—answer."

" I love the ground under his feet, and the air over his head, and everything he touches, and every word he says. I love all his looks, and all his actions, and him entirely and altogether. There now ! "

" And why ? "

" Nay, you are making a jest of it. It is exceedingly ill-natured. It's no jest to me ! " said the young lady, scowling and turning her face to the fire.

" I'm very far from jesting, Miss Catherine," I replied. " You love Mr. Edgar because he is handsome, and young, and cheerful, and rich, and loves you. The last, however, goes for nothing—you would love him without that probably ; and with it you wouldn't, unless he possessed the four former attractions."

" No ; to be sure not. I should only pity him—hate him, perhaps, if he were ugly and a clown."

" But there are several other handsome, rich young men in the world—handsomer, possibly, and richer than he is. What should hinder you from loving them ? "

" If there be any, they are out of my way. I've seen none like Edgar."

" You may see some. And he won't always be handsome, and young, and may not always be rich."

" He is now ; and I have only to do with the present. I wish you would speak rationally."

"Well, that settles it. If you have only to do with the present, marry Mr. Linton."

"I don't want your permission for that—I *shall* marry him; and yet you have not told me whether I'm right."

"Perfectly right, if people be right to marry only for the present. And now, let us hear what you are unhappy about. Your brother will be pleased; the old lady and gentleman will not object, I think; you will escape from a disorderly, comfortless home into a wealthy, respectable one; and you love Edgar, and Edgar loves you. All seems smooth and easy. Where is the obstacle?"

"*Here*, and *here*!" replied Catherine, striking one hand on her forehead and the other on her breast; "in whichever place the soul lives. In my soul and in my heart I'm convinced I'm wrong."

"That's very strange. I cannot make it out."

"It's my secret. But if you will not mock at me, I'll explain it. I can't do it distinctly, but I'll give you a feeling of how I feel."

She seated herself by me again; her countenance grew sadder and graver, and her clasped hands trembled.

"Nelly, do you never dream queer dreams?" she said suddenly, after some minutes' reflection.

"Yes; now and then," I answered.

"And so do I. I've dreamt in my life dreams that have stayed with me ever after, and changed my ideas; they've gone through and through me, like wine through water, and altered the colour of my mind. And this is one. I'm going to tell it; but take care not to smile at any part of it."

"Oh! don't, Miss Catherine!" I cried. "We're dismal enough without conjuring up ghosts and visions to perplex us. Come, come, be merry and like yourself! Look at little Hareton! *He's* dreaming nothing dreary. How sweetly he smiles in his sleep!"

"Yes; and how sweetly his father curses in his solitude! You remember him, I dare say, when he was just such another as that chubby thing—nearly as young and innocent. However, Nelly, I shall oblige you to listen; it's not long, and I've no power to be merry to-night."

"I won't hear it, I won't hear it!" I repeated hastily. I was superstitious about dreams then, and am still; and Catherine had an unusual gloom in her aspect that made me dread something from which I might shape a prophecy and foresee a fearful catastrophe. She was vexed, but she did not proceed. Apparently taking up another subject, she recommenced in a short time.

"If I were in heaven, Nelly, I should be extremely miserable."

"Because you are not fit to go there," I answered. "All sinners would be miserable in heaven."

"But it is not for that. I dreamt once that I was there."

"I tell you I won't hearken to your dreams, Miss Catherine! I'll go to bed," I interrupted again.

She laughed and held me down, for I made a motion to leave my chair.

"This is nothing," cried she. "I was only going to say that heaven did not seem to be my home, and I broke my heart with weeping to come back to earth; and the angels were so angry that they flung me out into the middle of the heath on the top of Wuthering Heights, where I woke sobbing for joy. That will do to explain my secret as well as the other. I've no more business to marry Edgar Linton than I have to be in heaven; and if the wicked man in there had not brought Heathcliff so low, I shouldn't have thought of it. It would degrade me to marry Heathcliff now, so he shall never know how I love him; and that not because he's handsome, Nelly, but because he's more myself than I am. Whatever our souls are made of, his and mine are the same; and Linton's is as different as a moonbeam from lightning, or frost from fire."

Ere this speech ended I became sensible of Heathcliff's presence. Having noticed a slight movement, I turned my head and saw him rise from the bench and steal out noiselessly. He had listened till he heard Catherine say it would degrade her to marry him, and then he stayed to hear no further. My companion, sitting on the ground, was prevented by the back of the settle from remarking his presence or departure; but I started and bade her hush.

"Why?" she asked, gazing nervously round.

"Joseph is here," I answered, catching opportunely the roll of his cart-wheels up the road, "and Heathcliff will come in with him. I'm not sure whether he were not at the door this moment."

"Oh, he couldn't overhear me at the door," said she. "Give me Hareton while you get the supper, and when it is ready ask me to sup with you. I want to cheat my uncomfortable conscience, and be convinced that Heathcliff has no notion of these things. He has not, has he? He does not know what being in love is?"

"I see no reason that he should not know, as well as you," I returned; "and if *you* are his choice, he'll be the most unfortunate creature that ever was born. As soon as you become Mrs. Linton, he loses friend, and love, and all. Have you considered how you'll bear the separation, and how he'll bear to be quite deserted in the world? Because, Miss Catherine——"

"He quite deserted! we separated!" she exclaimed with an accent of indignation. "Who is to separate us, pray? They'll meet the fate of Milo. Not as long as I live, Ellen—for no mortal creature. Every Linton on the face of the earth might melt into nothing before I could consent to forsake Heathcliff. Oh, that's not what I intend—that's not what I mean! I shouldn't be Mrs. Linton were such a price demanded! He'll be as much to me as he has been all his lifetime. Edgar must shake off his antipathy, and tolerate him, at least. He will, when he learns my true feelings towards him. Nelly, I see now—you think me a selfish wretch; but did it never strike you that if Heathcliff and I married, we should be beggars? Whereas, if I marry Linton,

I can aid Heathcliff to rise, and place him out of my brother's power."

"With your husband's money, Miss Catherine?" I asked. "You'll find him not so pliable as you calculate upon; and, though I'm hardly a judge, I think that's the worst motive you've given yet for being the wife of young Linton."

"It is not!" retorted she; "it is the best! The others were the satisfaction of my whims; and for Edgar's sake, too—to satisfy him. This is for the sake of one who comprehends in his person my feelings to Edgar and myself. I cannot express it, but surely you and everybody have a notion that there is or should be an existence of yours beyond you. What were the use of my creation if I were entirely contained here? My great miseries in this world have been Heathcliff's miseries, and I watched and felt each from the beginning. My great thought in living is himself. If all else perished, and *he* remained, *I* should still continue to be. And if all else remained, and he were annihilated, the universe would turn to a mighty stranger—I should not seem a part of it. My love for Linton is like the foliage in the woods; time will change it, I'm well aware, as winter changes the trees. My love for Heathcliff resembles the eternal rocks beneath—a source of little visible delight, but necessary. Nelly, I *am* Heathcliff! He's always, always in my mind—not as a pleasure, any more than I am always a pleasure to myself, but as my own being. So don't talk of our separation again. It is impracticable, and——"

She paused, and hid her face in the folds of my gown, but I jerked it forcibly away. I was out of patience with her folly.

"If I can make any sense of your nonsense, miss," I said, "it only goes to convince me that you are ignorant of the duties you undertake in marrying, or else that you are a wicked, unprincipled girl. But trouble me with no more secrets; I'll not promise to keep them."

"You'll keep that?" she asked eagerly.

" No, I'll not promise," I repeated.

She was about to insist, when the entrance of Joseph finished our conversation ; and Catherine removed her seat to a corner and nursed Hareton, while I made the supper. After it was cooked, my fellow-servant and I began to quarrel who should carry some to Mr. Hindley ; and we didn't settle it till all was nearly cold. Then we came to the agreement that we would let him ask if he wanted any, for we feared particularly to go into his presence when he had been some time alone.

" And how isn't that nowt comed in fro' th' field be this time ? What is he about ? girt idle seeght ! " demanded the old man, looking round for Heathcliff.

" I'll call him," I replied. " He's in the barn, I've no doubt "

I went and called, but got no answer. On returning, I whispered to Catherine that he had heard a good part of what she said, I was sure, and told how I saw him quit the kitchen just as she complained of her brother's conduct regarding him. She jumped up in a fine fright, flung Hareton on to the settle, and ran to seek for her friend herself, not taking leisure to consider why she was so flurried, or how her talk would have affected him. She was absent such a while that Joseph proposed we should wait no longer. He cunningly conjectured they were staying away in order to avoid hearing his protracted blessing. They were " ill eneugh for ony fahl manners," he affirmed. And on their behalf he added that night a special prayer to the usual quarter of an hour's supplication before meat, and would have tacked another to the end of the grace, had not his young mistress broken in upon him with a hurried command that he must run down the road, and wherever Heathcliff had rambled, find and make him re-enter directly.

" I want to speak to him, and I *must* before I go upstairs," she said. " And the gate is open. He is somewhere out of hearing, for he would not reply, though I shouted at the top of the fold as loud as I could."

Joseph objected at first. She was too much in earnest,

however, to suffer contradiction; and at last he placed his hat on his head and walked grumbling forth. Meantime, Catherine paced up and down the floor, exclaiming,—

"I wonder where he is—I wonder where he *can* be. What did I say, Nelly? I've forgotten. Was he vexed at my bad humour this afternoon? Dear! tell me what I've said to grieve him. I do wish he'd come. I do wish he would."

"What a noise for nothing!" I cried, though rather uneasy myself. "What a trifle scares you! It's surely no great cause of alarm that Heathcliff should take a moonlight saunter on the moors, or even lie too sulky to speak to us in the hay-loft. I'll engage he's lurking there. See if I don't ferret him out!"

I departed to renew my search. Its result was disappointment, and Joseph's quest ended in the same.

"Yon lad gets war un war!" observed he on re-entering. "He's left th' yate at t' full swing, and miss's pony has trodden dahn two rigs o' corn, and plottered through, raight o'er into t' meadow! Hahsomdiver, t' maister 'ull play t' devil to-morn, and he'll do weel. He's patience itsseln wi' sich careless, offald craters—patience itsseln he is! Bud he'll not be soa allus—yah's see, all on ye! Yah munn't drive him out of his heead for nowt!"

"Have you found Heathcliff, you ass?" interrupted Catherine. "Have you been looking for him, as I ordered?"

"I sud more likker look for th' horse," he replied. "It 'ud be to more sense. Bud I can look for norther horse nur man of a neeght loike this—as black as t' chimbley; und Heathcliff's noan t' chap to coom at *my* whistle. Happen he'll be less hard o' hearing wi' *ye*!"

It *was* a very dark evening for summer. The clouds appeared inclined to thunder, and I said we had better all sit down; the approaching rain would be certain to bring him home without further trouble. However, Catherine would not be persuaded into tranquillity. She kept wandering to and fro, from the gate to the door, in a state of agitation which permitted no repose, and at length took up a permanent situation on one side of the wall, near the road, where, heedless of my ex-postulations and the growling thunder, and the great drops that began to plash around her, she remained, calling at intervals, and then listening, and then crying outright. She beat Hareton, or any child, at a good passionate fit of crying.

About midnight, while we still sat up, the storm came rattling over the Heights in full fury. There was a violent wind, as well as thunder, and either one or the other split a tree off at the corner of the building ; a huge bough fell across the roof, and knocked down a portion of the east chimney stack, sending a clatter of stones and soot into the kitchen fire. We thought a bolt had fallen in the middle of us, and Joseph swung on to his knees, beseeching the Lord to remember the patriarchs Noah and Lot, and, as in former times, spare the righteous, though He smote the ungodly. I felt some sentiment that it must be a judgment on us also. The Jonah, in my mind, was Mr. Earnshaw ; and I shook the handle of his den, that I might ascertain if he were yet living. He replied audibly enough in a fashion which made my companion vociferate, more clamorously than before, that a wide distinction might be drawn between saints like himself and sinners like his master. But the uproar passed away in twenty minutes, leaving us all unharmed, excepting Cathy, who got thoroughly drenched for her obstinacy in refusing to take shelter, and standing bonnetless and shawl-less to catch as much water as she could with her hair and clothes. She came in and lay down on the settle, all soaked as she was, turning her face to the back and putting her hands before it.

" Well, miss ! " I exclaimed, touching her shoulder ; " you are not bent on getting your death, are you ? Do you know what o'clock it is ? Half-past twelve. Come, come to bed ! There's no use waiting longer on that foolish boy. He'll be gone to Gimmerton, and he'll stay there now. He guesses we shouldn't wake for him till this late hour—at least he guesses that only Mr. Hindley would be up; and he'd rather avoid having the door opened by the master."

"Nay, nay; he's noan at Gimmerton," said Joseph. "I's niver wonder but he's at t' bothom of a bog-hoile. This visitation worn't for nowt, and I wod hev ye to look out, miss; yah muh be t' next. Thank Hivin for all! All warks togither for gooid to them as is chozzen, and piked out fro' th' rubbidge. Yah knaw whet t' Scripture ses." And he began quoting several texts, referring us to chapters and verses where we might find them.

I, having vainly begged the wilful girl to rise and remove her wet things, left him preaching and her shivering, and betook myself to bed with little Hareton, who slept as fast as if every one had been sleeping round him. I heard Joseph read on a while afterwards; then I distinguished his slow step on the ladder, and then I dropped asleep.

Coming down somewhat later than usual, I saw, by the sunbeams piercing the chinks of the shutters, Miss Catherine still seated near the fireplace. The house door was ajar too; light entered from its unclosed windows. Hindley had come out, and stood on the kitchen hearth, haggard and drowsy.

"What ails you, Cathy?" he was saying when I entered; "you look as dismal as a drowned whelp. Why are you so damp and pale, child?"

"I've been wet!" she answered reluctantly, "and I'm cold; that's all."

"Oh, she is naughty!" I cried, perceiving the master to be tolerably sober. "She got steeped in the shower of yesterday evening, and there she has sat the night through, and I couldn't prevail on her to stir."

Mr. Earnshaw stared at us in surprise. "The night through!" he repeated. "What kept her up? Not fear of the thunder, surely? That was over hours since."

Neither of us wished to mention Heathcliff's absence as long as we could conceal it, so I replied I didn't know how she took it into her head to sit up, and she said nothing. The morning was fresh and cool. I threw back the lattice, and presently the room filled with sweet scents from the garden ; but Catherine called peevishly to me, " Ellen, shut the window. I'm starving ! " And her teeth chattered as she shrank closer to the almost extinguished embers.

" She's ill," said Hindley, taking her wrist ; " I suppose that's the reason she would not go to bed. Damn it ! I don't want to be troubled with more sickness here. What took you into the rain ? "

" Running after t' lads as usuald ! " croaked Joseph, catching an opportunity, from our hesitation, to thrust in his evil tongue. " If I war yah, maister, I'd just slam t' boards i' their faces all on 'em, gentle and simple. Never a day ut yah're off, but yon cat o' Linton comes sneaking hither ; and Miss Nelly—shoo's a fine lass— shoo sits watching for ye i' t' kitchen ; and as yah're in at one door, he's out at t'other, and then wer grand lady goes a-coorting of her side ! It's bonny behaviour, lurking amang t' fields after twelve o' t' night wi' that fahl, flaysome divil of a gipsy, Heathcliff ! They think *I'm* blind, but I'm noan—nowt ut t' soart ! I seed young Linton boath coming and going, and I seed *yah* " (directing his discourse to me), " yah gooid fur nowt, slattenly witch, nip up and bolt into th' house, t' minute yah heard t' maister's horse fit clatter up t' road."

" Silence, eavesdropper ! " cried Catherine ; " none of your insolence before me !—Edgar Linton came yesterday by chance, Hindley, and it was *I* who told him to be off, because I knew you would not like to have met him as you were."

" You lie, Cathy, no doubt," answered her brother, " and you are a confounded simpleton ! But never mind Linton at present ; tell me—were you not with Heathcliff last night ? Speak the truth, now. You need not be afraid of harming him. Though I hate him as much as ever, he did me a good turn a short time since that will make my conscience tender of breaking his neck. To prevent it, I shall send him about his business this very morning; and after he's gone, I'd advise you all to look sharp. I shall only have the more humour for you."

"I never saw Heathcliff last night," answered Catherine, beginning to sob bitterly, "and if you do turn him out of doors, I'll go with him. But perhaps you'll never have an opportunity; perhaps he's gone." Here she burst into uncontrollable grief, and the remainder of her words were inarticulate.

Hindley lavished on her a torrent of scornful abuse, and bade her get to her room immediately, or she shouldn't cry for nothing. I obliged her to obey; and I shall never forget what a scene she acted when we reached her chamber—it terrified me. I thought she was going mad, and I begged Joseph to run for the doctor. It proved the commencement of delirium. Mr. Kenneth, as soon as he saw her, pronounced her dangerously ill. She had a fever. He bled her, and he told me to let her live on whey and water-gruel, and take care she did not throw herself downstairs or out of the window; and then he left, for he had enough to do in the parish, where two or three miles was the ordinary distance between cottage and cottage.

Though I cannot say I made a gentle nurse, and Joseph and the master were no better, and though our patient was as wearisome and headstrong as a patient could be, she weathered it through. Old Mrs. Linton paid us several visits, to be sure, and set things to rights, and scolded and ordered us all; and when Catherine was convalescent she insisted on conveying her to Thrushcross Grange, for which deliverance we were very grateful; but the poor dame had reason to repent of her kindness. She and her husband both took the fever, and died within a few days of each other.

Our young lady returned to us, saucier and more passionate and haughtier than ever. Heathcliff had never been heard of since the evening of the thunderstorm; and one day I had the misfortune, when she had provoked me exceedingly, to lay the blame of his disappearance on her — where indeed it belonged, as she well knew. From that period, for several months, she ceased to hold any communication with me, save in the relation of a mere servant. Joseph fell under a ban also. He *would* speak his mind, and lecture her all the same as if she were a little girl; and she esteemed herself a woman, and our mistress, and thought that her recent illness gave her a claim to be treated with consideration. Then the doctor had said that she would not bear crossing much—she ought to have her own way; and it was nothing less than murder in her eyes for any one to presume to stand up and contradict her. From Mr. Earnshaw and his companions she kept aloof; and tutored by Kenneth, and serious threats of a fit that often attended her rages, her brother allowed her whatever she pleased to demand, and generally avoided aggravating her fiery temper. He was rather *too* indulgent in humouring her caprices—not from affection, but from pride. He wished earnestly to see her bring honour to the family by an alliance with the Lintons; and as long as she let him alone she might trample on us like slaves, for aught he cared. Edgar Linton, as multitudes have been before, and will be after him, was infatuated, and believed himself the happiest man alive on the day he led her to Gimmerton Chapel, three years subsequent to his father's death.

Much against my inclination, I was persuaded to leave Wuthering Heights and accompany her here. Little Hareton was nearly five years old, and I had just begun to teach him his letters. We made a sad parting, but Catherine's tears were more powerful than ours. When I refused to go, and when she found her entreaties did not move me, she went lamenting to her husband and brother. The former offered me munificent wages; the latter ordered me to pack up. He wanted no women in the house, he said, now that there was no mistress; and as to Hareton, the curate should take him in hand by-and-by. And so I had but one choice left—to do as I was ordered. I told the master he got rid of all decent people only to ride to ruin a little faster. I kissed Hareton, said good-bye, and since then he has been a stranger; and it's very queer to think it, but I've no doubt he has completely forgotten all about Ellen Dean, and that he was ever more than all the world to her, and she to him.

*   *   *   *   *

At this point of the housekeeper's story she chanced to glance towards the timepiece over the chimney, and was in amazement on seeing the minute-hand measure half-past one. She would not hear of staying a second longer—in truth, I felt rather disposed to defer the sequel of her narrative myself. And now that she is vanished to her rest, and I have meditated for another hour or two, I shall summon courage to go also, in spite of aching laziness of head and limbs.

CHAPTER X.

A CHARMING introduction to a hermit's life! Four weeks' torture, tossing, and sickness! Oh, these bleak winds, and bitter northern skies, and impassable roads, and dilatory country surgeons! And, oh, this dearth of the human physiognomy! and, worse than all, the terrible intimation of Kenneth that I need not expect to be out of doors till spring!

Mr. Heathcliff has just honoured me with a call. About seven days ago he sent me a brace of grouse—the last of the season. Scoundrel! He is not altogether guiltless in this illness of mine, and that I had a great mind to tell him; but, alas! how could I offend a man who was charitable enough to sit at my bedside a good hour, and talk on some other subject than pills and draughts, blisters, and leeches? This is quite an easy interval. I am too weak to read, yet I feel as if I could enjoy something interesting. Why not have up Mrs. Dean to finish her tale ? I can recollect its chief incidents as far as she had gone. Yes; I remember her hero had run off, and never been heard of for three years; and the heroine was married. I'll ring. She'll be delighted to find me capable of talking cheerfully. Mrs. Dean came.

"It wants twenty minutes, sir, to taking the medicine," she commenced.

"Away, away with it!" I replied. "I desire to have——"

"The doctor says you must drop the powders."

"With all my heart! Don't interrupt me. Come and take your seat here. Keep your fingers from that bitter phalanx of vials. Draw your knitting out of your pocket—that will do; now continue the history of Mr. Heathcliff, from where you left off to the present day. Did he finish his education on the Continent, and come back a gentleman ? or did he get a sizar's place at college, or escape to America, and earn honours by drawing blood from his foster-country, or make a fortune more promptly on the English highways ?"

"He may have done a little in all these vocations, Mr. Lockwood, but I couldn't give my word for any. I stated before that I didn't know how he gained his money, neither am I aware of the means he took to raise his mind from the savage ignorance into which it was sunk; but, with your leave, I'll proceed in my own fashion, if you think it will amuse and not weary you. Are you feeling better this morning ?"

"Much."

"That's good news.——I got Miss Catherine and myself to Thrushcross Grange, and, to my agreeable disappointment, she behaved infinitely better than I dared to expect. She seemed almost over-fond of Mr. Linton, and even to his sister she showed plenty of affection. They were both very attentive to her comfort, certainly. It was not the thorn bending to the honeysuckles, but the honeysuckles embracing the thorn. There were no mutual concessions—one stood erect and the others yielded ; and who *can* be ill-natured and bad-tempered when they encounter neither opposition nor indifference ? I observed that Mr. Edgar had a deep-rooted fear of ruffling her humour. He concealed it from her ; but if ever he heard me answer sharply, or saw any other servant grow cloudy at some imperious order of hers, he would show his trouble by a frown of displeasure that never darkened on his own account. He many a time spoke sternly to me about my pertness ; and averred that the stab of a knife could not inflict a worse pang than he suffered at seeing his lady vexed. Not to grieve a kind master, I learned to be less touchy ; and for the space of half a year the gunpowder lay as harmless as sand, because no fire came near to explode it. Catherine had seasons of gloom and silence now and then ; they were respected with sympathizing silence by her husband, who ascribed them to an alteration in her constitution, produced by her perilous illness, as she was never subject to depression of spirits before. The return of sunshine was welcomed by answering sunshine from him. I believe I may assert that they were really in possession of deep and growing happiness.

It ended. Well, we *must* be for ourselves in the long run ; the mild and generous are only more justly selfish than the domineering ; and it ended when circumstances caused each to feel that the one's interest was not the chief consideration in the other's thoughts. On a mellow evening in September I was coming from the garden with a heavy basket of apples which I had been gathering. It had got dusk, and the moon looked over the high wall of the court, causing undefined shadows to lurk in the corners of the numerous projecting portions of the building. I set my burden on the house steps by the kitchen door, and lingered to rest, and drew in a few more breaths of the soft, sweet air. My eyes were on the moon, and my back to the entrance, when I heard a voice behind me say,—

" Nelly, is that you ? "

It was a deep voice, and foreign in tone, yet there

was something in the manner of pronouncing my name which made it sound familiar. I turned about to discover who spoke, fearfully; for the doors were shut, and I had seen nobody on approaching the steps. Something stirred in the porch; and moving nearer, I distinguished a tall man dressed in dark clothes, with dark face and hair. He leant against the side, and held his fingers on the latch, as if intending to open for himself. "Who can it be?" I thought. "Mr. Earnshaw? Oh no! The voice has no resemblance to his."

"I have waited here an hour," he resumed, while I continued staring; "and the whole of that time all round has been as still as death. I dared not enter. You do not know me? Look, I'm not a stranger!"

A ray fell on his features; the cheeks were sallow and half covered with black whiskers, the brows lowering, the eyes deep-set and singular. I remembered the eyes.

"What!" I cried, uncertain whether to regard him as a worldly visitor, and I raised my hands in amazement. "What! you come back? Is it really you? Is it?"

"Yes, Heathcliff," he replied, glancing from me up to the windows, which reflected a score of glittering moons, but showed no lights from within. "Are they at home? Where is she? Nelly, you are not glad. You needn't be so disturbed. Is she here? Speak! I want to have one word with her—your mistress. Go, and say some person from Gimmerton desires to see her."

"How will she take it?" I exclaimed. "What will she do? The surprise bewilders me. It will put her out of her head. And you *are* Heathcliff, but altered! Nay, there's no comprehending it. Have you been for a soldier?"

"Go and carry my message," he interrupted impatiently. "I'm in hell till you do!"

He lifted the latch, and I entered; but when I got to the parlour where Mr. and Mrs. Linton were, I could not persuade myself to proceed. At length I resolved on making an excuse to ask if they would have the candles lighted, and I opened the door.

They sat together in a window whose lattice lay back against the wall, and displayed, beyond the garden trees and the wild green park, the valley of Gimmerton, with a long line of mist winding nearly to its top (for very soon after you pass the chapel, as you may have noticed, the sough that runs from the marshes joins a beck which follows the bend of the glen). Wuthering Heights rose above this silvery vapour, but our old house was invisible ; it rather dips down on the other side. Both the room and its occupants, and the scene they gazed on, looked wondrously peaceful. I shrank reluctantly from performing my errand, and was actually going away leaving it unsaid, after having put my question about the candles, when a sense of my folly compelled me to return and mutter, " A person from Gimmerton wishes to see you, ma'am."

" What does he want ? " asked Mrs. Linton.

" I did not question him," I answered.

" Well, close the curtains, Nelly," she said, " and bring up tea. I'll be back again directly."

She quitted the apartment. Mr. Edgar inquired carelessly who it was.

" Some one mistress does not expect," I replied. " That Heathcliff—you recollect him, sir—who used to live at Mr. Earnshaw's."

" What ! The gipsy—the ploughboy ? " he cried. " Why did you not say so to Catherine ? "

" Hush ! you must not call him by those names, master," I said. " She'd be sadly grieved to hear you. She was nearly heartbroken when he ran off. I guess his return will make a jubilee to her."

Mr. Linton walked to a window on the other side of the room that overlooked the court. He unfastened it and leant out. I suppose they were below, for he exclaimed quickly, " Don't stand there, love ! Bring the person in, if it be any one particular." Ere long

I heard the click of the latch, and Catherine flew up-stairs, breathless and wild, too excited to show gladness ; indeed, by her face, you would rather have surmised an awful calamity.

"O Edgar, Edgar !" she panted, flinging her arms round his neck. "O Edgar darling ! Heathcliff's come back—he is !" And she tightened her embrace to a squeeze.

"Well, well," cried her husband crossly, "don't strangle me for that. He never struck me as such a marvellous treasure. There is no need to be frantic."

"I know you didn't like him," she answered, repressing a little the intensity of her delight. "Yet, for my sake, you must be friends now. Shall I tell him to come up ?"

"Here ?" he said—"into the parlour ?"

"Where else ?" she asked.

He looked vexed, and suggested the kitchen as a more suitable place for him. Mrs. Linton eyed him with a droll expression—half angry, half laughing, at his fastidiousness.

"No," she added, after a while ; "I cannot sit in the kitchen.—Set two tables here, Ellen—one for your master and Miss Isabella, being gentry ; the other for Heathcliff and myself, being of the lower orders.—Will that please you, dear ? Or must I have a fire lighted elsewhere ? If so, give directions. I'll run down and secure my guest. I'm afraid the joy is too great to be real !"

She was about to dart off again, but Edgar arrested her.

"*You* bid him step up," he said, addressing me, "and, Catherine, try to be glad without being absurd. The whole household need not witness the sight of your welcoming a runaway servant as a brother."

I descended and found Heathcliff waiting under the porch, evidently anticipating an invitation to enter. He followed my guidance without waste of words, and I ushered him into the presence of the master and mis-tress, whose flushed cheeks betrayed signs of warm talking. But the lady's glowed with another feeling when her friend appeared at the door. She sprang forward, took both his hands, and led him to Linton; and then she seized Linton's reluctant fingers and crushed them into his. Now fully revealed by the fire and candle-light, I was amazed more than ever to behold the trans-formation of Heathcliff. He had grown a tall, athletic, well-formed man, beside whom my master seemed quite slender and youth-like. His upright carriage suggested the idea of his having been in the army. His coun-tenance was much older in expression and decision of feature than Mr. Linton's; it looked intelligent, and retained no marks of former degradation. A half-civilized ferocity lurked yet in the depressed brows and eyes full of black fire, but it was subdued, and his manner was even dignified—quite divested of roughness, though too stern for grace. My master's surprise equalled or exceeded mine. He remained for a minute at a loss how to address the ploughboy, as he had called him. Heathcliff dropped his slight hand, and stood looking at him coolly till he chose to speak.

"Sit down, sir," he said at length. "Mrs. Linton, recalling old times, would have me give you a cordial reception; and, of course, I am gratified when anything occurs to please her."

"And I also," answered Heathcliff, "especially if it be anything in which I have a part. I shall stay an hour or two willingly."

He took a seat opposite Catherine, who kept her gaze fixed on him as if she feared he would vanish were she to remove it. He did not raise his to her often—a quick glance now and then sufficed; but it flashed back, each time more confidently, the undisguised delight he drank from hers. They were too much absorbed in their mutual joy to suffer embarrassment. Not so Mr. Edgar. He grew pale with pure annoyance—a feeling that reached its climax when his lady rose, and stepping across the rug, seized Heathcliff's hands again, and laughed like one beside herself.

"I shall think it a dream to-morrow!" she cried.

" I shall not be able to believe that I have seen, and touched, and spoken to you once more. And yet, cruel Heathcliff ! you don't deserve this welcome. To be absent and silent for three years, and never to think of me ! "

" A little more than you have thought of me," he murmured. " I heard of your marriage, Cathy, not long since ; and while waiting in the yard below I meditated this plan—just to have one glimpse of your face, a stare of surprise, perhaps, and pretended pleasure ; afterwards settle my score with Hindley ; and then prevent the law by doing execution on myself. Your welcome has put these ideas out of my mind ; but beware of meeting me with another aspect next time ! Nay, you'll not drive me off again. You were really sorry for me, were you ? Well, there was cause. I've fought through a bitter life since I last heard your voice ; and you must forgive me, for I struggled only for you ! "

" Catherine, unless we are to have cold tea, please to come to the table," interrupted Linton, striving to preserve his ordinary tone, and a due measure of politeness. " Mr. Heathcliff will have a long walk, wherever he may lodge to-night, and I'm thirsty."

She took her post before the urn ; and Miss Isabella came, summoned by the bell ; then having handed their chairs forward, I left the room. The meal hardly endured ten minutes. Catherine's cup was never filled. She could neither eat nor drink. Edgar had made a slop in his saucer, and scarcely swallowed a mouthful. Their guest did not protract his stay that evening above an hour longer. I asked, as he departed, if he went to Gimmerton ?

" No ; to Wuthering Heights," he answered. " Mr. Earnshaw invited me when I called this morning."

Mr. Earnshaw invited *him* ! and *he* called on Mr. Earnshaw ! I pondered this sentence painfully after he was gone. Is he turning out a bit of a hypocrite, and coming into the country to work mischief under a cloak ? I mused. I had a presentiment in the bottom of my heart that he had better have remained away.

About the middle of the night I was wakened from my first nap by Mrs. Linton gliding into my chamber, taking a seat on my bedside, and pulling me by the hair to rouse me.

"I cannot rest, Ellen," she said, by way of apology. "And I want some living creature to keep me company in my happiness. Edgar is sulky because I'm glad of a thing that does not interest him. He refuses to open his mouth, except to utter pettish, silly speeches; and he affirmed I was cruel and selfish for wishing to talk when he was so sick and sleepy. He always contrives to be sick at the least cross! I gave a few sentences of commendation to Heathcliff, and he, either for a headache or a pang of envy, began to cry; so I got up and left him."

"What use is it praising Heathcliff to him?" I answered. "As lads they had an aversion to each other, and Heathcliff would hate just as much to hear him praised; it's human nature. Let Mr. Linton alone about him, unless you would like an open quarrel between them."

"But does it not show great weakness?" pursued she. "I'm not envious. I never feel hurt at the brightness of Isabella's yellow hair and the whiteness of her skin, at her dainty elegance and the fondness all the family exhibit for her. Even you, Nelly, if we have a dispute sometimes, you back Isabella at once; and I yield like a foolish mother. I call her a darling, and flatter her into a good temper. It pleases her brother to see us cordial, and that pleases me. But they are very much alike. They are spoiled children, and fancy the world was made for their accommodation; and though I humour both, I think a smart chastisement might improve them, all the same."

"You're mistaken, Mrs. Linton," said I. "They humour you. I know what there would be to do if they did not. You can well afford to indulge their passing whims as long as their business is to anticipate all your desires. You may, however, fall out at last over something of equal consequence to both sides; and then those you term weak are very capable of being as obstinate as you."

"And then we shall fight to the death, shan't we, Nelly?" she returned, laughing. "No; I tell you I have such faith in Linton's love that I believe I might kill him, and he wouldn't wish to retaliate."

I advised her to value him the more for his affection.

"I do," she answered; "but he needn't resort to whining for trifles. It is childish; and instead of melting into tears because I said that Heathcliff was now worthy of any one's regard, and it would honour the first gentleman in the country to be his friend, he ought to have said it for me, and been delighted from sympathy. He must get accustomed to him, and he may as well like him. Considering how Heathcliff has reason to object to him, I'm sure he behaved excellently."

"What do you think of his going to Wuthering Heights?" I inquired. "He is reformed in every respect, apparently—quite a Christian—offering the right hand of fellowship to his enemies all around!"

"He explained it," she replied. "I wonder as much as you. He said he called to gather information concerning me from you, supposing you resided there still; and Joseph told Hindley, who came out and fell to questioning him of what he had been doing, and how he had been living, and finally desired him to walk in. There were some persons sitting at cards. Heathcliff joined them. My brother lost some money to him; and finding him plentifully supplied, he requested that he would come again in the evening, to which he consented. Hindley is too reckless to select his acquaintance prudently. He doesn't trouble himself to reflect on the causes he might have for mistrusting one whom he has basely injured. But Heathcliff affirms his principal reason for resuming a connection with his ancient persecutor is a wish to install himself in quarters at walking distance from the Grange, and an attachment to the house where we lived together, and likewise a hope that I shall have more opportunities of seeing him there than I could have if he settled in Gimmerton. He means to offer liberal payment for permission to lodge at the Heights; and doubtless my brother's covetousness will prompt him to accept the terms. He was always greedy, though what he grasps with one hand he flings away with the other."

"It's a nice place for a young man to fix his dwelling in!" said I. "Have you no fear of the consequences, Mrs. Linton?"

"None for my friend," she replied. "His strong head will keep him from danger. A little for Hindley. But he can't be made morally worse than he is; and I stand between him and bodily harm. The event of this evening has reconciled me to God and humanity. I had risen in angry rebellion against Providence. Oh, I've endured very, very bitter misery, Nelly! If that creature knew how bitter, he'd be ashamed to cloud its removal with idle petulance. It was kindness for him which induced me to bear it alone. Had I expressed the agony I frequently felt, he would have been taught to long for its alleviation as ardently as I. However, it's over, and I'll take no revenge on his folly. I can afford to suffer anything hereafter. Should the meanest thing alive slap me on the cheek, I'd not only turn the other, but I'd ask pardon for provoking it; and as a proof I'll go make my peace with Edgar instantly. Good-night! I'm an angel!"

In this self-complacent conviction she departed; and the success of her fulfilled resolution was obvious on the morrow. Mr. Linton had not only abjured his peevishness (though his spirits seemed still subdued by Catherine's exuberance of vivacity), but he ventured no objection to her taking Isabella with her to Wuthering Heights in the afternoon; and she rewarded him with such a summer of sweetness and affection in return as made the house a paradise for several days, both master and servants profiting from the perpetual sunshine.

Heathcliff—Mr. Heathcliff, I should say in future—

used the liberty of visiting at Thrushcross Grange cautiously, at first. He seemed estimating how far its owner would bear his intrusion. Catherine, also, deemed it judicious to moderate her expressions of pleasure in receiving him ; and he gradually established his right to be expected. He retained a great deal of the reserve for which his boyhood was remarkable ; and that served to repress all startling demonstrations of feeling. My master's uneasiness experienced a lull, and further circumstances diverted it into another channel for a space.

His new source of trouble sprang from the not-anticipated misfortune of Isabella Linton evincing a sudden and irresistible attraction towards the tolerated guest. She was at that time a charming young lady of eighteen, infantile in manners, though possessed of keen wit, keen feelings, and a keen temper, too, if irritated. Her brother, who loved her tenderly, was appalled at this fantastic preference. Leaving aside the degradation of an alliance with a nameless man, and the possible fact that his property, in default of heirs male, might pass into such a one's power, he had sense to comprehend Heathcliff's disposition—to know that, though his exterior was altered, his mind was unchangeable and unchanged. And he dreaded that mind. It revolted him. He shrank forebodingly from the idea of committing Isabella to its keeping. He would have recoiled still more had he been aware that her attachment rose unsolicited, and was bestowed where it awakened no reciprocation of sentiment, for the minute he discovered its existence he laid the blame on Heathcliff's deliberate designing.

We had all remarked, during some time, that Miss Linton fretted and pined over something. She grew cross and wearisome, snapping at and teasing Catherine continually, at the imminent risk of exhausting her limited patience. We excused her, to a certain extent, on the plea of ill-health. She was dwindling and fading before our eyes. But one day, when she had been peculiarly wayward, rejecting her breakfast, complaining that the servants did not do what she told them ; that the mistress would allow her to be nothing in the house, and Edgar neglected her; that she had caught a cold with the doors being left open, and we let the parlour fire go out on purpose to vex her, with a hundred yet more frivolous accusations, Mrs. Linton peremptorily insisted that she should get to bed, and having scolded her heartily, threatened to send for the doctor. Mention of Kenneth caused her to exclaim instantly that her health was perfect, and it was only Catherine's harshness which made her unhappy.

"How can you say I am harsh, you naughty fondling?" cried the mistress, amazed at the unreasonable assertion. "You are surely losing your reason. When have I been harsh, tell me?"

"Yesterday," sobbed Isabella, "and now!"

"Yesterday!" said her sister-in-law. "On what occasion?"

"In our walk along the moor. You told me to ramble where I pleased, while you sauntered on with Mr. Heathcliff!"

"And that's your notion of harshness?" said Catherine, laughing. "It was no hint that your company was superfluous. We didn't care whether you kept with us or not. I merely thought Heathcliff's talk would have nothing entertaining for your ears."

"Oh no," wept the young lady; "you wished me away because you knew I liked to be there!"

"Is she sane?" asked Mrs. Linton, appealing to me. "I'll repeat our conversation, word for word, Isabella; and you point out any charm it could have had for you."

"I don't mind the conversation," she answered. "I wanted to be with——"

"Well?" said Catherine, perceiving her hesitate to complete the sentence.

"With him; and I won't be always sent off!" she continued, kindling up. "You are a dog in the manger, Cathy, and desire no one to be loved but yourself!"

"You are an impertinent little monkey!" exclaimed Mrs. Linton, in surprise. "But I'll not believe this idiocy. It is impossible that you can covet the admiration of Heathcliff—that you consider him an agreeable person! I hope I have misunderstood you, Isabella?"

"No, you have not," said the infatuated girl. "I love him more than ever you loved Edgar; and he might love me, if you would let him!"

"I wouldn't be you for a kingdom, then!" Catherine declared emphatically; and she seemed to speak sincerely.—"Nelly, help me to convince her of her madness. Tell her what Heathcliff is—an unreclaimed creature, without refinement, without cultivation, an arid wilderness of furze and whinstone. I'd as soon put that little canary into the park on a winter's day, as recommend you to bestow your heart on him. It is deplorable ignorance of his character, child, and nothing else, which makes that dream enter your head. Pray don't imagine that he conceals depths of benevolence and affection beneath a stern exterior. He's not a rough diamond, a pearl-containing oyster of a rustic. He's a fierce, pitiless, wolfish man. I never say to him, 'Let this or that enemy alone, because it would be ungenerous or cruel to harm them.' I say, 'Let them alone, because I should hate them to be wronged.' And he'd crush you like a sparrow's egg, Isabella, if he found you a troublesome charge. I know he couldn't love a Linton; and yet he'd be quite capable of marrying your fortune and expectations. Avarice is growing with him a besetting sin. There's my picture; and I'm his friend—so much so, that had he thought seriously to catch you, I should perhaps have held my tongue, and let you fall into his trap."

Miss Linton regarded her sister-in-law with indignation.

"For shame! for shame!" she repeated angrily; "you are worse than twenty foes, you poisonous friend!"

"Ah! you won't believe me, then?" said Catherine. "You think I speak from wicked selfishness?"

"I'm certain you do," retorted Isabella; "and I shudder at you!"

"Good!" cried the other. "Try for yourself, if that

be your spirit. I have done, and yield the argument to your saucy insolence."

"And I must suffer for her egotism!" she sobbed, as Mrs. Linton left the room. "All, all is against me. She has blighted my single consolation. But she uttered falsehoods, didn't she? Mr. Heathcliff is not a fiend. He has an honourable soul, and a true one, or how could he remember her?"

"Banish him from your thoughts, miss," I said. "He's a bird of bad omen—no mate for you. Mrs. Linton spoke strongly, and yet I can't contradict her. She is better acquainted with his heart than I, or any one besides; and she never would represent him as worse than he is. Honest people don't hide their deeds. How has he been living? How has he got rich? Why is he staying at Wuthering Heights, the house of a man whom he abhors? They say Mr. Earnshaw is worse and worse since he came. They sit up all night together continually, and Hindley has been borrowing money on his land, and does nothing but play and drink. I heard only a week ago—it was Joseph who told me—I met him at Gimmerton. 'Nelly,' he said, 'we's hae a crowner's 'quest enow, at ahr folks. One on 'em's a'most getten his finger cut off wi' hauding t'other fro' stickin hisseln loike a cawlf. That's maister, yah knaw, 'at's soa up o' going tuh t' grand 'sizes. He's noan feared o' t' bench o' judges, norther Paul, nur Peter, nur John, nur Matthew, nor noan on 'em, not he. He fair likes—he langs to set his brazened face agean 'em. And yon bonny lad Heathcliff, yah mind, he's a rare un! He can girn a laugh as well's onybody at a raight divil's jest. Does he niver say nowt of his fine living amang us, when he goes to t' Grange? This is t' way on't. Up at sundown; dice, brandy, cloised shutters, un can'le-light till next day at noon; then, t' fooil gangs banning un raving to his cham'er, makking dacent fowks dig thur fingers i' thur lugs fur varry shame; un the knave, why he can caint his brass, un ate, un sleep, un off to his neighbour's to gossip wi' t' wife.

I' course, he tells Dame Catherine how her fathur's goold runs into his pocket, and her fathur's son gallops down t' broad road, while he flees afore to oppen t' pikes!' Now, Miss Linton, Joseph is an old rascal, but no liar; and if his account of Heathcliff's conduct be true, you would never think of desiring such a husband, would you?"

"You are leagued with the rest, Ellen!" she replied. "I'll not listen to your slanders. What malevolence you must have to wish to convince me that there is no happiness in the world!"

Whether she would have got over this fancy if left to herself, or persevered in nursing it perpetually, I cannot say. She had little time to reflect. The day after, there was a justice meeting at the next town. My master was obliged to attend; and Mr. Heathcliff, aware of his absence, called rather earlier than usual. Catherine and Isabella were sitting in the library, on hostile terms, but silent—the latter alarmed at her recent indiscretion, and the disclosure she had made of her secret feelings in a transient fit of passion; the former, on mature consideration, really offended with her companion, and if she laughed again at her pertness, inclined to make it no laughing matter to *her*. She did laugh as she saw Heathcliff pass the window. I was sweeping the hearth, and I noticed a mischievous smile on her lips. Isabella, absorbed in her meditations, or a book, remained till the door opened; and it was too late to attempt an escape, which she would gladly have done had it been practicable.

"Come in; that's right!" exclaimed the mistress gaily, pulling a chair to the fire. "Here are two people sadly in need of a third to thaw the ice between them; and you are the very one we should both of us choose. Heathcliff, I'm proud to show you, at last, somebody that dotes on you more than myself. I expect you to feel flattered. Nay, it's not Nelly; don't look at her! My poor little sister-in-law is breaking her heart by mere contemplation of your physical and moral beauty.

It lies in your own power to be Edgar's brother.—No, no, Isabella; you shan't run off." she continued, arresting, with feigned playfulness, the confounded girl, who had risen indignantly.—" We were quarrelling like cats about you, Heathcliff, and I was fairly beaten in protestations of devotion and admiration; and, moreover, I was informed that if I would but have the manners to stand aside, my rival, as she will have herself to be, would shoot a shaft into your soul that would fix you for ever, and send my image into eternal oblivion!"

"Catherine!" said Isabella, calling up her dignity, and disdaining to struggle from the tight grasp that held her, "I'd thank you to adhere to the truth, and not slander me, even in joke.—Mr. Heathcliff, be kind enough to bid this friend of yours release me. She forgets that you and I are not intimate acquaintances; and what amuses her is painful to me beyond expression."

As the guest answered nothing, but took his seat, and looked thoroughly indifferent what sentiments she cherished concerning him, she turned and whispered an earnest appeal for liberty to her tormentor.

"By no means!" cried Mrs. Linton in answer. "I won't be named a dog in the manger again. You *shall* stay.—Now, then, Heathcliff, why don't you evince satisfaction at my pleasant news? Isabella swears that the love Edgar has for me is nothing to that she entertains for you. I'm sure she made some speech of the kind—did she not, Ellen? And she has fasted ever since the day before yesterday's walk, from sorrow and rage that I dispatched her out of your society under the idea of its being unacceptable."

"I think you belie her," said Heathcliff, twisting his chair to face them. "She wishes to be out of my society now, at any rate."

And he stared hard at the object of discourse, as one might do at a strange, repulsive animal—a centipede from the Indies, for instance, which curiosity leads one to examine in spite of the aversion it raises. The poor thing couldn't bear that. She grew white and red in rapid succession, and, while tears beaded her lashes, bent the strength of her small fingers to loosen the firm clutch of Catherine; and perceiving that as fast as she raised one finger off her arm another closed down, and she could not remove the whole together, she began to make use of her nails; and their sharpness presently ornamented the detainer's with crescents of red.

"There's a tigress!" exclaimed Mrs. Linton, setting her free, and shaking her hand with pain. "Begone, for God's sake, and hide your vixen face! How foolish to reveal those talons to *him!* Can't you fancy the conclusions he'll draw?—Look, Heathcliff! they are instruments that will do execution; you must beware of your eyes."

"I'd wrench them off her fingers if they ever menaced me," he answered brutally, when the door had closed after her. "But what did you mean by teasing the creature in that manner, Cathy? You were not speaking the truth, were you?"

"I assure you I was," she returned. "She has been dying for your sake several weeks, and raving about you this morning, and pouring forth a deluge of abuse, because I represented your failings in a plain light, for the purpose of mitigating her adoration. But don't notice it further. I wished to punish her sauciness—that's all. I like her too well, my dear Heathcliff, to let you absolutely seize and devour her up."

"And I like her too ill to attempt it," said he, "except in a very ghoulish fashion. You'd hear of odd things if I lived alone with that mawkish, waxen face. The most ordinary would be painting on its white the colours of the rainbow, and turning the blue eyes black, every day or two. They detestably resemble Linton's."

"Delectably!" observed Catherine. "They are dove's eyes—angel's!"

"She's her brother's heir, is she not?" he asked, after a brief silence.

"I should be sorry to think so," returned his companion. "Half a dozen nephews shall erase her title, please Heaven! Abstract your mind from the subject at present. You are too prone to covet your neighbour's goods. Remember *this* neighbour's goods are mine."

" If they were *mine*, they would be none the less that," said Heathcliff; " but though Isabella Linton may be silly, she is scarcely mad; and, in short, we'll dismiss the matter, as you advise."

From their tongues they did dismiss it; and Catherine, probably, from her thoughts. The other, I felt certain, recalled it often in the course of the evening. I saw him smile to himself—grin rather—and lapse into ominous musing whenever Mrs. Linton had occasion to be absent from the apartment.

I determined to watch his movements. My heart invariably cleaved to the master's, in preference to Catherine's side—with reason, I imagined, for he was kind, and trustful, and honourable; and she—she could not be called the *opposite*, yet she seemed to allow herself such wide latitude that I had little faith in her principles, and still less sympathy for her feelings. I wanted something to happen which might have the effect of freeing both Wuthering Heights and the Grange of Mr. Heathcliff quietly, leaving us as we had been prior to his advent. His visits were a continual nightmare to me, and, I suspected, to my master also. His abode at the Heights was an oppression past explaining. I felt that God had forsaken the stray sheep there to its own wicked wanderings, and an evil beast prowled between it and the fold, waiting his time to spring and destroy.

CHAPTER XI.

SOMETIMES, while meditating on these things in solitude, I've got up in a sudden terror, and put on my bonnet to go see how all was at the farm. I've persuaded my conscience that it was a duty to warn him how people talked regarding his ways; and then I've recollected his confirmed bad habits, and, hopeless of benefiting him, have flinched from re-entering the dismal house, doubting if I could bear to be taken at my word.

One time I passed the old gate, going out of my way, on a journey to Gimmerton. It was about the period that my narrative has reached—a bright, frosty afternoon, the ground bare, and the road hard and dry. I came to a stone where the highway branches off on to the moor at your left hand—a rough sand-pillar, with the letters W. H. cut on its north side, on the east, G., and on the south-west, T. G. It serves as a guide-post to the Grange, the Heights, and village. The sun shone yellow on its gray head, reminding me of summer; and I cannot say why, but all at once a gush of child's sensations flowed into my heart. Hindley and I held it a favourite spot twenty years before. I gazed long at the weather-worn block, and stooping down, perceived a hole near the bottom still full of snail-shells and pebbles, which we were fond of storing there with more perishable things; and, as fresh as reality, it appeared that I beheld my early playmate seated on the withered turf, his dark, square head bent forward, and his little hand scooping out the earth with a piece of slate. "Poor Hindley!" I exclaimed involuntarily. I started. My bodily eye was cheated into a momentary belief that the child lifted its face and stared straight into mine! It vanished in a twinkling; but immediately I felt an irresistible yearning to be at the Heights. Superstition urged me to comply with this impulse. Supposing he should be dead, I thought, or should die soon!— supposing it were a sign of death! The nearer I got to the house the more agitated I grew; and on catching sight of it I trembled every limb. The apparition had outstripped me. It stood looking through the gate. That was my first idea on observing an elf-locked, brown-eyed boy setting his ruddy countenance against the bars. Further reflection suggested this must be Hareton, *my* Hareton, not altered greatly since I left him, ten months since.

"God bless thee, darling!" I cried, forgetting instantaneously my foolish fears. "Hareton, it's Nelly—Nelly, thy nurse."

He retreated out of arm's length, and picked up a large flint.

"I am come to see thy father, Hareton," I added, guessing from the action that Nelly, if she lived in his memory at all, was not recognized as one with me.

He raised his missile to hurl it. I commenced a soothing speech, but could not stay his hand. The stone struck my bonnet; and then ensued, from the stammering lips of the little fellow, a string of curses, which, whether he comprehended them or not, were delivered with practised emphasis, and distorted his baby features into a shocking expression of malignity. You may be certain this grieved more than angered me. Fit to cry, I took an orange from my pocket, and offered it to propitiate him. He hesitated, and then snatched it from my hold, as if he fancied I only intended to tempt and disappoint him. I showed another, keeping it out of his reach.

"Who has taught you those fine words, my bairn?" I inquired—"the curate?"

"Damn the curate, and thee! Gie me that," he replied.

"Tell us where you got your lessons, and you shall have it," said I. "Who's your master?"

"Devil daddy," was his answer.

"And what do you learn from daddy?" I continued.

He jumped at the fruit. I raised it higher. "What does he teach you?" I asked.

"Naught," said he, "but to keep out of his gait. Daddy cannot bide me, because I swear at him."

"Ah! and the devil teaches you to swear at daddy?" I observed.

"Ay—nay," he drawled.

"Who, then?"

"Heathcliff."

I asked if he liked Mr. Heathcliff.

"Ay!" he answered again.

Desiring to have his reasons for liking him, I could only gather the sentences, " I known't. He pays dad back what he gies to me; he curses daddy for cursing me. He says I mun do as I will."

" And the curate does not teach you to read and write then ? " I pursued.

" No, I was told the curate should have his —— teeth dashed down his —— throat if he stepped over the threshold. Heathcliff had promised that ! "

I put the orange in his hand, and bade him tell his father that a woman called Nelly Dean was waiting to speak with him by the garden gate. He went up the walk, and entered the house; but instead of Hindley, Heathcliff appeared on the door stones; and I turned directly and ran down the road as hard as ever I could race, making no halt till I gained the guide-post, and feeling as scared as if I had raised a goblin. This is not much connected with Miss Isabella's affair, except that it urged me to resolve further on mounting vigilant guard, and doing my utmost to check the spread of such bad influence at the Grange, even though I should wake a domestic storm by thwarting Mrs. Linton's pleasure.

The next time Heathcliff came, my young lady chanced to be feeding some pigeons in the court. She had never spoken a word to her sister-in-law for three days; but she had likewise dropped her fretful complaining, and we found it a great comfort. Heathcliff had not the habit of bestowing a single unnecessary civility on Miss Linton, I knew. Now, as soon as he beheld her, his first precaution was to take a sweeping survey of the house-front. I was standing by the kitchen window, but I drew out of sight. He then stepped across the pavement to her, and said something. She seemed embarrassed and desirous of getting away; to prevent it, he laid his hand on her arm. She averted her face. He apparently put some question which she had no mind to answer. There was another rapid glance at the house; and supposing himself unseen, the scoundrel had the impudence to embrace her.

" Judas ! traitor ! " I ejaculated. " You are a hypocrite, too, are you—a deliberate deceiver ? "

" Who is, Nelly ? " said Catherine's voice at my elbow. I had been over-intent on watching the pair outside to mark her entrance.

" Your worthless friend ! " I answered warmly—" the sneaking rascal yonder. Ah, he has caught a glimpse of us ; he is coming in ! I wonder will he have the heart to find a plausible excuse for making love to miss, when he told you he hated her ? "

Mrs. Linton saw Isabella tear herself free, and run into the garden ; and a minute after Heathcliff opened the door. I couldn't withhold giving some loose to my indignation ; but Catherine angrily insisted on silence, and threatened to order me out of the kitchen, if I dared to be so presumptuous as to put in my insolent tongue.

" To hear you, people might think you were the mistress ! " she cried. " You want setting down in your right place !—Heathcliff, what are you about, raising this stir ? I said you must let Isabella alone ! I beg you will, unless you are tired of being received here, and wish Linton to draw the bolts against you ! "

" God forbid that he should try ! " answered the black villain. I detested him just then. " God keep him meek and patient ! Every day I grow madder after sending him to heaven ! "

" Hush ! " said Catherine, shutting the inner door. " Don't vex me. Why have you disregarded my request ? Did she come across you on purpose ? "

" What is it to you ? " he growled. " I have a right to kiss her, if she chooses ; and you have no right to object. I am not *your* husband ; *you* needn't be jealous of me."

" I'm not jealous *of* you," replied the mistress—" I'm jealous *for* you. Clear your face ; you shan't scowl at me ! If you like Isabella, you shall marry her. But do you like her ? Tell the truth, Heathcliff. There, you won't answer. I'm certain you don't."

" And would Mr. Linton approve of his sister marrying that man ? " I inquired.

" Mr. Linton should approve," returned my lady decisively.

" He might spare himself the trouble," said Heathcliff ; " I could do as well without his approbation. And as to you, Catherine, I have a mind to speak a few words now, while we are at it. I want you to be aware that I *know* you have treated me infernally— infernally ! Do you hear ? And if you flatter yourself that I don't perceive it, you are a fool ; and if you think I can be consoled by sweet words, you are an idiot ; and if you fancy I'll suffer unrevenged, I'll convince you of the contrary in a very little while. Meantime, thank you for telling me your sister-in-law's secret. I swear I'll make the most of it. And stand you aside."

" What new phase of his character is this ? " exclaimed Mrs. Linton, in amazement. " I've treated you infernally, and you'll take your revenge ! How will you take it, ungrateful brute ? How have I treated you infernally ? "

" I seek no revenge on you," replied Heathcliff, less vehemently. " That's not the plan. The tyrant grinds down his slaves, and they don't turn against him ; they crush those beneath them. You are welcome to torture me to death for your amusement, only allow me to amuse myself a little in the same style, and refrain from insult as much as you are able. Having levelled my palace, don't erect a hovel and complacently admire your own charity in giving me that for a home. If I imagined you really wished me to marry Isabel, I'd cut my throat ! "

" Oh, the evil is that I am *not* jealous, is it ? " cried Catherine. " Well, I won't repeat my offer of a wife. It is as bad as offering Satan a lost soul. Your bliss lies, like his, in inflicting misery. You prove it. Edgar is restored from the ill-temper he gave way to at your coming. I begin to be secure and tranquil ; and you, restless to know us at peace, appear resolved on exciting a quarrel. Quarrel with Edgar, if you please, Heathcliff, and deceive his sister. You'll hit on exactly the most efficient method of revenging yourself on me."

The conversation ceased. Mrs. Linton sat down by the fire, flushed and gloomy. The spirit which served her was growing intractable; she could neither lay nor control it. He stood on the hearth with folded arms, brooding on his evil thoughts; and in this position I left them to seek the master, who was wondering what kept Catherine below so long.

"Ellen," said he, when I entered, "have you seen your mistress?"

"Yes; she's in the kitchen, sir," I answered. "She's sadly put out by Mr. Heathcliff's behaviour; and, indeed, I do think it's time to arrange his visits on another footing. There's harm in being too soft, and now it's come to this——" And I related the scene in the court, and, as near as I dared, the whole subsequent dispute. I fancied it could not be very prejudicial to Mrs. Linton, unless she made it so afterwards by assuming the defensive for her guest. Edgar Linton had difficulty in hearing me to the close. His first words revealed that he did not clear his wife of blame.

"This is insufferable!" he exclaimed. "It is disgraceful that she should own him for a friend, and force his company on me! Call me two men out of the hall, Ellen. Catherine shall linger no longer to argue with the low ruffian. I have humoured her enough."

He descended, and bidding the servants wait in the passage, went, followed by me, to the kitchen. Its occupants had recommenced their angry discussion. Mrs. Linton, at least, was scolding with renewed vigour. Heathcliff had moved to the window, and hung his head, somewhat cowed by her violent rating apparently. He saw the master first, and made a hasty motion that she should be silent; which she obeyed abruptly, on discovering the reason of his intimation.

"How is this?" said Linton, addressing her. "What notion of propriety must you have to remain here, after the language which has been held to you by that black-guard? I suppose, because it is his ordinary talk, you think nothing of it. You are habituated to his baseness, and, perhaps, imagine I can get used to it too."

"Have you been listening at the door, Edgar?" asked the mistress, in a tone particularly calculated to provoke her husband, implying both carelessness and contempt of his irritation. Heathcliff, who had raised his eyes at the former speech, gave a sneering laugh at the latter—on purpose, it seemed, to draw Mr. Linton's attention to him. He succeeded; but Edgar did not mean to entertain him with any high flights of passion.

"I have been so far forbearing with you, sir," he said quietly—"not that I was ignorant of your miserable, degraded character, but I felt you were only partly responsible for that; and Catherine wishing to keep up your acquaintance, I acquiesced—foolishly. Your presence is a moral poison that would contaminate the most virtuous. For that cause, and to prevent worse consequences, I shall deny you hereafter admission into this house, and give notice now that I require your instant departure. Three minutes' delay will render it involuntary and ignominious."

Heathcliff measured the height and breadth of the speaker with an eye full of derision.

"Cathy, this lamb of yours threatens like a bull!" he said. "It is in danger of splitting its skull against my knuckles.—By God, Mr. Linton, I'm mortally sorry that you are not worth knocking down!"

My master glanced towards the passage, and signed me to fetch the men. He had no intention of hazarding a personal encounter. I obeyed the hint; but Mrs. Linton, suspecting something, followed; and when I attempted to call them, she pulled me back, slammed the door to, and locked it.

"Fair means!" she said, in answer to her husband's look of angry surprise. "If you have not courage to attack him, make an apology, or allow yourself to be beaten. It will correct you of feigning more valour than you possess. No, I'll swallow the key before you shall get it! I'm delightfully rewarded for my kindness to each! After constant indulgence of one's weak nature, and the other's bad one, I earn for thanks two samples of blind ingratitude, stupid to absurdity! Edgar, I was defending you and yours; and I wish Heathcliff may flog you sick for daring to think an evil thought of me!"

It did not need the medium of a flogging to produce that effect on the master. He tried to wrest the key from Catherine's grasp, and for safety she flung it into the hottest part of the fire; whereupon Mr. Edgar was taken with a nervous trembling, and his countenance grew deadly pale. For his life he could not avert that excess of emotion; mingled anguish and humiliation overcame him completely. He leant on the back of a chair, and covered his face.

"O heavens! In old days this would win you knighthood!" exclaimed Mrs. Linton. "We are vanquished! we are vanquished! Heathcliff would as soon lift a finger at you as a king would march his army against a colony of mice. Cheer up; you shan't be hurt! Your type is not a lamb; it's a sucking leveret."

"I wish you joy of the milk-blooded coward, Cathy!" said her friend. "I compliment you on your taste. And that is the slavering, shivering thing you preferred to me! I would not strike him with my fist, but I'd kick him with my foot, and experience considerable satisfaction. Is he weeping, or is he going to faint for fear?"

The fellow approached and gave the chair on which Linton rested a push. He'd better have kept his distance. My master quickly sprang erect, and struck him full on the throat a blow that would have levelled a slighter man. It took his breath for a minute; and while he choked, Mr. Linton walked out by the back door into the yard, and from thence to the front entrance.

"There! you've done with coming here," cried Catherine. "Get away, now. He'll return with a brace of pistols and half a dozen assistants. If he did overhear us, of course he'd never forgive you. You've

played me an ill turn, Heathcliff. But go—make haste !
I'd rather see Edgar at bay than you."

"Do you suppose I'm going with that blow burning
in my gullet ?" he thundered. "By hell, no ! I'll
crush his ribs in like a rotten hazel-nut before I cross
the threshold ! If I don't floor him now, I shall murder
him some time ; so, as you value his existence, let me
get at him !"

"He is not coming," I interposed, framing a bit of a
lie. "There's the coachman and the two gardeners.
You'll surely not wait to be thrust into the road by
them ! Each has a bludgeon ; and master will very
likely be watching from the parlour windows, to see
that they fulfil his orders."

The gardeners and coachman *were* there, but Linton
was with them. They had already entered the court.
Heathcliff, on second thoughts, resolved to avoid a
struggle against the three underlings. He seized the
poker, smashed the lock from the inner door, and made
his escape as they tramped in.

Mrs. Linton, who was very much excited, bade me
accompany her upstairs. She did not know my share
in contributing to the disturbance, and I was anxious
to keep her in ignorance.

"I'm nearly distracted, Nelly !" she exclaimed, throwing herself on the sofa. "A thousand smiths' hammers
are beating in my head ! Tell Isabella to shun me ; this
uproar is owing to her ; and should she or any one else
aggravate my anger at present, I shall get wild. And,
Nelly, say to Edgar, if you see him again to-night, that
I'm in danger of being seriously ill. I wish it may prove
true. He has startled and distressed me shockingly.
I want to frighten him. Besides, he might come and
begin a string of abuse or complainings. I'm certain I
should recriminate, and God knows where we should
end ! Will you do so, my good Nelly ? You are aware
that I am no way blamable in this matter. What
possessed him to turn listener ? Heathcliff's talk was
outrageous after you left us ; but I could soon have

diverted him from Isabella, and the rest meant nothing. Now all is dashed wrong, by the fool's craving to hear evil of self that haunts some people like a demon. Had Edgar never gathered our conversation, he would never have been the worse for it. Really, when he opened on me in that unreasonable tone of displeasure after I had scolded Heathcliff till I was hoarse for *him*, I did not care hardly what they did to each other — especially as I felt that, however the scene closed, we should all be driven asunder for nobody knows how long! Well, if I cannot keep Heathcliff for my friend—if Edgar will be mean and jealous—I'll try to break their hearts by breaking my own. That will be a prompt way of finishing all, when I am pushed to extremity. But it's a deed to be reserved for a forlorn hope; I'd not take Linton by surprise with it. To this point he has been discreet in dreading to provoke me. You must represent the peril of quitting that policy, and remind him of my passionate temper, verging, when kindled, on frenzy. I wish you could dismiss that apathy out of that countenance, and look rather more anxious about me."

The stolidity with which I received these instructions was, no doubt, rather exasperating, for they were delivered in perfect sincerity; but I believed a person who could plan the turning of her fits of passion to account beforehand might, by exerting her will, manage to control herself tolerably, even while under their influence; and I did not wish to "frighten" her husband, as she said, and multiply his annoyances for the purpose of serving her selfishness. Therefore I said nothing when I met the master coming towards the parlour; but I took the liberty of turning back to listen whether they would resume their quarrel together. He began to speak first.

"Remain where you are, Catherine," he said, without any anger in his voice, but with much sorrowful despondency. "I shall not stay. I am neither come to wrangle nor be reconciled; but I wish just to learn whether, after this evening's events, you intend to continue your intimacy with——"

"Oh, for mercy's sake," interrupted the mistress, stamping her foot—"for mercy's sake, let us hear no more of it now! Your cold blood cannot be worked into a fever. Your veins are full of ice-water; but mine are boiling, and the sight of such chillness makes them dance."

"To get rid of me, answer my question," persevered Mr. Linton. "You *must* answer it, and that violence does not alarm me. I have found that you can be as stoical as any one, when you please. Will you give up Heathcliff hereafter, or will you give up me? It is impossible for you to be *my* friend and *his* at the same time; and I absolutely *require* to know which you choose."

"I require to be let alone!" exclaimed Catherine furiously. "I demand it! Don't you see I can scarcely stand? Edgar, you—you leave me!"

She rang the bell till it broke with a twang. I entered leisurely. It was enough to try the temper of a saint, such senseless, wicked rages! There she lay dashing her head against the arm of the sofa, and grinding her teeth, so that you might fancy she would crash them to splinters! Mr. Linton stood looking at her in sudden compunction and fear. He told me to fetch some water. She had no breath for speaking. I brought a glass full; and as she would not drink, I sprinkled it on her face. In a few seconds she stretched herself out stiff, and turned up her eyes, while her cheeks, at once blanched and livid, assumed the aspect of death. Linton looked terrified.

"There is nothing in the world the matter," I whispered. I did not want him to yield, though I could not help being afraid in my heart.

"She has blood on her lips!" he said, shuddering.

"Never mind!" I answered tartly. And I told him how she had resolved, previous to his coming, on exhibiting a fit of frenzy. I incautiously gave the account aloud, and she heard me, for she started up, her hair flying over her shoulders, her eyes flashing, the muscles of her neck and arms standing out preternaturally. I made up my mind for broken bones at least; but she only glared about her for an instant, and then rushed from the room. The master directed me to follow. I did, to her chamber door. She hindered me from going farther by securing it against me.

As she never offered to descend to breakfast next morning, I went to ask whether she would have some carried up. "No!" she replied peremptorily. The same question was repeated at dinner and tea, and again on the morrow after, and received the same answer. Mr. Linton, on his part, spent his time in the library, and did not inquire concerning his wife's occupations. Isabella and he had had an hour's interview, during which he tried to elicit from her some sentiment of proper horror for Heathcliff's advances; but he could make nothing of her evasive replies, and was obliged to close the examination unsatisfactorily, adding, however, a solemn warning that if she were so insane as to encourage that worthless suitor, it would dissolve all bonds of relationship between herself and him.

CHAPTER XII.

WHILE Miss Linton moped about the park and garden, always silent, and almost always in tears, and her brother shut himself up among books that he never opened— wearying, I guessed, with a continual vague expectation that Catherine, repenting her conduct, would come of her own accord to ask pardon, and seek a reconciliation —and *she* fasted pertinaciously, under the idea, probably, that at every meal Edgar was ready to choke for her absence, and pride alone held him from running to cast himself at her feet, I went about my household duties, convinced that the Grange had but one sensible soul in its walls, and that lodged in my body. I wasted no condolences on miss, nor any expostulations on my mistress; nor did I pay much attention to the sighs of my master, who yearned to hear his lady's name, since he might not hear her voice. I determined they

should come about as they pleased for me; and though
it was a tiresomely slow process, I began to rejoice at
length in a faint dawn of its progress, as I thought at first.

Mrs. Linton on the third day unbarred her door, and
having finished the water in her pitcher and decanter,
desired a renewed supply, and a basin of gruel, for she
believed she was dying. That I set down as a speech
meant for Edgar's ears. I believed no such thing, so
I kept it to myself, and brought her some tea and dry
toast. She ate and drank eagerly, and sank back on
her pillow again, clenching her hands and groaning.
"Oh, I will die," she exclaimed, "since no one cares
anything about me. I wish I had not taken that."
Then a good while after I heard her murmur, "No, I'll
not die—he'd be glad—he does not love me at all—he
would never miss me!"

"Did you want anything, ma'am?" I inquired, still
preserving my external composure, in spite of her ghastly
countenance and strange, exaggerated manner.

"What is that apathetic being doing?" she demanded,
pushing the thick entangled locks from her wasted face.
"Has he fallen into a lethargy, or is he dead?"

"Neither," replied I, "if you mean Mr. Linton. He's
tolerably well, I think, though his studies occupy him
rather more than they ought. He is continually among
his books, since he has no other society."

I should not have spoken so if I had known her true
condition, but I could not get rid of the notion that
she acted a part of her disorder.

"Among his books!" she cried, confounded. "And
I dying—I on the brink of the grave! My God! does
he know how I'm altered?" continued she, staring at
her reflection in a mirror hanging against the opposite
wall. "Is that Catherine Linton? He imagines me in
a pet—in play, perhaps. Cannot you inform him that
it is frightful earnest? Nelly, if it be not too late, as
soon as I learn how he feels I'll choose between these
two—either to starve at once (that would be no punishment unless he had a heart), or to recover, and leave the

country. Are you speaking the truth about him now ?
Take care. Is he actually so utterly indifferent for my
life ? "

"Why, ma'am," I answered, "the master has no idea
of your being deranged ; and, of course, he does not
fear that you will let yourself die of hunger."

"You think not ? Cannot you tell him I will ? "
she returned. "Persuade him ; speak of your own
mind ; say you are certain I will ! "

"No, you forget, Mrs. Linton," I suggested, "that
you have eaten some food with a relish this evening,
and to-morrow you will perceive its good effects."

"If I were only sure it would kill him," she interrupted,
"I'd kill myself directly ! These three awful nights
I've never closed my lids ; and oh, I've been tormented !
I've been haunted, Nelly ! But I begin to fancy you
don't like me. How strange ! I thought, though everybody hated and despised each other, they could not
avoid loving me. And they have all turned to enemies
in a few hours. *They* have, I'm positive—the people
here. How dreary to meet death, surrounded by their
cold faces ! Isabella, terrified and repelled, afraid to
enter the room ; it would be so dreadful to watch Catherine
go ! And Edgar standing solemnly by to see it over ;
then offering prayers of thanks to God for restoring
peace to his house, and going back to his *books !* What
in the name of all that feels has he to do with *books*
when I am dying ? "

She could not bear the notion which I had put into
her head of Mr. Linton's philosophical resignation.
Tossing about, she increased her feverish bewilderment
to madness, and tore the pillow with her teeth ; then
raising herself up, all burning, desired that I would open
the window. We were in the middle of winter, the wind
blew strong from the north-east, and I objected. Both
the expressions flitting over her face and the changes
of her moods began to alarm me terribly, and brought
to my recollection her former illness, and the doctor's
injunction that she should not be crossed. A minute

previously she was violent; now, supported on one arm, and not noticing my refusal to obey her, she seemed to find childish diversion in pulling the feathers from the rents she had just made, and ranging them on the sheet according to their different species. Her mind had strayed to other associations.

"That's a turkey's," she murmured to herself, "and this is a wild duck's, and this is a pigeon's. Ah, they put pigeons' feathers in the pillows; no wonder I couldn't die! Let me take care to throw it on the floor when I lie down. And here is a moor-cock's; and this—I should know it among a thousand—it's a lapwing's. Bonny bird, wheeling over our heads in the middle of the moor. It wanted to get to its nest, for the clouds had touched the swells, and it felt rain coming. This feather was picked up from the heath; the bird was not shot. We saw its nest in the winter, full of little skeletons. Heathcliff set a trap over it, and the old ones dare not come. I made him promise he'd never shoot a lapwing after that, and he didn't. Yes, here are more! Did he shoot my lapwings, Nelly? Are they red, any of them? Let me look."

"Give over with that baby-work!" I interrupted, dragging the pillow away, and turning the holes towards the mattress, for she was removing its contents by handfuls. "Lie down and shut your eyes; you're wandering. There's a mess! The down is flying about like snow."

I went here and there collecting it.

"I see in you, Nelly," she continued dreamily, "an aged woman. You have gray hair and bent shoulders. This bed is the fairy cave under Peniston Crag, and you are gathering elf-bolts to hurt our heifers, pretending, while I am near, that they are only locks of wool. That's what you'll come to fifty years hence. I know you are not so now. I'm not wandering; you're mistaken, or else I should believe you really *were* that withered hag, and I should think I *was* under Peniston Crag; and I'm conscious it's night, and there are two candles on the table making the black press shine like jet."

" The black press ?   Where is that ? " I asked.   " You
are talking in your sleep ! "

" It's against the wall, as it always is," she replied.
" It *does* appear odd.   I see a face in it ! "

" There's no press in the room, and never was," said
I, resuming my seat, and looping up the curtain, that I
might watch her.

" Don't *you* see that face ? " she inquired, gazing
earnestly at the mirror.

And say what I could, I was incapable of making her
comprehend it to be her own ; so I rose and covered it
with a shawl.

" It's behind there still ! " she pursued anxiously.
" And it stirred.   Who is it ?   I hope it will not come
out when you are gone !   O Nelly, the room is haunted !
I'm afraid of being alone ! "

I took her hand in mine, and bade her be composed,
for a succession of shudders convulsed her frame, and she
would keep straining her gaze towards the glass.

" There's nobody here ! " I insisted.   " It was *yourself*,
Mrs. Linton.   You knew it a while since."

" Myself ! " she gasped ; " and the clock is striking
twelve !   It's true, then ; that's dreadful ! "

Her fingers clutched the clothes, and gathered them
over her eyes.   I attempted to steal to the door, with
an intention of calling her husband ; but I was summoned back by a piercing shriek.   The shawl had dropped
from the frame.

" Why, what *is* the matter ? " cried I.   " Who is
coward now ?   Wake up !   That is the glass—the mirror,
Mrs. Linton ; and you see yourself in it ; and there am
I too, by your side."

Trembling and bewildered, she held me fast, but the
horror gradually passed from her countenance.   Its paleness gave place to a glow of shame.

" Oh dear !   I thought I was at home," she sighed—
" I thought I was lying in my chamber at Wuthering
Heights.   Because I'm weak, my brain got confused,
and I screamed unconsciously.   Don't say anything,

ut stay with me. I dread sleeping. My dreams appall
ne."

"A sound sleep would do you good, ma'am," I an-
wered; "and I hope this suffering will prevent your
rying starving again."

"Oh, if I were but in my own bed in the old house!"
he went on bitterly, wringing her hands. "And that
vind sounding in the firs by the lattice. Do let me feel
t—it comes straight down the moor—do let me have one
reath!"

To pacify her, I held the casement ajar a few seconds.
A cold blast rushed through. I closed it, and returned
o my post. She lay still now, her face bathed in tears.
Exhaustion of body had entirely subdued her spirit.
Our fiery Catherine was no better than a wailing child.

"How long is it since I shut myself in here?" she
asked, suddenly reviving.

"It was Monday evening," I replied; "and this is
Thursday night, or rather Friday morning, at present."

"What! of the same week?" she exclaimed. "Only
that brief time?"

"Long enough to live on nothing but cold water and
ll-temper," observed I.

"Well, it seems a weary number of hours," she muttered doubtfully. "It must be more. I remember being
in the parlour after they had quarrelled, and Edgar being
cruelly provoking, and me running into this room desperate. As soon as ever I had barred the door, utter blackness overwhelmed me, and I fell on the floor. I couldn't
explain to Edgar how certain I felt of having a fit, or
going raging mad, if he persisted in teasing me. I had
no command of tongue or brain, and he did not guess
my agony perhaps; it barely left me sense to try to
escape from him and his voice. Before I recovered
sufficiently to see and hear, it began to be dawn; and,
Nelly, I'll tell you what I thought, and what has kept
recurring and recurring till I feared for my reason. I
thought as I lay there, with my head against that table
leg, and my eyes dimly discerning the gray square of

the window, that I was enclosed in the oak-panelled
bed at home; and my heart ached with some great
grief which, just waking, I could not recollect. I pon
dered, and worried myself to discover what it could
be; and, most strangely, the whole last seven years of
my life grew a blank! I did not recall that they had
been at all. I was a child; my father was just buried,
and my misery arose from the separation that Hindley
had ordered between me and Heathcliff. I was laid
alone, for the first time; and rousing from a dismal
doze, after a night of weeping, I lifted my hand to push
the panels aside. It struck the table-top! I swept it
along the carpet; and then memory burst in. My late
anguish was swallowed in a paroxysm of despair. I
cannot say why I felt so wildly wretched. It must
have been temporary derangement, for there is scarcely
cause. But, supposing at twelve years old I had been
wrenched from the Heights, and every early association,
and my all in all, as Heathcliff was at that time, and
been converted at a stroke into Mrs. Linton, the lady
of Thrushcross Grange, and the wife of a stranger, an
exile and outcast thenceforth from what had been my
world—you may fancy a glimpse of the abyss where I
grovelled! Shake your head as you will, Nelly, you
have helped to unsettle me! You should have spoken
to Edgar—indeed you should—and compelled him to
leave me quiet! Oh, I'm burning! I wish I were out
of doors! I wish I were a girl again, half savage and
hardy and free, and laughing at injuries, not maddening
under them! Why am I so changed? Why does my
blood rush into a hell of tumult at a few words? I'm
sure I should be myself were I once among the heather
on those hills. Open the window again wide—fasten it
open! Quick! Why don't you move?"

"Because I won't give you your death of cold," I
answered.

"You won't give me a chance of life, you mean,"
she said sullenly. "However, I'm not helpless yet;
I'll open it myself."

And sliding from the bed before I could hinder her,
he crossed the room, walking very uncertainly, threw
t back, and bent out, careless of the frosty air that
ut about her shoulders as keen as a knife. I entreated,
nd finally attempted to force her to retire. But I
oon found her delirious strength much surpassed mine
she *was* delirious, I became convinced by her subsequent
ctions and ravings). There was no moon, and every-
hing beneath lay in misty darkness. Not a light gleamed
rom any house, far or near—all had been extinguished
ong ago ; and those at Wuthering Heights were never
risible—still she asserted she caught their shining.

"Look !" she cried eagerly ; "that's my room with
he candle in it, and the tree swaying before it ; and the
ther candle is in Joseph's garret. Joseph sits up late,
loesn't he ? He's waiting till I come home, that he
nay lock the gate. Well, he'll wait a while yet. It's
 rough journey, and a sad heart to travel it ; and we
nust pass by Gimmerton Kirk to go that journey !
Ve've braved its ghosts often together, and dared each
ther to stand among the graves and ask them to come.
3ut, Heathcliff, if I dare you now, will you venture ?
f you do, I'll keep you. I'll not lie there by myself.
They may bury me twelve feet deep, and throw the
hurch down over me, but I won't rest till you are with
ne. I never will ! "

She paused, and resumed with a strange smile. " He's
onsidering ; he'd rather I'd come to him ! Find a way,
hen—not through that kirkyard. You are slow ! Be
ontent ; you always followed me ! "

Perceiving it vain to argue against her insanity, I was
lanning how I could reach something to wrap about
er, without quitting my hold of herself (for I could not
rust her alone by the gaping lattice), when, to my
onsternation, I heard the rattle of the door-handle,
nd Mr. Linton entered. He had only then come from
he library, and in passing through the lobby had
oticed our talking, and been attracted by curiosity, or
ear, to examine what it signified, at that late hour.

"O sir!" I cried, checking the exclamation risen t
his lips at the sight which met him, and the bleak atmos
phere of the chamber, "my poor mistress is ill, and sh
quite masters me. I cannot manage her at all. Pray
come and persuade her to go to bed. Forget you
anger, for she's hard to guide any way but her own."

"Catherine ill?" he said, hastening to us. "Shu
the window, Ellen!—Catherine! why——"

He was silent. The haggardness of Mrs. Linton'
appearance smote him speechless, and he could onl
glance from her to me in horrified astonishment.

"She's been fretting here," I continued, "and eatin
scarcely anything, and never complaining. She woul
admit none of us till this evening, and so we couldn'
inform you of her state, as we were not aware of it our
selves; but it is nothing."

I felt I uttered my explanations awkwardly. The
master frowned. "It is nothing, is it, Ellen Dean?"
he said sternly. "You shall account more clearly fo
keeping me ignorant of this!" And he took his wif
in his arms, and looked at her with anguish.

At first she gave him no glance of recognition; h
was invisible to her abstracted gaze. The delirium wa
not fixed, however; having weaned her eyes from con
templating the outer darkness, by degrees she centred
her attention on him, and discovered who it was tha
held her.

"Ah! you are come, are you, Edgar Linton?" sh
said, with angry animation. "You are one of thos
things that are ever found when least wanted, and whe
you are wanted, never! I suppose we shall have plenty
of lamentations now—I see we shall; but they can'
keep me from my narrow home out yonder—my resting
place, where I'm bound before spring is over! There i
is—not among the Lintons, mind, under the chapel
roof, but in the open air, with a head-stone; and you
may please yourself whether you go to them or come
to me!"

"Catherine, what have you done?" commenced the

master. "Am I nothing to you any more? Do you love that wretch Heath——"

"Hush!" cried Mrs. Linton—"hush, this moment! You mention that name, and I end the matter instantly by a spring from the window! What you touch at present you may have; but my soul will be on that hill-top before you lay hands on me again. I don't want you, Edgar. I'm past wanting you. Return to your books. I'm glad you possess a consolation, for all you had in me is gone."

"Her mind wanders, sir," I interposed—"she has been talking nonsense the whole evening; but let her have quiet and proper attendance, and she'll rally. Hereafter we must be cautious how we vex her."

"I desire no further advice from you," answered Mr. Linton. "You knew your mistress's nature, and you encouraged me to harass her. And not to give me one hint of how she has been these three days! It was heartless! Months of sickness could not cause such a change!"

I began to defend myself, thinking it too bad to be blamed for another's wicked waywardness. "I knew Mrs. Linton's nature to be headstrong and domineering," cried I, "but I didn't know that you wished to foster her fierce temper. I didn't know that, to humour her, I should wink at Mr. Heathcliff. I performed the duty of a faithful servant in telling you, and I have got a faithful servant's wages! Well, it will teach me to be careful next time. Next time you may gather intelligence for yourself."

"The next time you bring a tale to me you shall quit my service, Ellen Dean," he replied.

"You'd rather hear nothing about it, I suppose, then, Mr. Linton?" said I. "Heathcliff has your permission to come a-courting to miss, and to drop in at every opportunity your absence offers, on purpose to poison the mistress against you?"

Confused as Catherine was, her wits were alert at applying our conversation.

"Ah! Nelly has played traitor!" she exclaimed passionately—"Nelly is my hidden enemy! You witch! So you do seek elf-bolts to hurt us! Let me go, and I'll make her rue! I'll make her howl a recantation!"

A maniac's fury kindled under her brows. She struggled desperately to disengage herself from Linton's arms. I felt no inclination to tarry the event; and resolving to seek medical aid on my own responsibility, I quitted the chamber.

In passing the garden to reach the road, at a place where a bridle hook is driven into the wall, I saw something white moved irregularly, evidently by another agent than the wind. Notwithstanding my hurry, I stayed to examine it, lest ever after I should have the conviction impressed on my imagination that it was a creature of the other world. My surprise and perplexity were great on discovering, by touch more than vision, Miss Isabella's springer, Fanny, suspended by a handkerchief, and nearly at its last gasp. I quickly released the animal, and lifted it into the garden. I had seen it follow its mistress upstairs when she went to bed, and wondered much how it could have got out there, and what mischievous person had treated it so. While untying the knot round the hook, it seemed to me that I repeatedly caught the beat of horses' feet galloping at some distance; but there were such a number of things to occupy my reflections that I hardly gave the circumstance a thought, though it was a strange sound in that place at two o'clock in the morning.

Mr. Kenneth was fortunately just issuing from his house to see a patient in the village as I came up the street, and my account of Catherine Linton's malady induced him to accompany me back immediately. He was a plain, rough man; and he made no scruple to speak his doubts of her surviving this second attack, unless she were more submissive to his directions than she had shown herself before.

"Nelly Dean," said he, "I can't help fancying there's an extra cause for this. What has there been to do at the Grange ? We've odd reports up here. A stout, hearty lass like Catherine does not fall ill for a trifle ; and that sort of people should not, either. It's hard work bringing them through fevers and such things. How did it begin ? "

" The master will inform you," I answered ; " but you are acquainted with the Earnshaws' violent dispositions, and Mrs. Linton caps them all. I may say this : it commenced in a quarrel. She was struck during a tempest of passion with a kind of fit. That's her account, at least, for she flew off in the height of it, and locked herself up. Afterwards she refused to eat, and now she alternately raves and remains in a half dream, knowing those about her, but having her mind filled with all sorts of strange ideas and illusions."

" Mr. Linton will be sorry ? " observed Kenneth interrogatively.

" Sorry ? He'll break his heart should anything happen ! " I replied. " Don't alarm him more than necessary."

" Well, I told him to beware," said my companion ; " and he must bide the consequences of neglecting my warning. Hasn't he been intimate with Mr. Heathcliff lately ? "

" Heathcliff frequently visits at the Grange," answered I, " though more on the strength of the mistress having known him when a boy than because the master likes his company. At present he's discharged from the trouble of calling, owing to some presumptuous aspirations after Miss Linton which he manifested. I hardly think he'll be taken in again."

" And does Miss Linton turn a cold shoulder on him ? " was the doctor's next question.

" I'm not in her confidence," returned I, reluctant to continue the subject.

" No ; she's a sly one," he remarked, shaking his head. " She keeps her own counsel. But she's a real little fool. I have it from good authority that last night (and a pretty night it was) she and Heathcliff were walking in the plantation at the back of your house above two hours ; and he pressed her not to go in again, but just mount his horse and away with him. My informant said she could only put him off by pledging her word of honour to be prepared on their first meeting after that. When it was to be, he didn't hear ; but you urge Mr. Linton to look sharp."

This news filled me with fresh fears. I outstripped Kenneth, and ran most of the way back. The little dog was yelping in the garden yet. I spared a minute to open the gate for it, but instead of going to the house door, it coursed up and down snuffing the grass, and would have escaped to the road had I not seized and conveyed it in with me. On ascending to Isabella's room my suspicions were confirmed. It was empty. Had I been a few hours sooner, Mrs. Linton's illness might have arrested her rash step. But what could be done now ? There was a bare possibility of overtaking them if pursued instantly. *I* could not pursue them, however ; and I dare not rouse the family, and fill the place with confusion—still less unfold the business to my master, absorbed as he was in his present calamity, and having no heart to spare for a second grief. I saw nothing for it but to hold my tongue, and suffer matters to take their course ; and Kenneth being arrived, I went with a badly composed countenance to announce him. Catherine lay in a troubled sleep. Her husband had succeeded in soothing the excess of frenzy. He now hung over her pillow, watching every shade and every change of her painfully expressive features.

The doctor, on examining the case for himself, spoke hopefully to him of its having a favourable termination, if we could only preserve around her perfect and constant tranquillity. To me he signified the threatening danger was not so much death, as permanent alienation of intellect.

I did not close my eyes that night, nor did Mr. Linton —indeed, we never went to bed ; and the servants were all up long before the usual hour, moving through the house with stealthy tread, and exchanging whispers as they encountered each other in their vocations. Every one was active but Miss Isabella; and they began to remark how sound she slept. Her brother, too, asked if she had risen, and seemed impatient for her presence, and hurt that she showed so little anxiety for her sister-in-law. I trembled lest he should send me to call her; but I was spared the pain of being the first proclaimant of her flight. One of the maids, a thoughtless girl, who had been on an early errand to Gimmerton, came panting upstairs, open mouthed, and dashed into the chamber, crying,—

"Oh dear, dear! What mun we have next? Master, master, our young lady——"

"Hold your noise!" cried I hastily, enraged at her clamorous manner.

"Speak lower, Mary. What is the matter?" said Mr. Linton. "What ails your young lady?"

"She's gone, she's gone! Yon Heathcliff's run off wi' her!" gasped the girl.

"That is not true!" exclaimed Linton, rising in agitation. "It cannot be. How has the idea entered your head?—Ellen Dean, go and seek her. It is incredible. It cannot be."

As he spoke he took the servant to the door, and then repeated his demand to know her reasons for such an assertion.

"Why, I met on the road a lad that fetches milk here," she stammered, "and he asked whether we weren't in trouble at the Grange. I thought he meant for missis's sickness, so I answered yes. Then says he, 'There's somebody gone after 'em, I guess?' I stared. He saw I knew nought about it, and he told how a gentleman and lady had stopped to have a horse's shoe fastened at a blacksmith's shop, two miles out of Gimmerton, not very long after midnight; and how the blacksmith's lass had got up to spy who they were. She knew them both directly. And she noticed the man—Heathcliff it was, she felt certain; nob'dy could

mistake him, besides—put a sovereign in her father's
hand for payment. The lady had a cloak about her
face; but having desired a sup of water, while she
drank it fell back, and she saw her very plain. Heathcliff held both bridles as they rode on, and they set
their faces from the village, and went as fast as the rough
roads would let them. The lass said nothing to her
father, but she told it all over Gimmerton this morning."

I ran and peeped, for form's sake, into Isabella's
room, confirming, when I returned, the servant's statement. Mr. Linton had resumed his seat by the bed.
On my re-entrance he raised his eyes, read the meaning
of my blank aspect, and dropped them without giving
an order or uttering a word.

"Are we to try any measures for overtaking and
bringing her back?" I inquired. "How should we
do?"

"She went of her own accord," answered the master;
"she had a right to go if she pleased. Trouble me no
more about her. Hereafter she is only my sister in
name—not because I disown her, but because she has
disowned me."

And that was all he said on the subject. He did not
make a single inquiry further, or mention her in any
way, except directing me to send what property she had
in the house to her fresh home, wherever it was, when
I knew it.

CHAPTER XIII.

FOR two months the fugitives remained absent. In
those two months Mrs. Linton encountered and con-
quered the worst shock of what was denominated a
brain fever. No mother could have nursed an only
child more devotedly than Edgar tended her. Day and
night he was watching and patiently enduring all the
annoyances that irritable nerves and a shaken reason
could inflict; and though Kenneth remarked that
what he saved from the grave would only recompense

his care by forming the source of constant future anxiety —in fact, that his health and strength were being sacrificed to preserve a mere ruin of humanity—he knew no limits in gratitude and joy when Catherine's life was declared out of danger ; and hour after hour he would sit beside her, tracing the gradual return to bodily health, and flattering his too sanguine hopes with the illusion that her mind would settle back to its right balance also, and she would soon be entirely her former self.

The first time she left her chamber was at the commencement of the following March. Mr. Linton had put on her pillow, in the morning, a handful of golden crocuses. Her eye, long stranger to any gleam of pleasure, caught them in waking, and shone delighted as she gathered them eagerly together.

" These are the earliest flowers at the Heights," she exclaimed. " They remind me of soft thaw winds, and warm sunshine, and nearly melted snow. Edgar, is there not a south wind, and is not the snow almost gone ? "

" The snow in quite gone down here, darling," replied her husband, " and I only see two white spots on the whole range of moors. The sky is blue, and the larks are singing, and the becks and brooks are all brim full. Catherine, last spring at this time I was longing to have you under this roof; now I wish you were a mile or two up those hills ; the air blows so sweetly, I feel that it would cure you."

" I shall never be there but once more," said the invalid ; " and then you'll leave me, and I shall remain for ever. Next spring you'll long again to have me under this roof, and you'll look back and think you were happy to-day."

Linton lavished on her the kindest caresses, and tried to cheer her by the fondest words ; but, vaguely regarding the flowers, she let the tears collect on her lashes and stream down her cheeks unheeding. We knew she was really better, and therefore decided that long confinement to a single place produced much of this despondency, and it might be partially removed by a change of scene.

The master told me to light a fire in the many-weeks-deserted parlour, and to set an easy-chair in the sunshine by the window; and then he brought her down, and she sat a long while enjoying the genial heat, and, as we expected, revived by the objects round her, which, though familiar, were free from the dreary associations investing her hated sick chamber. By evening she seemed greatly exhausted, yet no arguments could persuade her to return to that apartment; and I had to arrange the parlour sofa for her bed, till another room could be prepared. To obviate the fatigue of mounting and descending the stairs, we fitted up this, where you lie at present, on the same floor with the parlour; and she was soon strong enough to move from one to the other, leaning on Edgar's arm. Ah, I thought myself she might recover, so waited on as she was. And there was double cause to desire it, for on her existence depended that of another: we cherished the hope that in a little while Mr. Linton's heart would be gladdened, and his lands secured from a stranger's gripe, by the birth of an heir.

I should mention that Isabella sent to her brother, some six weeks from her departure, a short note announcing her marriage with Heathcliff. It appeared dry and cold, but at the bottom was dotted in with pencil an obscure apology, and an entreaty for kind remembrance and reconciliation, if her proceeding had offended him, asserting that she could not help it then, and, being done, she had now no power to repeal it. Linton did not reply to this, I believe; and in a fortnight more I got a long letter which I considered odd, coming from the pen of a bride just out of the honeymoon. I'll read it, for I keep it yet. Any relic of the dead is precious if they were valued living.

DEAR ELLEN, it begins, I came last night to Wuthering Heights, and heard for the first time that Catherine has been, and is yet, very ill. I must not write to her, I suppose, and my brother is either too angry or too distressed to answer what I sent him. Still, I must write to somebody, and the only choice left me is you.

Inform Edgar that I'd give the world to see his face again—that my heart returned to Thrushcross Grange in twenty-four hours after I left it, and is there at this moment, full of warm feelings for him and Catherine. *I can't follow it, though* (those words are underlined); they need not expect me; and they may draw what conclusions they please, taking care, however, to lay nothing at the door of my weak will or deficient affection.

The remainder of the letter is for yourself alone. I want to ask you two questions; the first is—How did you contrive to preserve the common sympathies of human nature when you resided here ? I cannot recognize any sentiment which those around share with me.

The second question I have great interest in; it is this—Is Mr. Heathcliff a man ? If so, is he mad ? And if not, is he a devil ? I shan't tell my reasons for making this inquiry, but I beseech you to explain, if you can, what I have married—that is, when you call to see me; and you must call, Ellen, very soon. Don't write, but come, and bring me something from Edgar.

Now you shall hear how I have been received in my new home, as I am led to imagine the Heights will be. It is to amuse myself that I dwell on such subjects as the lack of external comforts; they never occupy my thoughts, except at the moment when I miss them. I should laugh and dance for joy if I found their absence was the total of my miseries, and the rest was an unnatural dream.

The sun set behind the Grange as we turned on to the moors : by that I judged it to be six o'clock ; and my companion halted half an hour to inspect the park and the gardens, and probably the place itself, as well as he could ; so it was dark when we dismounted in the paved yard of the farmhouse, and your old fellow-servant Joseph issued out to receive us by the light of a dip candle. He did it with a courtesy that redounded to his credit. His first act was to elevate his torch to a level with my face, squint malignantly, project his under lip, and turn away. Then he took the two horses and led them into the stables, reappearing for the purpose of locking the outer gate, as if we lived in an ancient castle.

Heathcliff stayed to speak to him, and I entered the kitchen—a dingy, untidy hole. I dare say you would not know it, it is so changed since it was in your charge. By the fire stood a ruffianly child, strong in limb and dirty in garb, with a look of Catherine in his eyes and about his mouth.

"This is Edgar's legal nephew," I reflected—"mine in a manner. I must shake hands, and—yes—I must kiss him. It is right to establish a good understanding at the beginning."

I approached, and attempting to take his chubby fist, said,—

"How do you do, my dear?"

He replied in a jargon I did not comprehend.

"Shall you and I be friends, Hareton?" was my next essay at conversation.

An oath, and a threat to set Throttler on me if I did not "frame off," rewarded my perseverance.

"Hey, Throttler, lad!" whispered the little wretch, rousing a half-bred bull-dog from its lair in a corner. "Now, wilt thou be ganging?" he asked authoritatively.

Love for my life urged a compliance. I stepped over the threshold to wait till the others should enter. Mr. Heathcliff was nowhere visible, and Joseph, whom I followed to the stables and requested to accompany me in, after staring and muttering to himself, screwed up his nose and replied,—

"Mim! mim! mim! Did iver Christian body hear aught like it? Minching un munching! How can I tell whet ye say?"

"I say I wish you to come with me into the house!" I cried, thinking him deaf, yet highly disgusted at his rudeness.

"None o' me. I getten summut else to do," he answered, and continued his work, moving his lantern jaws meanwhile, and surveying my dress and countenance (the former a great deal too fine, but the latter, I'm sure, as sad as he could desire) with sovereign contempt.

I walked round the yard and through a wicket to another door, at which I took the liberty of knocking, in hopes some more civil servant might show himself. After a short suspense it was opened by a tall, gaunt man, without neckerchief, and otherwise extremely slovenly; his features were lost in masses of shaggy hair that hung on his shoulders, and *his* eyes, too, were like a ghostly Catherine's with all their beauty annihilated.

"What's your business here?" he demanded grimly. "Who are you?"

"My name *was* Isabella Linton," I replied. "You've seen me before, sir. I'm lately married to Mr. Heathcliff, and he has brought me here—I suppose by your permission."

"Is he come back, then?" asked the hermit, glaring like a hungry wolf.

"Yes, we came just now," I said; "but he left me by the kitchen door, and when I would have gone in your little boy played sentinel over the place, and frightened me off by the help of a bull-dog."

"It's well the hellish villain has kept his word!" growled my future host, searching the darkness beyond me in expectation of discovering Heathcliff; and then he indulged in a soliloquy of execrations, and threats of what he would have done had the "fiend" deceived him.

I repented having tried this second entrance, and was almost inclined to slip away before he finished cursing; but ere I could execute that intention he ordered me in, and shut and refastened the door. There was a great fire, and that was all the light in the huge apartment, whose floor had grown a uniform gray, and the once brilliant pewter dishes, which used to attract my gaze when I was a girl, partook of a similar obscurity, created by tarnish and dust. I inquired whether I might call the maid, and be conducted to a bedroom. Mr. Earnshaw vouchsafed no answer. He walked up and down, with his hands in his pockets, apparently quite forgetting my presence; and his abstraction was evidently so deep, and his whole aspect so misanthropical, that I shrank from disturbing him again.

You'll not be surprised, Ellen, at my feeling particularly cheerless, seated in worse than solitude on that inhospitable hearth, and remembering that four miles distant lay my delightful home, containing the only people I loved on earth; and there might as well be the Atlantic to part us, instead of those four miles. I could not overpass them. I questioned with myself—Where must I turn for comfort? and (mind you don't tell Edgar or Catherine) above every sorrow beside, this rose pre-eminent — despair at finding nobody who could or would be my ally against Heathcliff. I had sought shelter at Wuthering Heights almost gladly, because I was secured by that arrangement from living alone with him; but he knew the people we were coming amongst, and he did not fear their intermeddling.

I sat and thought a doleful time. The clock struck eight, and nine, and still my companion paced to and fro, his head bent on his breast, and perfectly silent, unless a groan or a bitter ejaculation forced itself out at intervals. I listened to detect a woman's voice in the house, and filled the interim with wild regrets and dismal anticipations, which at last spoke audibly in irrepressible sighing and weeping. I was not aware how openly I grieved, till Earnshaw halted opposite, in his measured walk, and gave me a stare of newly-awakened surprise. Taking advantage of his recovered attention, I exclaimed,—

" I'm tired with my journey, and I want to go to bed! Where is the maidservant? Direct me to her, as she won't come to me."

" We have none," he answered. " You must wait on yourself."

" Where must I sleep, then?" I sobbed. I was beyond regarding self-respect, weighed down by fatigue and wretchedness.

"Joseph will show you Heathcliff's chamber," said he. "Open that door; he's in there."

I was going to obey, but he suddenly arrested me, and added in the strangest tone,—

"Be so good as to turn your lock and draw your bolt; don't omit it!"

"Well!" I said; "but why, Mr. Earnshaw?" I did not relish the notion of deliberately fastening myself in with Heathcliff.

"Look here!" he replied, pulling from his waistcoat a curiously constructed pistol, having a double-edged spring knife attached to the barrel. "That's a great tempter to a desperate man, is it not? I cannot resist going up with this every night and trying his door. If once I find it open, he's done for! I do it invariably, even though the minute before I have been recalling a hundred reasons that should make me refrain. It is some devil that urges me to thwart my own schemes by killing him. You fight against that devil for love as long as you may: when the time comes, not all the angels in heaven shall save him!"

I surveyed the weapon inquisitively. A hideous notion struck me. How powerful I should be, possessing such an instrument! I took it from his hand and touched the blade. He looked astonished at the expression my face assumed during a brief second; it was not horror —it was covetousness. He snatched the pistol back jealously, shut the knife, and returned it to its concealment.

"I don't care if you tell him," said he. "Put him on his guard, and watch for him. You know the terms we are on, I see. His danger does not shock you."

"What has Heathcliff done to you?" I asked. "In what has he wronged you, to warrant this appalling hatred? Wouldn't it be wiser to bid him quit the house?"

"No!" thundered Earnshaw. "Should he offer to

leave me, he's a dead man. Persuade him to attempt
it, and you are a murderess. Am I to lose *all* without
a chance of retrieval? Is Hareton to be a beggar?
Oh, damnation! I *will* have it back, and I'll have *his*
gold too, and then his blood, and hell shall have his
soul! It will be ten times blacker with that guest than
ever it was before!"

You've acquainted me, Ellen, with your old master's
habits. He is clearly on the verge of madness. He was
so last night at least. I shuddered to be near him, and
thought on the servant's ill-bred moroseness as com-
paratively agreeable. He now recommenced his moody
walk, and I raised the latch and escaped into the kitchen.
Joseph was bending over the fire, peering into a large
pan that swung above it, and a wooden bowl of oatmeal
stood on the settle close by. The contents of the pan
began to boil, and he turned to plunge his hand into
the bowl. I conjectured that this preparation was
probably for our supper, and being hungry, I resolved
it should be eatable; so, crying out sharply, "*I'll* make
the porridge!" I removed the vessel out of his reach,
and proceeded to take off my hat and riding-habit.
"Mr. Earnshaw," I continued, "directs me to wait on
myself. I will. I'm not going to act the lady among
you, for fear I should starve."

"Gooid Lord!" he muttered, sitting down and stroking his ribbed stockings from the knee to the ankle.
"If there's to be fresh ortherings, just when I getten
used to two maisters, if I mun hev a *mistress* set o'er my
heead, it's like time to be flitting. I niver *did* think to see
t' day that I mud lave th' owld place, but I doubt it's
nigh at hand!"

This lamentation drew no notice from me. I went
briskly to work, sighing to remember a period when it
would have been all merry fun, but compelled speedily
to drive off the remembrance. It racked me to recall
past happiness and the greater peril there was of conjuring up its apparition, the quicker the thible ran round,
and the faster the handfuls of meal fell into the water.

Joseph beheld my style of cookery with growing indignation.

"Thear!" he ejaculated. "Hareton, thou willn't sup thy porridge to-neeght; they'll be naught but lumps as big as my neive. Thear, agean! I'd fling in bowl un all, if I wer ye! There, pale t' guilp off, un then ye'll hae done wi't. Bang, bang. It's a mercy t' bothom isn't deaved out!"

It *was* rather a rough mess, I own, when poured into the basins. Four had been provided, and a gallon pitcher of new milk was brought from the dairy, which Hareton seized and commenced drinking and spilling from the expansive lip. I expostulated, and desired that he should have his in a mug, affirming that I could not taste the liquid treated so dirtily. The old cynic chose to be vastly offended at this nicety, assuring me repeatedly that "the barn was every bit as good" as I, "and every bit as wollsome," and wondering how I could fashion to be so conceited. Meanwhile the infant ruffian continued sucking, and glowered up at me defyingly as he slavered into the jug.

"I shall have my supper in another room," I said. "Have you no place you call a parlour?"

"*Parlour!*" he echoed sneeringly—"*parlour!* Nay, we've noa *parlours*. If yah dunnut loike wer company, there's maister's; un if yah dunnut loike maister, there's us."

"Then I shall go upstairs," I answered. "Show me a chamber."

I put my basin on a tray, and went myself to fetch some more milk. With great grumblings the fellow rose and preceded me in my ascent. We mounted to the garrets. He opened a door now and then to look into the apartments we passed.

"Here's a rahm," he said at last, flinging back a cranky board on hinges. "It's weel eneugh to ate a few porridge in. There's a pack o' corn i' t' corner, thear, meeterly clane. If ye're feared o' muckying yer grand silk cloes, spread yer hankerchir o' t' top on't."

The "rahm" was a kind of lumber-hole smelling strong of malt and grain, various sacks of which articles were piled around, leaving a wide, bare space in the middle.

"Why, man!" I exclaimed, facing him angrily, "this is not a place to sleep in. I wish to see my bedroom."

"*Bedrume!*" he repeated, in a tone of mockery. "Yah's see all t' *bedrumes* thear is. Yon's mine."

He pointed into the second garret, only differing from the first in being more naked about the walls, and having a large, low, curtainless bed with an indigo-coloured quilt at one end.

"What do I want with yours?" I retorted. "I suppose Mr. Heathcliff does not lodge at the top of the house, does he?"

"Oh, it's Maister *Hathecliff's* ye're wanting?" cried he, as if making a new discovery. "Couldn't ye ha' said soa, at onst? Un then I mud ha' telled ye, baht all this wark, that that's just one ye cannut see. He allas keeps it locked, un nob'dy iver mells on't but hisseln."

"You've a nice house, Joseph," I could not refrain from observing, "and pleasant inmates; and I think the concentrated essence of all the madness in the world took up its abode in my brain the day I linked my fate with theirs! However, that is not to the present purpose. There are other rooms. For Heaven's sake be quick, and let me settle somewhere!"

He made no reply to this adjuration, only plodding doggedly down the wooden steps, and halting before an apartment which, from that halt and the superior quality of its furniture, I conjectured to be the best one. There was a carpet—a good one—but the pattern was obliterated by dust; a fireplace hung with cut paper, dropping to pieces; a handsome oak bedstead with ample crimson curtains of rather expensive material and modern make, but they had evidently experienced rough usage —the vallances hung in festoons, wrenched from their rings, and the iron rod supporting them was bent in an arc on one side, causing the drapery to trail upon the floor. The chairs were also damaged, many of them severely, and deep indentations deformed the panels of the walls. I was endeavouring to gather resolution for entering and taking possession, when my fool of a guide announced, "This here is t' maister's." My supper by this time was cold, my appetite gone, and my patience exhausted. I insisted on being provided instantly with a place of refuge and means of repose.

"Whear the divil?" began the religious elder. "The Lord bless us! The Lord forgie us! Whear the *hell* wold ye gang, ye marred, wearisome nowt? Ye've seen all but Hareton's bit of a cham'er. There's not another hoile to lig down in i' th' hahse!"

I was so vexed, I flung my tray and its contents on the ground, and then seated myself at the stairs-head, hid my face in my hands, and cried.

"Ech! ech!" exclaimed Joseph. "Weel done, Miss Cathy! weel done, Miss Cathy! Howsiver, t' maister sall just tum'le o'er them brocken pots, un then we's hear summut—we's hear how it's to be. Gooid-for-naught madling! ye desarve pining fro' this to Churst-mas, flinging t' precious gifts o' God under fooit i' yer flaysome rages! But I'm mista'en if ye show yer sperrit lang. Will Hathecliff bide sich bonny ways, think ye? I nobbut wish he may catch ye i' that plisky. I nobbut wish he may."

And so he went on scolding to his den beneath, taking the candle with him, and I remained in the dark. The period of reflection succeeding this silly action compelled me to admit the necessity of smothering my pride and choking my wrath, and bestirring myself to remove its effects. An unexpected aid presently appeared in the shape of Throttler, whom I now recognized as a son of our old Skulker. It had spent its whelphood at the Grange, and was given by my father to Mr. Hindley. I fancy it knew me. It pushed its nose against mine by way of salute, and then hastened to devour the por-ridge, while I groped from step to step, collecting the shattered earthenware, and drying the spatters of milk from the banister with my pocket-handkerchief. Our labours were scarcely over when I heard Earnshaw's tread in the passage. My assistant tucked in his tail and pressed to the wall. I stole into the nearest door way. The dog's endeavour to avoid him was unsuccessful, as I guessed by a scutter downstairs, and a prolonged piteous yelping. I had better luck. He passed on entered his chamber, and shut the door. Directly after Joseph came up with Hareton, to put him to bed. I had found shelter in Hareton's room, and the old man on seeing me, said,—

"They's rahm for boath ye un yer pride now, I sud think, i' the hahse. It's empty; ye may hev it all to yerseln, un Him as allas maks a third i' sich ill company!"

Gladly did I take advantage of this intimation, and the minute I flung myself into a chair by the fire I nodded and slept. My slumber was deep and sweet, though over far too soon. Mr. Heathcliff awoke me. He had just come in, and demanded, in his loving manner, what I was doing there. I told him the cause of my staying up so late—that he had the key of our room in his pocket. The adjective *our* gave mortal offence. He swore it was not, nor ever should be mine, and he'd—— But I'll not repeat his language, nor describe his habitual conduct. He is ingenious and unresting in seeking to gain my abhorrence. I sometimes wonder at him with an intensity that deadens my fear; yet I assure you a tiger or a venomous serpent could not rouse terror in me equal to that which he wakens. He told me of Catherine's illness, and accused my brother of causing it, promising that I should be Edgar's proxy in suffering till he could get hold of him.

I do hate him—I am wretched—I have been a fool! Beware of uttering one breath of this to any one at the Grange. I shall expect you every day. Don't disappoint me.   ISABELLA.

————————

CHAPTER XIV.

As soon as I had perused this epistle I went to the master and informed him that his sister had arrived at the Heights, and sent me a letter expressing her sorrow for Mrs. Linton's situation, and her ardent desire to see him, with a wish that he would transmit to her, as early as possible, some token of forgiveness by me.

"Forgiveness!" said Linton. "I have nothing to forgive her, Ellen. You may call at Wuthering Heights this afternoon, if you like, and say that I am not *angry*, but I'm *sorry* to have lost her—especially as I can never think she'll be happy. It is out of the question my going to see her, however; we are eternally divided, and should she really wish to oblige me, let her persuade the villain she has married to leave the country."

"And you won't write her a little note, sir?" I asked imploringly.

"No," he answered; "it is needless. My communication with Heathcliff's family shall be as sparing as his with mine. It shall not exist."

Mr. Edgar's coldness depressed me exceedingly, and all the way from the Grange I puzzled my brains how to put more heart into what he said, when I repeated it, and how to soften his refusal of even a few lines to console Isabella. I dare say she had been on the watch for me since morning. I saw her looking through the lattice as I came up the garden causeway, and I nodded to her; but she drew back as if afraid of being observed. I entered without knocking. There never was such a dreary, dismal scene as the formerly cheerful house presented. I must confess that if I had been in the young lady's place I would, at least, have swept the hearth and wiped the tables with a duster. But she already partook of the pervading spirit of neglect which encompassed her. Her pretty face was wan and listless, her hair uncurled—some locks hanging lankly down, and some carelessly twisted round her head. Probably she had not touched her dress since yester evening. Hindley was not there. Mr. Heathcliff sat at a table, turning over some papers in his pocket-book; but he rose when I appeared, asked me how I did, quite friendly, and offered me a chair. He was the only thing there that seemed decent, and I thought he never looked better. So much had circumstances altered their positions that he would certainly have struck a stranger as a born and bred gentleman, and his wife as a thorough little slattern! She came forward eagerly to greet me, and held out one hand to take the expected letter. I shook my head. She wouldn't understand the hint, but followed me to a sideboard where I went to lay my bonnet, and importuned me in a whisper to give her directly what I had brought. Heathcliff guessed the meaning of her manœuvres, and said,—

"If you have got anything for Isabella—as no doubt you have, Nelly—give it to her. You needn't make a secret of it. We have no secrets between us."

"Oh, I have nothing," I replied, thinking it best to speak the truth at once. "My master bade me tell his sister that she must not expect either a letter or a visit from him at present. He sends his love, ma'am, and his wishes for your happiness, and his pardon for the grief you have occasioned; but he thinks that after this time his household and the household here should drop intercommunication, as nothing could come of keeping it up."

Mrs. Heathcliff's lip quivered slightly, and she returned to her seat in the window. Her husband took his stand on the hearthstone near me, and began to put questions concerning Catherine. I told him as much as I thought proper of her illness, and he extorted from me, by cross-examination, most of the facts connected with its origin. I blamed her, as she deserved, for bringing it all on herself, and ended by hoping that he would follow Mr. Linton's example, and avoid future interference with his family, for good or evil.

"Mrs. Linton is now just recovering," I said. "She'll

never be like she was, but her life is spared; and if you really have a regard for her, you'll shun crossing her way again—nay, you'll move out of this country entirely; and that you may not regret it, I'll inform you Catherine Linton is as different now from your old friend Catherine Earnshaw as that young lady is different from me. Her appearance is changed greatly, her character much more so; and the person who is compelled, of necessity, to be her companion will only sustain his affection hereafter by the remembrance of what she once was, by common humanity, and a sense of duty."

"That is quite possible," remarked Heathcliff, forcing himself to seem calm—"quite possible that your master should have nothing but common humanity and a sense of duty to fall back upon. But do you imagine that I shall leave Catherine to his *duty* and *humanity?* and can you compare my feelings respecting Catherine to his? Before you leave this house, I must exact a promise from you that you'll get me an interview with her. Consent or refuse, I *will* see her! What do you say?"

"I say, Mr. Heathcliff," I replied, "you must not. You never shall, through my means. Another encounter between you and the master would kill her altogether."

"With your aid that may be avoided," he continued; "and should there be danger of such an event—should he be the cause of adding a single trouble more to her existence—why, I think I shall be justified in going to extremes. I wish you had sincerity enough to tell me whether Catherine would suffer greatly from his loss; the fear that she would restrains me. And there you see the distinction between our feelings: had he been in my place, and I in his, though I hated him with a hatred that turned my life to gall, I never would have raised a hand against him. You may look incredulous if you please. I never would have banished him from her society as long as she desired his. The moment her regard ceased, I would have torn his heart out and drunk his blood! But till then—if you don't believe me you don't know me—till then I would have died by inches before I touched a single hair of his head!"

"And yet," I interrupted, "you have no scruples in completely ruining all hopes of her perfect restoration by thrusting yourself into her remembrance now, when she has nearly forgotten you, and involving her in a new tumult of discord and distress."

"You suppose she has nearly forgotten me?" he said. "O Nelly, you know she has not! You know as well as I do that for every thought she spends on Linton, she spends a thousand on me! At a most miserable period of my life I had a notion of the kind. It haunted me on my return to the neighbourhood last summer; but only her own assurance could make me admit the horrible idea again. And then Linton would be nothing, nor Hindley, nor all the dreams that ever I dreamt. Two words would comprehend my future—*death* and *hell*; existence, after losing her, would be hell. Yet I was a fool to fancy for a moment that she valued Edgar Linton's attachment more than mine. If he loved with all the powers of his puny being, he couldn't love as much in eighty years as I could in a day. And Catherine has a heart as deep as I have; the sea could be as readily contained in that horse-trough as her whole affection be monopolized by him. Tush! He is scarcely a degree dearer to her than her dog or her horse. It is not in him to be loved like me. How can she love in him what he has not?"

"Catherine and Edgar are as fond of each other as any two people can be," cried Isabella with sudden vivacity. "No one has a right to talk in that manner, and I won't hear my brother depreciated in silence!"

"Your brother is wondrous fond of you too, isn't he?" observed Heathcliff scornfully. "He turns you adrift on the world with surprising alacrity."

"He is not aware of what I suffer," she replied. "I didn't tell him that."

" You have been telling him something, then. You
ave written, have you ? "

" To say that I was married, I did write ; you saw the
ote."

" And nothing since ? "

" No."

" My young lady is looking sadly the worse for her
hange of condition," I remarked. " Somebody's love
omes short in her case obviously. Whose, I may
uess, but perhaps I shouldn't say."

" I should guess it was her own," said Heathcliff.
" She degenerates into a mere slut. She is tired of
rying to please me uncommonly early. You'd hardly
redit it, but the very morrow of our wedding she was
veeping to go home. However, she'll suit this house
o much the better for not being overnice, and I'll take
are she does not disgrace me by rambling abroad."

" Well, sir," returned I, " I hope you'll consider that
Mrs. Heathcliff is accustomed to be looked after and
vaited on, and that she has been brought up like an
only daughter, whom every one was ready to serve.
You must let her have a maid to keep things tidy about
er, and you must treat her kindly. Whatever be
our notion of Mr. Edgar, you cannot doubt that she
as a capacity for strong attachments, or she wouldn't
ave abandoned the elegances, and comforts, and friends
f her former home to fix contentedly in such a wilder-
ess as this with you."

" She abandoned them under a delusion," he an-
wered, " picturing in me a hero of romance, and ex-
ecting unlimited indulgences from my chivalrous
evotion. I can hardly regard her in the light of a
ational creature, so obstinately has she persisted in
orming a fabulous notion of my character, and acting
on the false impressions she cherished. But at last I
hink she begins to know me. I don't perceive the
illy smiles and grimaces that provoked me at first,
nd the senseless incapability of discerning that I was
n earnest when I gave her my opinion of her infatuation

and herself. It was a marvellous effort of perspicacit
to discover that I did not love her. I believed, at on
time, no lessons could teach her that. And yet it i
poorly learned, for this morning she announced, as
piece of appalling intelligence, that I had actually suc
ceeded in making her hate me — a positive labour c
Hercules, I assure you! If it be achieved, I have caus
to return thanks.—Can I trust your assertion, Isabella
Are you sure you hate me? If I let you alone for ha
a day, won't you come sighing and wheedling to m
again?—I dare say she would rather I had seemed al
tenderness before you; it wounds her vanity to hav
the truth exposed. But I don't care who knows tha
the passion was wholly on one side; and I never tol
her a lie about it. She cannot accuse me of showin
one bit of deceitful softness. The first thing she saw m
do on coming out of the Grange was to hang up her littl
dog, and when she pleaded for it, the first words I uttere
were a wish that I had the hanging of every being belong
ing to her, except one. Possibly she took that exceptio
for herself. But no brutality disgusted her. I suppos
she has an innate admiration of it, if only her preciou
person were secure from injury. Now, was it not th
depth of absurdity, of genuine idiocy, for that pitifu
slavish, mean-minded brach to dream that I could lov
her? Tell your master, Nelly, that I never, in all m
life, met with such an abject thing as she is. She eve
disgraces the name of Linton; and I've sometime
relented, from pure lack of invention, in my experiment
on what she could endure and still creep shamefull
cringing back. But tell him also to set his fraterna
and magisterial heart at ease; that I keep strictl
within the limits of the law. I have avoided, up to thi
period, giving her the slightest right to claim a separa
tion; and, what's more, she'd thank nobody for dividing
us. If she desired to go, she might; the nuisance o
her presence outweighs the gratification to be derive
from tormenting her."

"Mr. Heathcliff," said I, "this is the talk of a madman. Your wife, most likely, is convinced you are mad, and for that reason she has borne with you hitherto; but now that you say she may go, she'll doubtless avail herself of the permission.—You are not so bewitched, ma'am, are you, as to remain with him of your own accord?"

"Take care, Ellen!" answered Isabella, her eyes sparkling irefully. There was no misdoubting, by their expression, the full success of her partner's endeavours to make himself detested. "Don't put faith in a single word he speaks. He's a lying fiend—a monster, and not a human being! I've been told I might leave him before, and I've made the attempt, but I dare not repeat it. Only, Ellen, promise you'll not mention a syllable of his infamous conversation to my brother or Catherine. Whatever he may pretend, he wishes to provoke Edgar to desperation. He says he has married me on purpose to obtain power over him; and he shan't obtain it. I'll die first! I just hope—I pray—that he may forget his diabolical prudence and kill me! The single pleasure I can imagine is to die or to see him dead!"

"There—that will do for the present!" said Heathcliff.—"If you are called upon in a court of law you'll remember her language, Nelly. And take a good look at that countenance; she's near the point which would suit me.—No; you're not fit to be your own guardian, Isabella, now; and I, being your legal protector, must retain you in my custody, however distasteful the obligation may be. Go upstairs; I have something to say to Ellen Dean in private. That's not the way. Upstairs, I tell you! Why, this is the road upstairs, child."

He seized and thrust her from the room, and returned muttering,—

"I have no pity! I have no pity! The more the worms writhe, the more I yearn to crush out their entrails! It is a moral teething; and I grind with greater energy in proportion to the increase of pain."

" Do you understand what the word pity means ? "
I said, hastening to resume my bonnet. " Did you ever
feel a touch of it in your life ? "

"Put that down!" he interrupted, perceiving my
intention to depart. "You are not going yet. Come
here now, Nelly. I must either persuade or compel
you to aid me in fulfilling my determination to see
Catherine, and that without delay. I swear that I
meditate no harm. I don't desire to cause any disturbance, or to exasperate or insult Mr. Linton. I only
wish to hear from herself how she is, and why she has
been ill, and to ask if anything that I could do would
be of use to her. Last night I was in the Grange garden
six hours, and I'll return there to-night ; and every night
I'll haunt the place, and every day, till I find an opportunity of entering. If Edgar Linton meets me I shall
not hesitate to knock him down, and give him enough
to assure his quiescence while I stay. If his servants
oppose me I shall threaten them off with these pistols.
But wouldn't it be better to prevent my coming in
contact with them or their master ? And you could
do it so easily. I'd warn you when I came, and then
you might let me in unobserved, as soon as she was
alone, and watch till I departed, your conscience quite
calm. You would be hindering mischief."

I protested against playing that treacherous part in
my employer's house, and, besides, I urged the cruelty
and selfishness of his destroying Mrs. Linton's tranquillity for his satisfaction. " The commonest occurrence
startles her painfully," I said. " She's all nerves, and
she couldn't bear the surprise, I'm positive. Don't
persist, sir, or else I shall be obliged to inform my master
of your designs, and he'll take measures to secure his
house and its inmates from any such unwarrantable
intrusions ! "

" In that case, I'll take measures to secure you, woman," exclaimed Heathcliff. " You shall not leave
Wuthering Heights till to-morrow morning. It is a
foolish story to assert that Catherine could not bear to

see me; and as to surprising her, I don't desire it. You must prepare her; ask her if I may come. You say she never mentions my name, and that I am never mentioned to her. To whom should she mention me if I am a forbidden topic in the house? She thinks you are all spies for her husband. Oh, I've no doubt she's in hell among you! I guess by her silence, as much as anything, what she feels. You say she is often restless and anxious-looking. Is that a proof of tranquillity? You talk of her mind being unsettled. How the devil could it be otherwise in her frightful isolation? And that insipid, paltry creature attending her from *duty* and *humanity*, from *pity* and *charity!* He might as well plant an oak in a flower-pot, and expect it to thrive, as imagine he can restore her to vigour in the soil of his shallow cares! Let us settle it at once. Will you stay here, and am I to fight my way to Catherine over Linton and his footman? or will you be my friend, as you have been hitherto, and do what I request? Decide, because there is no reason for my lingering another minute if you persist in your stubborn ill-nature."

Well, Mr. Lockwood, I argued and complained, and flatly refused him fifty times; but in the long run he forced me to an agreement. I engaged to carry a letter from him to my mistress; and should she consent, I promised to let him have intelligence of Linton's next absence from home, when he might come, and get in as he was able. I wouldn't be there, and my fellow-servants should be equally out of the way. Was it right or wrong? I fear it was wrong, though expedient. I thought I prevented another explosion by my compliance, and I thought, too, it might create a favourable crisis in Catherine's mental illness. And then I remembered Mr. Edgar's stern rebuke of my carrying tales, and I tried to smooth away all disquietude on the subject by affirming, with frequent iteration, that that betrayal of trust, if it merited so harsh an appellation, should be the last. Notwithstanding, my journey homeward was sadder than my journey thither, and many misgivings

I had ere I could prevail on myself to put the missive into Mrs. Linton's hand.

But here is Kenneth. I'll go down and tell him how much better you are. My history is *dree*, as we say, and will serve to while away another morning.

* * * * * *

Dree and dreary, I reflected, as the good woman descended to receive the doctor, and not exactly of the kind which I should have chosen to amuse me. But never mind. I'll extract wholesome medicines from Mrs. Dean's bitter herbs; and firstly, let me beware the fascination that lurks in Catherine Heathcliff's brilliant eyes. I should be in a curious taking if I surrendered my heart to that young person, and the daughter turned out a second edition of the mother.

CHAPTER XV.

ANOTHER week over, and I am so many days nearer health and spring! I have now heard all my neighbour's history, at different sittings, as the housekeeper could spare time from more important occupations. I'll continue it in her own words, only a little condensed. She is, on the whole, a very fair narrator, and I don't think I could improve her style.

In the evening, she said—the evening of my visit to the Heights—I knew, as well as if I saw him, that Mr. Heathcliff was about the place; and I shunned going out, because I still carried his letter in my pocket, and didn't want to be threatened or teased any more. I had made up my mind not to give it till my master went somewhere, as I could not guess how its receipt would affect Catherine. The consequence was that it did not reach her before the lapse of three days. The fourth was Sunday, and I brought it into her room after the family were gone to church. There was a manservant left to keep the house with me, and we generally made a practice of locking the doors during the hours of service; but on that occasion the weather was so warm and pleasant that I set them wide open, and, to fulfil my engagement, as I knew who would be coming, I told my companion that the mistress wished very much for some oranges, and he must run over to the village and get a few, to be paid for on the morrow. He departed, and I went upstairs.

Mrs. Linton sat in a loose, white dress, with a light shawl over her shoulders, in the recess of the open window as usual. Her thick, long hair had been partly removed at the beginning of her illness, and now she wore it simply combed in its natural tresses over her temples and neck. Her appearance was altered, as I had told Heathcliff; but when she was calm there seemed unearthly beauty in the change. The flash of her eyes had been succeeded by a dreamy and melancholy softness; they no longer gave the impression of looking at the objects around her; they appeared always to gaze beyond, and far beyond—you would have said out of this world. Then the paleness of her face—its haggard aspect having vanished as she recovered flesh—and the peculiar expression arising from her mental state, though painfully suggestive of their causes, added to the touching interest which she awakened, and—invariably to me, I know, and to any person who saw her, I should think—refuted more tangible proofs of convalescence, and stamped her as one doomed to decay.

A book lay spread on the sill before her, and the scarcely perceptible wind fluttered its leaves at intervals. I believe Linton had laid it there, for she never endeavoured to divert herself with reading or occupation of any kind, and he would spend many an hour in trying to entice her attention to some subject which had formerly been her amusement. She was conscious of his aim, and in her better moods endured his efforts placidly, only showing their uselessness by now and then suppressing a wearied sigh, and checking him at last with the saddest of smiles and kisses. At other times she would turn petulantly away, and hide her face in her hands, or

even push him off angrily; and then he took care to
let her alone, for he was certain of doing no good.

Gimmerton chapel bells were still ringing, and the
full, mellow flow of the beck in the valley came soothingly
on the ear. It was a sweet substitute for the yet absent
murmur of the summer foliage which drowned that
music about the Grange when the trees were in leaf. At
Wuthering Heights it always sounded on quiet days
following a great thaw or a season of steady rain. And
of Wuthering Heights Catherine was thinking as she
listened—that is, if she thought or listened at all; but
she had the vague, distant look I mentioned before, which
expressed no recognition of material things either by
ear or eye.

"There's a letter for you, Mrs. Linton," I said, gently
inserting it in one hand that rested on her knee. "You
must read it immediately, because it wants an answer.
Shall I break the seal?" "Yes," she answered, without altering the direction of her eyes. I opened it; it
was very short. "Now," I continued, "read it."
She drew away her hand, and let it fall. I replaced it
in her lap, and stood waiting till it should please her
to glance down; but that movement was so long delayed
that at last I resumed,—

"Must I read it, ma'am? It is from Mr. Heathcliff."
There was a start and a troubled gleam of recollection, and a struggle to arrange her ideas. She lifted
the letter, and seemed to peruse it, and when she came
to the signature she sighed; yet still I found she had
not gathered its import, for, upon my desiring to hear
her reply, she merely pointed to the name and gazed at
me with mournful and questioning eagerness.

"Well, he wishes to see you," said I, guessing her
need of an interpreter. "He's in the garden by this
time, and impatient to know what answer I shall bring."

As I spoke I observed a large dog lying on the sunny
grass beneath raise its ears as if about to bark, and then,
smoothing them back, announce, by a wag of the tail,
that some one approached whom it did not consider a

tranger.   Mrs. Linton bent forward and listened breath-
essly.   The minute after a step traversed the hall.   The
pen house was too tempting for Heathcliff to resist
valking in.   Most likely he supposed that I was inclined
o shirk my promise, and so resolved to trust to his own
udacity.   With straining eagerness Catherine gazed
owards the entrance of her chamber.   He did not hit
he right room directly.   She motioned me to admit
im, but he found it out ere I could reach the door,
nd in a stride or two was at her side, and had her
rasped in his arms.

He neither spoke nor loosed his hold for some five
ninutes, during which period he bestowed more kisses
han ever he gave in his life before, I dare say; but then
ny mistress had kissed him first, and I plainly saw that
e could hardly bear, for downright agony, to look into
er face.   The same conviction had stricken him as me,
rom the instant he beheld her, that there was no pros-
ect of ultimate recovery there; she was fated, sure to die.

"O Cathy! O my life! how can I bear it?" was
he first sentence he uttered, in a tone that did not
eek to disguise his despair.   And now he stared at her
o earnestly that I thought the very intensity of his
aze would bring tears into his eyes; but they burned
vith anguish—they did not melt.

"What now?" said Catherine, leaning back and
eturning his look with a suddenly clouded brow.   Her
umour was a mere vane for constantly varying ca-
rices.   "You and Edgar have broken my heart, Heath-
liff!   And you both come to bewail the deed to me, as
 you were the people to be pitied!   I shall not pity
ou, not I.   You have killed me—and thriven on it, I
hink.   How strong you are!   How many years do you
nean to live after I am gone?"

Heathcliff had knelt on one knee to embrace her.   He
ttempted to rise, but she seized his hair and kept him
lown.

"I wish I could hold you," she continued bitterly,
till we were both dead!   I shouldn't care what you

suffered. I care nothing for your sufferings. Why
shouldn't *you* suffer? I do! Will you forget me?
Will you be happy when I am in the earth? Will you
say twenty years hence, 'That's the grave of Catherine
Earnshaw. I loved her long ago, and was wretched to
lose her; but it is past. I've loved many others since.
My children are dearer to me than she was, and at death
I shall not rejoice that I am going to her; I shall be sorry
that I must leave them.' Will you say so, Heathcliff?"

"Don't torture me till I'm as mad as yourself," cried
he, wrenching his head free and grinding his teeth.

The two, to a cool spectator, made a strange and fearful picture. Well might Catherine deem that heaven
would be a land of exile to her, unless with her mortal
body she cast away her moral character also. Her
present countenance had a wild vindictiveness in its
white cheek, and a bloodless lip and a scintillating eye;
and she retained in her closed fingers a portion of the
locks she had been grasping. As to her companion,
while raising himself with one hand, he had taken her
arm with the other, and so inadequate was his stock of
gentleness to the requirements of her condition that on
his letting go I saw four distinct impressions left blue in
the colourless skin.

"Are you possessed with a devil," he pursued savagely,
"to talk in that manner to me when you are dying?
Do you reflect that all those words will be branded in
my memory, and eating deeper eternally after you have
left me? You know you lie to say I have killed you;
and, Catherine, you know that I could as soon forget
you as my existence! Is it not sufficient for your infernal selfishness that, while you are at peace, I shall
writhe in the torments of hell?"

"I shall not be at peace," moaned Catherine, recalled
to a sense of physical weakness by the violent, unequal
throbbing of her heart, which beat visibly and audibly
under this excess of agitation. She said nothing further
till the paroxysm was over, then she continued more
kindly,—

"I'm not wishing you greater torment than I have, Heathcliff. I only wish us never to be parted; and should a word of mine distress you hereafter, think I feel the same distress underground, and for my own sake forgive me! Come here and kneel down again. You never harmed me in your life. Nay, if you nurse anger, that will be worse to remember than my harsh words. Won't you come here again? Do!"

Heathcliff went to the back of her chair and leant over, but not so far as to let her see his face, which was livid with emotion. She bent round to look at him. He would not permit it. Turning abruptly, he walked to the fireplace, where he stood, silent, with his back towards us. Mrs. Linton's glance followed him suspiciously. Every movement woke a new sentiment in her. After a pause and a prolonged gaze she resumed, addressing me in accents of indignant disappointment,—

"Oh, you see, Nelly, he would not relent a moment to keep me out of the grave! *That* is how I'm loved! Well, never mind. That is not *my* Heathcliff. I shall love mine yet, and take him with me; he's in my soul. And," added she musingly, "the thing that irks me most is this shattered prison, after all. I'm tired of being enclosed here. I'm wearying to escape into that glorious world, and to be always there—not seeing it dimly through tears, and yearning for it through the walls of an aching heart, but really with it and in it. Nelly, you think you are better and more fortunate than I, in full health and strength. You are sorry for me. Very soon that will be altered. I shall be sorry for *you*. I shall be incomparably beyond and above you all. I *wonder* he won't be near me!" she went on to herself. "I thought he wished it.—Heathcliff dear, you should not be sullen now. Do come to me, Heathcliff."

In her eagerness she rose and supported herself on the arm of the chair. At that earnest appeal he turned to her, looking absolutely desperate. His eyes, wide and wet, at last flashed fiercely on her; his breast heaved convulsively. An instant they held asunder,

and then how they met I hardly saw, but Catherine made
a spring, and he caught her, and they were locked in
an embrace from which I thought my mistress would
never be released alive—in fact, to my eyes, she seemed
directly insensible. He flung himself into the nearest
seat, and on my approaching hurriedly to ascertain if
she had fainted, he gnashed at me and foamed like a
mad dog, and gathered her to him with greedy jealousy.
I did not feel as if I were in the company of a creature of
my own species. It appeared that he would not understand, though I spoke to him, so I stood off and held
my tongue in great perplexity.

A movement of Catherine's relieved me a little
presently. She put up her hand to clasp his neck, and
bring her cheek to his as he held her ; while he, in return,
covering her with frantic caresses, said wildly,—

"You teach me now how cruel you've been—cruel
and false. *Why* did you despise me ? *Why* did you
betray your own heart, Cathy ? I have not one word
of comfort. You deserve this. You have killed yourself. Yes, you may kiss me, and cry, and wring out my
kisses and tears ; they'll blight you—they'll damn
you. You loved me ; then what *right* had you to leave
me ? What right—answer me—for the poor fancy you
felt for Linton ? Because misery, and degradation, and
death, and nothing that God or Satan could inflict
would have parted us, *you*, of your own will, did it.
I have not broken your heart—*you* have broken it ;
and in breaking it you have broken mine. So much the
worse for me that I am strong. Do I want to live ?
What kind of living will it be when you—— O God !
would *you* like to live with your soul in the grave ? "

"Let me alone ! let me alone ! " sobbed Catherine.
"If I've done wrong, I'm dying for it. It is enough !
You left me too ; but I won't upbraid you. I forgive
you. Forgive me."

"It is hard to forgive, and to look at those eyes, and
feel those wasted hands," he answered. "Kiss me again,
and don't let me see your eyes. I forgive what you have

one to me. I love *my* murderer—but *yours*! How
an I?"

They were silent—their faces hid against each other,
nd washed by each other's tears. At least, I suppose
he weeping was on both sides, as it seemed Heathcliff
ould weep on a great occasion like this.

I grew very uncomfortable, meanwhile, for the after-
oon wore fast away, the man whom I had sent off
eturned from his errand, and I could distinguish by
he shine of the western sun up the valley a concourse
hickening outside Gimmerton chapel porch.

"Service is over," I announced. "My master will be
ere in half an hour."

Heathcliff groaned a curse, and strained Catherine
loser. She never moved.

Ere long I perceived a group of the servants passing
p the road towards the kitchen wing. Mr. Linton was
ot far behind. He opened the gate himself, and saun-
ered slowly up, probably enjoying the lovely afternoon,
hat breathed as soft as summer.

"Now he is here!" I exclaimed. "For Heaven's
ake hurry down! You'll not meet any one on the
ront stairs. Do be quick, and stay among the trees
ill he is fairly in."

"I must go, Cathy," said Heathcliff, seeking to ex-
ricate himself from his companion's arms. "But if
live I'll see you again before you are asleep. I won't
tray five yards from your window."

"You must not go!" she answered, holding him as
irmly as her strength allowed. "You *shall* not, I tell
ou."

"For one hour," he pleaded earnestly.

"Not for one minute," she replied.

"I *must*; Linton will be up immediately," persisted
he alarmed intruder.

He would have risen and unfixed her fingers by the
ct; she clung fast, gasping. There was mad resolu-
ion in her face.

"No!" she shrieked. "Oh, don't, don't go! It is

the last time ! Edgar will not hurt us. Heathcliff, shall die ! I shall die ! "

" Damn the fool ! There he is ! " cried Heathclif sinking back into his seat. " Hush, my darling ! Hus hush, Catherine ! I'll stay. If he shot me so, I'd e pire with a blessing on my lips."

And there they were fast again. I heard my mast mounting the stairs. The cold sweat ran from my for head ; I was horrified.

" Are you going to listen to her ravings ? " I sai passionately. " She does not know what she say Will you ruin her because she has not wit to help he self ? Get up ! You could be free instantly. That the most diabolical deed that ever you did. We a all done for—master, mistress, and servant."

I wrung my hands and cried out, and Mr. Linto hastened his step at the noise. In the midst of m agitation I was sincerely glad to observe that Catherine arms had fallen relaxed, and her head hung down.

" She's fainted or dead," I thought ; " so much the better. Far better that she should be dead than linge ing a burden and a misery-maker to all about her."

Edgar sprang to his unbidden guest, blanched wit astonishment and rage. What he meant to do I canno tell. However, the other stopped all demonstrations a once by placing the lifeless-looking form in his arms.

" Look there ! " he said. " Unless you be a fien help her first ; then you shall speak to me ! "

He walked into the parlour and sat down. M Linton summoned me, and with great difficulty, an after resorting to many means, we managed to restor her to sensation ; but she was all bewildered. Sh sighed and moaned, and knew nobody. Edgar, in h anxiety for her, forgot her hated friend. I did no I went at the earliest opportunity and besought him t depart, affirming that Catherine was better, and he shoul hear from me in the morning how she passed the night.

" I shall not refuse to go out of doors," he answered " but I shall stay in the garden ; and, Nelly, mind yo

eep your word to-morrow. I shall be under those
rch trees. Mind! or I pay another visit, whether
inton be in or not."

He sent a rapid glance through the half-open door
f the chamber, and, ascertaining that what I stated was
pparently true, delivered the house of his luckless
resence.

CHAPTER XVI.

ABOUT twelve o'clock that night was born the Catherine
ou saw at Wuthering Heights—a puny seven months'
hild; and two hours after, the mother died, having
ever recovered sufficient consciousness to miss Heath-
liff or know Edgar. The latter's distraction at his
ereavement is a subject too painful to be dwelt on;
ts after effects showed how deep the sorrow sank. A
reat addition, in my eyes, was his being left without
n heir. I bemoaned that as I gazed on the feeble
rphan, and I mentally abused old Linton for—what
vas only natural partiality—the securing his estate to
is own daughter instead of his son's. An unwelcomed
nfant it was, poor thing! It might have wailed out of
ife and nobody cared a morsel, during those first hours
f existence. We redeemed the neglect afterwards, but
ts beginning was as friendless as its end is likely to be.

Next morning—bright and cheerful out of doors—
tole softened in through the blinds of the silent room,
nd suffused the couch and its occupant with a mellow,
ender glow. Edgar Linton had his head laid on the
illow, and his eyes shut. His young and fair features
vere almost as deathlike as those of the form beside
im, and almost as fixed; but *his* was the hush of ex-
austed anguish, and *hers* of perfect peace. Her brow
mooth, her lids closed, her lips wearing the expression
f a smile—no angel in heaven could be more beautiful
han she appeared. And I partook of the infinite calm
n which she lay. My mind was never in a holier frame
han while I gazed on that untroubled image of Divine

rest. I instinctively echoed the words she had uttered
a few hours before. "Incomparably beyond and above
us all! Whether still on earth or now in heaven, her
spirit is at home with God!"

I don't know if it be a peculiarity in me, but I am
seldom otherwise than happy while watching in the
chamber of death, should no frenzied or despairing
mourner share the duty with me. I see a repose that
neither earth nor hell can break, and I feel an assurance
of the endless and shadowless hereafter—the eternity
they have entered—where life is boundless in its dura-
tion, and love in its sympathy, and joy in its fullness.
I noticed on that occasion how much selfishness there
is even in a love like Mr. Linton's, when he so regretted
Catherine's blessed release. To be sure, one might have
doubted, after the wayward and impatient existence
she had led, whether she merited a haven of peace at
last. One might doubt in seasons of cold reflection, but
not then, in the presence of her corpse. It asserted its
own tranquillity, which seemed a pledge of equal quiet
to its former inhabitants.

Do you believe such people *are* happy in the other
world, sir? I'd give a great deal to know.

I declined answering Mrs. Dean's question, which
struck me as something heterodox. She proceeded,—

Retracing the course of Catherine Linton, I fear we
have no right to think she is; but we'll leave her with
her Maker.

The master looked asleep, and I ventured soon after
sunrise to quit the room and steal out to the pure re-
freshing air. The servants thought me gone to shake off
the drowsiness of my protracted watch; in reality, my
chief motive was seeing Mr. Heathcliff. If he had
remained among the larches all night he would have
heard nothing of the stir at the Grange—unless, perhaps,
he might catch the gallop of the messenger going to
Gimmerton. If he had come nearer he would probably
be aware, from the lights flitting to and fro, and the opening and shutting of the outer doors, that all was not

right within. I wished yet feared to find him. I felt
the terrible news must be told, and I longed to get it
over; but *how* to do it I did not know. He was there
—at least a few yards farther in the park—leant against
an old ash tree, his hat off, and his hair soaked with
the dew that had gathered on the budded branches,
and fell pattering round him. He had been standing a
long time in that position, for I saw a pair of ousels passing
and repassing scarcely three feet from him, busy in building their nest, and regarding his proximity no more than
that of a piece of timber. They flew off at my approach,
and he raised his eyes and spoke.

"She's dead!" he said. "I've not waited for you to
learn that. Put your handkerchief away; don't snivel
before me. Damn you all! she wants none of *your* tears!"

I was weeping as much for him as her; we do sometimes pity creatures that have none of the feeling either
for themselves or others. When I first looked into his
face, I perceived that he had got intelligence of the
catastrophe; and a foolish notion struck me that his
heart was quelled, and he prayed, because his lips moved,
and his gaze was bent on the ground.

"Yes, she's dead!" I answered, checking my sobs
and drying my cheeks — "gone to heaven, I hope,
where we may, every one, join her, if we take due warning and leave our evil ways to follow good!"

"Did *she* take due warning, then?" asked Heathcliff,
attempting a sneer. "Did she die like a saint? Come,
give me a true history of the event. How did——"

He endeavoured to pronounce the name, but could
not manage it; and compressing his mouth he held a
silent combat with his inward agony, defying, meanwhile,
my sympathy with an unflinching ferocious stare. "How
did she die?" he resumed at last, fain, notwithstanding
his hardihood, to have a support behind him; for,
after the struggle, he trembled, in spite of himself, to
his very finger-ends.

"Poor wretch!" I thought, "you have a heart and
nerves the same as your brother men! Why should you

be anxious to conceal them? Your pride cannot blin[
God. You tempt Him to wring them till He force
a cry of humiliation."

"Quietly as a lamb!" I answered aloud. "Sh[
drew a sigh, and stretched herself, like a child reviving
and sinking again to sleep; and five minutes after
felt one little pulse at her heart, and nothing more!"

"And—did she ever mention me?" he asked, hesi
tating, as if he dreaded the answer to his question woul[
introduce details that he could not bear to hear.

"Her senses never returned. She recognized nobod[
from the time you left her," I said. "She lies with [
sweet smile on her face, and her latest ideas wandere[
back to pleasant early days. Her life closed in a gentl[
dream. May she wake as kindly in the other world!"

"May she wake in torment!" he cried with frightfu[
vehemence, stamping his foot and groaning in a sudde[
paroxysm of ungovernable passion. "Why, she's [
liar to the end. Where is she? Not *there*—not i[
heaven — not perished — where? — Oh! you said yo[
cared nothing for my sufferings! And I pray one praye[
—I repeat it till my tongue stiffens—Catherine Earn
shaw, may you not rest as long as I am living! Yo[
said I killed you—haunt me. then! The murdered d[
haunt their murderers, I believe. I know that ghost[
have wandered on earth. Be with me always—take an[
form—drive me mad—only *do* not leave me in this abyss
where I cannot find you! O God! it is unutterable
I *cannot* live without my life! I *cannot* live without m[
soul!"

He dashed his head against the knotted trunk, and
lifting up his eyes, howled—not like a man, but like [
savage beast being goaded to death with knives an[
spears. I observed several splashes of blood about th[
bark of the tree, and his hand and forehead were bot[
stained; probably the scene I witnessed was a repetitio[
of others acted during the night. It hardly moved m[
compassion—it appalled me; still I felt reluctant t[
quit him so. But the moment he recollected himsel[

enough to notice me watching, he thundered a command for me to go, and I obeyed. He was beyond my skill to quiet or console.

Mrs. Linton's funeral was appointed to take place on the Friday following her decease, and till then her coffin remained uncovered and strewn with flowers and scented leaves in the great drawing-room. Linton spent his days and nights there, a sleepless guardian; and—a circumstance concealed from all but me—Heathcliff spent his nights, at least, outside, equally a stranger to repose. I held no communication with him. Still, I was conscious of his design to enter, if he could; and on the Tuesday, a little after dark, when my master, from sheer fatigue, had been compelled to retire a couple of hours, I went and opened one of the windows, moved by his perseverance to give him a chance of bestowing on the faded image of his idol one final adieu. He did not omit to avail himself of the opportunity, cautiously and briefly—too cautiously to betray his presence by the slightest noise. Indeed, I shouldn't have discovered that he had been there, except for the disarrangement of the drapery about the corpse's face, and for observing on the floor a curl of light hair fastened with a silver thread, which, on examination, I ascertained to have been taken from a locket hung round Catherine's neck. Heathcliff had opened the trinket and cast out its contents, replacing them by a black lock of his own. I twisted the two, and enclosed them together.

Mr. Earnshaw was, of course, invited to attend the remains of his sister to the grave. He sent no excuse, but he never came; so that, besides her husband, the mourners were wholly composed of tenants and servants. Isabella was not asked.

The place of Catherine's interment, to the surprise of the villagers, was neither in the chapel under the carved monument of the Lintons, nor yet by the tombs of her own relations outside. It was dug on a green slope in a corner of the kirkyard, where the wall is so low that heath and bilberry plants have climbed over it from the moor, and peat mould almost buries it. Her husband lies in the same spot now, and they have each a simple headstone above, and a plain gray block at their feet, to mark the graves.

CHAPTER XVII.

THAT Friday made the last of our fine days for a month. In the evening the weather broke; the wind shifted from south to north-east, and brought rain first, and then sleet and snow. On the morrow one could hardly imagine that there had been three weeks of summer— the primroses and crocuses were hidden under windy drifts, the larks were silent, the young leaves of the early trees smitten and blackened. And dreary, and chill, and dismal, that morrow did creep over! My master kept his room; I took possession of the lonely parlour, converting it into a nursery, and there I was, sitting with the moaning doll of a child laid on my knee, rocking it to and fro, and watching, meanwhile, the still driving flakes build up the uncurtained window, when the door opened, and some person entered, out of breath and laughing. My anger was greater than my astonishment for a minute. I supposed it one of the maids, and I cried,—

"Have done! How dare you show your giddiness here? What would Mr. Linton say if he heard you?"

"Excuse me," answered a familiar voice; "but I know Edgar is in bed, and I cannot stop myself."

With that the speaker came forward to the fire, panting and holding her hand to her side.

"I have run the whole way from Wuthering Heights," she continued, after a pause, "except where I've flown. I couldn't count the number of falls I've had. Oh, I'm aching all over! Don't be alarmed! There shall be an explanation as soon as I can give it, only just have the goodness to step out and order the carriage to take me on to Gimmerton, and tell a servant to seek up a few clothes in my wardrobe."

The intruder was Mrs. Heathcliff. She certainly seemed in no laughing predicament. Her hair streamed on her shoulders, dripping with snow and water; she was dressed in the girlish dress she commonly wore, befitting her age more than her position—a low frock with short sleeves, and nothing on either head or neck. The frock was of light silk, and clung to her with wet, and her feet were protected merely by thin slippers; add to this a deep cut under one ear, which only the cold prevented from bleeding profusely, a white face scratched and bruised, and a frame hardly able to support itself, through fatigue, and you may fancy my first fright was not much allayed when I had had leisure to examine her.

"My dear young lady," I exclaimed, "I'll stir nowhere, and hear nothing, till you have removed every article of your clothes, and put on dry things; and certainly you shall not go to Gimmerton to-night, so it is needless to order the carriage."

"Certainly I shall," she said— "walking or riding. Yet I've no objection to dress myself decently. And— Ah, see how it flows down my neck now! The fire does make it smart."

She insisted on my fulfilling her directions before she would let me touch her; and not till after the coachman had been instructed to get ready, and a maid set to pack up some necessary attire, did I obtain her consent for binding the wound, and helping to change her garments.

"Now, Ellen," she said, when my task was finished and she was seated in an easy-chair on the hearth, with a cup of tea before her, "you sit down opposite me, and put poor Catherine's baby away. I don't like to see it. You mustn't think I care little for Catherine because I behaved so foolishly on entering. I've cried, too, bitterly—yes, more than any one else has reason to cry. We parted unreconciled, you remember, and I shan't forgive myself. But, for all that, I was not going to sympathize with him—the brute beast! Oh, give me the poker! This is the last thing of his I have about me." She slipped the gold ring from her third finger, and threw it on the floor. "I'll smash it!" she continued, striking it with childish spite, "and then I'll burn it!" And she took and dropped the misused article among the coals. "There! he shall buy another if he gets me back again. He'd be capable of coming to seek me, to tease Edgar. I dare not stay, lest that notion should possess his wicked head! And besides, Edgar has not been kind, has he? And I won't come suing for his assistance, nor will I bring him into more trouble. Necessity compelled me to seek shelter here, though, if I had not learned he was out of the way, I'd have halted at the kitchen, washed my face, warmed myself, got you to bring what I wanted, and departed again to anywhere out of the reach of my accursed—of that incarnate goblin! Ah, he was in such a fury! If he had caught me! It's a pity Earnshaw is not his match in strength. I wouldn't have run till I'd seen him all but demolished, had Hindley been able to do it."

"Well, don't talk so fast, miss," I interrupted; "you'll disorder the handkerchief I have tied round your face, and make the cut bleed again. Drink your tea, and take breath, and give over laughing; laughter is sadly out of place under this roof, and in your condition!"

"An undeniable truth," she replied. "Listen to that child! It maintains a constant wail. Send it out of my hearing for an hour; I shan't stay any longer."

I rang the bell and committed it to a servant's care, and then I inquired what had urged her to escape from Wuthering Heights in such an unlikely plight, and where she meant to go, as she refused remaining with us.

"I ought and I wish to remain," answered she—"to cheer Edgar and take care of the baby, for two things, and because the Grange is my right home. But I tell you he wouldn't let me. Do you think he could bear to see me grow fat and merry, could bear to think that we were tranquil, and not resolve on poisoning our comfort? Now, I have the satisfaction of being sure that he detests me to the point of its annoying him seriously to have me within earshot or eyesight. I notice, when I enter his presence, the muscles of his countenance are involuntarily distorted into an expression of hatred, partly arising from his knowledge of the good causes I have to feel that sentiment for him, and partly from original aversion. It is strong enough to make me feel pretty certain that he would not chase me over England supposing I contrived a clear escape, and therefore I must get quite away. I've recovered from my first desire to be killed by him; I'd rather he'd kill himself! He has extinguished my love effectually, and so I'm at my ease. I can recollect yet how I loved him, and can dimly imagine that I could still be loving him, if—no, no! Even if he had doted on me, the devilish nature would have revealed its existence somehow. Catherine had an awfully perverted taste to esteem him so dearly, knowing him so well. Monster! Would that he could be blotted out of creation and out of my memory!"

"Hush, hush! He's a human being," I said. "Be more charitable. There are worse men than he is yet."

"He's not a human being," she retorted, "and he has no claim on my charity. I gave him my heart, and he took and pinched it to death, and flung it back to me. People feel with their hearts, Ellen; and since he has destroyed mine, I have not power to feel for him, and I would not, though he groaned from this to his dying day, and wept tears of blood for Catherine! No, indeed, indeed, I wouldn't!" And here Isabella began to cry; but, immediately dashing the water from her lashes, she recommenced. "You asked, what has driven me to flight at last? I was compelled to attempt it, because I had succeeded in rousing his rage a pitch above his malignity. Pulling out the nerves with red-hot pincers requires more coolness than knocking on the head. He was worked up to forget the fiendish prudence he boasted of, and proceeded to murderous violence. I experienced pleasure in being able to exasperate him ; the sense of pleasure woke my instinct of self-preservation, so I fairly broke free ; and if ever I come into his hands again, he is welcome to a signal revenge.

" Yesterday, you know, Mr. Earnshaw should have been at the funeral. He kept himself sober for the purpose, tolerably sober—not going to bed mad at six o'clock and getting up drunk at twelve. Consequently he rose, in suicidal low spirits, as fit for the church as for a dance ; and instead, he sat down by the fire and swallowed gin or brandy by tumblerfuls.

" Heathcliff—I shudder to name him !—has been a stranger in the house from last Sunday till to-day. Whether the angels have fed him, or his kin beneath, I cannot tell ; but he has not eaten a meal with us for nearly a week. He has just come home at dawn, and gone upstairs to his chamber, locking himself in—as if anybody dreamt of coveting his company ! There he has continued, praying like a Methodist—only the deity he implored is senseless dust and ashes ; and God, when addressed, was curiously confounded with his own black father ! After concluding these precious orisons —and they lasted generally till he grew hoarse and his voice was strangled in his throat—he would be off again, always straight down to the Grange ! I wonder Edgar did not send for a constable, and give him into custody. For me, grieved as I was about Catherine, it was impossible to avoid regarding this season of deliverance from degrading oppression as a holiday.

" I recovered spirits sufficient to hear Joseph's eternal lectures without weeping, and to move up and down the house less with the foot of a frightened thief than formerly. You wouldn't think that I should cry at anything Joseph could say ; but he and Hareton are detestable companions. I'd rather sit with Hindley, and hear his awful talk, than with ' t' little maister ' and his stanch supporter, that odious old man ! When Heathcliff is in, I'm often obliged to seek the kitchen and their society, or starve among the damp uninhabited chambers. When he is not, as was the case this week, I establish a table and chair at one corner of the house fire, and never mind how Mr. Earnshaw may occupy himself ; and he does not interfere with my arrangements. He is quieter now than he used to be, if no one provokes him—more sullen and depressed and less furious. Joseph affirms he's sure he's an altered man, that the Lord has touched his heart, and he is saved ' so as by fire.' I'm puzzled to detect signs of the favourable change ; but it is not my business.

" Yester-evening I sat in my nook reading some old books till late on towards twelve. It seemed so dismal to go upstairs, with the wild snow blowing outside, and my thoughts continually reverting to the kirkyard and the new-made grave. I dared hardly lift my eyes from the page before me, that melancholy scene so instantly usurped its place. Hindley sat opposite, his head leant on his hand, perhaps meditating on the same subject. He had ceased drinking at a point below irrationality, and had neither stirred nor spoken during two or three hours. There was no sound through the house but the moaning wind, which shook the windows every now and then, the faint crackling of the coals, and the click of my snuffers as I removed at intervals the long wick of the candle. Hareton and Joseph were probably fast asleep in bed. It was very, very sad ; and while I read I sighed, for it seemed as if all joy had vanished from the world, never to be restored.

" The doleful silence was broken at length by the sound of the kitchen latch. Heathcliff had returned from his watch earlier than usual, owing, I suppose, to the sudden storm. That entrance was fastened, and we heard him coming round to get in by the other. I rose with an irrepressible expression of what I felt on my lips, which induced my companion, who had been staring towards the door, to turn and look at me.

" ' I'll keep him out five minutes,' he exclaimed. ' You won't object ?'

"'No; you may keep him out the whole night for me,' I answered. 'Do; put the key in the lock, and draw the bolts.'

"Earnshaw accomplished this ere his guest reached the front. He then came and brought his chair to the other side of my table, leaning over it, and searching in my eyes for a sympathy with the burning hate that gleamed from his. As he both looked and felt like an assassin, he couldn't exactly find that; but he discovered enough to encourage him to speak.

"'You and I,' he said, 'have each a great debt to settle with the man out yonder. If we were neither of us cowards, we might combine to discharge it. Are you as soft as your brother? Are you willing to endure to the last, and not once attempt a repayment?'

"'I'm weary of enduring now,' I replied, 'and I'd be glad of a retaliation that wouldn't recoil on myself; but treachery and violence are spears pointed at both ends. They wound those who resort to them worse than their enemies.'

"'Treachery and violence are a just return for treachery and violence!' cried Hindley. 'Mrs. Heathcliff, I'll ask you to do nothing but sit still and be dumb. Tell me now, can you? I'm sure you would have as much pleasure as I in witnessing the conclusion of the fiend's existence. He'll be *your* death unless you overreach him; and he'll be *my* ruin. Damn the hellish villain! He knocks at the door as if he were master here already! Promise to hold your tongue, and before that clock strikes —it wants three minutes of one—you're a free woman!'

"He took the implements which I described to you in my letter from his breast, and would have turned down the candle. I snatched it away, however, and seized his arm.

"'I'll not hold my tongue,' I said; 'you mustn't touch him. Let the door remain shut, and be quiet.'

"'No! I've formed my resolution, and by God I'll execute it!' cried the desperate being. 'I'll do you a kindness in spite of yourself, and Hareton justice! And you needn't trouble your head to screen me; Catherine is gone. Nobody alive would regret me, or be ashamed, though I cut my throat this minute; and it's time to make an end!'

"I might as well have struggled with a bear or reasoned with a lunatic. The only resource left me was to run to a lattice and warn his intended victim of the fate which awaited him.

"'You'd better seek shelter somewhere else to-night,' I exclaimed, in rather a triumphant tone. 'Mr. Earnshaw has a mind to shoot you, if you persist in endeavouring to enter.'

"'You'd better open the door, you ——,' he answered, addressing me by some elegant term that I don't care to repeat.

"'I shall not meddle in the matter,' I retorted again. 'Come in and get shot, if you please. I've done my duty.'

"With that I shut the window and returned to my place by the fire, having too small a stock of hypocrisy at my command to pretend any anxiety for the danger that menaced him. Earnshaw swore passionately at me, affirming that I loved the villain yet, and calling me all sorts of names for the base spirit I evinced. And I, in my secret heart (and conscience never reproached me), thought what a blessing it would be for *him* should Heathcliff put him out of misery; and what a blessing for *me* should he send Heathcliff to his right abode! As I sat nursing these reflections, the casement behind me was banged on to the floor by a blow from the latter individual, and his black countenance looked blightingly through. The stanchions stood too close to suffer his shoulders to follow, and I smiled, exulting in my fancied security. His hair and clothes were whitened with snow, and his sharp cannibal teeth, revealed by cold and wrath, gleamed through the dark.

"'Isabella, let me in, or I'll make you repent!' he 'girned,' as Joseph calls it.

"'I cannot commit murder,' I replied. 'Mr. Hindley stands sentinel with a knife and loaded pistol.'

" ' Let me in by the kitchen door,' he said.

" ' Hindley will be there before me,' I answered; ' and that's a poor love of yours that cannot bear a shower of snow ! We were left at peace in our beds as long as the summer moon shone, but the moment a blast of winter returns, you must run for shelter ! Heathcliff, if I were you, I'd go stretch myself over her grave and die like a faithful dog. The world is surely not worth living in now, is it ? You had distinctly impressed on me the idea that Catherine was the whole joy of your life. I can't imagine how you think of surviving her loss.'

" ' He's there, is he ? ' exclaimed my companion, rushing to the gap. ' If I can get my arm out I can hit him ! '

" I'm afraid, Ellen, you'll set me down as really wicked ; but you don't know all, so don't judge. I wouldn't have aided or abetted an attempt on even *his* life for anything. Wish that he were dead, I must ; and therefore I was fearfully disappointed, and unnerved by terror for the consequences of my taunting speech, when he flung himself on Earnshaw's weapon and wrenched it from his grasp.

" The charge exploded, and the knife, in springing back, closed into its owner's wrist. Heathcliff pulled it away by main force, slitting up the flesh as it passed on, and thrust it dripping into his pocket. He then took a stone, struck down the division between two windows, and sprang in. His adversary had fallen senseless with excessive pain and the flow of blood that gushed from an artery or a large vein. The ruffian kicked and trampled on him, and dashed his head repeatedly against the flags, holding me with one hand meantime to prevent me summoning Joseph. He exerted preterhuman self-denial in abstaining from finishing him completely ; but getting out of breath he finally desisted, and dragged the apparently inanimate body on to the settle. There he tore off the sleeve of Earnshaw's coat, and bound up the wound with brutal roughness, spitting and cursing during the operation as energetically as he had kicked before. Being at liberty, I lost no time in seeking the old servant, who, having gathered by degrees the purport of my hasty tale, hurried below, gasping as he descended the steps two at once.

"'What is ther to do now—what is ther to do now?'

"'There's this to do,' thundered Heathcliff, 'that your master's mad; and should he last another month, I'll have him to an asylum. And how the devil did you come to fasten me out, you toothless hound? Don't stand muttering and mumbling there. Come, I'm not going to nurse him. Wash that stuff away; and mind the sparks of your candle—it is more than half brandy.'

"'And so ye've been murthering on him!' exclaimed Joseph, lifting his hands and eyes in horror. 'If iver I seed a seeght loike this! May the Lord——'

"Heathcliff gave him a push on to his knees in the middle of the blood, and flung a towel to him; but instead of proceeding to dry it up, he joined his hands and began a prayer, which excited my laughter from its odd phraseology. I was in the condition of mind to be shocked at nothing; in fact, I was as reckless as some malefactors show themselves at the foot of the gallows.

"'Oh, I forgot you,' said the tyrant. 'You shall do that. Down with you! And you conspire with him against me, do you, viper? There, that is work fit for you!'

"He shook me till my teeth rattled, and pitched me beside Joseph, who steadily concluded his supplications, and then rose, vowing he would set off for the Grange directly. Mr. Linton was a magistrate, and though he had fifty wives dead, he should inquire into this. He was so obstinate in his resolution that Heathcliff deemed it expedient to compel from my lips a recapitulation of what had taken place, standing over me, heaving with malevolence, as I reluctantly delivered the account in answer to his questions. It required a great deal of labour to satisfy the old man that Heathcliff was not the aggressor, especially with my hardly-wrung replies.

However, Mr. Earnshaw soon convinced him that he was alive still. Joseph hastened to administer a dose of spirits, and by their succour his master presently regained motion and consciousness. Heathcliff, aware that his opponent was ignorant of the treatment received while insensible, called him deliriously intoxicated, and said he should not notice his atrocious conduct further, but advised him to get to bed. To my joy, he left us, after giving this judicious counsel, and Hindley stretched himself on the hearthstone. I departed to my own room, marvelling that I had escaped so easily.

"This morning when I came down, about half an hour before noon, Mr. Earnshaw was sitting by the fire deadly sick. His evil genius, almost as gaunt and ghastly, leant against the chimney. Neither appeared inclined to dine; and, having waited till all was cold on the table, I commenced alone. Nothing hindered me from eating heartily, and I experienced a certain sense of satisfaction and superiority as, at intervals, I cast a look towards my silent companions, and felt the comfort of a quiet conscience within me. After I had done, I ventured on the unusual liberty of drawing near the fire, going round Earnshaw's seat, and kneeling in the corner beside him.

"Heathcliff did not glance my way, and I gazed up, and contemplated his features almost as confidently as if they had been turned to stone. His forehead, that I once thought so manly, and that I now think so diabolical, was shaded with a heavy cloud; his basilisk eyes were nearly quenched by sleeplessness, and weeping, perhaps, for the lashes were wet then; his lips devoid of their ferocious sneer, and sealed in an expression of unspeakable sadness. Had it been another, I would have covered my face in the presence of such grief. In *his* case, I was gratified; and, ignoble as it seems to insult a fallen enemy, I couldn't miss this chance of sticking in a dart. His weakness was the only time when I could taste the delight of paying wrong for wrong."

"Fie, fie, miss!" I interrupted. "One might suppose

you had never opened a Bible in your life. If God afflict your enemies, surely that ought to suffice you. It is both mean and presumptuous to add your torture to His."

"In general I'll allow that it would be, Ellen," she continued; "but what misery laid on Heathcliff could content me, unless I have a hand in it? I'd rather he suffered *less*, if I might cause his sufferings, and he might *know* that I was the cause. Oh, I owe him so much! On only one condition can I hope to forgive him. It is, if I may take an eye for an eye, a tooth for a tooth, for every wrench of agony return a wrench, reduce him to my level; as he was the first to injure, make him the first to implore pardon; and then—why, then, Ellen, I might show you some generosity. But it is utterly impossible I can ever be revenged, and therefore I cannot forgive him. Hindley wanted some water, and I handed him a glass, and asked him how he was.

"'Not as ill as I wish,' he replied. 'But leaving out my arm, every inch of me is as sore as if I had been fighting with a legion of imps.'

"'Yes, no wonder,' was my next remark. 'Catherine used to boast that she stood between you and bodily harm. She meant that certain persons would not hurt you for fear of offending her. It's well people don't *really* rise from their grave, or last night she might have witnessed a repulsive scene! Are not you bruised and cut over your chest and shoulders?'

"'I can't say,' he answered; 'but what do you mean? Did he dare to strike me when I was down?'

"'He trampled on and kicked you, and dashed you on the ground,' I whispered. 'And his mouth watered to tear you with his teeth, because he's only half man—not so much—and the rest fiend.'

"Mr. Earnshaw looked up, like me, to the countenance of our mutual foe, who, absorbed in his anguish, seemed insensible to anything around him. The longer he stood, the plainer his reflections revealed their blackness through his features.

"'Oh, if God would but give me strength to strangle

him in my last agony, I'd go to hell with joy,' groaned the impatient man, writhing to rise, and sinking back in despair, convinced of his inadequacy for the struggle.

"'Nay, it's enough that he has murdered one of you,' I observed aloud. 'At the Grange, every one knows your sister would have been living now had it not been for Mr. Heathcliff. After all, it is preferable to be hated than loved by him. When I recollect how happy we were, how happy Catherine was before he came, I'm fit to curse the day.'

"Most likely Heathcliff noticed more the truth of what was said than the spirit of the person who said it. His attention was roused, I saw, for his eyes rained down tears among the ashes, and he drew his breath in suffocating sighs. I stared full at him, and laughed scornfully. The clouded windows of hell flashed a moment towards me; the fiend which usually looked out, however, was so dimmed and drowned that I did not fear to hazard another sound of derision.

"'Get up, and begone out of my sight,' said the mourner.

"I guessed he uttered those words, at least, though his voice was hardly intelligible.

"'I beg your pardon,' I replied. 'But I loved Catherine too; and her brother requires attendance, which, for her sake, I shall supply. Now that she's dead, I see her in Hindley. Hindley has exactly her eyes, if you had not tried to gouge them out, and made them black and red; and her——'

"'Get up, wretched idiot, before I stamp you to death!' he cried, making a movement that caused me to make one also.

"'But, then,' I continued, holding myself ready to flee, 'if poor Catherine had trusted you, and assumed the ridiculous, contemptible, degrading title of Mrs. Heathcliff, she would soon have presented a similar picture. *She* wouldn't have borne your abominable behaviour quietly. Her detestation and disgust must have found voice.'

" The back of the settle and Earnshaw's person interposed between me and him ; so instead of endeavouring
to reach me, he snatched a dinner knife from the table
and flung it at my head. It struck beneath my ear,
and stopped the sentence I was uttering ; but, pulling it
out, I sprang to the door and delivered another, which
I hope went a little deeper than his missile. The last
glimpse I caught of him was a furious rush on his part,
checked by the embrace of his host ; and both fell
locked together on the hearth. In my flight through the
kitchen I bade Joseph speed to his master. I knocked
over Hareton, who was hanging a litter of puppies from
a chair-back in the doorway ; and, blest as a soul
escaped from purgatory, I bounded, leaped, and flew
down the steep road ; then, quitting its windings, shot
direct across the moor, rolling over banks, and wading
through marshes, precipitating myself, in fact, towards
the beacon light of the Grange. And far rather would
I be condemned to a perpetual dwelling in the infernal
regions than, even for one night, abide beneath the
roof of Wuthering Heights again."

Isabella ceased speaking, and took a drink of tea ; then
she rose, and bidding me put on her bonnet and a great
shawl I had brought, and turning a deaf ear to my
entreaties for her to remain another hour, she stepped
on to a chair, kissed Edgar's and Catherine's portraits,
bestowed a similar salute on me, and descended to the
carriage, accompanied by Fanny, who yelped wild with
joy at recovering her mistress. She was driven away,
never to revisit this neighbourhood ; but a regular
correspondence was established between her and my
master when things were more settled. I believe her
new abode was in the south, near London ; there she
had a son born, a few months subsequent to her escape.
He was christened Linton, and, from the first, she reported him to be an ailing, peevish creature.

Mr. Heathcliff, meeting me one day in the village,
inquired where she lived. I refused to tell. He remarked that it was not of any moment, only she must

beware of coming to her brother. She should not b
with him, if he had to keep her himself. Though
would give no information, he discovered, through som
of the other servants, both her place of residence an
the existence of the child. Still he didn't molest her
for which forbearance she might thank his aversion,
suppose. He often asked about the infant, when h
saw me; and on hearing its name, smiled grimly, an
observed,—

"They wish me to hate it too, do they?"

"I don't think they wish you to know anything abou
it," I answered.

"But I'll have it," he said, "when I want it. The
may reckon on that."

Fortunately its mother died before the time arrived
some thirteen years after the decease of Catherine, whe
Linton was twelve or a little more.

On the day succeeding Isabella's unexpected visit,
had no opportunity of speaking to my master. H
shunned conversation, and was fit for discussing nothing
When I could get him to listen, I saw it pleased him tha
his sister had left her husband, whom he abhorred wit
an intensity which the mildness of his nature woul
scarcely seem to allow. So deep and sensitive was hi
aversion that he refrained from going anywhere wher
he was likely to see or hear of Heathcliff. Grief an
that together transformed him into a complete hermit
He threw up his office of magistrate, ceased even t
attend church, avoided the village on all occasions, an
spent a life of entire seclusion within the limits of hi
park and grounds, only varied by solitary rambles o
the moors and visits to the grave of his wife, mostly a
evening, or early morning before other wanderers wer
abroad. But he was too good to be thoroughly un
happy long. *He* didn't pray for Catherine's soul t
haunt him. Time brought resignation and a melan
choly sweeter than common joy. He recalled her memor
with ardent, tender love, and hopeful aspiring to th
better world, where he doubted not she was gone.

And he had earthly consolation and affections also. For a few days, I said, he seemed regardless of the puny successor to the departed; that coldness melted as fast as snow in April, and ere the tiny thing could stammer a word or totter a step, it wielded a despot's sceptre in his heart. It was named Catherine; but he never called it the name in full, as he had never called the first Catherine short, probably because Heathcliff had a habit of doing so. The little one was always Cathy; it formed to him a distinction from the mother, and yet a connection with her; and his attachment sprang from its relation to her far more than from its being his own.

I used to draw a comparison between him and Hindley Earnshaw, and perplex myself to explain satisfactorily why their conduct was so opposite in similar circumstances. They had both been fond husbands, and were both attached to their children; and I could not see how they shouldn't both have taken the same road, for good or evil. But, I thought in my mind, Hindley, with apparently the stronger head, has shown himself sadly the worse and the weaker man. When his ship struck, the captain abandoned his post; and the crew, instead of trying to save her, rushed into riot and confusion, leaving no hope for their luckless vessel. Linton, on the contrary, displayed the true courage of a loyal and faithful soul. He trusted God, and God comforted him. One hoped, and the other despaired. They chose their own lots, and were righteously doomed to endure them. But you'll not want to hear my moralizing, Mr. Lockwood; you'll judge as well as I can all these things. At least, you'll think you will, and that's the same. The end of Earnshaw was what might have been expected: it followed fast on his sister's; there were scarcely six months between them. We at the Grange never got a very succinct account of his state preceding it; all that I did learn was on occasion of going to aid in the preparations for the funeral. Mr. Kenneth came to announce the event to my master.

"Well, Nelly," said he, riding into the yard one morn-

ing, too early not to alarm me with an instant presentiment of bad news, " it's yours and my turn to go into
mourning at present. Who's given us the slip now, do
you think ? "

" Who ? " I asked in a flurry.

" Why, guess," he returned, dismounting, and slinging
his bridle on a hook by the door. " And nip up the
corner of your apron. I'm certain you'll need it."

" Not Mr. Heathcliff, surely ? " I exclaimed.

" What ! would you have tears for him ? " said the
doctor. " No, Heathcliff's a tough young fellow ; he
looks blooming to-day. I've just seen him. He's rapidly
regaining flesh since he lost his better half."

" Who is it, then, Mr. Kenneth ? " I repeated impatiently.

" Hindley Earnshaw—your old friend Hindley," he
replied, " and my wicked gossip, though he's been too
wild for me this long while. There ! I said we should
draw water. But cheer up. He died true to his character—drunk as a lord. Poor lad ! I'm sorry, too. One
can't help missing an old companion, though he had the
worst tricks with him that ever man imagined, and has
done me many a rascally turn. He's barely twenty
seven, it seems ; that's your own age. Who would have
thought you were born in one year ? "

I confess this blow was greater to me than the shock
of Mrs. Linton's death. Ancient associations lingered
round my heart. I sat down in the porch and wept
as for a blood relation, desiring Mr. Kenneth to get
another servant to introduce him to the master.
could not hinder myself from pondering on the question
" Had he had fair play ? " Whatever I did, that idea
would bother me. It was so tiresomely pertinacious that
I resolved on requesting leave to go to Wuthering Heights
and assist in the last duties to the dead. Mr. Linton
was extremely reluctant to consent, but I pleaded
eloquently for the friendless condition in which he lay
and I said my old master and foster-brother had a
claim on my services as strong as his own. Besides,

reminded him that the child Hareton was his wife's nephew, and, in the absence of nearer kin, he ought to act as its guardian ; and he ought to and must inquire how the property was left, and look over the concerns of his brother-in-law. He was unfit for attending to such matters then, but he bade me speak to his lawyer, and at length permitted me to go. His lawyer had been Earnshaw's also. I called at the village, and asked him to accompany me. He shook his head, and advised that Heathcliff should be let alone, affirming, if the truth were known, Hareton would be found little else than a beggar.

"His father died in debt," he said ; "the whole property is mortgaged, and the sole chance for the natural heir is to allow him an opportunity of creating some interest in the creditor's heart, that he may be inclined to deal leniently towards him."

When I reached the Heights, I explained that I had come to see everything carried on decently ; and Joseph, who appeared in sufficient distress, expressed satisfaction at my presence. Mr. Heathcliff said he did not perceive that I was wanted ; but I might stay and order the arrangements for the funeral, if I chose.

"Correctly," he remarked, "that fool's body should be buried at the cross-roads, without ceremony of any kind. I happened to leave him ten minutes yesterday afternoon, and in that interval he fastened the two doors of the house against me, and he has spent the night in drinking himself to death deliberately ! We broke in this morning, for we heard him snorting like a horse ; and there he was, laid over the settle ; flaying and scalping would not have wakened him. I sent for Kenneth, and he came, but not till the beast had changed into carrion. He was both dead and cold and stark ; and so you'll allow it was useless making more stir about him."

The old servant confirmed this statement, but muttered,—

"I'd rayther he'd goan hisseln for t' doctor ! I sud ha' taen tent o' t' maister better nor him ; and he warn't deead when I left, naught o' t' soart !"

I insisted on the funeral being respectable. Mr. Heath-cliff said I might have my own way there too; only, he desired me to remember that the money for the whole affair came out of his pocket. He maintained a hard, careless deportment, indicative of neither joy nor sorrow; if anything, it expressed a flinty gratification at a piece of difficult work successfully executed. I observed once, indeed, something like exultation in his aspect; it was just when the people were bearing the coffin from the house. He had the hypocrisy to repre-sent a mourner; and previous to following with Hareton, he lifted the unfortunate child on to the table, and muttered, with peculiar gusto, " Now, my bonny lad, you are *mine !* And we'll see if one tree won't grow as crooked as another, with the same wind to twist it ! " The unsuspecting thing was pleased at this speech. He played with Heathcliff's whiskers, and stroked his cheek; but I divined its meaning, and observed tartly, " That boy must go back with me to Thrushcross Grange, sir. There is nothing in the world less yours than he is."

" Does Linton say so ? " he demanded.

" Of course ; he has ordered me to take him," I replied.

" Well," said the scoundrel, " we'll not argue the subject now ; but I have a fancy to try my hand at rearing a young one, so intimate to your master that I must supply the place of this with my own, if he attempt to remove it. I don't engage to let Hareton go un-disputed, but I'll be pretty sure to make the other come ! Remember to tell him."

This hint was enough to bind our hands. I repeated its substance on my return ; and Edgar Linton, little interested at the commencement, spoke no more of interfering. I'm not aware that he could have done it to any purpose, had he been ever so willing.

The guest was now the master of Wuthering Heights. He held firm possession, and proved to the attorney— who, in his turn, proved it to Mr. Linton—that Earnshaw had mortgaged every yard of land he owned for cash to supply his mania for gaming; and he, Heathcliff, was the mortgagee. In that manner Hareton, who should now be the first gentleman in the neighbourhood, was reduced to a state of complete dependence on his father's inveterate enemy, and lives in his own house as a servant, deprived of the advantage of wages, quite unable to right himself, because of his friendlessness and his ignorance that he has been wronged.

CHAPTER XVIII.

THE twelve years, continued Mrs. Dean, following that dismal period were the happiest of my life. My greatest troubles in their passage rose from our little lady's trifling illnesses, which she had to experience in common with all children, rich and poor. For the rest, after the first six months, she grew like a larch, and could walk and talk too, in her own way, before the heath blossomed a second time over Mrs. Linton's dust. She was the most winning thing that ever brought sunshine into a desolate house—a real beauty in face, with the Earnshaws' handsome dark eyes, but the Lintons' fair skin and small features and yellow curling hair. Her spirit was high, though not rough, and qualified by a heart sensitive and lively to excess in its affections. That capacity for intense attachments reminded me of her mother. Still she did not resemble her, for she could be soft and mild as a dove, and she had a gentle voice and pensive expression. Her anger was never furious, her love never fierce. It was deep and tender. However, it must be acknowledged, she had faults to foil her gifts. A propensity to be saucy was one; and a perverse will, that indulged children invariably acquire, whether they be good-tempered or cross. If a servant chanced to vex her, it was always, "I shall tell papa!" And if he reproved her, even by a look, you would have thought it a heart-breaking business. I don't believe he ever did speak a harsh word to her. He took her education entirely on himself, and made it an amusement. Fortunately, curiosity and a quick intellect made her an apt scholar. She learned rapidly and eagerly, and did honour to his teaching.

Till she reached the age of thirteen, she had not once been beyond the range of the park by herself. Mr. Linton would take her with him a mile or so outside, on rare occasions ; but he trusted her to no one else. Gimmerton was an unsubstantial name in her ears ; the chapel the only building she had approached or entered, except her own home. Wuthering Heights and Mr. Heathcliff did not exist for her. She was a perfect recluse, and, apparently, perfectly contented. Sometimes, indeed, while surveying the country from her nursery window, she would observe,—

"Ellen, how long will it be before I can walk to the top of those hills ? I wonder what lies on the other side. Is it the sea ? "

" No, Miss Cathy," I would answer ; " it is hills again, just like these."

" And what are those golden rocks like when you stand under them ? " she once asked.

The abrupt descent of Peniston Crags particularly attracted her notice, especially when the setting sun shone on it and the topmost heights, and the whole extent of landscape besides lay in shadow. I explained that they were bare masses of stone, with hardly enough earth in their clefts to nourish a stunted tree.

" And why are they bright so long after it is evening here ? " she pursued.

" Because they are a great deal higher up than we are," replied I ; " you could not climb them—they are too high and steep. In winter the frost is always there before it comes to us ; and deep into summer I have found snow under that black hollow on the north-east side."

" Oh, you have been on them ! " she cried gleefully. " Then I can go, too, when I am a woman. Has papa been, Ellen ? "

"Papa would tell you, miss," I answered hastily, "that they are not worth the trouble of visiting. The moors, where you ramble with him, are much nicer; and Thrushcross Park is the finest place in the world."

"But I know the park, and I don't know those," she murmured to herself. "And I should delight to look round me from the brow of that tallest point. My little pony Minny shall take me some time."

One of the maids mentioning the Fairy Cave quite turned her head with a desire to fulfil this project. She teased Mr. Linton about it, and he promised she should have the journey when she got older. But Miss Catherine measured her age by months, and, "Now, am I old enough to go to Peniston Crags?" was the constant question in her mouth. The road thither wound close by Wuthering Heights. Edgar had not the heart to pass it, so she received as constantly the answer, "Not yet, love; not yet."

I said Mrs. Heathcliff lived above a dozen years after quitting her husband. Her family were of a delicate constitution. She and Edgar both lacked the ruddy health that you will generally meet in these parts. What her last illness was I am not certain. I conjecture they died of the same thing—a kind of fever, slow at its commencement, but incurable, and rapidly consuming life towards the close. She wrote to inform her brother of the probable conclusion of a four months' indisposition under which she had suffered, and entreated him to come to her, if possible, for she had much to settle, and she wished to bid him adieu, and deliver Linton safely into his hands. Her hope was, that Linton might be left with him, as he had been with her. His father, she would fain convince herself, had no desire to assume the burden of his maintenance or education. My master hesitated not a moment in complying with her request. Reluctant as he was to leave home at ordinary calls, he flew to answer this, commending Catherine to my peculiar vigilance, in his absence, with reiterated orders that she

must not wander out of the park, even under my escort.
He did not calculate on her going unaccompanied.

He was away three weeks. The first day or two my
charge sat in a corner of the library, too sad for either
reading or playing. In that quiet state she caused me
little trouble; but it was succeeded by an interval of
impatient fretful weariness; and being too busy and
too old then to run up and down amusing her, I hit on
a method by which she might entertain herself. I used
to send her on her travels round the grounds, now on
foot and now on a pony, indulging her with a patient
audience of all her real and imaginary adventures, when
she returned.

The summer shone in full prime, and she took such a
taste for this solitary rambling that she often contrived
to remain out from breakfast till tea; and then the
evenings were spent in recounting her fanciful tales.
did not fear her breaking bounds, because the gates were
generally locked, and I thought she would scarcely
venture forth alone, if they had stood wide open. Unluckily, my confidence proved misplaced. Catherine came
to me one morning at eight o'clock, and said she was
that day an Arabian merchant, going to cross the desert
with his caravan, and I must give her plenty of pro-
vision for herself and beasts—a horse and three camels,
personated by a large hound and a couple of pointers.
I got together good store of dainties, and slung them in
a basket on one side of the saddle; and she sprang up
as gay as a fairy, sheltered by her wide-brimmed hat
and gauze veil from the July sun, and trotted off with
a merry laugh, mocking my cautious counsel to avoid
galloping and come back early. The naughty thing
never made her appearance at tea. One traveller, the
hound, being an old dog and fond of its ease, returned
but neither Cathy, nor the pony, nor the two pointers
were visible in any direction. I dispatched emissaries
down this path and that path, and at last went wandering in search of her myself. There was a labourer
working at a fence round a plantation, on the border

of the grounds. I inquired of him if he had seen our young lady.

"I saw her at morn," he replied. "She would have me to cut her a hazel switch, and then she leapt her Galloway over the hedge yonder, where it is lowest, and galloped out of sight."

You may guess how I felt at hearing this news. It struck me directly she must have started for Peniston Crags. "What will become of her?" I ejaculated, pushing through a gap which the man was repairing, and making straight to the highroad. I walked as if for a wager, mile after mile, till a turn brought me in view of the Heights; but no Catherine could I detect far or near. The Crags lie about a mile and a half beyond Mr. Heathcliff's place, and that is four from the Grange, so I began to fear night would fall ere I could reach them. "And what if she should have slipped in clambering among them," I reflected, "and been killed or broken some of her bones?" My suspense was truly painful; and at first it gave me delightful relief to observe, in hurrying by the farmhouse, Charlie, the fiercest of the pointers, lying under a window, with swelled head and bleeding ear. I opened the wicket and ran to the door, knocking vehemently for admittance. A woman whom I knew, and who formerly lived at Gimmerton, answered. She had been servant there since the death of Mr. Earnshaw.

"Ah," said she, "you are come a-seeking your little mistress! Don't be frightened. She's here safe; but I'm glad it isn't the master."

"He is not at home, then, is he?" I panted, quite breathless with quick walking and alarm.

"No, no," she replied; "both he and Joseph are off, and I think they won't return this hour or more. Step in and rest you a bit."

I entered, and beheld my stray lamb seated on the hearth, rocking herself in a little chair that had been her mother's when a child. Her hat was hung against the wall, and she seemed perfectly at home, laughing and chattering, in the best spirits imaginable, to Hareton—now a great, strong lad of eighteen—who stared at her with considerable curiosity and astonishment, comprehending precious little of the fluent succession of remarks and questions which her tongue never ceased pouring forth.

"Very well, miss!" I exclaimed, concealing my joy under an angry countenance. "This is your last ride till papa comes back. I'll not trust you over the threshold again, you naughty, naughty girl!"

"Aha, Ellen!" she cried gaily, jumping up and running to my side. "I shall have a pretty story to tell to-night And so you've found me out. Have you ever been here in your life before?"

"Put that hat on, and home at once," said I. "I'm dreadfully grieved at you, Miss Cathy; you've done extremely wrong. It's no use pouting and crying; that won't repay the trouble I've had, scouring the country after you. To think how Mr. Linton charged me to keep you in; and you stealing off so! It shows you are a cunning little fox, and nobody will put faith in you any more."

"What have I done?" sobbed she, instantly checked "Papa charged me nothing. He'll not scold me, Ellen he's never cross like you."

"Come, come!" I repeated. "I'll tie the ribbon Now, let us have no petulance. Oh, for shame! You thirteen years old, and such a baby!"

This exclamation was caused by her pushing the hat from her head, and retreating to the chimney out of my reach.

"Nay," said the servant; "don't be hard on the bonny lass, Mrs. Dean. We made her stop. She'd fain have ridden forwards, afeard you should be uneasy Hareton offered to go with her, and I thought he should It's a wild road over the hills."

Hareton, during the discussion, stood with his hands in his pockets, too awkward to speak, though he looked as if he did not relish my intrusion.

"How long am I to wait?" I continued, disregarding

the woman's interference. "It will be dark in ten minutes.—Where is the pony, Miss Cathy? And where is Phœnix? I shall leave you, unless you be quick; so please yourself."

"The pony is in the yard," she replied, "and Phœnix is shut in there. He's bitten, and so is Charlie. I was going to tell you all about it; but you are in a bad temper, and don't deserve to hear."

I picked up her hat, and approached to reinstate it; but perceiving that the people of the house took her part, she commenced capering round the room; and on my giving chase, ran like a mouse over and under and behind the furniture, rendering it ridiculous for me to pursue. Hareton and the woman laughed, and she joined them, and waxed more impertinent still, till I cried, in great irritation,—

"Well, Miss Cathy, if you were aware whose house this is, you'd be glad enough to get out."

"It's *your* father's, isn't it?" said she, turning to Hareton.

"Nay," he replied, looking down, and blushing bashfully.

He could not stand a steady gaze from her eyes, though they were just his own.

"Whose, then—your master's?" she asked.

He coloured deeper, with a different feeling, muttered an oath, and turned away.

"Who is his master?" continued the tiresome girl, appealing to me. "He talked about 'our house,' and 'our folk.' I thought he had been the owner's son. And he never said miss. He should have done, shouldn't he, if he's a servant?"

Hareton grew black as a thunder-cloud at this childish speech. I silently shook my questioner, and at last succeeded in equipping her for departure.

"Now, get my horse," she said, addressing her unknown kinsman as she would one of the stable-boys at the Grange. "And you may come with me. I want to see where the goblin-hunter rises in the marsh, and to hear about the *fairishes*, as you call them. But make haste! What's the matter? Get my horse, I say."

"I'll see thee damned before I be *thy* servant!" growled the lad.

"You'll see me *what?*" asked Catherine in surprise.

"Damned, thou saucy witch!" he replied.

"There, Miss Cathy, you see you have got into pretty company," I interposed. "Nice words to be used to a young lady! Pray don't begin to dispute with him. Come, let us seek for Minny ourselves, and begone."

"But, Ellen," cried she, staring, fixed in astonishment, "how dare he speak so to me? Mustn't he be made to do as I ask him?—You wicked creature, I shall tell papa what you said. Now, then!"

Hareton did not appear to feel this threat, so the tears sprang into her eyes with indignation. "You bring the pony," she exclaimed, turning to the woman, "and let my dog free this moment!"

"Softly, miss," answered she addressed; "you'll lose nothing by being civil. Though Mr. Hareton there be not the master's son, he's your cousin; and I was never hired to serve you."

"*He* my cousin!" cried Cathy, with a scornful laugh.

"Yes, indeed," responded her reprover.

"O Ellen! don't let them say such things," she pursued, in great trouble. "Papa is gone to fetch my cousin from London. My cousin is a gentleman's son. That my——" She stopped, and wept outright, upset at the bare notion of relationship with such a clown.

"Hush, hush!" I whispered; "people can have many cousins, and of all sorts, Miss Cathy, without being any the worse for it; only they needn't keep their company if they be disagreeable and bad."

"He's not—he's not my cousin, Ellen!" she went on, gathering fresh grief from reflection, and flinging herself into my arms for refuge from the idea.

I was much vexed at her and the servant for their mutual revelations, having no doubt of Linton's approaching arrival, communicated by the former, being reported to Mr. Heathcliff, and feeling as confident that Catherine's first thought on her father's return would be to seek an explanation of the latter's assertion concerning her rude-bred kindred. Hareton, recovering from his disgust at being taken for a servant, seemed moved by her distress; and having fetched the pony round to the door, he took, to propitiate her, a fine crooked-legged terrier-whelp from the kennel, and putting it into her hand bade her whist, for he meant nought. Pausing in her lamentations, she surveyed him with a glance of awe and horror, then burst forth anew.

I could scarcely refrain from smiling at this antipathy to the poor fellow, who was a well-made, athletic youth, good-looking in features, and stout and healthy, but attired in garments befitting his daily occupations of working on the farm and lounging among the moors after rabbits and game. Still, I thought I could detect in his physiognomy a mind owning better qualities than his father ever possessed—good things lost amid a wilderness of weeds, to be sure, whose rankness far over-topped their neglected growth; yet, notwithstanding, evidence of a wealthy soil, that might yield luxuriant crops under other and favourable circumstances. Mr. Heathcliff, I believe, had not treated him physically ill —thanks to his fearless nature, which offered no temptation to that course of oppression. He had none of the timid susceptibility that would have given zest to ill-treatment, in Heathcliff's judgment. He appeared to have bent his malevolence on making him a brute. He was never taught to read or write, never rebuked for any bad habit which did not annoy his keeper, never led a single step towards virtue or guarded by a single precept against vice. And from what I heard, Joseph contributed much to his deterioration by a narrow-minded partiality which prompted him to flatter and pet him, as a boy, because he was the head of the old family. And as he had been in the habit of accusing Catherine Earnshaw and Heathcliff, when children, of putting the master past his patience, and compelling him

to seek solace in drink by what he termed their "offald
ways," so at present he laid the whole burden of Hareton's
faults on the shoulders of the usurper of his property
If the lad swore, he wouldn't correct him, nor however
culpably he behaved. It gave Joseph satisfaction
apparently, to watch him go the worst lengths. He
allowed that the lad was ruined, that his soul was abandoned to perdition; but then he reflected that Heathcliff
must answer for it. Hareton's blood would be required
at his hands; and there lay immense consolation in that
thought. Joseph had instilled into him a pride of name
and of his lineage. He would, had he dared, have fostered
hate between him and the present owner of the Heights
but his dread of that owner amounted to superstition
and he confined his feelings regarding him to muttered
innuendoes and private comminations. I don't pretend
to be intimately acquainted with the mode of living
customary in those days at Wuthering Heights. I only
speak from hearsay, for I saw little. The villagers
affirmed Mr. Heathcliff was *near*, and a cruel hard
landlord to his tenants; but the house inside had regained its ancient aspect of comfort under female manage-
ment, and the scenes of riot common in Hindley's time
were not now enacted within its walls. The master was
too gloomy to seek companionship with any people, good
or bad; and he is yet.

This, however, is not making progress with my story
Miss Cathy rejected the peace-offering of the terrier,
and demanded her own dogs, Charlie and Phœnix.
They came limping, and hanging their heads; and we
set out for home, sadly out of sorts, every one of us.
I could not wring from my little lady how she had spent
the day, except that, as I supposed, the goal of her
pilgrimage was Peniston Crags; and she arrived without
adventure to the gate of the farmhouse, when Hareton
happened to issue forth, attended by some canine followers, who attacked her train. They had a smart
battle before their owners could separate them; that
formed an introduction. Catherine told Hareton who

she was, and where she was going, and asked him to show her the way, finally beguiling him to accompany her. He opened the mysteries of the Fairy Cave and twenty other queer places. But, being in disgrace, I was not favoured with a description of the interesting objects she saw. I could gather, however, that her guide had been a favourite till she hurt his feelings by addressing him as a servant, and Heathcliff's house-keeper hurt hers by calling him her cousin. Then the language he had held to her rankled in her heart; she who was always "love," and "darling," and "queen," and "angel," with everybody at the Grange, to be insulted so shockingly by a stranger! She did not comprehend it; and hard work I had to obtain a promise that she would not lay the grievance before her father. I explained how he objected to the whole household at the Heights, and how sorry he would be to find she had been there; but I insisted most on the fact that if she revealed my negligence of his orders, he would perhaps be so angry that I should have to leave; and Cathy couldn't bear that prospect. She pledged her word, and kept it, for my sake. After all, she was a sweet little girl.

CHAPTER XIX.

A LETTER, edged with black, announced the day of my master's return. Isabella was dead; and he wrote to bid me get mourning for his daughter, and arrange a room, and other accommodations, for his youthful nephew. Catherine ran wild with joy at the idea of welcoming her father back, and indulged most sanguine anticipations of the innumerable excellences of her "real" cousin. The evening of their expected arrival came. Since early morning she had been busy ordering her own small affairs; and now, attired in her new black frock—poor thing! her aunt's death impressed her with no definite sorrow—she obliged me, by constant worrying, to walk with her down through the grounds to meet them.

"Linton is just six months younger than I am," she chattered, as we strolled leisurely over the swells and hollows of mossy turf, under shadow of the trees. "How delightful it will be to have him for a playfellow! Aunt Isabella sent papa a beautiful lock of his hair. It was lighter than mine—more flaxen, and quite as fine. I have it carefully preserved in a little glass box; and I've often thought what pleasure it would be to see its owner. Oh! I am happy—and papa, dear, dear papa! Come, Ellen, let us run! Come, run!"

She ran, and returned and ran again, many times before my sober footsteps reached the gate; and then she seated herself on the grassy bank beside the path, and tried to wait patiently; but that was impossible. She couldn't be still a minute.

"How long they are!" she exclaimed. "Ah, I see some dust on the road; they are coming? No! When will they be here? May we not go a little way—half a mile, Ellen—only just half a mile? Do say yes—to that clump of birches at the turn!"

I refused stanchly. At length her suspense was ended; the travelling carriage rolled in sight. Miss Cathy shrieked and stretched out her arms, as soon as she caught her father's face looking from the window. He descended, nearly as eager as herself; and a considerable interval elapsed ere they had a thought to spare for any but themselves. While they exchanged caresses, I took a peep in to see after Linton. He was asleep in a corner, wrapped in a warm, fur-lined cloak, as if it had been winter—a pale, delicate, effeminate boy, who might have been taken for my master's younger brother, so strong was the resemblance; but there was a sickly peevishness in his aspect that Edgar Linton never had. The latter saw me looking; and having shaken hands, advised me to close the door and leave him undisturbed, for the journey had fatigued him. Cathy would fain have taken one glance, but her father told her to come, and they walked together up the park, while I hastened before to prepare the servants.

"Now, darling," said Mr. Linton, addressing his daughter, as they halted at the bottom of the front steps, "your cousin is not so strong or so merry as you are, and he has lost his mother, remember, a very short time since ; therefore, don't expect him to play and run about with you directly. And don't harass him much by talking. Let him be quiet this evening, at least, will you ?"

"Yes, yes, papa," answered Catherine ; "but I do want to see him, and he hasn't once looked out."

The carriage stopped, and the sleeper being roused was lifted to the ground by his uncle.

"This is your cousin Cathy, Linton," he said, putting their little hands together. "She's fond of you already ; and mind you don't grieve her by crying to-night. Try to be cheerful now ; the travelling is at an end, and you have nothing to do but rest and amuse yourself as you please."

"Let me go to bed, then," answered the boy, shrinking from Catherine's salute ; and he put up his fingers to remove incipient tears.

"Come, come, there's a good child," I whispered, leading him in. "You'll make her weep too. See how sorry she is for you !"

I do not know whether it was sorrow for him, but his cousin put on as sad a countenance as himself, and returned to her father. All three entered, and mounted to the library, where tea was laid ready. I proceeded to remove Linton's cap and mantle, and placed him on a chair by the table ; but he was no sooner seated than he began to cry afresh. My master inquired what was the matter.

"I can't sit on a chair," sobbed the boy.

"Go to the sofa, then, and Ellen shall bring you some tea," answered his uncle patiently.

He had been greatly tried during the journey, I felt convinced, by his fretful ailing charge. Linton slowly trailed himself off, and lay down. Cathy carried a foot-stool and her cup to his side. At first she sat silent ; but that could not last. She had resolved to make a pet of her little cousin, as she would have him to be ; and she commenced stroking his curls, and kissing his cheek, and offering him tea in her saucer, like a baby. This pleased him, for he was not much better. He dried his eyes, and lightened into a faint smile.

"Oh, he'll do very well," said the master to me, after watching them a minute—"very well, if we can keep him, Ellen. The company of a child of his own age will instil new spirit into him soon, and by wishing for strength he'll gain it."

"Ay, if we can keep him ! " I mused to myself, and sore misgivings came over me that there was slight hope of that. And then, I thought, however will that weakling live at Wuthering Heights ? Between his father and Hareton, what playmates and instructors they'll be ! Our doubts were presently decided—even earlier than I expected. I had just taken the children upstairs, after tea was finished, and seen Linton asleep—he would not suffer me to leave him till that was the case ; I had come down, and was standing by the table in the hall, lighting a bedroom candle for Mr. Edgar, when a maid stepped out of the kitchen and informed me that Mr. Heathcliff's servant Joseph was at the door, and wished to speak with the master.

"I shall ask him what he wants first," I said, in considerable trepidation. "A very unlikely hour to be troubling people, and the instant they have returned from a long journey. I don't think the master can see him."

Joseph had advanced through the kitchen as I uttered these words, and now presented himself in the hall. He was donned in his Sunday garments, with his most sancti-monious and sourest face ; and, holding his hat in one hand and his stick in the other, he proceeded to clean his shoes on the mat.

"Good-evening, Joseph," I said coldly. "What business brings you here to-night ? "

"It's Maister Linton I mun spake to," he answered, waving me disdainfully aside.

"Mr. Linton is going to bed; unless you have something particular to say, I'm sure he won't hear it now," I continued. "You had better sit down in there, and entrust your message to me."

"Which is his rahm?" pursued the fellow, surveying the range of closed doors.

I perceived he was bent on refusing my mediation, so very reluctantly I went up to the library, and announced the unseasonable visitor, advising that he should be dismissed till next day. Mr. Linton had no time to empower me to do so, for Joseph mounted close at my heels, and pushing into the apartment, planted himself at the far side of the table, with his two fists clapped on the head of his stick, and began in an elevated tone, as if anticipating opposition,—

"Hatheliff has sent me for his lad, and I munn't goa back 'bout him."

Edgar Linton was silent a minute; an expression of exceeding sorrow overcast his features. He would have pitied the child on his own account; but recalling Isabella's hopes and fears, and anxious wishes for her son, and her commendations of him to his care, he grieved bitterly at the prospect of yielding him up, and searched in his heart how it might be avoided. No plan offered itself. The very exhibition of any desire to keep him would have rendered the claimant more peremptory. There was nothing left but to resign him. However, he was not going to rouse him from his sleep.

"Tell Mr. Heathcliff," he answered calmly, "that his son shall come to Wuthering Heights to-morrow. He is in bed, and too tired to go the distance now. You may also tell him that the mother of Linton desired him to remain under my guardianship; and at present his health is very precarious."

"Noa!" said Joseph, giving a thud with his prop on the floor, and assuming an authoritative air; "noa! that means naught. Hatheliff maks noa 'count o' t' mother, nor ye norther, but he'll hev his lad, und I mun tak him; soa now ye knaw!"

"You shall not to-night!" answered Linton decisively.
"Walk downstairs at once, and repeat to your master
what I have said.—Ellen, show him down.—Go!"

And aiding the indignant elder with a lift by the arm,
he rid the room of him, and closed the door.

"Varrah weell!" shouted Joseph, as he slowly drew
off.   "To-morn, he's come hisseln; and thrust *him* out,
if ye darr!"

CHAPTER XX.

To obviate the danger of this threat being fulfilled, Mr.
Linton commissioned me to take the boy home early, on
Catherine's pony; and said he,—

"As we shall now have no influence over his destiny,
good or bad, you must say nothing of where he is gone
to my daughter.   She cannot associate with him hereafter, and it is better for her to remain in ignorance of
his proximity, lest she should be restless and anxious
to visit the Heights.   Merely tell her his father sent for
him suddenly, and he has been obliged to leave us."

Linton was very reluctant to be roused from his bed
at five o'clock, and astonished to be informed that he
must prepare for further travelling; but I softened off
the matter by stating that he was going to spend some
time with his father, Mr. Heathcliff, who wished to see
him so much, he did not like to defer the pleasure till
he should recover from his late journey.

"My father!" he cried, in strange perplexity.   "Mamma
never told me I had a father.   Where does he live?   I'd
rather stay with uncle."

"He lives a little distance from the Grange," I replied,
"just beyond those hills—not so far, but you may walk
over here when you get hearty.   And you should be
glad to go home, and to see him.   You must try to love
him, as you did your mother, and then he will love you."

"But why have I not heard of him before?" asked
Linton.   "Why didn't mamma and he live together,
as other people do?"

"He had business to keep him in the north," I answered, "and your mother's health required her to reside in the south."

"And why didn't mamma speak to me about him?" persevered the child. "She often talked of uncle, and I learned to love him long ago. How am I to love papa? I don't know him."

"Oh, all children love their parents," I said. "Your mother, perhaps, thought you would want to be with him if she mentioned him often to you. Let us make haste. An early ride on such a beautiful morning is much preferable to an hour's more sleep."

"Is *she* to go with us," he demanded—"the little girl I saw yesterday?"

"Not now," replied I.

"Is uncle?" he continued.

"No; I shall be your companion there," I said.

Linton sank back on his pillow and fell into a brown study.

"I won't go without uncle," he cried at length. "I can't tell where you mean to take me."

I attempted to persuade him of the naughtiness of showing reluctance to meet his father. Still he obstinately resisted any progress towards dressing, and I had to call for my master's assistance in coaxing him out of bed. The poor thing was finally got off, with several delusive assurances that his absence should be short, that Mr. Edgar and Cathy would visit him, and other promises, equally ill-founded, which I invented and reiterated at intervals throughout the way. The pure heather-scented air, the bright sunshine, and the gentle canter of Minny relieved his despondency after a while. He began to put questions concerning his new home and its inhabitants with greater interest and liveliness.

"Is Wuthering Heights as pleasant a place as Thrushcross Grange?" he inquired, turning to take a last glance into the valley, whence a light mist mounted and formed a fleecy cloud on the skirts of the blue.

"It is not so buried in trees," I replied, "and it is not

quite so large, but you can see the country beautifully all round, and the air is healthier for you—fresher and dryer. You will perhaps think the building old and dark at first, though it is a respectable house—the next best in the neighbourhood. And you will have such nice rambles on the moors. Hareton Earnshaw—that is Miss Cathy's other cousin, and so yours in a manner—will show you all the sweetest spots; and you can bring a book in fine weather, and make a green hollow your study; and now and then your uncle may join you in a walk. He does frequently walk out on the hills."

"And what is my father like?" he asked. "Is he as young and handsome as uncle?"

"He's as young," said I; "but he has black hair and eyes, and looks sterner, and he is taller and bigger altogether. He'll not seem to you so gentle and kind at first, perhaps, because it is not his way; still, mind you be frank and cordial with him; and naturally he'll be fonder of you than any uncle, for you are his own."

"Black hair and eyes!" mused Linton. "I can't fancy him. Then I am not like him, am I?"

"Not much," I answered; not a morsel, I thought, surveying with regret the white complexion and slim frame of my companion, and his large languid eyes—his mother's eyes, save that, unless a morbid touchiness kindled them a moment, they had not a vestige of her sparkling spirit.

"How strange that he should never come to see mamma and me!" he murmured. "Has he ever seen me? If he has, I must have been a baby. I remember not a single thing about him."

"Why, Master Linton," said I, "three hundred miles is a great distance; and ten years seem very different in length to a grown-up person compared with what they do to you. It is probable Mr. Heathcliff proposed going from summer to summer, but never found a convenient opportunity; and now it is too late. Don't trouble him with questions on the subject; it will disturb him for no good."

The boy was fully occupied with his own cogitations for the remainder of the ride, till we halted before the farmhouse garden gate. I watched to catch his impressions in his countenance. He surveyed the carved front and low-browed lattices, the straggling gooseberry bushes and crooked firs, with solemn intentness, and then shook his head. His private feelings entirely disapproved of the exterior of his new abode. But he had sense to postpone complaining. There might be compensation within. Before he dismounted I went and opened the door. It was half-past six; the family had just finished breakfast; the servant was clearing and wiping down the table. Joseph stood by his master's chair, telling some tale concerning a lame horse, and Hareton was preparing for the hay-field.

"Hullo, Nelly!" said Mr. Heathcliff when he saw me. "I feared I should have to come down and fetch my property myself. You've brought it, have you? Let us see what we can make of it."

He got up and strode to the door. Hareton and Joseph followed in gaping curiosity. Poor Linton ran a frightened eye over the faces of the three.

"Sure-ly," said Joseph, after a grave inspection, "he's swopped wi' ye, maister, an' yon's his lass!"

Heathcliff, having stared his son into an ague of confusion, uttered a scornful laugh.

"God! what a beauty! what a lovely, charming thing!" he exclaimed. "Haven't they reared it on snails and sour milk, Nelly? Oh, damn my soul! but that's worse than I expected, and the devil knows I was not sanguine!"

I bade the trembling and bewildered child get down and enter. He did not thoroughly comprehend the meaning of his father's speech, or whether it were intended for him; indeed, he was not yet certain that the grim, sneering stranger was his father. But he clung to me with growing trepidation; and on Mr. Heathcliff's taking a seat and bidding him "come hither," he hid his face on my shoulder and wept.

"Tut, tut!" said Heathcliff, stretching out a hand and dragging him roughly between his knees, and then holding up his head by the chin. "None of that nonsense! We're not going to hurt thee, Linton. Isn't that thy name? Thou art thy mother's child entirely! Where is *my* share in thee, puling chicken?"

He took off the boy's cap and pushed back his thick flaxen curls, felt his slender arms and his small fingers, during which examination Linton ceased crying, and lifted his great blue eyes to inspect the inspector.

"Do you know me?" asked Heathcliff, having satisfied himself that the limbs were all equally frail and feeble.

"No," said Linton, with a gaze of vacant fear.

"You've heard of me, I dare say?"

"No," he replied again.

"No! What a shame of your mother, never to waken your filial regard for me! You are my son, then, I'll tell you; and your mother was a wicked slut to leave you in ignorance of the sort of father you possessed. Now, don't wince and colour up. Though it *is* something to see you have not white blood. Be a good lad, and I'll do for you.—Nelly, if you be tired, you may sit down; if not, get home again. I guess you'll report what you hear and see to the cipher at the Grange; and this thing won't be settled while you linger about it."

"Well," replied I, "I hope you'll be kind to the boy, Mr. Heathcliff, or you'll not keep him long; and he's all you have akin in the wide world that you will ever know, remember."

"I'll be *very* kind to him, you needn't fear," he said, laughing. "Only nobody else must be kind to him. I'm jealous of monopolizing his affection. And to begin my kindness, Joseph, bring the lad some breakfast.—Hareton, you infernal calf, begone to your work.—Yes, Nell," he added, when they had departed, "my son is prospective owner of your place, and I should not wish him to die till I was certain of being his successor. Besides, he's *mine*, and I want the triumph of seeing *my* descendant fairly lord of their estates—my child hiring their children to till their father's lands for wages. That is the sole consideration which can make me endure the whelp. I despise him for himself, and hate him for the memories he revives. But that consideration is sufficient. He's safe with me, and shall be tended as carefully as your master tends his own. I have a room upstairs furnished for him in handsome style. I've engaged a tutor also to come three times a week, from twenty miles distance, to teach him what he pleases to learn. I've ordered Hareton to obey him; and, in fact, I've arranged everything with a view to preserve the superior and the gentleman in him, above his associates. I do regret, however, that he so little deserves the trouble. If I wished any blessing in the world, it was to find him a worthy object of pride; and I'm bitterly disappointed with the whey-faced whining wretch!"

While he was speaking, Joseph returned bearing a basin of milk-porridge, and placed it before Linton, who stirred round the homely mess with a look of aversion, and affirmed he could not eat it. I saw the old man-servant shared largely in his master's scorn of the child, though he was compelled to retain the sentiment in his heart, because Heathcliff plainly meant his underlings to hold him in honour.

"Cannot ate it?" repeated he, peering in Linton's face, and subduing his voice to a whisper, for fear of being overheard. "But Maister Hareton nivir ate naught else, when he wer a little un; and what wer gooid eneugh for him's gooid eneugh for ye, I's rayther think."

"I *shan't* eat it!" answered Linton snappishly. "Take it away."

Joseph snatched up the food indignantly, and brought it to us.

"Is there aught ails th' victuals?" he asked, thrusting the tray under Heathcliff's nose.

"What should ail them?" he said.

"Wah!" answered Joseph, "yon dainty chap says he cannut ate 'em. But I guess it's raight. His mother

wer just soa : we wer a'most too mucky to sow t' cor
for makking her breead."

"Don't mention his mother to me," said the maste
angrily. "Get him something that he can eat, that's
all.—What is his usual food, Nelly ?"

I suggested boiled milk or tea ; and the housekeepe
received instructions to prepare some. Come, I reflected
his father's selfishness may contribute to his comfort
He perceives his delicate constitution, and the necessity
of treating him tolerably. I'll console Mr. Edgar by
acquainting him with the turn Heathcliff's humour has
taken. Having no excuse for lingering longer, I slipped
out, while Linton was engaged in timidly rebuffing the
advances of a friendly sheep-dog. But he was too much
on the alert to be cheated. As I closed the door, I
heard a cry, and a frantic repetition of the words,—

"Don't leave me ! I'll not stay here ! I'll not stay
here ! "

Then the latch was raised and fell. They did not
suffer him to come forth. I mounted Minny, and urged
her to a trot ; and so my brief guardianship ended.

CHAPTER XXI.

WE had sad work with little Cathy that day. She rose
in high glee, eager to join her cousin, and such passionate
tears and lamentations followed the news of his departure
that Edgar himself was obliged to soothe her by affirming he should come back soon. He added, however,
"if I can get him," and there were no hopes of that.
This promise poorly pacified her ; but time was more
potent ; and though still at intervals she inquired of
her father when Linton would return, before she did see
him again his features had waxed so dim in her memory
that she did not recognize him.

When I chanced to encounter the housekeeper of Wuthering Heights, in paying business visits to Gimmerton,
I used to ask how the young master got on, for he lived

almost as secluded as Catherine herself, and was never to be seen. I could gather from her that he continued in weak health, and was a tiresome inmate. She said Mr. Heathcliff seemed to dislike him ever longer and worse, though he took some trouble to conceal it. He had an antipathy to the sound of his voice, and could not do at all with his sitting in the same room with him many minutes together. There seldom passed much talk between them. Linton learned his lessons and spent his evenings in a small apartment they called the parlour, or else lay in bed all day, for he was constantly getting coughs, and colds, and aches, and pains of some sort.

"And I never knew such a faint-hearted creature," added the woman, "nor one so careful of hisseln. He *will* go on if I leave the window open a bit late in the evening. Oh, it's killing, a breath of night air! And he must have a fire in the middle of summer; and Joseph's bacca pipe is poison; and he must always have sweets and dainties, and always miik, milk for ever, heeding naught how the rest of us are pinched in winter; and there he'll sit, wrapped in his furred cloak in his chair by the fire, with some toast and water or other slop on the hob to sip at; and if Hareton, for pity, comes to amuse him—Hareton is not bad-natured, though he's rough—they're sure to part, one swearing and the other crying. I believe the master would relish Earnshaw's thrashing him to a mummy, if he were not his son; and I'm certain he would be fit to turn him out of doors if he knew half the nursing he gives hisseln. But then he won't go into danger of temptation. He never enters the parlour, and should Linton show those ways in the house where he is, he sends him upstairs directly."

I divined from this account that utter lack of sympathy had rendered young Heathcliff selfish and disagreeable, if he were not so originally; and my interest in him consequently decayed, though still I was moved with a sense of grief at his lot, and a wish that he had been left with us. Mr. Edgar encouraged me to gain information. He thought a great deal about him, I

fancy, and would have run some risk to see him ; and
he told me once to ask the housekeeper whether he ever
came into the village. She said he had only been twice
on horseback, accompanying his father, and both times
he pretended to be quite knocked up for three or four
days afterwards. That housekeeper left, if I recollect
rightly, two years after he came, and another, whom I
did not know, was her successor. She lives there still.

Time wore on at the Grange in its former pleasant way
till Miss Cathy reached sixteen. On the anniversary of
her birth we never manifested any signs of rejoicing,
because it was also the anniversary of my late mistress'
death. Her father invariably spent that day alone in the
library, and walked at dusk as far as Gimmerton kirkyard, where he would frequently prolong his stay beyond
midnight. Therefore Catherine was thrown on her own
resources for amusement. This 20th of March was a
beautiful spring day, and when her father had retired
my young lady came down dressed for going out, and
said she asked to have a ramble on the edge of the moor
with me. Mr. Linton had given her leave, if we went
only a short distance and were back within the hour.

" So make haste, Ellen ! " she cried. " I know where
I wish to go—where a colony of moor game are settled :
I want to see whether they have made their nest
yet."

" That must be a good distance up," I answered ;
" They don't breed on the edge of the moor."

" No, it's not," she said. " I've gone very near with
papa."

I put on my bonnet and sallied out, thinking nothing
more of the matter. She bounded before me, and returned to my side, and was off again like a young grey-
hound ; and at first I found plenty of entertainment in
listening to the larks singing far and near, and enjoying
the sweet, warm sunshine, and watching her, my pet
and my delight, with her golden ringlets flying loose
behind, and her bright cheek, as soft and pure in its
bloom as a wild rose, and her eyes radiant with cloud-

ess pleasure. She was a happy creature, and an angel, n those days. It's a pity she could not be content.

"Well," said I, "where are your moor-game, Miss Cathy? We should be at them. The Grange park fence s a great way off now."

"Oh, a little farther—only a little farther, Ellen," was er answer continually. "Climb to that hillock, pass hat bank, and by the time you reach the other side I hall have raised the birds."

But there were so many hillocks and banks to climb nd pass that at length I began to be weary, and told er we must halt and retrace our steps. I shouted to er, as she had outstripped me a long way. She either lid not hear or did not regard, for she still sprang on, nd I was compelled to follow. Finally she dived into hollow, and before I came in sight of her again she was wo miles nearer Wuthering Heights than her own home ; nd I beheld a couple of persons arrest her, one of whom felt convinced was Mr. Heathcliff himself.

Cathy had been caught in the fact of plundering, or at east hunting out the nests of the grouse. The Heights vere Heathcliff's land, and he was reproving the poacher.

"I've neither taken any nor found any," she said, as toiled to them, expanding her hands in corroboration f the statement. "I didn't mean to take them ; but apa told me there were quantities up here, and I wished o see the eggs."

Heathcliff glanced at me with an all-meaning smile, xpressing his acquaintance with the party, and, conse-uently, his malevolence towards it, and demanded who papa" was.

"Mr. Linton of Thrushcross Grange," she replied. I thought you did not know me, or you wouldn't ave spoken in that way."

"You suppose papa is highly esteemed and respected, hen ?" he said sarcastically.

"And what are you ?" inquired Catherine, gazing uriously on the speaker. "That man I've seen before. s he your son ?"

She pointed to Hareton, the other individual, who had gained nothing but increased bulk and strength by the addition of two years to his age; he seemed as awkward and rough as ever.

"Miss Cathy," I interrupted, "it will be three hours instead of one that we are out presently. We really must go back."

"No, that man is not my son," answered Heathcliff, pushing me aside. "But I have one, and you have seen him before too; and though your nurse is in a hurry, I think both you and she would be the better for a little rest. Will you just turn this nab of heath and walk into my house? You'll get home earlier for the ease, and you shall receive a kind welcome."

I whispered Catherine that she mustn't on any account accede to the proposal. It was entirely out of the question.

"Why?" she asked aloud. "I'm tired of running, and the ground is dewy. I can't sit here. Let us go, Ellen. Besides, he says I have seen his son. He's mistaken, I think; but I guess where he lives—at the farmhouse I visited in coming from Peniston Crags. Don't you?"

"I do.—Come, Nelly, hold your tongue; it will be a treat for her to look in on us.—Hareton, get forwards with the lass.—You shall walk with me, Nelly."

"No, she's not going to any such place," I cried, struggling to release my arm, which he had seized; but she was almost at the door-stones already, scampering round the brow at full speed. Her appointed companion did not pretend to escort her; he shied off by the roadside and vanished.

"Mr. Heathcliff, it's very wrong," I continued. "You know you mean no good. And there she'll see Linton, and all will be told as soon as ever we return; and I shall have the blame."

"I want her to see Linton," he answered. "He's looking better these few days. It's not often he's fit to be seen. And we'll soon persuade her to keep the visit secret. Where is the harm of it?"

"The harm of it is that her father would hate me if he found I suffered her to enter your house; and I am convinced you have a bad design in encouraging her to do so," I replied.

"My design is as honest as possible. I'll inform you of its whole scope," he said—"that the two cousins may fall in love, and get married. I'm acting generously to your master. His young chit has no expectations, and should she second my wishes, she'll be provided for at once as joint successor with Linton."

"If Linton died," I answered, "and his life is quite uncertain, Catherine would be the heir."

"No, she would not," he said. "There is no clause in the will to secure it so. His property would go to me. But to prevent disputes I desire their union, and am resolved to bring it about."

"And I am resolved she shall never approach your house with me again," I returned, as we reached the gate, where Miss Cathy waited our coming.

Heathcliff bade me be quiet, and preceding us up the path, hastened to open the door. My young lady gave him several looks, as if she could not exactly make up her mind what to think of him; but now he smiled when he met her eye, and softened his voice in addressing her; and I was foolish enough to imagine the memory of her mother might disarm him from desiring her injury. Linton stood on the hearth. He had been out walking in the fields, for his cap was on, and he was calling to Joseph to bring him dry shoes. He had grown all of his age, still wanting some months of sixteen. His features were pretty yet, and his eye and complexion brighter than I remembered them, though with merely temporary lustre borrowed from the salubrious air and genial sun.

"Now, who is that?" asked Mr. Heathcliff, turning to Cathy. "Can you tell?"

"Your son?" she said, having doubtfully surveyed first one and then the other.

"Yes, yes," answered he. "But is this the only time

you have beheld him ? Think ! Ah ! you have a short memory.—Linton, don't you recall your cousin that you used to tease us so with wishing to see ?"

"What, Linton ! " cried Cathy, kindling into joyful surprise at the name. "Is that little Linton ? He's taller than I am !—Are you Linton ?"

The youth stepped forward and acknowledged himself. She kissed him fervently, and they gazed with wonder at the change time had wrought in the appearance of each. Catherine had reached her full height ; her figure was both plump and slender, elastic as steel, and her whole aspect sparkling with health and spirits. Linton's looks and movements were very languid, and his form extremely slight ; but there was a grace in his manner that mitigated these defects, and rendered him not unpleasing. After exchanging numerous marks of fondness with him, his cousin went to Mr. Heathcliff, who lingered by the door, dividing his attention between the objects inside and those that lay without—pretending, that is to observe the latter, and really noting the former alone.

"And you are my uncle, then ! " she cried, reaching up to salute him. "I thought I liked you, though you were cross at first. Why don't you visit at the Grange with Linton ? To live all these years such close neighbours, and never see us, is odd. What have you done so for ?"

"I visited it once or twice too often before you were born," he answered. "There—damn it ! If you have any kisses to spare, give them to Linton—they are thrown away on me."

"Naughty Ellen ! " exclaimed Catherine, flying to attack me next with her lavish caresses. "Wicked Ellen, to try to hinder me from entering ! But I'll take this walk every morning in future—may I, uncle ?— and sometimes bring papa. Won't you be glad to see us ?"

"Of course ! " replied the uncle, with a hardly suppressed grimace, resulting from his deep aversion to both the proposed visitors. "But stay," he continued, turning towards the young lady. "Now I think of it, I'd better tell you. Mr. Linton has a prejudice against me. We quarrelled at one time of our lives with unchristian ferocity, and if you mention coming here to him he'll put a veto on your visits altogether. Therefore you must not mention it, unless you be careless of seeing your cousin hereafter. You may come if you will, but you must not mention it."

"Why did you quarrel?" asked Catherine, considerably crestfallen.

"He thought me too poor to wed his sister," answered Heathcliff, "and was grieved that I got her. His pride was hurt, and he'll never forgive it."

"That's wrong!" said the young lady. "Some time I'll tell him so. But Linton and I have no share in your quarrel. I'll not come here then; he shall come to the Grange."

"It will be too far for me," murmured her cousin; "to walk four miles would kill me. No, come here, Miss Catherine, now and then—not every morning, but once or twice a week."

The father launched towards his son a glance of bitter contempt.

"I am afraid, Nelly, I shall lose my labour," he muttered to me. "Miss Catherine, as the ninny calls her, will discover his value, and send him to the devil. Now, if it had been Hareton! Do you know that, twenty times a day, I covet Hareton, with all his degradation? I'd have loved the lad had he been some one else. But I think he's safe from *her* love. I'll pit him against that paltry creature, unless it bestir itself briskly. We calculate it will scarcely last till it is eighteen. Oh, confound the vapid thing! He's absorbed in drying his feet, and never looks at her.—Linton!"

"Yes, father," answered the boy.

"Have you nothing to show your cousin anywhere about—not even a rabbit or a weasel's nest? Take her into the garden before you change your shoes, and into the stable to see your horse."

"Wouldn't you rather sit here?" asked Linton, addressing Cathy in a tone which expressed reluctance to move again.

"I don't know," she replied, casting a longing look to the door, and evidently eager to be active.

He kept his seat, and shrank closer to the fire. Heathcliff rose and went into the kitchen, and from thence to the yard, calling out for Hareton. Hareton responded, and presently the two re-entered. The young man had been washing himself, as was visible by the glow on his cheeks and his wetted hair.

"Oh, I'll ask *you*, uncle," cried Miss Cathy, recollecting the housekeeper's assertion. "That is not my cousin, is he?"

"Yes," he replied—"your mother's nephew. Don't you like him?"

Catherine looked queer.

"Is he not a handsome lad?" he continued.

The uncivil little thing stood on tiptoe, and whispered a sentence in Heathcliff's ear. He laughed. Hareton darkened. I perceived he was very sensitive to suspected slights, and had obviously a dim notion of his inferiority. But his master or guardian chased the frown by exclaiming,—

"You'll be the favourite among us, Hareton! She says you are a—— What was it? Well, something very flattering. Here! you go with her round the farm. And behave like a gentleman, mind! Don't use any bad words; and don't stare when the young lady is not looking at you, and be ready to hide your face when she is; and when you speak, say your words slowly, and keep your hands out of your pockets. Be off, and entertain her as nicely as you can."

He watched the couple walking past the window. Earnshaw had his countenance completely averted from his companion. He seemed studying the familiar landscape with a stranger's and an artist's interest. Catherine took a sly look at him, expressing small admiration. She then turned her attention to seeking out objects of amusement for herself, and tripped merrily on, lilting a tune to supply the lack of conversation.

"I've tied his tongue," observed Heathcliff. "He'll not venture a single syllable all the time! Nelly, you recollect me at his age—nay, some years younger. Did I ever look so stupid—so 'gaumless,' as Joseph calls it?"

"Worse," I replied, "because more sullen with it."

"I've a pleasure in him," he continued, reflecting aloud. "He has satisfied my expectations. If he were a born fool I should not enjoy it half so much. But he's no fool; and I can sympathize with all his feelings, having felt them myself. I know what he suffers now, for instance, exactly. It is merely a beginning of what he shall suffer, though. And he'll never be able to emerge from his bathos of coarseness and ignorance. I've got him faster than his scoundrel of a father secured me, and lower, for he takes a pride in his brutishness. I've taught him to scorn everything extra-animal as silly and weak. Don't you think Hindley would be proud of his son if he could see him—almost as proud as I am of mine? But there's this difference: one is gold put to the use of paving-stones, and the other is tin polished to ape a service of silver. *Mine* has nothing valuable about it, yet I shall have the merit of making it go as far as such poor stuff can go. *His* had first-rate qualities, and they are lost, rendered worse than unavailing. *I* have nothing to regret; *he* would have more than any but me are aware of. And the best of it is, Hareton is damnably fond of me! You'll own that I've outmatched Hindley there. If the dead villain could rise from his grave to abuse me for his offspring's wrongs, I should have the fun of seeing the said offspring fight him back again, indignant that he should dare to rail at the one friend he has in the world."

Heathcliff chuckled a fiendish laugh at the idea. I made no reply, because I saw that he expected none. Meantime our young companion, who sat too removed from us to hear what was said, began to evince symptoms

of uneasiness, probably repenting that he had denied
himself the treat of Catherine's society for fear of a little
fatigue. His father remarked the restless glances wandering to the window, and the hand irresolutely extended
towards his cap.

"Get up, you idle boy!" he exclaimed, with assumed
heartiness. "Away after them! They are just at the
corner, by the stand of hives."

Linton gathered his energies, and left the hearth. The
lattice was open, and as he stepped out I heard Cathy
inquiring of her unsociable attendant what was that
inscription over the door? Hareton stared up, and
scratched his head like a true clown.

"It's some damnable writing," he answered. "I
cannot read it."

"Can't read it?" cried Catherine. "I can read it
it's English. But I want to know why it is there."

Linton giggled—the first appearance of mirth he had
exhibited.

"He does not know his letters," he said to his cousin.
"Could you believe in the existence of such a colossal
dunce?"

"Is he all as he should be?" asked Miss Cathy seriously, "or is he simple—not right? I've questioned
him twice now, and each time he looked so stupid I
think he does not understand me. I can hardly understand *him*, I'm sure."

Linton repeated his laugh, and glanced at Hareton
tauntingly, who certainly did not seem quite clear of
comprehension at that moment.

"There's nothing the matter but laziness—is there,
Earnshaw?" he said. "My cousin fancies you are an
idiot. There you experience the consequence of scorning
'book-larning,' as you would say.—Have you noticed,
Catherine, his frightful Yorkshire pronunciation?"

"Why, where the devil is the use on't?" growled
Hareton, more ready in answering his daily companion.
He was about to enlarge further, but the two youngsters
broke into a noisy fit of merriment, my giddy miss being

delighted to discover that she might turn his strange talk to matter of amusement.

"Where is the use of the devil in that sentence?" tittered Linton. "Papa told you not to say any bad words, and you can't open your mouth without one. Do try to behave like a gentleman—now do!"

"If thou weren't more a lass than a lad, I'd fell thee this minute, I would, pitiful lath of a crater!" retorted the angry boor, retreating, while his face burned with mingled rage and mortification, for he was conscious of being insulted, and embarrassed how to resent it.

Mr. Heathcliff having overheard the conversation as well as I, smiled when he saw him go, but immediately afterwards cast a look of singular aversion on the flippant pair, who remained chattering in the doorway, the boy finding animation enough while discussing Hareton's faults and deficiencies and relating anecdotes of his goings-on, and the girl relishing his pert and spiteful sayings, without considering the ill-nature they evinced. I began to dislike more than to compassionate Linton, and to excuse his father, in some measure, for holding him cheap.

We stayed till afternoon—I could not tear Miss Cathy away sooner; but happily my master had not quitted his apartment, and remained ignorant of our prolonged absence. As we walked home I would fain have enlightened my charge on the characters of the people we had quitted, but she got it into her head that I was prejudiced against them.

"Aha!" she cried, "you take papa's side, Ellen. You are partial, I know, or else you wouldn't have cheated me so many years into the notion that Linton lived a long way from here. I'm really extremely angry, only I'm so pleased I can't show it. But you must hold your tongue about my uncle. He's *my* uncle, remember, and I'll scold papa for quarrelling with him."

And so she ran on, till I relinquished the endeavour to convince her of her mistake. She did not mention

the visit that night, because she did not see Mr. Linton.
Next day it all came out, sadly to my chagrin. And
still I was not altogether sorry. I thought the burden
of directing and warning would be more efficiently borne
by him than me. But he was too timid in giving satis-
factory reasons for his wish that she should shun connection with the household of the Heights, and Catherine
liked good reasons for every restraint that harassed her
petted will.

"Papa!" she exclaimed, after the morning's saluta-
tions, "guess whom I saw yesterday in my walk on the
moors. Ah, papa, you started! You've not done right,
have you, now? I saw—— But listen, and you shall
hear how I found you out, and Ellen, who is in league
with you, and yet pretended to pity me so when I kept
hoping, and was always disappointed about Linton's
coming back."

She gave a faithful account of her excursion and its
consequences; and my master, though he cast more than
one reproachful look at me, said nothing till she had
concluded. Then he drew her to him, and asked if she
knew why he had concealed Linton's near neighbourhood from her. Could she think it was to deny her a
pleasure that she might harmlessly enjoy?

"It was because you disliked Mr. Heathcliff," she
answered.

"Then you believe I care more for my own feelings
than yours, Cathy?" he said. "No, it was not because
I disliked Mr. Heathcliff, but because Mr. Heathcliff
dislikes me, and is a most diabolical man, delighting to
wrong and ruin those he hates, if they give him the
slightest opportunity. I knew that you could not keep
up an acquaintance with your cousin without being
brought into contact with him, and I knew he would
detest you on my account; so for your own good, and
nothing else, I took precautions that you should not
see Linton again. I meant to explain this some time
as you grew older, and I'm sorry I delayed it."

"But Mr. Heathcliff was quite cordial, papa," oberved Catherine, not at all convinced; " and *he* didn't object to our seeing each other. He said I might come to his house when I pleased, only I must not tell you, because you had quarrelled with him, and would not forgive him for marrying Aunt Isabella. And you won't. *You* are the one to be blamed. He is willing to let *us* be friends—at least, Linton and I—and you are not."

My master, perceiving that she would not take his word for her uncle-in-law's evil disposition, gave a hasty sketch of his conduct to Isabella, and the manner in which Wuthering Heights became his property. He could not bear to discourse long upon the topic, for though he spoke little of it, he still felt the same horror and detestation of his ancient enemy that had occupied his heart ever since Mrs. Linton's death. " She might have been living yet if it had not been for him!" was his constant bitter reflection; and in his eyes Heathcliff seemed a murderer. Miss Cathy—conversant with no bad deeds except her own slight acts of disobedience, injustice, and passion, arising from hot temper and thoughtlessness, and repented of on the day they were committed—was amazed at the blackness of spirit that could brood on and cover revenge for years, and deliberately prosecute its plans without a visitation of remorse. She appeared so deeply impressed and shocked at this new view of human nature, excluded from all her studies and all her ideas till now, that Mr. Edgar deemed it unnecessary to pursue the subject. He merely added,—

" You will know hereafter, darling, why I wish you to avoid his house and family. Now return to your old employments and amusements, and think no more about them."

Catherine kissed her father and sat down quietly to her lessons for a couple of hours, according to custom; then she accompanied him into the grounds, and the whole day passed as usual. But in the evening, when he had retired to her room, and I went to help her to undress, I found her crying on her knees by the bedside.

"Oh, fie, silly child!" I exclaimed. "If you had an real griefs you'd be ashamed to waste a tear on thi little contrariety. You never had one shadow of sub stantial sorrow, Miss Catherine. Suppose, for a minute that master and I were dead, and you were by yoursel in the world; how would you feel then? Compare th present occasion with such an affliction as that, and b thankful for the friends you have, instead of covetin more."

"I'm not crying for myself, Ellen," she answered– "it's for him. He expected to see me again to-morrow and there he'll be so disappointed; and he'll wait fo me, and I shan't come."

"Nonsense!" said I. "Do you imagine he ha thought as much of you as you have of him? Hasn' he Hareton for a companion? Not one in a hundre would weep at losing a relation they had just seen twice for two afternoons. Linton will conjecture how it is and trouble himself no further about you."

"But may I not write a note to tell him why I canno come," she asked, rising to her feet, "and just sen those books I promised to lend him? His books ar not as nice as mine, and he wanted to have them ex tremely when I told him how interesting they were May I not, Ellen?"

"No, indeed! no, indeed!" replied I, with decisio "Then he would write to you, and there'd never be a end of it. No, Miss Catherine, the acquaintance mus be dropped entirely; so papa expects, and I shall se that it is done."

"But how can one little note——" she recommence putting on an imploring countenance.

"Silence!" I interrupted. "We'll not begin wit your little notes. Get into bed."

She threw at me a very naughty look—so naughty tha I would not kiss her good-night at first. I covered he up and shut her door in great displeasure, but repentin half-way, I returned softly, and lo! there was mis standing at the table with a bit of blank paper befor

her and a pencil in her hand, which she guiltily slipped
out of sight on my entrance.

"You'll get nobody to take that, Catherine," I said, "if
you write it; and at present I shall put out your candle."

I set the extinguisher on the flame, receiving as I did
so a slap on my hand, and a petulant "Cross thing!"
I then quitted her again, and she drew the bolt in one of
her worst, most peevish humours. The letter was fin-
shed and forwarded to its destination by a milk-fetcher
who came from the village; but that I did not learn till
some time afterwards. Weeks passed on, and Cathy
recovered her temper, though she grew wondrous fond
of stealing off to corners by herself; and often, if I came
near her suddenly while reading, she would start and
bend over the book, evidently desirous to hide it, and I
detected edges of loose paper sticking out beyond the
eaves. She also got a trick of coming down early in
the morning and lingering about the kitchen, as if she
were expecting the arrival of something; and she had a
small drawer in a cabinet in the library which she would
rifle over for hours, and whose key she took special
care to remove when she left it.

One day, as she inspected this drawer, I observed that
the playthings and trinkets which recently formed its
contents were transmuted into bits of folded paper.
My curiosity and suspicions were aroused. I determined
to take a peep at her mysterious treasures: so at night,
as soon as she and my master were safe upstairs, I
searched and readily found among my house-keys one
that would fit the lock. Having opened, I emptied the
whole contents into my apron, and took them with me
to examine at leisure in my own chamber. Though I
could not but suspect, I was still surprised to discover
that they were a mass of correspondence—daily, almost,
it must have been—from Linton Heathcliff, answers to
documents forwarded by her. The earlier dated were
embarrassed and short; gradually, however, they ex-
panded into copious love-letters, foolish, as the age of
the writer rendered natural, yet with touches here and

8

there which I thought were borrowed from a more ex
perienced source. Some of them struck me as singularl
odd compounds of ardour and flatness, commencing i
strong feeling, and concluding in the affected, word
style that a schoolboy might use to a fancied, incorporea
sweetheart. Whether they satisfied Cathy I don't know
but they appeared very worthless trash to me. Afte
turning over as many as I thought proper, I tied then
in a handkerchief and set them aside, relocking th
vacant drawer.

Following her habit, my young lady descended early
and visited the kitchen. I watched her go to the doo
on the arrival of a certain little boy, and while the dairy
maid filled his can, she tucked something into his jacke
pocket, and plucked something out. I went round b
the garden and laid wait for the messenger, who fough
valorously to defend his trust, and we spilt the mill
between us; but I succeeded in abstracting the epistle
and threatening serious consequences if he did not lool
sharp home, I remained under the wall and peruse
Miss Cathy's affectionate composition. It was mor
simple and more eloquent than her cousin's—very prett
and very silly. I shook my head, and went meditatin
into the house. The day being wet, she could not diver
herself with rambling about the park, so, at the conclusio
of her morning studies, she resorted to the solace of th
drawer. Her father sat reading at the table, and I, o
purpose, had sought a bit of work in some unrippe
fringes of the window curtain, keeping my eye steadil
fixed on her proceedings. Never did any bird flying bacl
to a plundered nest which it had left brimful of chirpin
young ones express more complete despair in its anguishe
cries and flutterings than she by her single "Oh!"
and the change that transfigured her late happy counte
nance. Mr. Linton looked up.

"What is the matter, love? Have you hurt your
self?" he said.

His tone and look assured her _he_ had not been th
discoverer of the hoard.

"No, papa," she gasped.—"Ellen! Ellen! come up-stairs! I'm sick!"

I obeyed her summons, and accompanied her out.

"O Ellen, you have got them!" she commenced im-mediately, dropping on her knees, when we were en-closed alone. "Oh, give them to me, and I'll never, never do so again! Don't tell papa. You have not told papa, Ellen? Say you have not. I've been ex-ceedingly naughty, but I won't do it any more!"

With a grave severity in my manner I bade her stand up.

"So," I exclaimed, "Miss Catherine, you are tolerably far on, it seems; you may well be ashamed of them. A fine bundle of trash you study in your leisure hours, to be sure. Why, it's good enough to be printed. And what do you suppose the master will think when I dis-play it before him? I haven't shown it yet, but you needn't imagine I shall keep your ridiculous secrets. For shame! And you must have led the way in writing such absurdities. He would not have thought of be-ginning, I'm certain.'

"I didn't! I didn't!" sobbed Cathy, fit to break her heart. "I didn't once think of loving him till——"

"_Loving!_" cried I, as scornfully as I could utter the word. "_Loving!_ Did anybody ever hear the like? I might just as well talk of loving the miller who comes once a year to buy our corn. Pretty loving, indeed! And both times together you have seen Linton hardly four hours in your life! Now here is the babyish trash. I'm going with it to the library, and we'll see what your father says to such _loving_."

She sprang at her precious epistles, but I held them above my head; and then she poured out further frantic entreaties that I would burn them—do anything rather than show them. And being really fully as much in-clined to laugh as scold—for I esteemed it all girlish vanity—I at length relented in a measure, and asked,—

"If I consent to burn them, will you promise faith-fully neither to send nor receive a letter again, nor a

book (for I perceive you have sent him books), nor locks
of hair, nor rings, nor playthings ? "

"We don't send playthings !" cried Catherine, her
pride overcoming her shame.

"Nor anything at all then, my lady," I said. "Unless
you will, here I go."

"I promise, Ellen !" she cried, catching my dress
"Oh, put them in the fire !—do, do ! "

But when I proceeded to open a place with the poker
the sacrifice was too painful to be borne. She earnestly
supplicated that I would spare her one or two.

"One or two, Ellen, to keep for Linton's sake ! "

I unknotted the handkerchief, and commenced dropping them in from an angle, and the flame curled up the
chimney.

"I will have one, you cruel wretch," she screamed,
darting her hand into the fire and drawing forth some
half-consumed fragments, at the expense of her fingers.

"Very well ; and I will have some to exhibit to papa !"
I answered, shaking back the rest into the bundle, and
turning anew to the door.

She emptied her blackened pieces into the flames, and
motioned me to finish the immolation. It was done. I
stirred up the ashes, and interred them under a shovelful
of coals ; and she mutely, and with a sense of intense
injury, retired to her private apartment. I descended to
tell my master that the young lady's qualm of sickness
was almost gone, but I judged it best for her to lie down
a while. She wouldn't dine ; but she reappeared at tea,
pale and red about the eyes, and marvellously subdued
in outward aspect. Next morning I answered the letter
by a slip of paper inscribed, "Master Heathcliff is requested to send no more notes to Miss Linton, as she
will not receive them." And thenceforth the little boy
came with vacant pockets.

CHAPTER XXII.

SUMMER drew to an end, and early autumn. It was past Michaelmas; but the harvest was late that year, and a few of our fields were still uncleared. Mr. Linton and his daughter would frequently walk out among the reapers. At the carrying of the last sheaves they stayed till dusk, and the evening happening to be chill and damp, my master caught a bad cold, that settled obstinately on his lungs, and confined him indoors throughout the whole of the winter, nearly without intermission.

Poor Cathy, frightened from her little romance, had been considerably sadder and duller since its abandonment; and her father insisted on her reading less, and taking more exercise. She had his companionship no longer. I esteemed it a duty to supply its lack, as much as possible, with mine—an inefficient substitute, for I could only spare two or three hours from my numerous diurnal occupations to follow her footsteps, and then my society was obviously less desirable than his.

On an afternoon in October or the beginning of November, a fresh, watery afternoon, when the turf and paths were rustling with moist, withered leaves, and the cold blue sky was half hidden by clouds—dark gray streamers, rapidly mounting from the west and boding abundant rain—I requested my young lady to forego her ramble, because I was certain of showers. She refused, and I unwillingly donned a cloak and took my umbrella to accompany her on a stroll to the bottom of the park— a formal walk which she generally affected if low-spirited (and that she invariably was when Mr. Edgar had been worse than ordinary)—a thing never known from his confession, but guessed both by her and me from his increased silence and the melancholy of his countenance. She went sadly on. There was no running or bounding now, though the chill wind might well have tempted her to race. And often, from the side of my eye, I could

detect her raising a hand and brushing something of
her cheek. I gazed round for a means of diverting her
thoughts. On one side of the road rose a high, rough
bank, where hazels and stunted oaks, with their roots
half exposed, held uncertain tenure. The soil was too
loose for the latter, and strong winds had blown some
nearly horizontal. In summer Miss Catherine delighted
to climb along these trunks, and sit in the branches
swinging twenty feet above the ground; and I, pleased
with her agility and her light, childish heart, still considered it proper to scold every time I caught her at such
an elevation, but so that she knew there was no necessity
for descending. From dinner to tea she would lie in
her breeze-rocked cradle, doing nothing except singing
old songs—my nursery lore—to herself, or watching the
birds, joint tenants, feed and entice their young ones to
fly; or nestling with closed lids, half thinking, half
dreaming, happier than words can express.

"Look, miss!" I exclaimed, pointing to a nook under
the roots of one twisted tree; "winter is not here yet.
There's a little flower up yonder—the last bud from the
multitude of bluebells that clouded those turf steps in
July with a lilac mist. Will you clamber up and pluck
it to show to papa?"

Cathy stared a long time at the lonely blossom trembling in its earthy shelter, and replied at length,—

"No, I'll not touch it. But it looks melancholy, does
it not, Ellen?"

"Yes," I observed—"about as starved and sackless
as you. Your cheeks are bloodless. Let us take hold
of hands and run. You're so low I dare say I shall keep
up with you."

"No," she repeated, and continued sauntering on,
pausing at intervals to muse over a bit of moss, or a tuft
of blanched grass, or a fungus spreading its bright orange
among the heaps of brown foliage; and ever and anon
her hand was lifted to her averted face.

"Catherine, why are you crying, love?" I asked,
approaching and putting my arm over her shoulder.

" You mustn't cry because papa has a cold. Be thankful it is nothing worse."

She now put no further restraint on her tears; her breath was stifled by sobs.

" Oh, it *will* be something worse!" she said. " And what shall I do when papa and you leave me, and I am by myself ? I can't forget your words, Ellen; they are always in my ear. How life will be changed, how dreary the world will be, when papa and you are dead!"

" None can tell whether you won't die before us," I replied. " It's wrong to anticipate evil. We'll hope there are years and years to come before any of us go. Master is young, and I am strong and hardly forty-five. My mother lived till eighty, a canty dame to the last. And suppose Mr. Linton were spared till he saw sixty, that would be more years than you have counted, miss. And would it not be foolish to mourn a calamity above twenty years beforehand ? "

" But Aunt Isabella was younger than papa," she remarked, gazing up with timid hope to seek further consolation.

" Aunt Isabella had not you and me to nurse her," I replied. " She wasn't as happy as master; she hadn't as much to live for. All you need do is to wait well on your father, and cheer him by letting him see you cheerful, and avoid giving him anxiety on any subject. Mind that, Cathy. I'll not disguise but you might kill him if you were wild and reckless, and cherished a foolish, fanciful affection for the son of a person who would be glad to have him in his grave, and allowed him to discover that you fretted over the separation he has judged it expedient to make."

" I fret about nothing on earth except papa's illness," answered my companion. " I care for nothing in comparison with papa. And I'll never—never—oh, never, while I have my senses, do an act or say a word to vex him. I love him better than myself, Ellen, and I know it by this : I pray every night that I may live after

him, because I would rather be miserable than that
he should be. That proves I love him better than
myself."

"Good words," I replied. "But deeds must prove it
also. And after he is well, remember you don't forget
resolutions formed in the hour of fear."

As we talked, we neared a door that opened on the
road ; and my young lady, lightening into sunshine
again, climbed up and seated herself on the top of the
wall, reaching over to gather some hips that bloomed
scarlet on the summit branches of the wild rose trees
shadowing the highway side. The lower fruit had disappeared, but only birds could touch the upper, except
from Cathy's present station. In stretching to pull them,
her hat fell off, and as the door was locked she proposed
scrambling down to recover it. I bade her be cautious
lest she got a fall, and she nimbly disappeared. But the
return was no such easy matter. The stones were smooth
and neatly cemented, and the rose bushes and blackberry
stragglers could yield no assistance in reascending. I,
like a fool, didn't recollect that till I heard her laughing
and exclaiming,—

"Ellen, you'll have to fetch the key, or else I must
run round to the porter's lodge. I can't scale the ram-
parts on this side."

"Stay where you are," I answered. "I have my
bundle of keys in my pocket. Perhaps I may manage
to open it ; if not, I'll go."

Catherine amused herself with dancing to and fro
before the door, while I tried all the large keys in succession. I had applied the last, and found that none
would do. So, repeating my desire that she would remain there, I was about to hurry home as fast as I could,
when an approaching sound arrested me. It was the
trot of a horse. Cathy's dance stopped also.

"Who is that ?" I whispered.

"Ellen, I wish you could open the door," whispered
back my companion anxiously.

"Ho, Miss Linton !" cried a deep voice (the rider's) ;

" I'm glad to meet you. Don't be in haste to enter, for I have an explanation to ask and obtain."

" I shan't speak to you, Mr. Heathcliff," answered Catherine. " Papa says you are a wicked man, and you hate both him and me ; and Ellen says the same."

" That is nothing to the purpose," said Heathcliff. (He it was.) " I don't hate my son, I suppose, and it is concerning him that I demand your attention. Yes, you have cause to blush. Two or three months since were you not in the habit of writing to Linton—making love in play, eh ? You deserved, both of you, flogging for that—you especially, the elder, and less sensitive, as it turns out. I've got your letters, and if you give me any pertness I'll send them to your father. I presume you grew weary of the amusement and dropped it, didn't you ? Well, you dropped Linton with it into a Slough of Despond. He was in earnest—in love, really. As true as I live, he's dying for you, breaking his heart at your fickleness—not figuratively, but actually. Though Hareton has made him a standing jest for six weeks, and I have used more serious measures, and attempted to frighten him out of his idiocy, he gets worse daily ; and he'll be under the sod before summer unless you restore him ! "

" How can you lie so glaringly to the poor child ? " I called from the inside. " Pray ride on ! How can you deliberately get up such paltry falsehoods ?—Miss Cathy, I'll knock the lock off with a stone. You won't believe that vile nonsense. You can feel in yourself it is impossible that a person should die for love of a stranger."

" I was not aware there were eavesdroppers," muttered the detected villain. " Worthy Mrs. Dean, I like you, but I don't like your double-dealing," he added aloud. " How could *you* lie so glaringly as to affirm I hated the ' poor child,' and invent bugbear stories to terrify her from my door-stones ? Catherine Linton (the very name warms me), my bonny lass, I shall be from home all this week ; go and see if I have not spoken truth ; do—there's a darling ! Just imagine your father in my place, and

Linton in yours ; then think how you would value your careless lover if he refused to stir a step to comfort you when your father himself entreated him ; and don't, from pure stupidity, fall into the same error. I swear, on my salvation, he's going to his grave, and none but you can save him ! "

The lock gave way, and I issued out.

" I swear Linton is dying," repeated Heathcliff, looking hard at me. " And grief and disappointment are hastening his death. Nelly, if you won't let her go, you can walk over yourself. But I shall not return till this time next week ; and I think your master himself would scarcely object to her visiting her cousin."

" Come in," said I, taking Cathy by the arm and half forcing her to re-enter ; for she lingered, viewing with troubled eyes the features of the speaker, too stern to express his inward deceit.

He pushed his horse close, and bending down, observed,—

" Miss Catherine, I'll own to you that I have little patience with Linton ; and Hareton and Joseph have less. I'll own that he's with a harsh set. He pines for kindness as well as love, and a kind word from you would be his best medicine. Don't mind Mrs. Dean's cruel cautions, but be generous, and contrive to see him. He dreams of you day and night, and cannot be persuaded that you don't hate him, since you neither write nor call."

I closed the door and rolled a stone to assist the loosened lock in holding it, and spreading my umbrella, I drew my charge underneath, for the rain began to drive through the moaning branches of the trees, and warned us to avoid delay. Our hurry prevented any comment on the encounter with Heathcliff as we stretched towards home, but I divined instinctively that Catherine's heart was clouded now in double darkness. Her features were so sad they did not seem hers. She evidently regarded what she had heard as every syllable true.

The master had retired to rest before we came in.

Cathy stole to his room to inquire how he was; he had fallen asleep. She returned, and asked me to sit with her in the library. We took our tea together, and afterwards she lay down on the rug, and told me not to talk, for she was weary. I got a book, and pretended to read. As soon as she supposed me absorbed in my occupation she recommenced her silent weeping; it appeared, at present, her favourite diversion. I suffered her to enjoy it a while, then I expostulated, deriding and ridiculing all Mr. Heathcliff's assertions about his son, as if I were certain she would coincide. Alas! I hadn't skill to counteract the effect his account had produced; it was just what he intended.

"You may be right, Ellen," she answered, "but I shall never feel at ease till I know. And I must tell Linton it is not my fault that I don't write, and convince him that I shall not change."

What use were anger and protestations against her silly credulity? We parted that night hostile, but next day beheld me on the road to Wuthering Heights by the side of my wilful young mistress's pony. I couldn't bear to witness her sorrow, to see her pale dejected countenance and heavy eyes; and I yielded, in the faint hope that Linton himself might prove, by his reception of us, how little of the tale was founded on fact.

CHAPTER XXIII.

THE rainy night had ushered in a misty morning, half frost, half drizzle, and temporary brooks crossed our path, gurgling from the uplands. My feet were thoroughly wetted. I was cross and low—exactly the humour suited for making the most of these disagreeable things. We entered the farmhouse by the kitchen way, to ascertain whether Mr. Heathcliff were really absent, because I put slight faith in his own affirmation.

Joseph seemed sitting in a sort of elysium alone, beside a roaring fire, a quart of ale on the table near him, bristling with large pieces of toasted oat-cake, and his black, short pipe in his mouth. Catherine ran to the hearth to warm herself. I asked if the master was in. My question remained so long unanswered that I thought the old man had grown deaf, and repeated it louder.

"Na—ay!" he snarled, or rather screamed through his nose. "Na—ay! yah muh goa back whear yah coom frough."

"Joseph!" cried a peevish voice, simultaneously with me, from the inner room. "How often am I to call you? There are only a few red ashes now. Joseph! come this moment."

Vigorous puffs and a resolute stare into the grate declared he had no ear for this appeal. The house-keeper and Hareton were invisible—one gone on an errand, and the other at his work probably. We knew Linton's tones, and entered.

"Oh, I hope you'll die in a garret, starved to death," said the boy, mistaking our approach for that of his negligent attendant.

He stopped on observing his error. His cousin flew to him.

"Is that you, Miss Linton?" he said, raising his head from the arm of the great chair in which he reclined. "No, don't kiss me; it takes my breath. Dear me! Papa said you would call," continued he, after recovering a little from Catherine's embrace, while she stood by looking very contrite. "Will you shut the door, if you please? You left it open; and those—those *detestable* creatures won't bring coals to the fire. It's so cold!"

I stirred up the cinders, and fetched a scuttleful my-self. The invalid complained of being covered with ashes; but he had a tiresome cough, and looked feverish and ill, so I did not rebuke his temper.

"Well, Linton," murmured Catherine, when his cor-rugated brow relaxed, "are you glad to see me? Can I do you any good?"

"Why didn't you come before?" he asked. "You should have come, instead of writing. It tired me dreadfully writing those long letters. I'd far rather have talked to you. Now, I can neither bear to talk nor anything else. I wonder where Zillah is! Will you"—looking at me—"step into the kitchen and see?"

I had received no thanks for my other service, and being unwilling to run to and fro at his behest, I replied,—

"Nobody is out there but Joseph."

"I want to drink," he exclaimed fretfully, turning away. "Zillah is constantly gadding off to Gimmerton since papa went; it's miserable! And I'm obliged to come down here: they resolved never to hear me upstairs."

"Is your father attentive to you, Master Heathcliff?" I asked, perceiving Catherine to be checked in her friendly advances.

"Attentive? He makes *them* a little more attentive at least," he cried. "The wretches! Do you know, Miss Linton, that brute Hareton laughs at me! I hate him! Indeed, I hate them all! They are odious beings."

Cathy began searching for some water; she lighted on a pitcher in the dresser, filled a tumbler, and brought it. He bade her add a spoonful of wine from a bottle on the table; and having swallowed a small portion, appeared more tranquil, and said she was very kind.

"And are you glad to see me?" asked she, reiterating her former question, and pleased to detect the faint dawn of a smile.

"Yes, I am. It's something new to hear a voice like yours!" he replied. "But I have been vexed because you wouldn't come. And papa swore it was owing to me. He called me a pitiful, shuffling, worthless thing, and said you despised me, and if he had been in my place he would be more the master of the Grange than your father by this time. But you don't despise me, do you, Miss——"

"I wish you would say Catherine, or Cathy," interrupted my young lady. "Despise you? No! Next to papa and Ellen, I love you better than anybody living.

I don't love Mr. Heathcliff, though, and I dare not come when he returns. Will he stay away many days?"

"Not many," answered Linton; "but he goes on to the moors frequently since the shooting season commenced, and you might spend an hour or two with me in his absence. Do say you will. I think I should not be peevish with you. You'd not provoke me, and you'd always be ready to help me, wouldn't you?"

"Yes," said Catherine, stroking his long soft hair. "If I could only get papa's consent I'd spend half my time with you. Pretty Linton! I wish you were my brother."

"And then you would like me as well as your father?" observed he more cheerfully. "But papa says you would love me better than him and all the world if you were my wife; so I'd rather you were that."

"No, I should never love anybody better than papa," she returned gravely. "And people hate their wives sometimes, but not their sisters and brothers; and if you were the latter you would live with us, and papa would be as fond of you as he is of me."

Linton denied that people ever hated their wives, but Cathy affirmed they did, and in her wisdom instanced his own father's aversion to her aunt. I endeavoured to stop her thoughtless tongue. I couldn't succeed till everything she knew was out. Master Heathcliff, much irritated, asserted her relation was false.

"Papa told me, and papa does not tell falsehoods," she answered pertly.

"*My* papa scorns yours!" cried Linton. "He calls him a sneaking fool."

"Yours is a wicked man," retorted Catherine, "and you are very naughty to dare to repeat what he says. He must be wicked to have made Aunt Isabella leave him as she did."

"She didn't leave him," said the boy. "You shan't contradict me."

"She did," cried my young lady.

"Well, I'll tell *you* something," said Linton. "Your mother hated your father. Now then."

"Oh!" exclaimed Catherine, too enraged to continue.

"And she loved mine," added he.

"You little liar! I hate you now!" she panted, and her face grew red with passion.

"She did! she did!" sang Linton, sinking into the recess of his chair, and leaning back his head to enjoy the agitation of the other disputant, who stood behind.

"Hush, Master Heathcliff!" I said. "That's your father's tale too, I suppose."

"It isn't. You hold your tongue!" he answered.— "She did! she did, Catherine! She did! she did!"

Cathy, beside herself, gave the chair a violent push, and caused him to fall against one arm. He was immediately seized by a suffocating cough that soon ended his triumph. It lasted so long that it frightened even me. As to his cousin, she wept with all her might, aghast at the mischief she had done, though she said nothing. I held him till the fit exhausted itself. Then he thrust me away, and leant his head down silently. Catherine quelled her lamentations also, took a seat opposite, and looked solemnly into the fire.

"How do you feel now, Master Heathcliff?" I inquired, after waiting ten minutes.

"I wish *she* felt as I do," he replied—"spiteful, cruel thing! Hareton never touches me; he never struck me in his life. And I was better to-day; and there——" His voice died in a whimper.

"*I* didn't strike you!" muttered Cathy, chewing her lip to prevent another burst of emotion.

He sighed and moaned like one under great suffering, and kept it up for a quarter of an hour, on purpose to distress his cousin, apparently, for whenever he caught a stifled sob from her he put renewed pain and pathos into the inflections of his voice.

"I'm sorry I hurt you, Linton," she said at length, racked beyond endurance. "But *I* couldn't have been hurt by that little push, and I had no idea that you could either. You're not much, are you, Linton? Don't let

me go home thinking I've done you harm. Answer!
Speak to me!"

"I can't speak to you," he murmured. "You've hurt
me so that I shall lie awake all night choking with this
cough. If you had it you'd know what it was; but *you'll*
be comfortably asleep while I'm in agony, and nobody
near me. I wonder how you would like to pass those
fearful nights." And he began to wail aloud, for very
pity of himself.

"Since you are in the habit of passing dreadful nights,"
I said, "it won't be miss who spoils your ease; you'd
be the same had she never come. However, she shall
not disturb you again; and perhaps you'll get quieter
when we leave you."

"Must I go?" asked Catherine dolefully, bending over
him. "Do you want me to go, Linton?"

"You can't alter what you've done," he replied pet-
tishly, shrinking from her, "unless you alter it for the
worse by teasing me into a fever."

"Well, then, I must go?" she repeated.

"Let me alone, at least," said he. "I can't bear your
talking."

She lingered, and resisted my persuasions to departure
a tiresome while; but as he neither looked up nor spoke
she finally made a movement to the door, and I followed.
We were recalled by a scream. Linton had slid from his
seat on to the hearth-stone, and lay writhing in the mere
perverseness of an indulged plague of a child, determined
to be as grievous and harassing as it can. I thoroughly
gauged his disposition from his behaviour, and saw at
once it would be folly to attempt humouring him. Not
so my companion. She ran back in terror, knelt down,
and cried, and soothed, and entreated, till he grew quiet
from lack of breath, by no means from compunction at
distressing her.

"I shall lift him on to the settle," I said, "and he may
roll about as he pleases. We can't stop to watch him.
I hope you are satisfied, Miss Cathy, that *you* are not
the person to benefit him, and that his condition of

health is not occasioned by attachment to you. Now, then, there he is! Come away. As soon as he knows there is nobody by to care for his nonsense, he'll be glad to lie still."

She placed a cushion under his head, and offered him some water. He rejected the latter, and tossed uneasily on the former, as if it were a stone or a block of wood. She tried to put it more comfortably.

"I can't do with that," he said; "it's not high enough."

Catherine brought another to lay above it.

"That's *too* high," murmured the provoking thing.

"How must I arrange it, then?" she asked despairingly.

He twined himself up to her, as she half knelt by the settle, and converted her shoulder into a support.

"No, that won't do," I said. "You'll be content with the cushion, Master Heathcliff. Miss has wasted too much time on you already; we cannot remain five minutes longer."

"Yes, yes; we can!" replied Cathy. "He's good and patient now. He's beginning to think I shall have far greater misery than he will to-night if I believe he is the worse for my visit, and then I dare not come again.— Tell the truth about it, Linton; for I mustn't come if I have hurt you."

"You must come, to cure me," he answered. "You ought to come, because you have hurt me; you know you have extremely. I was not as ill when you entered as I am at present—was I?"

"But you've made yourself ill by crying and being in a passion."

"I didn't do it all," said his cousin. "However, we'll be friends now. And you want me—you would wish to see me sometimes, really?"

"I told you I did," he replied impatiently. "Sit on the settle and let me lean on your knee. That's as mamma used to do, whole afternoons together. Sit quite still and don't talk; but you may sing a song, if you can sing, or you may say a nice long interesting ballad—one of those you promised to teach me—or a story. I'd rather have a ballad, though. Begin."

Catherine repeated the longest she could remember. The employment pleased both mightily. Linton would have another, and after that another, notwithstanding my strenuous objections; and so they went on until the clock struck twelve, and we heard Hareton in the court, returning for his dinner.

"And to-morrow, Catherine—will you be here to-morrow?" asked young Heathcliff, holding her frock as she rose reluctantly.

"No," I answered, "nor next day neither." She, however, gave a different response evidently, for his forehead cleared as she stooped and whispered in his ear.

"You won't go to-morrow, recollect, miss," I commenced, when we were out of the house. "You are not dreaming of it, are you?"

She smiled.

"Oh, I'll take good care," I continued. "I'll have that lock mended, and you can escape by no way else."

"I can get over the wall," she said, laughing. "The Grange is not a prison, Ellen, and you are not my gaoler. And besides, I'm almost seventeen; I'm a woman. And I'm certain Linton would recover quickly if he had me to look after him. I'm older than he is, you know, and wiser—less childish, am I not? And he'll soon do as I direct him, with some slight coaxing. He's a pretty little darling when he's good. I'd make such a pet of him if he were mine. We should never quarrel, should we, after we were used to each other? Don't you like him, Ellen?"

"Like him!" I exclaimed. "The worst-tempered bit of a sickly slip that ever struggled into its teens. Happily, as Mr. Heathcliff conjectured, he'll not win twenty. I doubt whether he'll see spring, indeed. And small loss to his family whenever he drops off. And lucky it is for us that his father took him: the kinder he was treated, the more tedious and selfish he'd be. I'm glad you have no chance of having him for a husband, Miss Catherine."

My companion waxed serious at hearing this speech. To speak of his death so regardlessly wounded her feelings.

"He's younger than I," she answered, after a protracted pause of meditation, "and he ought to live the longest. He will—he must live as long as I do. He's as strong now as when he first came into the north; I'm positive of that. It's only a cold that ails him—the same as papa has. You say papa will get better, and why shouldn't he?"

"Well, well," I cried, "after all we needn't trouble ourselves; for listen, miss—and mind I'll keep my word: if you attempt going to Wuthering Heights again, with or without me, I shall inform Mr. Linton; and unless he allow it, the intimacy with your cousin must not be revived."

"It has been revived," muttered Cathy sulkily.

"Must not be continued, then," I said.

"We'll see," was her reply; and she set off at a gallop, leaving me to toil in the rear.

We both reached home before our dinner-time; my master supposed we had been wandering through the park, and therefore he demanded no explanation of our absence. As soon as I entered I hastened to change my soaked shoes and stockings, but sitting such a while at the Heights had done the mischief. On the succeeding morning I was laid up, and during three weeks I remained incapacitated for attending to my duties—a calamity never experienced prior to that period, and never, I am thankful to say, since.

My little mistress behaved like an angel in coming to wait on me and cheer my solitude. The confinement brought me exceedingly low—it is wearisome to a stirring, active body; but few have slighter reasons for complaint than I had. The moment Catherine left Mr. Linton's room she appeared at my bedside. Her day was divided between us; no amusement usurped a minute. She neglected her meals, her studies, and her

play, and she was the fondest nurse that ever watched.
She must have had a warm heart, when she loved her
father so, to give so much to me. I said her days were
divided between us; but the master retired early, and
I generally needed nothing after six o'clock; thus the
evening was her own. Poor thing! I never considered
what she did with herself after tea. And though frequently, when she looked in to bid me good-night,
remarked a fresh colour in her cheeks and a pinkness
over her slender fingers, instead of fancying the hue borrowed from a cold ride across the moors, I laid it to the
charge of a hot fire in the library.

CHAPTER XXIV.

AT the close of three weeks I was able to quit my chamber and move about the house; and on the first occasion
of my sitting up in the evening I asked Catherine to
read to me, because my eyes were weak. We were in
the library, the master having gone to bed. She consented, rather unwillingly, I fancied; and imagining my
sort of books did not suit her, I bade her please herself
in the choice of what she perused. She selected one of
her own favourites, and got forward steadily about an
hour; then came frequent questions.

"Ellen, are not you tired? Hadn't you better lie
down now? You'll be sick keeping up so long, Ellen."

"No, no, dear; I'm not tired," I returned continually.

Perceiving me immovable, she essayed another method
of showing her disrelish for her occupation. It changed
to yawning and stretching, and—

"Ellen, I'm tired."

"Give over, then, and talk," I answered.

That was worse. She fretted and sighed, and looked
at her watch till eight, and finally went to her room
completely overdone with sleep, judging by her peevish
heavy look, and the constant rubbing she inflicted on
her eyes. The following night she seemed more im-

patient still, and on the third from recovering my company she complained of a headache and left me. I thought her conduct odd; and having remained alone a long while, I resolved on going and inquiring whether she were better, and asking her to come and lie on the sofa, instead of upstairs in the dark. No Catherine could I discover upstairs, and none below. The servants affirmed they had not seen her. I listened at Mr. Edgar's door; all was silence. I returned to her apartment, extinguished my candle, and seated myself in the window.

The moon shone bright; a sprinkling of snow covered the ground, and I reflected that she might possibly have taken it into her head to walk about the garden for refreshment. I did detect a figure creeping along the inner fence of the park, but it was not my young mistress. On its merging into the light I recognized one of the grooms. He stood a considerable period, viewing the carriage-road through the grounds, then started off at a brisk pace, as if he had detected something, and reappeared presently leading miss's pony; and there she was, just dismounted, and walking by its side. The man took his charge stealthily across the grass towards the stable. Cathy entered by the casement window of the drawing-room, and glided noiselessly up to where I awaited her. She put the door gently to, slipped off her snowy shoes, untied her hat, and was proceeding, unconscious of my espionage, to lay aside her mantle, when I suddenly rose and revealed myself. The surprise petrified her an instant; she uttered an inarticulate exclamation, and stood fixed.

"My dear Miss Catherine," I began, too vividly impressed by her recent kindness to break into a scold, "where have you been riding out at this hour? And why should you try to deceive me by telling a tale? Where have you been? Speak!"

"To the bottom of the park," she stammered. "I didn't tell a tale."

"And nowhere else?" I demanded.

"No," was the muttered reply.

"O Catherine!" I cried sorrowfully. "You know you have been doing wrong, or you wouldn't be driven to uttering an untruth to me. That does grieve me. I'd rather be three months ill than hear you frame a deliberate lie."

She sprang forward, and bursting into tears, threw her arms round my neck.

"Well, Ellen, I'm so afraid of you being angry," she said. "Promise not to be angry, and you shall know the very truth. I hate to hide it."

We sat down in the window-seat. I assured her I would not scold, whatever her secret might be, and I guessed it, of course; so she commenced,—

"I've been to Wuthering Heights, Ellen, and I've never missed going a day since you fell ill, except thrice before and twice after you left your room. I gave Michael books and pictures to prepare Minny every evening, and to put her back in the stable. You mustn't scold *him* either, mind. I was at the Heights by half-past six, and generally stayed till half-past eight, and then galloped home. It was not to amuse myself that I went; I was often wretched all the time. Now and then I was happy—once in a week perhaps. At first I expected there would be sad work persuading you to let me keep my word to Linton, for I had engaged to call again next day when we quitted him; but as you stayed upstairs on the morrow, I escaped that trouble. While Michael was refastening the lock of the park door in the afternoon, I got possession of the key, and told him how my cousin wished me to visit him, because he was sick and couldn't come to the Grange, and how papa would object to my going; and then I negotiated with him about the pony. He is fond of reading, and he thinks of leaving soon to get married; so he offered, if I would lend him books out of the library, to do what I wished; but I preferred giving him my own, and that satisfied him better.

"On my second visit Linton seemed in lively spirits;

and Zillah (that is their housekeeper) made us a clean room and a good fire, and told us that, as Joseph was out at a prayer-meeting, and Hareton Earnshaw was off with his dogs—robbing our woods of pheasants, as I heard afterwards—we might do what we liked. She brought me some warm wine and gingerbread, and appeared exceedingly good-natured; and Linton sat in the arm-chair, and I in the little rocking-chair on the hearth-stone, and we laughed and talked so merrily, and found so much to say. We planned where we would go, and what we would do in summer. I needn't repeat that, because you would call it silly.

"One time, however, we were near quarrelling. He said the pleasantest manner of spending a hot July day was lying from morning till evening on a bank of heath in the middle of the moors, with the bees humming dreamily about among the bloom, and the larks singing high up overhead, and the blue sky and bright sun shining steadily and cloudlessly. That was his most perfect idea of heaven's happiness. Mine was rocking in a rustling green tree, with a west wind blowing, and bright white clouds flitting rapidly above, and not only larks, but throstles, and blackbirds, and linnets, and cuckoos pouring out music on every side, and the moors seen at a distance, broken into cool, dusky dells, but close by great swells of long grass undulating in waves to the breeze, and woods and sounding water, and the whole world awake and wild with joy. He wanted all to lie in an ecstasy of peace; I wanted all to sparkle and dance in a glorious jubilee. I said his heaven would be only half alive, and he said mine would be drunk; I said I should fall asleep in his, and he said he could not breathe in mine, and began to grow very snappish. At last we agreed to try both, as soon as the right weather came; and then we kissed each other and were friends.

"After sitting still an hour, I looked at the great room with its smooth uncarpeted floor, and thought how nice it would be to play in if we removed the table; and I asked Linton to call Zillah in to help us, and we'd have

a game at blind-man's buff. She should try to catch us
you used to, you know, Ellen. He wouldn't. Ther
was no pleasure in it, he said. But he consented to pla
at ball with me. We found two in a cupboard, among
heap of old toys, tops, and hoops, and battledores, an
shuttlecocks. One was marked C. and the other H.
wished to have the C., because that stood for Catherine
and the H. might be for Heathcliff, his name ; but th
bran came out of H., and Linton didn't like it. I bea
him constantly, and he got cross again, and coughed, an
returned to his chair. That night, though, he easily re
covered his good-humour. He was charmed with tw
or three pretty songs—*your* songs, Ellen ; and when
was obliged to go he begged and entreated me to com
the following evening, and I promised. Minny and
went flying home as light as air, and I dreamt c
Wuthering Heights and my sweet darling cousin til
morning.

"On the morrow I was sad, partly because you wer
poorly, and partly that I wished my father knew an
approved of my excursions ; but it was beautiful moon
light after tea, and as I rode on the gloom cleared.
shall have another happy evening, I thought to myself
and, what delights me more, my pretty Linton will.
trotted up their garden, and was turning round to th
back, when that fellow Earnshaw met me, took my bridle
and bade me go in by the front entrance. He patte
Minny's neck, and said she was a bonny beast, and ap
peared as if he wanted me to speak to him. I only tol
him to leave my horse alone, or else it would kick him
He answered in his vulgar accent, ' It wouldn't do mitc
hurt if it did,' and surveyed its legs with a smile.
was half inclined to make it try ; however, he moved
off to open the door, and as he raised the latch he looke
up to the inscription above, and said, with a stupi
mixture of awkwardness and elation,—

"' Miss Catherine, I can read yon now.'

"' Wonderful !' I exclaimed. ' Pray let us hear you
you *are* grown clever.'

" He spelt, and drawled over by syllables, the name. 'Hareton Earnshaw.'

" ' And the figures ? ' I cried encouragingly, perceiving that he came to a dead halt.

" ' I cannot tell them yet,' he answered.

" ' Oh, you dunce!' I said, laughing heartily at his failure.

" The fool stared, with a grin hovering about his lips, and a scowl gathering over his eyes, as if uncertain whether he might not join in my mirth—whether it were not pleasant familiarity, or what it really was, contempt. I settled his doubts by suddenly retrieving my gravity and desiring him to walk away, for I came to see Linton, not him. He reddened—I saw that by the moonlight—dropped his hand from the latch, and skulked off, a picture of mortified vanity. He imagined himself to be as accomplished as Linton, I suppose, because he could spell his own name, and was marvellously discomfited that I didn't think the same."

" Stop, Miss Catherine dear ! " I interrupted. " I shall not scold, but I don't like your conduct there. If you had remembered that Hareton was your cousin as much as Master Heathcliff, you would have felt how improper it was to behave in that way. At least, it was praiseworthy ambition for him to desire to be as accomplished as Linton, and probably he did not learn merely to show off. You had made him ashamed of his ignorance before, I have no doubt, and he wished to remedy it and please you. To sneer at his imperfect attempt was very bad breeding. Had *you* been brought up in his circumstances, would you be less rude ? He was as quick and as intelligent a child as ever you were, and I'm hurt that he should be despised now, because that base Heathcliff has treated him so unjustly."

" Well, Ellen, you won't cry about it, will you ? " she exclaimed, surprised at my earnestness. " But wait, and you shall hear if he conned his A B C to please me, and if it were worth while being civil to the brute. I entered. Linton was lying on the settle, and half got up to welcome me.

"'I'm ill to-night, Catherine, love,' he said; 'and you must have all the talk, and let me listen. Come and sit by me. I was sure you wouldn't break your word, and I'll make you promise again before you go.'

"I knew now that I mustn't tease him, as he was ill, and I spoke softly, and put no questions, and avoided irritating him in any way. I had brought some of my nicest books for him. He asked me to read a little of one, and I was about to comply, when Earnshaw burst the door open, having gathered venom with reflection. He advanced direct to us, seized Linton by the arm, and swung him off the seat.

"'Get to thy own room!' he said, in a voice almost inarticulate with passion; and his face looked swelled and furious. 'Take her there if she comes to see thee: thou shalln't keep me out of this. Begone wi' ye both!'

"He swore at us, and left Linton no time to answer, nearly throwing him into the kitchen; and he clenched his fist as I followed, seemingly longing to knock me down. I was afraid for a moment, and I let one volume fall; he kicked it after me, and shut us out. I heard a malignant, crackly laugh by the fire, and turning, beheld that odious Joseph standing rubbing his bony hands, and quivering.

"'I wer sure he'd sarve ye out! He's a grand lad! He's getten t' raight sperrit in him! _He_ knaws—ay, he knaws as weel as I do—who sud be t' maister yonder! Ech, ech, ech! He made ye skift properly! Ech, ech, ech!'

"'Where must we go?' I asked of my cousin, disregarding the old wretch's mockery.

"Linton was white and trembling. He was not pretty then, Ellen—oh no! He looked frightful, for his thin face and large eyes were wrought into an expression of frantic, powerless fury. He grasped the handle of the door, and shook it; it was fastened inside.

"'If you don't let me in I'll kill you! if you don't let me in I'll kill you!' he rather shrieked than said. 'Devil! devil! I'll kill you! I'll kill you!'

"Joseph uttered his croaking laugh again.

" ' Thear, that's t' father ! ' he cried. ' That's father ! We've allas summut o' either side in us. Niver heed, Hareton, lad—dunnut be 'feard—he cannot get at thee ! '

" I took hold of Linton's hands and tried to pull him away, but he shrieked so shockingly that I dared not proceed. At last his cries were choked by a dreadful fit of coughing. Blood gushed from his mouth, and he fell on the ground. I ran into the yard, sick with terror, and called for Zillah as loud as I could. She soon heard me. She was milking the cows in a shed behind the barn, and hurrying from her work she inquired what there was to do. I hadn't breath to explain. Dragging her in, I looked about for Linton. Earnshaw had come out to examine the mischief he had caused, and he was then conveying the poor thing upstairs. Zillah and I ascended after him ; but he stopped me at the top of the steps, and said I shouldn't go in—I must go home. I exclaimed that he had killed Linton, and I *would* enter. Joseph locked the door, and declared I should do ' no sich stuff,' and asked me whether I were ' bahn to be as mad as him.' I stood crying till the house-keeper reappeared. She affirmed he would be better in a bit, but he couldn't do with that shrieking and din ; and she took me and nearly carried me into the house.

" Ellen, I was ready to tear my hair off my head. I sobbed and wept so that my eyes were almost blind ; and the ruffian you have such sympathy with stood opposite, presuming every now and then to bid me ' wisht,' and denying that it was his fault ; and finally, frightened by my assertions that I would tell papa, and that he should be put in prison and hanged, he commenced blubbering himself, and hurried out to hide his cowardly agitation. Still I was not rid of him. When at length they compelled me to depart, and I had got some hundred yards off the premises, he suddenly issued from the shadow of the roadside, and checked Minny and took hold of me.

" ' Miss Catherine, I'm ill grieved,' he began, ' but it's rayther too bad——'

"I gave him a cut with my whip, thinking perhaps he would murder me. He let go, thundering one of his horrid curses, and I galloped home more than half out of my senses.

"I didn't bid you good-night that evening, and I didn't go to Wuthering Heights the next. I wished to go exceedingly, but I was strangely excited, and dreaded to hear that Linton was dead, sometimes, and sometimes shuddered at the thought of encountering Hareton. On the third day I took courage—at least I couldn't bear longer suspense, and stole off once more. I went at five o'clock, and walked, fancying I might manage to creep into the house and up to Linton's room unobserved. However, the dogs gave notice of my approach. Zillah received me, and saying 'the lad was mending nicely,' showed me into a small, tidy, carpeted apartment, where, to my inexpressible joy, I beheld Linton laid on a little sofa, reading one of my books. But he would neither speak to me nor look at me through a whole hour, Ellen ; he has such an unhappy temper. And what quite confounded me, when he did open his mouth it was to utter the falsehood that I had occasioned the uproar, and Hareton was not to blame ! Unable to reply, except passionately, I got up and walked from the room. He sent after me a faint 'Catherine !' He did not reckon on being answered so. But I wouldn't turn back ; and the morrow was the second day on which I stayed at home, nearly determined to visit him no more. But it was so miserable going to bed and getting up, and never hearing anything about him, that my resolution melted into air before it was properly formed. It *had* appeared wrong to take the journey once, now it seemed wrong to refrain. Michael came to ask if he must saddle Minny ; I said 'Yes,' and considered myself doing a duty as she bore me over the hills. I was forced to pass the front windows to get to the court : it was no use trying to conceal my presence.

"'Young master is in the house,' said Zillah, as she saw me making for the parlour. I went in. Earnshaw vas there also, but he quitted the room directly. Linon sat in the great armchair half asleep. Walking up o the fire, I began in a serious tone, partly meaning it o be true,—

"'As you don't like me, Linton, and as you think I ome on purpose to hurt you, and pretend that I do so very time, this is our last meeting. Let us say good-ye ; and tell Mr. Heathcliff that you have no wish to ee me, and that he mustn't invent any more falsehoods n the subject.'

"'Sit down and take your hat off, Catherine,' he nswered. 'You are so much happier than I am, you ught to be better. Papa talks enough of my defects nd shows enough scorn of me to make it natural I hould doubt myself. I doubt whether I am not alto-ether as worthless as he calls me frequently ; and then feel so cross and bitter, I hate everybody ! I *am* vorthless, and bad in temper, and bad in spirit, almost lways, and if you choose you *may* say good-bye ; you'll et rid of an annoyance. Only, Catherine, do me this ustice : believe that if I might be as sweet, and as kind, and as good as you are, I would be—as willingly, nd more so, than as happy and as healthy. And believe hat your kindness has made me love you deeper than f I deserved your love ; and though I couldn't and annot help showing my nature to you, I regret it and epent it, and shall regret and repent it till I die !'

"I felt he spoke the truth, and I felt I must forgive im ; and though he should quarrel the next moment, must forgive him again. We were reconciled ; but we ried, both of us, the whole time I stayed—not entirely or sorrow, yet I *was* sorry Linton had that distorted nature. He'll never let his friends be at ease, and he'll ever be at ease himself. I have always gone to his ittle parlour since that night, because his father re-urned the day after.

"About three times, I think, we have been merry and hopeful, as we were the first evening ; the rest of my visits were dreary and troubled—now with his selfish-

ness and spite, and now with his sufferings; but I've
learned to endure the former with nearly as little resent-
ment as the latter. Mr. Heathcliff purposely avoids
me; I have hardly seen him at all. Last Sunday
indeed, coming earlier than usual, I heard him abusing
poor Linton cruelly for his conduct of the night before
I can't tell how he knew of it, unless he listened. Linton
had certainly behaved provokingly. However, it was
the business of nobody but me, and I interrupted Mr
Heathcliff's lecture by entering and telling him so. He
burst into a laugh, and went away, saying he was glad
I took that view of the matter. Since then I've told
Linton he must whisper his bitter things. Now, Ellen
you have heard all. I can't be prevented from going to
Wuthering Heights except by inflicting misery on two
people; whereas, if you'll only not tell papa, my going
need disturb the tranquillity of none. You'll not tell
will you? It will be very heartless if you do."

"I'll make up my mind on that point by to-morrow,
Miss Catherine," I replied. "It requires some study;
and so I'll leave you to your rest, and go think it over."

I thought it over aloud, in my master's presence,
walking straight from her room to his, and relating the
whole story, with the exception of her conversations
with her cousin, and any mention of Hareton. Mr.
Linton was alarmed and distressed, more than he would
acknowledge to me. In the morning Catherine learned
my betrayal of her confidence, and she learned also that
her secret visits were to end. In vain she wept and
writhed against the interdict, and implored her father
to have pity on Linton. All she got to comfort her was
a promise that he would write and give him leave to
come to the Grange when he pleased, but explaining that
he must no longer expect to see Catherine at Wuthering
Heights. Perhaps, had he been aware of his nephew's
disposition and state of health, he would have seen fit
to withhold even that slight consolation.

CHAPTER XXV.

"THESE things happened last winter, sir," said Mrs. Dean—"hardly more than a year ago. Last winter I did not think, at another twelve months' end, I should be amusing a stranger to the family with relating them! Yet who knows how long you'll be a stranger? You're too young to rest always contented, living by yourself, and I some way fancy no one could see Catherine Linton and not love her. You smile; but why do you look so lively and interested when I talk about her? and why have you asked me to hang her picture over your fireplace? and why——"

"Stop, my good friend!" I cried. "It may be very possible that I should love her, but would she love me? I doubt it too much to venture my tranquillity by running into temptation. And then my home is not here. I'm of the busy world, and to its arms I must return. Go on. Was Catherine obedient to her father's commands?"

"She was," continued the housekeeper. "Her affection for him was still the chief sentiment in her heart; and he spoke without anger—he spoke in the deep tenderness of one about to leave his treasure amid perils and foes, where his remembered words would be the only aid that he could bequeath to guide her. He said to me a few days afterwards,—

"'I wish my nephew would write, Ellen, or call. Tell me sincerely what you think of him. Is he changed for the better, or is there a prospect of improvement as he grows a man?'

"'He's very delicate, sir,' I replied, 'and scarcely likely to reach manhood; but this I can say, he does not resemble his father. And if Miss Catherine had the misfortune to marry him, he would not be beyond her control, unless she were extremely and foolishly indulgent. However, master, you'll have plenty of time to get acquainted with him, and see whether he would suit her. It wants four years and more to his being of age.'

Edgar sighed, and walking to the window, looked out towards Gimmerton Kirk. It was a misty afternoon, but the February sun shone dimly, and we could just distinguish the two fir-trees in the yard, and the sparely scattered gravestones.

"I've prayed often," he half soliloquized, "for the approach of what is coming, and now I begin to shrink and fear it. I thought the memory of the hour I came down that glen a bridegroom would be less sweet than the anticipation that I was soon, in a few months, or possibly weeks, to be carried up and laid in its lonely hollow. Ellen, I've been very happy with my little Cathy; through winter nights and summer days she was a living hope at my side. But I've been as happy musing by myself among those stones, under that old church, lying through the long June evenings on the green mound of her mother's grave, and wishing, yearning for the time when I might lie beneath it. What can I do for Cathy? How must I quit her? I'd not care one moment for Linton being Heathcliff's son, nor for his taking her from me, if he could console her for my loss. I'd not care that Heathcliff gained his ends, and triumphed in robbing me of my last blessing. But should Linton be unworthy—only a feeble tool to his father—I cannot abandon her to him. And, hard though it be to crush her buoyant spirit, I must persevere in making her sad while I live, and leaving her solitary when I die. Darling! I'd rather resign her to God, and lay her in the earth before me."

"Resign her to God as it is, sir," I answered; "and if we should lose you—which may He forbid—under His providence I'll stand her friend and counsellor to the last. Miss Catherine is a good girl; I don't fear that she will go wilfully wrong; and people who do their duty are always finally rewarded."

Spring advanced, yet my master gathered no real strength, though he resumed his walks in the grounds with his daughter. To her inexperienced notions this itself was a sign of convalescence. And then his cheek was often flushed, and his eyes were bright; she felt sure of his recovery. On her seventeenth birthday he did not visit the churchyard. It was raining, and I observed,—

"You'll surely not go out to-night, sir?"

He answered,—

"No, I'll defer it this year a little longer."

He wrote again to Linton, expressing his great desire to see him; and had the invalid been presentable, I've no doubt his father would have permitted him to come. As it was, being instructed, he returned an answer, intimating that Mr. Heathcliff objected to his calling at the Grange; but his uncle's kind remembrance delighted him, and he hoped to meet him sometimes in his rambles, and personally to petition that his cousin and he might not remain long so utterly divided.

That part of his letter was simple and probably his own. Heathcliff knew he could plead eloquently for Catherine's company, then.

"I do not ask," he said, "that she may visit here, but am I never to see her because my father forbids me to go to her home, and you forbid her to come to mine? Do, now and then, ride with her towards the Heights, and let us exchange a few words in your presence. We have done nothing to deserve this separation; and you are not angry with me—you have no reason to dislike me, you allow, yourself. Dear uncle, send me a kind note to-morrow, and leave to join you anywhere you please, except at Thrushcross Grange. I believe an interview would convince you that my father's character is not mine. He affirms I am more your nephew than his son; and though I have faults which render me unworthy of Catherine, she has excused them, and for her sake you should also. You inquire after my health. It is better; but while I remain cut off from all hope, and doomed to solitude or the society of those who never did and never will like me, how can I be cheerful and well?"

9

Edgar, though he felt for the boy, could not conser to grant his request, because he could not accompan Catherine. He said in summer perhaps they might mee Meantime he wished him to continue writing at interval and engaged to give him what advice and comfort h was able by letter, being well aware of his hard positio in his family. Linton complied, and had he been ur restrained, would probably have spoiled all by filling hi epistles with complaints and lamentations; but hi father kept a sharp watch over him, and of course ir sisted on every line that my master sent being show So, instead of penning his peculiar personal suffering and distresses, the themes constantly uppermost in hi thoughts, he harped on the cruel obligation of bein held asunder from his friend and love, and gently int mated that Mr. Linton must allow an interview soor or he should fear he was purposely deceiving him wit empty promises.

Cathy was a powerful ally at home, and between ther they at length persuaded my master to acquiesce in thei having a ride or a walk together about once a weel under my guardianship, and on the moors nearest th Grange—for June found him still declining. Thoug he had set aside yearly a portion of his income for m young lady's fortune, he had a natural desire that sh might retain—or at least return in a short time to- the house of her ancestors; and he considered her onl prospect of doing that was by a union with his hei He had no idea that the latter was failing almost a fast as himself, nor had any one, I believe. No docto visited the Heights, and no one saw Master Heathcli to make report of his condition among us. I, for m part, began to fancy my forebodings were false, and tha he must be actually rallying, when he mentioned ridin and walking on the moors, and seemed so earnest in pur suing his object. I could not picture a father treating dying child as tyrannically and wickedly as I afterwar learned Heathcliff had treated him, to compel thi apparent eagerness, his efforts redoubling the more im

ninently his avaricious and unfeeling plans were threat-
ned with defeat by death.

CHAPTER XXVI.

UMMER was already past its prime when Edgar reluc-
antly yielded his assent to their entreaties, and Catherine
nd I set out on our first ride to join her cousin. It was
 close, sultry day, devoid of sunshine, but with a sky
oo dappled and hazy to threaten rain ; and our place
f meeting had been fixed at the guide-stone by the cross-
oads. On arriving there, however, a little herd-boy,
ispatched as a messenger, told us that—

"Maister Linton wer just o' this side th' Heights, and
e'd be mitch obleeged to us to gang on a bit further."

"Then Master Linton has forgot the first injunction
 his uncle," I observed. "He bade us keep on the
range land, and here we are off at once."

"Well, we'll turn our horses' heads round when we
ach him," answered my companion; "our excursion
all lie towards home."

But when we reached him, and that was scarcely a
uarter of a mile from his own door, we found he had
o horse, and we were forced to dismount and leave ours
 graze. He lay on the heath awaiting our approach,
d did not rise till we came within a few yards. Then
 walked so feebly, and looked so pale, that I immedi-
ely exclaimed,—

"Why, Master Heathcliff, you are not fit for enjoying
ramble this morning. How ill you do look !"

Catherine surveyed him with grief and astonishment.
e changed the ejaculation of joy on her lips to one of
arm, and the congratulation on their long-postponed
eeting to an anxious inquiry whether he were worse
an usual.

"No; better—better ! " he panted, trembling, and re-
ining her hand as if he needed its support, while his
ge blue eyes wandered timidly over her, the hollow-

ness round them transforming to haggard wildness th
languid expression they once possessed.

"But you have been worse," persisted his cousin—
"worse than when I saw you last. You are thinner
and——"

"I'm tired," he interrupted hurriedly. It is too ho
for walking; let us rest here. And in the morning
often feel sick. Papa says I grow so fast."

Badly satisfied, Cathy sat down, and he reclined be
side her.

"This is something like your paradise," said she, mak
ing an effort at cheerfulness. "You recollect the tw
days we agreed to spend in the place and way eac
thought pleasantest? This is nearly yours, only ther
are clouds; but then they are so soft and mellow, it i
nicer than sunshine. Next week, if you can, we'll rid
down to the Grange Park and try mine."

Linton did not appear to remember what she talke
of, and he had evidently great difficulty in sustainin
any kind of conversation. His lack of interest in th
subjects she started, and his equal incapacity to con
tribute to her entertainment, were so obvious that sh
could not conceal her disappointment. An indefinit
alteration had come over his whole person and manne
The pettishness that might be caressed into fondnes
had yielded to a listless apathy; there was less of th
peevish temper of a child which frets and teases on pu
pose to be soothed, and more of the self-absorbed moros
ness of a confirmed invalid, repelling consolation, an
ready to regard the good-humoured mirth of others a
an insult. Catherine perceived, as well as I did, that h
held it rather a punishment than a gratification to endu
our company, and she made no scruple of proposin
presently, to depart. That proposal unexpectedly rouse
Linton from his lethargy, and threw him into a strang
state of agitation. He glanced fearfully towards th
Heights, begging she would remain another half-hour a
least.

"But I think," said Cathy, "you'd be more comfor

ble at home than sitting here; and I cannot amuse
ou to-day, I see, by my tales, and songs, and chatter.
ou have grown wiser than I in these six months; you
ave little taste for my diversions now—or else, if I could
muse you, I'd willingly stay."

"Stay to rest yourself," he replied. "And, Catherine,
on't think or say that I'm *very* unwell. It is the heavy
eather and heat that make me dull; and I walked about,
efore you came, a great deal for me. Tell uncle I'm in
olerable health, will you?"

"I'll tell him that *you* say so, Linton. I couldn't
ffirm that you are," observed my young lady, wonder-
ng at his pertinacious assertion of what was evidently
n untruth.

"And be here again next Thursday," continued he,
hunning her puzzled gaze. "And give him my thanks
or permitting you to come—my best thanks, Catherine.
And—and if you *did* meet my father, and he asked you
bout me, don't lead him to suppose that I've been
xtremely silent and stupid. Don't look sad and down-
ast, as you *are* doing; he'll be angry."

"I care nothing for his anger," exclaimed Cathy,
magining she would be its object.

"But I do," said her cousin, shuddering. "*Don't* pro-
oke him against me, Catherine, for he is very hard."

"Is he severe to you, Master Heathcliff?" I inquired.
Has he grown weary of indulgence, and passed from
assive to active hatred?"

Linton looked at me, but did not answer; and after
keeping her seat by his side another ten minutes, during
which his head fell drowsily on his breast, and he uttered
nothing except suppressed moans of exhaustion or pain,
Cathy began to seek solace in looking for bilberries, and
haring the produce of her researches with me. She did
not offer them to him, for she saw further notice would
only weary and annoy.

"Is it half an hour now, Ellen?" she whispered in
my ear at last. "I can't tell why we should stay. He's
asleep, and papa will be wanting us back."

"Well, we must not leave him asleep," I answered
"Wait till he wakes, and be patient. You were migh
eager to set off, but your longing to see poor Linto
has soon evaporated."

"Why did *he* wish to see me?" returned Catherin
"In his crossest humours, formerly, I liked him bett
than I do in his present curious mood. It's just as if
were a task he was compelled to perform—this intervie
—for fear his father should scold him. But I'm hard
going to come to give Mr. Heathcliff pleasure, whatev
reason he may have for ordering Linton to undergo th
penance. And though I'm glad he's better in healt
I'm sorry he's so much less pleasant, and so much le
affectionate to me."

"You think *he is* better in health, then?" I said.

"Yes," she answered, "because he always made suc
a great deal of his sufferings, you know. He is no
tolerably well, as he told me to tell papa; but he
better, very likely."

"There you differ with me, Miss Cathy," I remarked
"I should conjecture him to be far worse."

Linton here started from his slumber in bewildere
terror, and asked if any one had called his name.

"No," said Catherine, "unless in dreams. I canno
conceive how you manage to doze out of doors, in th
morning."

"I thought I heard my father," he gasped, glancin
up to the frowning nab above us. "You are sure no
body spoke?"

"Quite sure," replied his cousin. "Only Ellen and
were disputing concerning your health. Are you trul
stronger, Linton, than when we separated in winter
If you be, I'm certain one thing is not stronger—you
regard for me. Speak! Are you?"

The tears gushed from Linton's eyes as he answere
"Yes, yes, I am!" And still under the spell of th
imaginary voice, his gaze wandered up and down t
detect its owner.

Cathy rose. "For to-day we must part," she sai

'And I won't conceal that I have been sadly disap-pointed with our meeting, though I'll mention it to no-body but you—not that I stand in awe of Mr. Heathcliff."

"Hush!" murmured Linton; "for God's sake, hush! He's coming." And he clung to Catherine's arm, striv-ing to detain her; but at that announcement she hastily disengaged herself and whistled to Minny, who obeyed her like a dog.

"I'll be here next Thursday," she cried, springing to the saddle. "Good-bye.—Quick, Ellen!"

And so we left him, scarcely conscious of our departure, so absorbed was he in anticipating his father's approach.

Before we reached home, Catherine's displeasure soft-ened into a perplexed sensation of pity and regret, largely blended with vague, uneasy doubts about Linton's actual circumstances, physical and social, in which I partook, though I counselled her not to say much, for a second journey would make us better judges. My master requested an account of our ongoings. His nephew's offering of thanks was duly delivered, Miss Cathy gently touching on the rest. I also threw little light on his inquiries, for I hardly knew what to hide and what to reveal.

CHAPTER XXVII.

SEVEN days glided away, every one marking its course by the henceforth rapid alteration of Edgar Linton's state. The havoc that months had previously wrought was now emulated by the inroads of hours. Catherine we would fain have deluded yet; but her own quick spirit refused to delude her; it divined in secret, and brooded on the dreadful probability, gradually ripening into certainty. She had not the heart to mention her ride when Thursday came round. I mentioned it for her, and obtained permission to order her out of doors; for the library, where her father stopped a short time daily —the brief period he could bear to sit up—and his chamber, had become her whole world. She grudged

each moment that did not find her bending over his
pillow or seated by his side. Her countenance grew
wan with watching and sorrow, and my master gladly
dismissed her to what he flattered himself would be a
happy change of scene and society, drawing comfort
from the hope that she would not now be left entirely
alone after his death.

He had a fixed idea, I guessed by several observations
he let fall, that, as his nephew resembled him in person,
he would resemble him in mind, for Linton's letters
bore few or no indications of his defective character.
And I, through pardonable weakness, refrained from correcting the error, asking myself what good there would be
in disturbing his last moments with information that he
had neither power nor opportunity to turn to account.

We deferred our excursion till the afternoon—a golden
afternoon of August, every breath from the hills so full
of life that it seemed, whoever respired it, though dying,
might revive. Catherine's face was just like the landscape—shadows and sunshine flitting over it in rapid
succession ; but the shadows rested longer, and the sunshine was more transient ; and her poor little heart
reproached itself for even that passing forgetfulness of
its cares.

We discerned Linton watching at the same spot he
had selected before. My young mistress alighted, and
told me that, as she was resolved to stay a very little
while, I had better hold the pony and remain on horseback ; but I dissented. I wouldn't risk losing sight of
the charge committed to me a minute, so we climbed the
slope of heath together. Master Heathcliff received us
with greater animation on this occasion—not the animation of high spirits though, nor yet of joy ; it looked
more like fear.

"It is late," he said, speaking short and with difficulty. "Is not your father very ill ? I thought you
wouldn't come."

"*Why* won't you be candid ?" cried Catherine, swallowing her greeting. "Why cannot you say at once

you don't want me? It is strange, Linton, that for the second time you have brought me here on purpose, apparently, to distress us both, and for no reason besides."

Linton shivered, and glanced at her, half supplicating, half ashamed; but his cousin's patience was not sufficient to endure this enigmatical behaviour.

"My father *is* very ill," she said; "and why am I called from his bedside? Why didn't you send to absolve me from my promise when you wished I wouldn't keep it? Come! I desire an explanation; playing and trifling are completely banished out of my mind, and I can't dance attendance on your affectations now!"

"My affectations!" he murmured; "what are they? For Heaven's sake, Catherine, don't look so angry! Despise me as much as you please. I am a worthless, cowardly wretch—I can't be scorned enough; but I'm too mean for your anger. Hate my father, and spare me for contempt."

"Nonsense!" cried Catherine in a passion. "Foolish, silly boy! And there! he trembles, as if I were really going to touch him! You needn't bespeak contempt, Linton; anybody will have it spontaneously at your service. Get off! I shall return home. It is folly dragging you from the hearthstone, and pretending—what do we pretend? Let go my frock! If I pitied you for crying and looking so very frightened, you should spurn such pity.—Ellen, tell him how disgraceful this conduct is.—Rise, and don't degrade yourself into an abject reptile—*don't!*"

With streaming face and an expression of agony Linton had thrown his nerveless frame along the ground. He seemed convulsed with exquisite terror.

"Oh!" he sobbed, "I cannot bear it! Catherine, Catherine, I'm a traitor too, and I dare not tell you! But leave me, and I shall be killed! *Dear* Catherine, my life is in your hands; and you have said you loved me, and if you did, it wouldn't harm you. You'll not go then, kind, sweet, good Catherine? And perhaps you *will* consent—and he'll let me die with you!"

My young lady, on witnessing his intense anguish, stooped to raise him. The old feeling of indulgent tenderness overcame her vexation, and she grew thoroughly moved and alarmed.

"Consent to what ?" she asked. "To stay ? Tell me the meaning of this strange talk, and I will. You contradict your own words and distract me. Be calm and frank, and confess at once all that weighs on your heart. You wouldn't injure me, Linton, would you ? You wouldn't let any enemy hurt me, if you could prevent it ? I'll believe you are a coward for yourself, but not a cowardly betrayer of your best friend."

"But my father threatened me," gasped the boy, clasping his attenuated fingers, "and I dread him—I dread him ! I *dare* not tell ! "

"Oh, well," said Catherine, with scornful compassion, "keep your secret. *I'm* no coward. Save yourself. I'm not afraid."

Her magnanimity provoked his tears. He wept wildly, kissing her supporting hands, and yet could not summon courage to speak out. I was cogitating what the mystery might be, and determined Catherine should never suffer to benefit him or any one else, by my good-will, when, hearing a rustle among the ling, I looked up and saw Mr. Heathcliff almost close upon us, descending the Heights. He didn't cast a glance towards my companions, though they were sufficiently near for Linton's sobs to be audible, but hailing me in the almost hearty tone he assumed to none besides, and the sincerity of which I couldn't avoid doubting, he said,—

"It is something to see you so near to my house, Nelly. How are you at the Grange ? Let us hear. The rumour goes," he added in a lower tone, "that Edgar Linton is on his deathbed ; perhaps they exaggerate his illness ?"

"No. My master is dying," I replied ; "it is true enough. A sad thing it will be for us all, but a blessing for him."

"How long will he last, do you think ?" he asked.

" I don't know," I said.

" Because," he continued, looking at the two young people, who were fixed under his eye—Linton appeared as if he could not venture to stir or raise his head, and Catherine could not move on his account—" because that lad yonder seems determined to beat me, and I'd thank his uncle to be quick and go before him. Hullo! has the whelp been playing that game long? I *did* give him some lessons about snivelling. Is he pretty lively with Miss Linton generally?"

" Lively? No; he has shown the greatest distress," I answered. "To see him, I should say that, instead of rambling with his sweetheart on the hills, he ought to be in bed, under the hands of a doctor."

" He shall be in a day or two," muttered Heathcliff. "But first—— Get up, Linton! get up!" he shouted. " Don't grovel on the ground there. Up, this moment!"

Linton had sunk prostrate again in another paroxysm of helpless fear, caused by his father's glance towards him, I suppose; there was nothing else to produce such humiliation. He made several efforts to obey, but his little strength was annihilated for the time, and he fell back again with a moan. Mr. Heathcliff advanced, and lifted him to lean against a ridge of turf.

" Now," said he, with curbed ferocity, " I'm getting angry, and if you don't command that paltry spirit of yours—— *Damn* you! get up directly!"

" I will, father," he panted. " Only let me alone, or I shall faint. I've done as you wished, I'm sure. Catherine will tell you that I—that I—have been cheerful. —Ah! keep by me, Catherine. Give me your hand."

" Take mine," said his father. " Stand on your feet. There now; she'll lend you her arm. That's right; look at *her*.—You would imagine I was the devil himself, Miss Linton, to excite such horror. Be so kind as to walk home with him, will you? He shudders if I touch him."

" Linton dear!" whispered Catherine, " I can't go to Wuthering Heights; papa has forbidden me. He'll not harm you. Why are you so afraid?"

"I can never re-enter that house," he answered. "I'm *not* to re-enter it without you."

"Stop!" cried his father. "We'll respect Catherine's filial scruples.—Nelly, take him in, and I'll follow your advice concerning the doctor without delay."

"You'll do well," replied I. "But I must remain with my mistress; to mind your son is not my business."

"You are very stiff," said Heathcliff—"I know that; but you'll force me to pinch the baby and make it scream before it moves your charity.—Come, then, my hero. Are you willing to return, escorted by me?"

He approached once more, and made as if he would seize the fragile being; but, shrinking back, Linton clung to his cousin, and implored her to accompany him, with a frantic importunity that admitted no denial. However I disapproved, I couldn't hinder her. Indeed, how could she have refused him herself? What was filling him with dread we had no means of discerning; but there he was, powerless under its gripe, and any addition seemed capable of shocking him into idiocy. We reached the threshold. Catherine walked in, and I stood waiting till she had conducted the invalid to a chair, expecting her out immediately, when Mr. Heathcliff, pushing me forward, exclaimed,—

"My house is not stricken with the plague, Nelly, and I have a mind to be hospitable to-day. Sit down, and allow me to shut the door."

He shut and locked it also. I started.

"You shall have tea before you go home," he added. "I am by myself. Hareton is gone with some cattle to the Lees, and Zillah and Joseph are off on a journey of pleasure; and though I'm used to being alone, I'd rather have some interesting company, if I can get it. —Miss Linton, take your seat by *him*. I give you what I have; the present is hardly worth accepting, but I have nothing else to offer. It is Linton I mean. How she does stare! It's odd what a savage feeling I have to anything that seems afraid of me. Had I been born where laws are less strict and tastes less dainty, I should treat myself to a slow vivisection of those two as an evening's amusement."

He drew in his breath, struck the table, and swore to himself, " By hell, I hate them ! "

" I'm not afraid of you ! " exclaimed Catherine, who could not hear the latter part of his speech. She stepped close up, her black eyes flashing with passion and resolution. " Give me that key. I will have it ! " she said. " I wouldn't eat or drink here if I were starving."

Heathcliff had the key in his hand that remained on the table. He looked up, seized with a sort of surprise at her boldness, or possibly reminded by her voice and glance of the person from whom she had inherited it. She snatched at the instrument, and half succeeded in getting it out of his loosened fingers ; but her action recalled him to the present—he recovered it speedily.

" Now, Catherine Linton," he said, " stand off, or I shall knock you down, and that will make Mrs. Dean mad."

Regardless of this warning, she captured his closed hand and its contents again. " We *will* go ! " she repeated, exerting her utmost efforts to cause the iron muscles to relax ; and finding that her nails made no impression, she applied her teeth pretty sharply. Heathcliff glanced at me a glance that kept me from interfering a moment. Catherine was too intent on his fingers to notice his face. He opened them suddenly, and resigned the object of dispute ; but ere she had well secured it, he seized her with the liberated hand, and pulling her on his knee, administered with the other a shower of terrific slaps on both sides of the head, each sufficient to have fulfilled his threat, had she been able to fall.

At this diabolical violence I rushed on him furiously. " You villain ! " I began to cry, " you villain ! " A touch on the chest silenced me. I am stout, and soon put out of breath ; and what with that and the rage, I staggered dizzily back, and felt ready to suffocate or to burst a blood-vessel. The scene was over in two minutes. Catherine, released, put her two hands to her temples,

and looked just as if she were not sure whether her ears
were off or on. She trembled like a reed, poor thing,
and leant against the table perfectly bewildered.

"I know how to chastise children, you see," said the
scoundrel grimly, as he stooped to repossess himself of
the key, which had dropped to the floor. "Go to Linton
now, as I told you, and cry at your ease. I shall be your
father to-morrow—all the father you'll have in a few
days—and you shall have plenty of that. You can
bear plenty; you're no weakling. You shall have a
daily taste, if I catch such a devil of a temper in your
eyes again!"

Cathy ran to me instead of Linton, and knelt down and
put her burning cheek on my lap, weeping aloud. Her
cousin had shrunk into a corner of the settle, as quiet as
a mouse, congratulating himself, I dare say, that the cor-
rection had lighted on another than him. Mr. Heathcliff, perceiving us all confounded, rose, and expeditiously
made the tea himself. The cups and saucers were laid
ready. He poured it out, and handed me a cup.

"Wash away your spleen," he said. "And help your
own naughty pet and mine. It is not poisoned, though
I prepared it. I'm going out to seek your horses."

Our first thought, on his departure, was to force an
exit somewhere. We tried the kitchen door, but that
was fastened outside. We looked at the windows; they
were too narrow for even Cathy's little figure.

"Master Linton," I cried, seeing we were regularly
imprisoned, "you know what your diabolical father is
after, and you shall tell us, or I'll box your ears, as he
has done your cousin's."

"Yes, Linton, you must tell," said Catherine. "It
was for your sake I came, and it will be wickedly ungrateful if you refuse."

"Give me some tea—I'm thirsty—and then I'll tell
you," he answered.—"Mrs. Dean, go away. I don't
like you standing over me.—Now, Catherine, you are
letting your tears fall into my cup. I won't drink that.
Give me another."

Catherine pushed another to him, and wiped her face. I felt disgusted at the little wretch's composure, since he was no longer in terror for himself. The anguish he had exhibited on the moor subsided as soon as ever he entered Wuthering Heights, so I guessed he had been menaced with an awful visitation of wrath if he failed in decoying us there; and that accomplished, he had no further immediate fears.

"Papa wants us to be married," he continued, after sipping some of the liquid. "And he knows your papa wouldn't let us marry now, and he's afraid of my dying if we wait; so we are to be married in the morning, and you are to stay here all night; and if you do as he wishes, you shall return home next day, and take me with you."

"Take you with her, pitiful changeling!" I exclaimed. "*You* marry! Why, the man is mad, or he thinks us fools every one. And do you imagine that beautiful young lady, that healthy, hearty girl, will tie herself to a little perishing monkey like you? Are you cherishing the notion that *anybody*, let alone Miss Catherine Linton, would have you for a husband? You want whipping for bringing us in here at all, with your dastardly puling tricks; and—don't look so silly now! I've a very good mind to shake you severely for your contemptible treachery and your imbecile conceit."

I did give him a slight shaking, but it brought on the cough, and he took to his ordinary resource of moaning and weeping, and Catherine rebuked me.

"Stay all night? No," she said, looking slowly round. "Ellen, I'll burn that door down, but I'll get out."

And she would have commenced the execution of her threat directly, but Linton was up in alarm for his dear self again. He clasped her in his two feeble arms, sobbing,—

"Won't you have me, and save me?—not let me come to the Grange? O darling Catherine, you mustn't go and leave, after all! You *must* obey my father—you *must!*"

"I must obey my own," she replied, "and relieve him from this cruel suspense. The whole night! What would he think? He'll be distressed already. I'll either break or burn a way out of the house. Be quiet! You're in no danger. But if you hinder me—— Linton, I love papa better than you!"

The mortal terror he felt of Mr. Heathcliff's anger restored to the boy his coward's eloquence. Catherine was near distraught; still she persisted that she must go home, and tried entreaty in her turn, persuading him to subdue his selfish agony. While they were thus occupied, our gaoler re-entered.

"Your beasts have trotted off," he said, "and—— Now, Linton! snivelling again? What has she been doing to you? Come, come; have done, and get to bed. In a month or two, my lad, you'll be able to pay her back her present tyrannies with a vigorous hand. You're pining for pure love, are you not?—nothing else in the world; and she shall have you! There, to bed! Zillah won't be here to-night. You must undress yourself. Hush! hold your noise! Once in your own room, I'll not come near you. You needn't fear. By chance you've managed tolerably. I'll look to the rest."

He spoke these words, holding the door open for his son to pass; and the latter achieved his exit exactly as a spaniel might which suspected the person who attended on it of designing a spiteful squeeze. The lock was resecured. Heathcliff approached the fire, where my mistress and I stood silent. Catherine looked up, and instinctively raised her hand to her cheek. His neighbourhood revived a painful sensation. Anybody else would have been incapable of regarding the childish act with sternness, but he scowled on her and muttered,—

"Oh! you are not afraid of me? Your courage is well disguised; you *seem* damnably afraid!"

"I *am* afraid now," she replied, "because, if I stay, papa will be miserable; and how can I endure making him miserable when he—when he—— Mr. Heathcliff, *let* me go home! I promise to marry Linton; papa would like me to, and I love him. Why should you wish to force me to do what I'll willingly do of myself?"

"Let him dare to force you!" I cried. "There's law n the land—thank God there is!—though we be in an out-of-the-way place. I'd inform if he were my own son. And it's felony, without benefit of clergy."

"Silence!" said the ruffian. "To the devil with your clamour! I don't want *you* to speak.—Miss Linton, I shall enjoy myself remarkably in thinking your father will be miserable; I shall not sleep for satisfaction. You could have hit on no surer way of fixing your residence under my roof for the next twenty-four hours than informing me that such an event would follow. As to your promise to marry Linton, I'll take care you shall keep it, for you shall not quit this place till it is fulfilled."

"Send Ellen, then, to let papa know I'm safe!" exclaimed Catherine, weeping bitterly; "or marry me now. Poor papa!—Ellen, he'll think we're lost. What shall we do?"

"Not he! He'll think you are tired of waiting on him, and run off for a little amusement," answered Heathcliff. "You cannot deny that you entered my house of your own accord, in contempt of his injunctions to the contrary. And it is quite natural that you should desire amusement at your age, and that you would weary of nursing a sick man, and that man *only* your father. Catherine, his happiest days were over when your days began. He cursed you, I dare say, for coming into the world (I did, at least), and it would just do if he cursed you as *he* went out of it. I'd join him. I don't love you. How should I? Weep away. As far as I can see, it will be your chief diversion hereafter, unless Linton make amends for other losses; and your provident parent appears to fancy he may. His letters of advice and consolation entertained me vastly. In his last he recommended my jewel to be careful of his, and kind to her when he got her. Careful and kind—that's paternal. But Linton requires his whole stock of care and kindness for himself. Linton can play the little tyrant well. He'll undertake to torture any number of cats, if their teeth be drawn and their claws pared. You'll be able to tell his uncle fine tales of his *kindness* when you get home again, I assure you."

"You're right there!" I said: "explain your son's character; show his resemblance to yourself; and then, I hope, Miss Cathy will think twice before she takes the cockatrice!"

"I don't much mind speaking of his amiable qualities now," he answered, "because she must either accept him or remain a prisoner, and you along with her, till your master dies. I can detain you both, quite concealed, here. If you doubt, encourage her to retract her word, and you'll have an opportunity of judging."

"I'll not retract my word," said Catherine. "I'll marry him within this hour, if I may go to Thrushcross Grange afterwards. Mr. Heathcliff, you're a cruel man, but you're not a fiend; and you won't, from *mere* malice, destroy irrevocably all my happiness. If papa thought I had left him on purpose, and if he died before I returned, could I bear to live? I've given over crying, but I'm going to kneel here at your knee; and I'll not get up, and I'll not take my eyes from your face till you look back at me! No, don't turn away—*do* look! You'll see nothing to provoke you. I don't hate you. I'm not angry that you struck me. Have you never loved *anybody* in all your life, uncle? *never?* Ah! you must look once. I'm so wretched, you can't help being sorry and pitying me."

"Keep your eft's fingers off, and move, or I'll kick you!" cried Heathcliff, brutally repulsing her. "I'd rather be hugged by a snake. How the devil can you dream of fawning on me? I *detest* you!"

He shrugged his shoulders, shook himself, indeed, as if his flesh crept with aversion, and thrust back his chair, while I got up and opened my mouth to commence a downright torrent of abuse. But I was rendered dumb in the middle of the first sentence by a threat that I should be shown into a room by myself the very next syllable I uttered. It was growing dark. We heard a sound of voices at the garden gate. Our host hurried out instantly. *He* had his wits about him; *we* had not. There was a talk of two or three minutes, and he returned alone.

"I thought it had been your cousin Hareton," I observed to Catherine. "I wish he would arrive. Who knows but he might take our part?"

"It was three servants sent to seek you from the Grange," said Heathcliff, overhearing me. "You should have opened a lattice and called out; but I could swear that chit is glad you didn't. She's glad to be obliged to stay, I'm certain."

At learning the chance we had missed we both gave vent to our grief without control, and he allowed us to wail on till nine o'clock. Then he bade us go upstairs, through the kitchen, to Zillah's chamber; and I whispered my companion to obey. Perhaps we might contrive to get through the window there, or into a garret, and out by its skylight. The window, however, was narrow, like those below, and the garret trap was safe from our attempts, for we were fastened in as before. We neither of us lay down. Catherine took her station by the lattice, and watched anxiously for morning, a deep sigh being the only answer I could obtain to my frequent entreaties that she would try to rest. I seated myself in a chair, and rocked to and fro, passing harsh judgment on my many derelictions of duty, from which, it struck me then, all the misfortunes of my employers sprang. It was not the case in reality, I am aware, but it was in my imagination that dismal night; and I thought Heathcliff himself less guilty than I.

At seven o'clock he came and inquired if Miss Linton had risen. She ran to the door immediately, and answered, "Yes." "Here, then," he said, opening it, and pulling her out. I rose to follow, but he turned the lock again. I demanded my release.

"Be patient," he replied. "I'll send up your breakfast in a while."

I thumped on the panels and rattled the latch angrily, and Catherine asked why I was still shut up? He answered, I must try to endure it another hour; and they

went away. I endured it two or three hours. At length
I heard a footstep—not Heathcliff's.

"I've brought you something to eat," said a voice.
"Oppen t' door!"

Complying eagerly, I beheld Hareton, laden with food
enough to last me all day.

"Tak it," he added, thrusting the tray into my hand.

"Stay one minute," I began.

"Nay," cried he, and retired, regardless of any prayers
I could pour forth to detain him.

And there I remained enclosed the whole day, and the
whole of the next night, and another, and another.
Five nights and four days I remained altogether, seeing
nobody but Hareton, once every morning; and he was
a model of a gaoler—surly and dumb, and deaf to every
attempt at moving his sense of justice or compassion.

CHAPTER XXVIII.

ON the fifth morning, or rather afternoon, a different
step approached, lighter and shorter, and this time the
person entered the room. It was Zillah, donned in her
scarlet shawl, with a black silk bonnet on her head, and
a willow basket swung to her arm.

"Eh, dear, Mrs. Dean!" she exclaimed. "Well,
there is a talk about you at Gimmerton. I never thought
but you were sunk in the Blackhorse marsh, and missy
with you, till master told me you'd been found, and he'd
lodged you here! What! and you must have got on
an island, sure. And how long were you in the hole?
Did master save you, Mrs. Dean? But you're not so
thin—you've not been so poorly, have you?"

"Your master is a true scoundrel!" I replied. "But
he shall answer for it. He needn't have raised that tale.
It shall all be laid bare."

"What do you mean?" asked Zillah. "It's not his
tale. They tell that in the village, about your being
lost in the marsh; and I calls to Earnshaw, when I

come in, ' Eh, they's queer things, Mr. Hareton, happened since I went off. It's a sad pity of that likely young lass, and cant Nelly Dean.' He stared. I thought he had not heard aught, so I told him the rumour. The master listened, and he just smiled to himself and said, ' If they have been in the marsh, they are out now, Zillah. Nelly Dean is lodged, at this minute, in your room. You can tell her to flit when you go up; here is the key. The bog-water got into her head, and she would have run home quite flighty, but I fixed her till she came round to her senses. You can bid her go to the Grange at once, if she be able, and carry a message from me that her young lady will follow in time to attend the squire's funeral.' "

"Mr. Edgar is not dead?" I gasped. "O Zillah, Zillah!"

"No, no. Sit you down, my good mistress," she replied; "you're right sickly yet. He's not dead. Dr. Kenneth thinks he may last another day. I met him on the road and asked."

Instead of sitting down, I snatched my outdoor things and hastened below, for the way was free. On entering the house I looked about for some one to give information of Catherine. The place was filled with sunshine, and the door stood wide open, but nobody seemed at hand. As I hesitated whether to go off at once or return and seek my mistress, a slight cough drew my attention to the hearth. Linton lay on the settle, sole tenant, sucking a stick of sugar-candy, and pursuing my movements with apathetic eyes. "Where is Miss Catherine?" I demanded sternly, supposing I could frighten him into giving intelligence by catching him thus alone. He sucked on like an innocent.

"Is she gone?" I said.

"No," he replied; "she's upstairs. She's not to go; we won't let her."

"You won't let her, little idiot!" I exclaimed. "Direct me to her room immediately, or I'll make you sing out sharply."

"Papa would make you sing out if you attempted to get there," he answered. "He says I'm not to be soft with Catherine. She's my wife, and it's shameful that she should wish to leave me. He says she hates me and wants me to die, that she may have my money. But she shan't have it, and she shan't go home—she never shall! She may cry and be sick as much as she pleases!"

He resumed his former occupation, closing his lids as if he meant to drop asleep.

"Master Heathcliff," I resumed, "have you forgotten all Catherine's kindness to you last winter, when you affirmed you loved her, and when she brought you books and sang you songs, and came many a time through wind and snow to see you? She wept to miss one evening, because you would be disappointed; and you felt then that she was a hundred times too good to you, and now you believe the lies your father tells, though you know he detests you both. And you join him against her. That's fine gratitude, is it not?"

The corner of Linton's mouth fell, and he took the sugar-candy from his lips.

"Did she come to Wuthering Heights because she hated you?" I continued. "Think for yourself! As to your money, she does not even know that you will have any. And you say she's sick, and yet you leave her alone up there in a strange house — *you* who have felt what it is to be so neglected! You could pity your own sufferings, and she pitied them too, but you won't pity hers! I shed tears, Master Heathcliff, you see— an elderly woman, and a servant merely; and you, after pretending such affection, and having reason to worship her almost, store every tear you have for yourself, and lie there quite at ease. Ah! you're a heartless, selfish boy!"

"I can't stay with her," he answered crossly. "I'll not stay by myself. She cries so I can't bear it. And she won't give over, though I say I'll call my father. I did call him once, and he threatened to strangle her if she was not quiet; but she began again the instant he left the room, moaning and grieving all night long, though I screamed for vexation that I couldn't sleep."

"Is Mr. Heathcliff out?" I inquired, perceiving that the wretched creature had no power to sympathize with his cousin's mental tortures.

"He's in the court," he replied, "talking to Dr. Kenneth, who says uncle is dying, truly, at last. I'm glad, for I shall be master of the Grange after him. Catherine always spoke of it as *her* house. It isn't hers. It's mine. Papa says everything she has is mine. All her nice books are mine. She offered to give me them, and her pretty birds, and her pony Minny, if I would get the key of our room and let her out; but I told her she had nothing to give—they were all, all mine. And then she cried, and took a little picture from her neck, and said I should have that—two pictures in a gold case, on one side her mother, and on the other uncle, when they were young. That was yesterday. I said *they* were mine too, and tried to get them from her. The spiteful thing wouldn't let me; she pushed me off, and hurt me. I shrieked out; that frightens her. She heard papa coming, and she broke the hinges and divided the case, and gave me her mother's portrait. The other she attempted to hide; but papa asked what was the matter, and I explained it. He took the one I had away, and ordered her to resign hers to me. She refused, and he—he struck her down, and wrenched it off the chain, and crushed it with his foot."

"And were you pleased to see her struck?" I asked, having my designs in encouraging his talk.

"I winked," he answered. "I wink to see my father strike a dog or a horse; he does it so hard. Yet I was glad at first. She deserved punishing for pushing me. But when papa was gone she made me come to the window, and showed me her cheek cut on the inside, against her teeth, and her mouth filling with blood; and then she gathered up the bits of the picture, and went and sat down with her face to the wall, and she has never

spoken to me since, and I sometimes think she can'
speak for pain. I don't like to think so ; but she's a
naughty thing for crying continually, and she looks so
pale and wild, I'm afraid of her.''

" And you can get the key if you choose ? " I said.

" Yes, when I am upstairs," he answered. " But I
can't walk upstairs now.''

" In what apartment is it ? " I asked.

" Oh," he cried, " I shan't tell *you* where it is ! It
is our secret. Nobody, neither Hareton nor Zillah, is to
know. There ! you've tired me ; go away, go away
And he turned his face on to his arm, and shut his eyes
again.

I considered it best to depart without seeing Mr. Heath
cliff, and bring a rescue for my young lady from the
Grange. On reaching it, the astonishment of my fellow
servants to see me, and their joy also, was intense ; and
when they heard that their little mistress was safe, two
or three were about to hurry up and shout the news at
Mr. Edgar's door ; but I bespoke the announcement of
it myself. How changed I found him even in those few
days ! He lay an image of sadness and resignation
waiting his death. Very young he looked ; though his
actual age was thirty-nine, one would have called him
ten years younger, at least. He thought of Catherine, for
he murmured her name. I touched his hand and spoke.

" Catherine is coming, dear master," I whispered
" She is alive and well, and will be here, I hope, to-night.'

I trembled at the first effects of this intelligence. He
half rose up, looked eagerly round the apartment, and
then sank back in a swoon. As soon as he recovered
related our compulsory visit and detention at the Heights
I said Heathcliff forced me to go in, which was not quite
true. I uttered as little as possible against Linton, nor
did I describe all his father's brutal conduct, my inten
tions being to add no bitterness, if I could help it, to his
already overflowing cup.

He divined that one of his enemy's purposes was to
secure the personal property, as well as the estate, to

his son, or rather himself; yet why he did not wait till his decease was a puzzle to my master, because ignorant how nearly he and his nephew would quit the world together. However, he felt that his will had better be altered. Instead of leaving Catherine's fortune at her own disposal, he determined to put it in the hands of trustees for her use during life, and for her children, if she had any, after her. By that means it could not fall to Mr. Heathcliff, should Linton die.

Having received his orders, I dispatched a man to fetch the attorney, and four more, provided with serviceable weapons, to demand my young lady of her gaoler. Both parties were delayed very late. The single servant returned first. He said Mr. Green, the lawyer, was out when he arrived at his house, and he had to wait two hours for his re-entrance; and then Mr. Green told him he had a little business in the village that must be done, but he would be at Thrushcross Grange before morning. The four men came back unaccompanied also. They brought word that Catherine was ill—too ill to quit her room—and Heathcliff would not suffer them to see her. I scolded the stupid fellows well for listening to that tale, which I would not carry to my master, resolving to take a whole bevy up to the Heights at daylight, and storm it literally, unless the prisoner were quietly surrendered to us. Her father *shall* see her, I vowed, and vowed again, if that devil be killed on his own doorstones in trying to prevent it!

Happily I was spared the journey and the trouble. I had gone downstairs at three o'clock to fetch a jug of water, and was passing through the hall with it in my hand, when a sharp knock at the front door made me jump. "Oh! it is Green," I said, recollecting myself—"only Green;" and I went on, intending to send somebody else to open it; but the knock was repeated, not loud, and still importunately. I put the jug on the banister and hastened to admit him myself. The harvest moon shone clear outside. It was not the attorney. My own sweet little mistress sprang on my neck, sobbing,—

" Ellen ! Ellen ! is papa alive ? "

" Yes ! " I cried—" yes, my angel, he is ! God be thanked, you are safe with us again ! "

She wanted to run, breathless as she was, upstairs to Mr. Linton's room, but I compelled her to sit down on a chair, and made her drink, and washed her pale face, chafing it into a faint colour with my apron. Then I said I must go first and tell of her arrival, imploring her to say she should be happy with young Heathcliff. She stared, but soon comprehending why I counselled her to utter the falsehood, she assured me she would not complain.

I couldn't abide to be present at their meeting. I stood outside the chamber door a quarter of an hour, and hardly ventured near the bed then. All was composed, however. Catherine's despair was as silent as her father's joy. She supported him calmly, in appearance, and he fixed on her features his raised eyes, that seemed dilating with ecstasy.

He died blissfully, Mr. Lockwood ; he died so. Kissing her cheek, he murmured,—

" I am going to her ; and you, darling child, shall come to us," and never stirred or spoke again, but continued that rapt, radiant gaze till his pulse imperceptibly stopped and his soul departed. None could have noticed the exact minute of his death, it was so entirely without a struggle.

Whether Catherine had spent her tears, or whether the grief were too weighty to let them flow, she sat there dry-eyed till the sun rose ; she sat till noon, and would still have remained brooding over that deathbed, but I insisted on her coming away and taking some repose. It was well I succeeded in removing her, for at dinner-time appeared the lawyer, having called at Wuthering Heights to get his instructions how to behave. He had sold himself to Mr. Heathcliff ; that was the cause of his delay in obeying my master's summons. Fortunately, no thought of worldly affairs crossed the latter's mind, to disturb him, after his daughter's arrival.

Mr. Green took upon himself to order everything and everybody about the place. He gave all the servants but me notice to quit. He would have carried his delegated authority to the point of insisting that Edgar Linton should not be buried beside his wife, but in the chapel with his family. There was the will, however, to hinder that, and my loud protestations against any infringement of its directions. The funeral was hurried over. Catherine, Mrs. Linton Heathcliff now, was suffered to stay at the Grange till her father's corpse had quitted it.

She told me that her anguish had at last spurred Linton to incur the risk of liberating her. She heard the men I sent disputing at the door, and she gathered the sense of Heathcliff's answer. It drove her desperate. Linton, who had been conveyed up to the little parlour soon after I left, was terrified into fetching the key before his father reascended. He had the cunning to unlock and relock the door, without shutting it; and when he should have gone to bed, he begged to sleep with Hareton, and his petition was granted for once. Catherine stole out before break of day. She dare not try the doors, lest the dogs should raise an alarm. She visited the empty chambers and examined their windows, and luckily lighting on her mother's, she got easily out of its lattice, and on to the ground by means of the fir-tree close by. Her accomplice suffered for his share in the escape, notwithstanding his timid contrivances.

CHAPTER XXIX.

THE evening after the funeral, my young lady and I were seated in the library, now musing mournfully, one of us despairingly, on our loss, now venturing conjectures as to the gloomy future.

We had just agreed the best destiny which could await Catherine would be a permission to continue resident at the Grange—at least during Linton's life—he being allowed to join her there, and I to remain as housekeeper. That seemed rather too favourable an arrangement to be hoped for, and yet I did hope, and began to cheer up under the prospect of retaining my home and my employment, and, above all, my beloved young mistress, when a servant—one of the discarded ones, not yet departed—rushed hastily in, and said " that devil Heathcliff " was coming through the court ; should he fasten the door in his face ?

If we had been mad enough to order that proceeding, we had not time. He made no ceremony of knocking or announcing his name. He was master, and availed himself of the master's privilege to walk straight in without saying a word. The sound of our informant's voice directed him to the library. He entered, and motioning him out, shut the door.

It was the same room into which he had been ushered, as a guest, eighteen years before. The same moon shone through the window, and the same autumn landscape lay outside. We had not yet lighted a candle, but all the apartment was visible, even to the portraits on the wall—the splendid head of Mrs. Linton, and the graceful one of her husband. Heathcliff advanced to the hearth. Time had little altered his person either. There was the same man, his dark face rather sallower and more composed, his frame a stone or two heavier, perhaps, and no other difference. Catherine had risen, with an impulse to dash out, when she saw him.

" Stop ! " he said, arresting her by the arm. " No more runnings away ! Where would you go ? I'm come to fetch you home, and I hope you will be a dutiful daughter, and not encourage my son to further disobedience. I was embarrassed how to punish him when I discovered his part in the business—he's such a cobweb, a pinch would annihilate him—but you'll see by his look that he has received his due. I brought him down one evening, the day before yesterday, and just set him in a chair, and never touched him afterwards. I sent Hareton out, and we had the room to ourselves. In two hours I called Joseph to carry him up again ; and since then my presence is as potent on his nerves as a ghost, and I fancy he sees me often, though I am not near. Hareton says he wakes and shrieks in the night by the hour together, and calls you to protect him from me; and whether you like your precious mate or not, you must come. He's your concern now; I yield all my interest in him to you."

"Why not let Catherine continue here," I pleaded, "and send Master Linton to her? As you hate them both, you'd not miss them. They *can* only be a daily plague to your unnatural heart."

"I'm seeking a tenant for the Grange," he answered, "and I want my children about me, to be sure. Besides, that lass owes me her services for her bread. I'm not going to nurture her in luxury and idleness after Linton has gone. Make haste and get ready now, and don't oblige me to compel you."

"I shall," said Catherine. "Linton is all I have to love in the world, and though you have done what you could to make him hateful to me, and me to him, you *cannot* make us hate each other. And I defy you to hurt him when I am by, and I defy you to frighten me."

"You are a boastful champion," replied Heathcliff, "but I don't like you well enough to hurt him; you shall get the full benefit of the torment as long as it lasts. It is not I who will make him hateful to you; it is his own sweet spirit. He's as bitter as gall at your desertion and its consequences. Don't expect thanks for this noble devotion. I heard him draw a pleasant picture to Zillah of what he would do if he were as strong as I. The inclination is there, and his very weakness will sharpen his wits to find a substitute for strength."

"I know he has a bad nature," said Catherine: "he's your son. But I'm glad I've a better, to forgive it; and I know he loves me, and for that reason I love him. Mr. Heathcliff, *you* have *nobody* to love you; and however miserable you make us, we shall still have the revenge of thinking that your cruelty arises from your greater misery. You *are* miserable, are you not?—

lonely, like the devil, and envious like him? *Nobody* loves you—*nobody* will cry for you when you die. I wouldn't be you."

Catherine spoke with a kind of dreary triumph. She seemed to have made up her mind to enter into the spirit of her future family, and draw pleasure from the griefs of her enemies.

"You shall be sorry to be yourself presently," said her father-in-law, "if you stand there another minute. Begone, witch, and get your things!"

She scornfully withdrew. In her absence I began to beg for Zillah's place at the Heights, offering to resign mine to her; but he would suffer it on no account. He bade me be silent; and then, for the first time, allowed himself a glance round the room and a look at the pictures. Having studied Mrs. Linton's, he said,—

"I shall have that home—not because I need it, but——" He turned abruptly to the fire, and continued, with what, for lack of a better word, I must call a smile —"I'll tell you what I did yesterday. I got the sexton, who was digging Linton's grave, to remove the earth off her coffin-lid, and I opened it. I thought, once, I would have stayed there. When I saw her face again— it is hers yet—he had hard work to stir me; but he said it would change if the air blew on it, and so I struck one side of the coffin loose, and covered it up—not Linton's side, damn him! I wish he'd been soldered in lead. And I bribed the sexton to pull it away when I'm laid there, and slide mine out too. I'll have it made so. And then, by the time Linton gets to us he'll not know which is which."

"You are very wicked, Mr. Heathcliff!" I exclaimed. "Were you not ashamed to disturb the dead?"

"I disturbed nobody, Nelly," he replied, "and I gave some ease to myself. I shall be a great deal more comfortable now, and you'll have a better chance of keeping me underground when I get there. Disturbed her! No! She has disturbed me, night and day, through eighteen years, incessantly, remorselessly, till yesternight;

and yesternight I was tranquil. I dreamt I was sleeping the last sleep by that sleeper, with my heart stopped and my cheek frozen against hers."

" And if she had been dissolved into earth, or worse, what would you have dreamt of then ? " I said.

" Of dissolving with her, and being more happy still;" he answered. " Do you suppose I dread any change of that sort ? I expected such a transformation on raising the lid, but I'm better pleased that it should not commence till I share it. Besides, unless I had received a distinct impression of her passionless features, that strange feeling would hardly have been removed. It began oddly. You know I was wild after she died, and eternally, from dawn to dawn, praying her to return to me her spirit. I have a strong faith in ghosts ; I have a conviction that they can and do exist among us. The day she was buried there came a fall of snow. In the evening I went to the churchyard. It blew bleak as winter ; all round was solitary. I didn't fear that her fool of a husband would wander up the den so late, and no one else had business to bring them there. Being alone, and conscious two yards of loose earth was the sole barrier between us, I said to myself, ' I'll have her in my arms again ! If she be cold, I'll think it is this north wind that chills *me ;* and if she be motionless, it is sleep.' I got a spade from the toolhouse, and began to delve with all my might. It scraped the coffin. I fell to work with my hands. The wood commenced cracking about the screws. I was on the point of attaining my object, when it seemed that I heard a sigh from some one above, close at the edge of the grave, and bending down. ' If I can only get this off,' I muttered, ' I wish they may shovel in the earth over us both ! ' and I wrenched at it more desperately still. There was another sigh close at my ear. I appeared to feel the warm breath of it displacing the sleet-laden wind. I knew no living thing in flesh and blood was by ; but as certainly as you perceive the approach to some substantial body in the dark, though it cannot be discerned, so certainly I felt that

Cathy was there—not under me, but on the earth. A
sudden sense of relief flowed from my heart through
every limb. I relinquished my labour of agony, and
turned consoled at once, unspeakably consoled. Her
presence was with me ; it remained while I refilled the
grave, and led me home. You may laugh if you will,
but I was sure I should see her there. I was sure she
was with me, and I could not help talking to her. Having
reached the Heights, I rushed eagerly to the door. It
was fastened, and, I remember, that accursed Earnshaw
and my wife opposed my entrance. I remember stopping to kick the breath out of him, and then hurrying
upstairs to my room and hers. I looked round impatiently ; I felt her by me ; I could *almost* see her, and
yet I *could not !* I ought to have sweat blood then
from the anguish of my yearning, from the fervour of
my supplications to have but one glimpse. I had not
one. She showed herself, as she often was in life, a
devil to me ! And since then, sometimes more and
sometimes less, I've been the sport of that intolerable
torture—infernal ! keeping my nerves at such a stretch
that, if they had not resembled catgut, they would long
ago have relaxed to the feebleness of Linton's. When
I sat in the house with Hareton it seemed that on going
out I should meet her ; when I walked on the moors I
should meet her coming in ; when I went from home I
hastened to return. She *must* be somewhere at the
Heights, I was certain. And when I slept in her chamber, I was beaten out of that. I couldn't lie there, for
the moment I closed my eyes she was either outside
the window, or sliding back the panels, or entering the
room, or even resting her darling head on the same
pillow as she did when a child, and I must open my
lids to see. And so I opened and closed them a hundred
times a night, to be always disappointed. It racked me
I've often groaned aloud, till that old rascal Joseph no
doubt believed that my conscience was playing the
fiend inside of me. Now, since I've seen her, I'm
pacified—a little. It was a strange way of killing—no

by inches, but by fractions of hairbreadths—to beguile me with the spectre of a hope through eighteen years!"

Mr. Heathcliff paused and wiped his forehead. His hair clung to it, wet with perspiration; his eyes were fixed on the red embers of the fire, the brows not contracted, but raised next the temples, diminishing the grim aspect of his countenance, but imparting a peculiar look of trouble and a painful appearance of mental tension towards one absorbing subject. He only half addressed me, and I maintained silence. I didn't like to hear him talk. After a short period he resumed his meditation on the picture, took it down and leant it against the sofa to contemplate it at better advantage; and while so occupied Catherine entered, announcing that she was ready, when her pony should be saddled.

"Send that over to-morrow," said Heathcliff to me; then turning to her, he added, "You may do without your pony. It is a fine evening, and you'll need no ponies at Wuthering Heights, for what journeys you make your own feet will serve you. Come along."

"Good-bye, Ellen!" whispered my dear little mistress. As she kissed me, her lips felt like ice. "Come and see me, Ellen; don't forget."

"Take care you do no such thing, Mrs. Dean!" said her new father. "When I wish to speak to you I'll come here. I want none of your prying at my house."

He signed her to precede him, and casting back a look that cut my heart, she obeyed. I watched them from the window walk down the garden. Heathcliff fixed Catherine's arm under his, though she disputed the act at first evidently, and with rapid strides he hurried her into the alley, whose trees concealed them.

CHAPTER XXX.

HAVE paid a visit to the Heights, but I have not seen her since she left. Joseph held the door in his hand when I called to ask after her, and wouldn't let me pass.

10

He said Mrs. Linton was " thrang," and the master wa
not in. Zillah has told me something of the way the
go on, otherwise I should hardly know who was dead an
who living. She thinks Catherine haughty, and does no
like her, I can guess by her talk. My young lady aske
some aid of her when she first came, but Mr. Heathcli
told her to follow her own business, and let his daughter
in-law look after herself ; and Zillah willingly acquiesced
being a narrow-minded, selfish woman. Catherine evince
a child's annoyance at this neglect, repaid it with con
tempt, and thus enlisted my informant among her ene
mies as securely as if she had done her some great wrong
I had a long talk with Zillah about six weeks ago, ;
little before you came, one day when we forgathered o
the moor ; and this is what she told me.

" The first thing Mrs. Linton did," she said, " on he
arrival at the Heights, was to run upstairs, without ever
wishing good-evening to me and Joseph ; she shut her
self into Linton's room, and remained till morning
Then, while the master and Earnshaw were at breakfast
she entered the house and asked all in a quiver if th
doctor might be sent for ; her cousin was very ill.

"' We know that,' answered Heathcliff ; ' but his lif
is not worth a farthing, and I won't spend a farthing o
him.'

"' But I cannot tell how to do,' she said ; ' and i
nobody will help me, he'll die.'

"' Walk out of the room,' cried the master, ' and let m
never hear a word more about him. None here car
what becomes of him. If you do, act the nurse ; if yo
do not, lock him up and leave him.'

" Then she began to bother me, and I said I'd ha
enough plague with the tiresome thing. We each ha
our tasks, and hers was to wait on Linton ; Mr. Heath
cliff bade me leave that labour to her.

" How they managed together I can't tell. I fanc
he fretted a great deal, and moaned hisseln night an
day ; and she had precious little rest, one could gues
by her white face and heavy eyes. She sometimes cam

into the kitchen all wildered like, and looked as if she would fain beg assistance. But I was not going to disobey the master—I never dare disobey him, Mrs. Dean; and though I thought it wrong that Kenneth should not be sent for, it was no concern of mine either to advise or complain, and I always refused to meddle. Once or twice, after we had gone to bed, I've happened to open my door again and seen her sitting crying on the stairs' top; and then I've shut myself in quick, for fear of being moved to interfere. I did pity her then, I'm sure; still I didn't wish to lose my place, you know.

" At last, one night she came boldly into my chamber, and frightened me out of my wits by saying,—

" ' Tell Mr. Heathcliff that his son is dying. I'm sure he is, this time. Get up instantly, and tell him.'

" Having uttered this speech, she vanished again. I lay a quarter of an hour listening and trembling. Nothing stirred—the house was quiet.

" She's mistaken, I said to myself. He's got over it. I needn't disturb them. And I began to doze. But my sleep was marred a second time by a sharp ringing of the bell—the only bell we have, put up on purpose for Linton; and the master called to me to see what was the matter, and inform them that he wouldn't have that noise repeated.

" I delivered Catherine's message. He cursed to himself, and in a few minutes came out with a lighted candle, and proceeded to their room. I followed. Mrs. Heathcliff was seated by the bedside with her hands folded on her knees. Her father-in-law went up, held the light to Linton's face, looked at him, and touched him. Afterwards he turned to her.

" ' Now, Catherine,' he said, ' how do you feel ? '

" She was dumb.

" ' How do you feel, Catherine ? ' he repeated.

" ' He's safe, and I'm free,' she answered. ' I should feel well, but,' she continued, with a bitterness she couldn't conceal, ' you have left me so long to struggle against death alone that I feel and see only death. I feel like death.'

" And she looked like it too. I gave her a little wine. Hareton and Joseph, who had been wakened by the ringing and the sound of feet, and heard our talk from outside, now entered. Joseph was fain, I believe, of the lad's removal; Hareton seemed a thought bothered, though he was more taken up with staring at Catherine than thinking of Linton. But the master bade him get off to bed again; we didn't want his help. He afterwards made Joseph remove the body to his chamber, and told me to return to mine, and Mrs. Heathcliff remained by herself.

" In the morning he sent me to tell her she must come down to breakfast. She had undressed, and appeared going to sleep, and said she was ill, at which I hardly wondered. I informed Mr. Heathcliff, and he replied,—

" ' Well, let her be till after the funeral, and go up now and then to get her what is needful; and as soon as she seems better, tell me.' "

Cathy stayed upstairs a fortnight, according to Zillah, who visited her twice a day, and would have been rather more friendly, but her attempts at increasing kindness were proudly and promptly repelled.

Heathcliff went up once to show her Linton's will. He had bequeathed the whole of his and what had been her movable property to his father. The poor creature was threatened or coaxed into that act during her week's absence when his uncle died. The lands, being a minor, he could not meddle with. However, Mr. Heathcliff has claimed and kept them in his wife's right and his also—I suppose legally. At any rate, Catherine, destitute of cash and friends, cannot disturb his possession.

" Nobody," said Zillah, " ever approached her door, except that once, but I; and nobody asked anything about her. The first occasion of her coming down into the house was on a Sunday afternoon. She had cried out, when I carried up her dinner, that she couldn't bear any longer being in the cold; and I told her the master was going to Thrushcross Grange, and Earnshaw and I needn't hinder her from descending; so, as soon as she heard Heathcliff's horse trot off, she made her appearance, donned in black, and her yellow curls combed back behind her ears as plain as a Quaker. She couldn't comb them out.

" Joseph and I generally go to chapel on Sundays." The kirk, you know, has no minister now, explained Mrs. Dean, and they call the Methodists' or Baptists' place (I can't say which it is) at Gimmerton a chapel. " Joseph has gone," she continued, " but I thought proper to bide at home. Young folks are always the better for an elder's overlooking; and Hareton, with all his bashfulness, isn't a model of nice behaviour. I let him know that his cousin would very likely sit with us, and she had been always used to see the Sabbath respected, so he had as good leave his guns and bits of indoor work alone while she stayed. He coloured up at the news, and cast his eyes over his hands and clothes. The train-oil and gunpowder were shoved out of sight in a minute. I saw he meant to give her his company, and I guessed by his way he wanted to be presentable; so, laughing as I durst not laugh when the master is by, I offered to help him, if he would, and joked at his confusion. He grew sullen, and began to swear.

" Now, Mrs. Dean," Zillah went on, seeing me not pleased by her manner, " you happen think your young lady too fine for Mr. Hareton, and happen you're right, but I own I should love well to bring her pride a peg lower. And what will all her learning and her daintiness do for her now ? She's as poor as you or I—poorer, I'll be bound. You're saving, and I'm doing my little all that road."

Hareton allowed Zillah to give him her aid, and she flattered him into a good humour. So, when Catherine came, half forgetting her former insults, he tried to make himself agreeable, by the housekeeper's account.

" Missis walked in," she said, " as chill as an icicle, and as high as a princess. I got up and offered her my seat in the armchair. No, she turned up her nose at my civility. Earnshaw rose too and bade her come to the settle, and sit close by the fire; he was sure she was starved.

" ' I've been starved a month and more,' she answered, resting on the word as scornful as she could.

" And she got a chair for herself, and placed it at a distance from both of us. Having sat till she was warm, she began to look round, and discovered a number of books in the dresser. She was instantly upon her feet again, stretching to reach them; but they were too high up. Her cousin, after watching her endeavours a while, at last summoned courage to help her. She held her frock, and he filled it with the first that came to hand.

" That was a great advance for the lad. She didn't thank him, still he felt gratified that she had accepted his assistance, and ventured to stand behind as she examined them, and even to stoop and point out what struck his fancy in certain old pictures which they contained. Nor was he daunted by the saucy style in which she jerked the page from his finger. He contented himself with going a bit farther back, and looking at her instead of the book. She continued reading, or seeking for something to read. His attention became, by degrees, quite centred in the study of her thick, silky curls. Her face he couldn't see, and she couldn't see him. And, perhaps not quite awake to what he did, but attracted like a child to a candle, at last he proceeded from staring to touching. He put out his hand and stroked one curl, as gently as if it were a bird. He might have stuck a knife into her neck, she started round in such a taking.

" ' Get away this moment! How dare you touch me! Why are you stopping there?' she cried in a tone of disgust. 'I can't endure you! I'll go upstairs again if you come near me.'

" Mr. Hareton recoiled, looking as foolish as he could do. He sat down in the settle very quiet, and she con-

inued turning over her volumes another half-hour.
Finally Earnshaw crossed over and whispered to me,—

" ' Will you ask her to read to us, Zillah ? I'm stalled
of doing naught ; and I do like—I could like to hear
her. Dunnot say I wanted it, but ask of yourseln.'

" ' Mr. Hareton wishes you would read to us, ma'am,'
I said immediately. ' He'd take it very kind—he'd be
much obliged.'

" She frowned, and looking up, answered,—

" ' Mr. Hareton and the whole set of you will be
good enough to understand that I reject any pretence at
kindness you have the hypocrisy to offer ! I despise
you, and will have nothing to say to any of you ! When
I would have given my life for one kind word, even to
see one of your faces, you all kept off. But I won't
complain to you. I'm driven down here by the cold,
not either to amuse you or enjoy your society.'

" ' What could I ha' done ? ' began Earnshaw. ' How
was I to blame ? '

" ' Oh, you are an exception,' answered Mrs. Heathcliff. ' I never missed such a concern as you.'

" ' But I offered more than once, and asked,' he said,
kindling up at her pertness—' I asked Mr. Heathcliff to
let me wake for you——'

" ' Be silent ! I'll go out of doors, or anywhere, rather
than have your disagreeable voice in my ear,' said my
lady.

" Hareton muttered she might go to hell, for him,
and unslinging his gun, restrained himself from his
Sunday occupations no longer. He talked now freely
enough, and she presently saw fit to retreat to her solitude ; but the frost had set in, and, in spite of her pride,
she was forced to condescend to our company more and
more. However, I took care there should be no further
scorning at my good nature. Ever since I've been as
stiff as herself, and she has no lover or liker among us ;
and she does not deserve one, for, let them say the least
word to her, and she'll curl back without respect of any
one. She'll snap at the master himself, and as good as

dares him to thrash her; and the more hurt she gets the more venomous she grows."

At first, on hearing this account from Zillah, I determined to leave my situation, take a cottage, and get Catherine to come and live with me; but Mr. Heathcliff would as soon permit that as he would set up Hareton in an independent house, and I can see no remedy at present, unless she could marry again, and that scheme it does not come within my province to arrange.

*   *   *   *   *

Thus ended Mrs. Dean's story. Notwithstanding the doctor's prophecy, I am rapidly recovering strength; and though it be only the second week in January, I propose getting out on horseback in a day or two, and riding over to Wuthering Heights to inform my landlord that I shall spend the next six months in London; and, if he likes, he may look out for another tenant to take the place after October. I would not pass another winter here for much.

CHAPTER XXXI.

YESTERDAY was bright, calm, and frosty. I went to the Heights as I proposed. My housekeeper entreated me to bear a little note from her to her young lady, and I did not refuse, for the worthy woman was not conscious of anything odd in her request. The front door stood open, but the jealous gate was fastened, as at my last visit. I knocked, and invoked Earnshaw from among the garden beds. He unchained it, and I entered. The fellow is as handsome a rustic as need be seen. I took particular notice of him this time; but then he does his best, apparently, to make the least of his advantages.

I asked if Mr. Heathcliff were at home. He answered, No, but he would be in at dinner-time. It was eleven o'clock, and I announced my intention of going in and waiting for him, at which he immediately flung down his tools and accompanied me, in the office of watchdog, not as a substitute for the host.

We entered together. Catherine was there, making herself useful in preparing some vegetables for the approaching meal. She looked more sulky and less spirited than when I had seen her first. She hardly raised her eyes to notice me, and continued her employment with the same disregard to common forms of politeness as before, never returning my bow and good-morning by the slightest acknowledgment.

" She does not seem so amiable," I thought, " as Mrs. Dean would persuade me to believe. She's a beauty, it is true, but not an angel."

Earnshaw surlily bade her remove her things to the kitchen. " Remove them yourself," she said, pushing them from her as soon as she had done, and retiring to a stool by the window, where she began to carve figures of birds and beasts out of the turnip parings in her lap. I approached her, pretending to desire a view of the garden, and, as I fancied, adroitly dropped Mrs. Dean's note on to her knee, unnoticed by Hareton ; but she asked aloud, " What is that ? " and chucked it off.

" A letter from your old acquaintance, the housekeeper at the Grange," I answered, annoyed at her exposing my kind deed, and fearful lest it should be imagined a missive of my own. She would gladly have gathered it up at this information, but Hareton beat her. He seized and put it in his waistcoat, saying Mr. Heathcliff should look at it first. Thereat Catherine silently turned her face from us, and very stealthily drew out her pocket-handkerchief and applied it to her eyes ; and her cousin, after struggling a while to keep down his softer feelings, pulled out the letter and flung it on the floor beside her, as ungraciously as he could. Catherine caught and perused it eagerly ; then she put a few questions to me concerning the inmates, rational and irrational, of her former home, and gazing towards the hills, murmured in soliloquy,—

" I should like to be riding Minny down there ! I should like to be climbing up there ! Oh ! I'm tired— I'm *stalled*, Hareton ! " And she leant her pretty head

back against the sill, with half a yawn and half a sigh,
and lapsed into an aspect of abstracted sadness, neither
caring nor knowing whether we remarked her.

"Mrs. Heathcliff," I said, after sitting some time mute,
"you are not aware that I am an acquaintance of yours—
so intimate that I think it strange you won't come and
speak to me. My housekeeper never wearies of talking
about and praising you, and she'll be greatly disappointed
if I return with no news of or from you, except that you
received her letter and said nothing."

She appeared to wonder at this speech, and asked,—

"Does Ellen like you?"

"Yes, very well," I replied hesitatingly.

"You must tell her," she continued, "that I would
answer her letter, but I have no materials for writing—
not even a book from which I might tear a leaf."

"No books!" I exclaimed. "How do you contrive
to live here without them? if I may take the liberty
to inquire. Though provided with a large library, I'm
frequently very dull at the Grange. Take my books
away, and I should be desperate."

"I was always reading when I had them," said Catherine; "and Mr. Heathcliff never reads, so he took it
into his head to destroy my books. I have not had a
glimpse of one for weeks. Only once I searched through
Joseph's store of theology, to his great irritation.—And
once, Hareton, I came upon a secret stock in your room
—some Latin and Greek, and some tales and poetry, all
old friends. I brought the last here, and you gathered
them, as a magpie gathers silver spoons, for the mere
love of stealing—they are of no use to you; or else you
concealed them in the bad spirit that as you cannot
enjoy them nobody else shall. Perhaps *your* envy counselled Mr. Heathcliff to rob me of my treasures? But
I've most of them written on my brain and printed in
my heart, and you cannot deprive me of those."

Earnshaw blushed crimson when his cousin made this
revelation of his private literary accumulations, and
stammered an indignant denial of her accusations.

"Mr. Hareton is desirous of increasing his amount of knowledge," I said, coming to his rescue. "He is not *envious* but *emulous* of your attainments. He'll be a clever scholar in a few years."

"And he wants me to sink into a dunce meantime," answered Catherine. "Yes, I hear him trying to spell and read to himself, and pretty blunders he makes.—I wish you would repeat 'Chevy Chase' as you did yesterday; it was extremely funny. I heard you, and I heard you turning over the dictionary to seek out the hard words, and then cursing because you couldn't read their explanations."

The young man evidently thought it too bad that he should be laughed at for his ignorance, and then laughed at for trying to remove it. I had a similar notion; and remembering Mrs. Dean's anecdote of his first attempt at enlightening the darkness in which he had been reared, I observed,—

"But, Mrs. Heathcliff, we have each had a commencement, and each stumbled and tottered on the threshold. Had our teachers scorned instead of aiding us, we should stumble and totter yet."

"Oh!" she replied, "I don't wish to limit his acquirements. Still, he has no right to appropriate what is mine, and make it ridiculous to me with his vile mistakes and mispronunciations. Those books, both prose and verse, are consecrated to me by other associations, and I hate to have them debased and profaned in his mouth. Besides, of all, he has selected my favourite pieces that I love the most to repeat, as if out of deliberate malice.'

Hareton's chest heaved in silence a minute. He laboured under a severe sense of mortification and wrath, which it was no easy task to suppress. I rose, and, from a gentlemanly idea of relieving his embarrassment, took up my station in the doorway, surveying the external prospect as I stood. He followed my example, and left the room, but presently reappeared, bearing half a dozen volumes in his hands, which he threw into Catherine's lap, exclaiming,—

" Take them ! I never want to hear, or read, or think
of them again ! "

" I won't have them now," she answered. " I shall
connect them with you, and hate them."

She opened one that had obviously been often turned
over, and read a portion in the drawling tone of a be-
ginner, then laughed and threw it from her. " And
listen," she continued provokingly, commencing a verse
of an old ballad in the same fashion.

But his self-love would endure no further torment. I
heard, and not altogether disapprovingly, a manual
check given to her saucy tongue. The little wretch had
done her utmost to hurt her cousin's sensitive though
uncultivated feelings, and a physical argument was the
only mode he had of balancing the account and repay-
ing its effects on the inflictor. He afterwards gathered
the books and hurled them on the fire. I read in his
countenance what anguish it was to offer that sacrifice
to spleen. I fancied that as they consumed he recalled
the pleasure they had already imparted and the triumph
and ever-increasing pleasure he had anticipated from
them, and I fancied I guessed the incitement to his
secret studies also. He had been content with daily
labour and rough animal enjoyments till Catherine
crossed his path. Shame at her scorn, and hope of her
approval, were his first prompters to higher pursuits ;
and, instead of guarding him from one and winning him
to the other, his endeavours to raise himself had produced
just the contrary result.

" Yes, that's all the good that such a brute as you can
get from them ! " cried Catherine, sucking her damaged
lip, and watching the conflagration with indignant eyes.

" You'd *better* hold your tongue now," he answered
fiercely.

And his agitation precluded further speech. He advanced hastily to the entrance, where I made way for
him to pass. But ere he had crossed the door-stones
Mr. Heathcliff, coming up the causeway, encountered
him, and laying hold of his shoulder, asked,—

"What's to do now, my lad?"

"Naught, naught," he said, and broke away to enjoy his grief and anger in solitude.

Heathcliff gazed after him and sighed.

"It will be odd if I thwart myself," he muttered, unconscious that I was behind him. "But when I look for his father in his face, I find *her* every day more. How the devil is he so like? I can hardly bear to see him."

He bent his eyes to the ground and walked moodily in. There was a restless, anxious expression in his countenance I had never remarked there before, and he looked sparer in person. His daughter-in-law, on perceiving him through the window, immediately escaped to the kitchen, so that I remained alone.

"I'm glad to see you out of doors again, Mr. Lockwood," he said, in reply to my greeting, "from selfish motives partly. I don't think I could readily supply your loss in this desolation. I've wondered more than once what brought you here."

"An idle whim, I fear, sir," was my answer, "or else an idle whim is going to spirit me away. I shall set out for London next week, and I must give you warning that I feel no disposition to retain Thrushcross Grange beyond the twelve months I agreed to rent it. I believe I shall not live there any more."

"Oh, indeed; you're tired of being banished from the world, are you?" he said. "But if you be coming to plead off paying for a place you won't occupy, your journey is useless. I never relent in exacting my due from any one."

"I'm coming to plead off nothing about it," I exclaimed, considerably irritated. "Should you wish it, I'll settle with you now." And I drew my notebook from my pocket.

"No, no," he replied coolly; "you'll leave sufficient behind to cover your debts if you fail to return. I'm not in such a hurry. Sit down and take your dinner with us. A guest that is safe from repeating his visit can generally be made welcome.—Catherine, bring the thing in. Where are you?"

Catherine reappeared, bearing a tray of knives and forks

"You may get your dinner with Joseph," muttered Heathcliff aside, "and remain in the kitchen till he i gone."

She obeyed his directions very punctually; perhap she had no temptation to transgress. Living among clowns and misanthropists, she probably cannot appreci ate a better class of people when she meets them.

With Mr. Heathcliff, grim and saturnine, on the on hand, and Hareton, absolutely dumb, on the other, made a somewhat cheerless meal, and bade adieu early I would have departed by the back way, to get a las glimpse of Catherine and annoy old Joseph; but Hareto received orders to lead up my horse, and my host himsel escorted me to the door, so I could not fulfil my wish.

"How dreary life gets over in that house!" I reflected while riding down the road. "What a realization c something more romantic than a fairy tale it would hav been for Mrs. Linton Heathcliff had she and I struck u an attachment, as her good nurse desired, and migrate together into the stirring atmosphere of the town!"

CHAPTER XXXII.

1802.—This September I was invited to devastate th moors of a friend in the north, and on my journey to h abode I unexpectedly came within fifteen miles of Gin merton. The ostler at a roadside public-house was hol ing a pail of water to refresh my horses, when a cart o very green oats, newly reaped, passed by, and he re marked,—

"Yon's frough Gimmerton, nah! They're allas thre wick after other folk wi' ther harvest."

"Gimmerton!" I repeated. My residence in tha locality had already grown dim and dreamy. "Ah! know. How far is it from this?"

"Happen fourteen mile o'er th' hills, and a rough road," he answered.

A sudden impulse seized me to visit Thrushcross Grange. It was scarcely noon, and I conceived that I might as well pass the night under my own roof as in an inn. Besides, I could spare a day easily to arrange matters with my landlord, and thus save myself the trouble of invading the neighbourhood again. Having rested a while, I directed my servant to inquire the way to the village, and with great fatigue to our beasts we managed the distance in some three hours.

I left him there, and proceeded down the valley alone. The gray church looked grayer, and the lonely church-yard lonelier. I distinguished a moor sheep cropping the short turf on the graves. It was sweet, warm weather —too warm for travelling ; but the heat did not hinder me from enjoying the delightful scenery above and below. Had I seen it nearer August I'm sure it would have tempted me to waste a month among its solitudes. In winter nothing more dreary, in summer nothing more divine, than those glens shut in by hills, and those bluff, bold swells of heath.

I reached the Grange before sunset, and knocked for admittance ; but the family had retreated into the back premises, I judged, by one thin, blue wreath curling from the kitchen chimney, and they did not hear. I rode into the court. Under the porch a girl of nine or ten sat knitting, and an old woman reclined on the house-steps, smoking a meditative pipe.

"Is Mrs. Dean within ? " I demanded of the dame.

"Mistress Dean ? Nay ! " she answered, "shoo doesn't bide here ; shoo's up at th' Heights."

"Are you the housekeeper, then ? " I continued.

"Eea, aw keep th' hause," she replied.

"Well, I'm Mr. Lockwood, the master. Are there any rooms to lodge me in, I wonder ? I wish to stay all night."

"T' maister ! " she cried in astonishment. "Whet ! whoiver knew yah wur coming ? Yah sud ha' send

word. They's nowt norther dry nor mensful abaht t'
place, nowt there isn't."

She threw down her pipe and bustled in; the girl followed, and I entered too. Soon perceiving that her report was true, and, moreover, that I had almost upset
her wits by my unwelcome apparition, I bade her be
composed. I would go out for a walk, and meantime
she must try to prepare a corner of a sitting-room for
me to sup in, and a bedroom to sleep in. No sweeping
and dusting—only good fire and dry sheets were necessary. She seemed willing to do her best, though she
thrust the hearth-brush into the grates in mistake for
the poker, and malappropriated several other articles of
her craft; but I retired, confiding in her energy for a
resting-place against my return. Wuthering Heights was
the goal of my proposed excursion. An afterthought
brought me back when I had quitted the court.

"All well at the Heights?" I inquired of the woman.

"Eea, f'r owt ee knaw," she answered, skurrying away
with a pan of hot cinders.

I would have asked why Mrs. Dean had deserted the
Grange, but it was impossible to delay her at such a
crisis, so I turned away and made my exit, rambling
leisurely along with the glow of a sinking sun behind,
and the mild glory of a rising moon in front—one fading
and the other brightening—as I quitted the park and
climbed the stony by-road branching off to Mr. Heathcliff's dwelling. Before I arrived in sight of it, all that
remained of day was a beamless amber light along the
west; but I could see every pebble on the path, and
every blade of grass, by that splendid moon. I had
neither to climb the gate nor to knock: it yielded to my
hand. That is an improvement, I thought. And I
noticed another by the aid of my nostrils—a fragrance
of stocks and wallflowers wafted on the air from amongst
the homely fruit-trees.

Both doors and lattices were open; and yet, as is
usually the case in a coal district, a fine, red fire illuminated
the chimney. The comfort which the eye derives from

t renders the extra heat endurable. But the house of Wuthering Heights is so large that the inmates have plenty of space for withdrawing out of its influence, and accordingly what inmates there were had stationed themselves not far from one of the windows. I could both see them and hear them talk before I entered, and looked and listened in consequence, being moved thereto by a mingled sense of curiosity and envy that grew as I lingered.

"Con-*trary!*" said a voice as sweet as a silver bell. "That for the third time, you dunce! I'm not going to tell you again. Recollect, or I'll pull your hair."

"Contrary, then," answered another, in deep but softened tones. "And now, kiss me for minding so well."

"No; read it over first correctly, without a single mistake."

The male speaker began to read. He was a young man, respectably dressed and seated at a table, having a book before him. His handsome features glowed with pleasure, and his eyes kept impatiently wandering from the page to a small white hand over his shoulder, which recalled him by a smart slap on the cheek whenever its owner detected such signs of inattention. Its owner stood behind, her light, shining ringlets blending at intervals with his brown locks, as she bent to superintend his studies; and her face—it was lucky he could not see her face, or he would never have been so steady. I could, and I bit my lip in spite at having thrown away the chance I might have had of doing something besides staring at its smiting beauty.

The task was done—not free from further blunders; but the pupil claimed a reward, and received at least five kisses, which, however, he generously returned. Then they came to the door, and from their conversation I judged they were about to issue out and have a walk on the moors. I supposed I should be condemned in Hareton Earnshaw's heart, if not by his mouth, to the lowest pit in the infernal regions if I showed my unfortunate person in his neighbourhood then ; and feeling very mean and malignant, I skulked round to seek refuge in the kitchen. There was unobstructed admittance on that side also, and at the door sat my old friend Nelly Dean, sewing and singing a song, which was often interrupted from within by harsh words of scorn and intolerance, uttered in far from musical accents.

"I'd rayther, by th' hauf, hev 'em swearing i' my lugs froh morn to neeght nor hearken ye hahsiver !" said the tenant of the kitchen, in answer to an unheard speech of Nelly's. "It's a blazing shame that I cannot oppen t' blessed Book but yah set up them glories to Sattan, and all t' flaysome wickednesses that iver were born into th' warld ! Oh ! ye're a raight nowt, and shoo's another, and that poor lad'll be lost atween ye. Poor lad !" he added, with a groan ; "he's witched, I'm sartin on't ! O Lord, judge 'em, for there's norther law nor justice among wer rullers !"

"No, or we should be sitting in flaming fagots, I suppose," retorted the singer. "But wisht, old man, and read your Bible like a Christian, and never mind me. This is 'Fairy Annie's Wedding'—a bonny tune ; it goes to a dance."

Mrs. Dean was about to recommence when I advanced ; and recognizing me directly, she jumped to her feet, crying,—

"Why, bless you, Mr. Lockwood ! How could you think of returning in this way ? All's shut up at Thrushcross Grange. You should have given us notice."

"I've arranged to be accommodated there for as long as I shall stay," I answered. "I depart again tomorrow. And how are you transplanted here, Mrs. Dean ? Tell me that."

"Zillah left, and Mr. Heathcliff wished me to come soon after you went to London, and stay till you returned. But step in, pray. Have you walked from Gimmerton this evening ?"

"From the Grange," I replied. "And while they make me lodging room there, I want to finish my busi-

ness with your master, because I don't think of having
another opportunity in a hurry."

"What business, sir?" said Nelly, conducting me into
the house. "He's gone out at present, and won't return soon."

"About the rent," I answered.

"Oh! then it is with Mrs. Heathcliff you must settle,"
she observed, "or rather with me. She has not learned
to manage her affairs yet, and I act for her; there's nobody else."

I looked surprised.

"Ah! you have not heard of Heathcliff's death, I
see," she continued.

"Heathcliff dead!" I exclaimed, astonished. "How
long ago?"

"Three months since. But sit down, and let me take
your hat, and I'll tell you all about it. Stop; you have
had nothing to eat, have you?"

"I want nothing; I have ordered supper at home.
You sit down too. I never dreamt of his dying. Let
me hear how it came to pass. You say you don't expect them back for some time—the young people?"

"No. I have to scold them every evening for their
late rambles, but they don't care for me. At least have
a drink of our old ale; it will do you good; you seem
weary."

She hastened to fetch it before I could refuse, and I
heard Joseph asking whether "it warn't a crying scandal
that she should have followers at her time of life. And
then, to get them jocks out o' t' maister's cellar! He fair
shaamed to 'bide still and see it."

She did not stay to retaliate, but re-entered in a
minute, bearing a reaming silver pint, whose contents I
lauded with becoming earnestness. And afterwards she
furnished me with the sequel of Heathcliff's history. He
had a "queer" end, as she expressed it.

I was summoned to Wuthering Heights within a fortnight of your leaving us, she said, and I obeyed joyfully,
for Catherine's sake. My first interview with her grieved

and shocked me—she had altered so much since our sepa
ration. Mr. Heathcliff did not explain his reasons fo
taking a new mind about my coming here; he only tol
me he wanted me, and he was tired of seeing Catherine
I must make the little parlour my sitting-room, and keep
her with me. It was enough if he were obliged to see
her once or twice a day. She seemed pleased at this
arrangement; and by degrees I smuggled over a great
number of books and other articles that had formed her
amusement at the Grange, and flattered myself we should
get on in tolerable comfort. The delusion did not last
long. Catherine, contented at first, in a brief space grew
irritable and restless. For one thing, she was forbidden
to move out of the garden, and it fretted her sadly to
be confined to its narrow bounds as spring drew on; for
another, in following the house I was forced to quit her
frequently, and she complained of loneliness. She preferred quarrelling with Joseph in the kitchen to sitting
at peace in her solitude. I did not mind their skir-
mishes; but Hareton was often obliged to seek the kitchen
also when the master wanted to have the house to himself; and though in the beginning she either left it at
his approach, or quietly joined in my occupations, and
shunned remarking or addressing him, and though he
was always as sullen and silent as possible, after a while
she changed her behaviour and became incapable of
letting him alone, talking at him, commenting on his
stupidity and idleness, expressing her wonder how he
could endure the life he lived, how he could sit a whole
evening staring into the fire and dozing.

"He's just like a dog, is he not, Ellen?" she once
observed, "or a cart-horse? He does his work, eats his
food, and sleeps eternally. What a blank, dreary mind
he must have!—Do you ever dream, Hareton? And
if you do, what is it about? But you can't speak to
me!"

Then she looked at him, but he would neither open
his mouth nor look again.

"He's perhaps dreaming now," she continued. "He

twitched his shoulder as Juno twitches hers. Ask him,
Ellen."

"Mr. Hareton will ask the master to send you upstairs, if you don't behave," I said. He had not only
twitched his shoulder but clenched his fist, as if tempted
to use it.

"I know why Hareton never speaks when I am in
the kitchen," she exclaimed on another occasion. "He
is afraid I shall laugh at him. Ellen, what do you think?
He began to teach himself to read once, and because I
laughed he burned his books and dropped it. Was he
not a fool?"

"Were not you naughty?" I said. "Answer me that."

"Perhaps I was," she went on, "but I did not expect
him to be so silly.—Hareton, if I gave you a book, would
you take it now? I'll try."

She placed one she had been perusing on his hand.
He flung it off, and muttered, if she did not give over he
would break her neck.

"Well, I shall put it here," she said—"in the table
drawer; and I'm going to bed."

Then she whispered me to watch whether he touched
it, and departed. But he would not come near it; and
so I informed her in the morning, to her great disappointment. I saw she was sorry for his persevering sulkiness
and indolence. Her conscience reproved her for fright-
ening him off improving himself. She had done it
effectually. But her ingenuity was at work to remedy
the injury. While I ironed or pursued other such
stationary employments as I could not well do in the
parlour, she would bring some pleasant volume and read
it aloud to me. When Hareton was there she generally
paused in an interesting part and left the book lying
about—that she did repeatedly; but he was as obstinate
as a mule, and, instead of snatching at her bait, in wet
weather he took to smoking with Joseph; and they sat
like automatons, one on each side of the fire, the elder
happily too deaf to understand her wicked nonsense, as
he would have called it, the younger doing his best **to**

seem to disregard it. On fine evenings the latter fol
lowed his shooting expeditions, and Catherine yawned
and sighed, and teased me to talk to her, and ran off
into the court or garden the moment I began, and as a
last resource cried and said she was tired of living—her
life was useless.

Mr. Heathcliff, who grew more and more disinclined to
society, had almost banished Earnshaw from his apart
ment. Owing to an accident at the commencement of
March, he became for some days a fixture in the kitchen.
His gun burst while out on the hills by himself ; a splinter
cut his arm, and he lost a good deal of blood before he
could reach home. The consequence was that, perforce,
he was condemned to the fireside and tranquillity till
he made it up again. It suited Catherine to have him
there. At any rate, it made her hate her room upstairs
more than ever ; and she would compel me to find out
business below, that she might accompany me.

On Easter Monday Joseph went to Gimmerton fair
with some cattle, and in the afternoon I was busy getting
up linen in the kitchen. Earnshaw sat, morose as usual,
at the chimney-corner, and my little mistress was beguiling an idle hour with drawing pictures on the window
panes, varying her amusement by smothered bursts of
songs, and whispered ejaculations, and quick glances of
annoyance and impatience in the direction of her cousin,
who steadfastly smoked, and looked into the grate. At
a notice that I could do with her no longer intercepting
my light, she removed to the hearthstone. I bestowed
little attention on her proceedings, but presently I heard
her begin,—

" I've found out, Hareton, that I want—that I'm glad
—that I should like you to be my cousin now, if you
had not grown so cross to me and so rough."

Hareton returned no answer.

" Hareton, Hareton, Hareton ! do you hear ? " she
continued.

" Get off wi' ye ! " he growled, with uncompromising
gruffness.

" Let me take that pipe," she said, cautiously advancing her hand and abstracting it from his mouth.

Before he could attempt to recover it, it was broken and behind the fire. He swore at her and seized another.

" Stop," she cried ; " you must listen to me first ; and I can't speak while those clouds are floating in my face."

" Will you go to the devil ! " he exclaimed ferociously, " and let me be ! "

" No," she persisted, " I won't. I can't tell what to do to make you talk to me, and you are determined not to understand. When I call you stupid, I don't mean anything. I don't mean that I despise you. Come, you shall take notice of me, Hareton. You are my cousin, and you shall own me."

" I shall have naught to do wi' you and your mucky pride, and your damned mocking tricks ! " he answered. ' I'll go to hell, body and soul, before I look sideways after you again. Side out o' t' gate now, this minute ! "

Catherine frowned and retreated to the window-seat chewing her lip, and endeavouring, by humming an eccentric tune, to conceal a growing tendency to sob.

" You should be friends with your cousin, Mr. Hareton," I interrupted, " since she repents of her sauciness. It would do you a great deal of good ; it would make you another man to have her for a companion."

" A companion ! " he cried, " when she hates me, and does not think me fit to wipe her shoon ! Nay ! if it made me a king, I'd not be scorned for seeking her good-will any more."

" It is not I who hate you ; it is you who hate me ! " wept Cathy, no longer disguising her trouble. " You hate me as much as Mr. Heathcliff does, and more."

" You're a damned liar," began Earnshaw. " Why have I made him angry by taking your part, then, a hundred times, and that when you sneered at and despised me, and—— Go on plaguing me, and I'll step in yonder and say you worried me out of the kitchen."

"I didn't know you took my part," she answered
drying her eyes, "and I was miserable and bitter a
everybody; but now I thank you, and beg you to for
give me. What can I do besides?"

She returned to the hearth, and frankly extended he
hand. He blackened and scowled like a thundercloud
and kept his fists resolutely clenched, and his gaze fixed
on the ground. Catherine, by instinct, must have divine
it was obdurate perversity, and not dislike, that prompte
this dogged conduct, for, after remaining an instant un
decided, she stooped and impressed on his cheek a gentl
kiss. The little rogue thought I had not seen her, and
drawing back, she took her former station by the win
dow, quite demurely. I shook my head reprovingly
and then she blushed and whispered,—

"Well, what should I have done, Ellen? He wouldn'
shake hands, and he wouldn't look; I must show him
some way that I like him—that I want to be friends."

Whether the kiss convinced Hareton I cannot tell
He was very careful, for some minutes, that his fac
should not be seen; and when he did raise it, he wa
sadly puzzled where to turn his eyes.

Catherine employed herself in wrapping a handsom
book neatly in white paper, and having tied it with
bit of ribbon, and addressed it to "Mr. Hareton Earn
shaw," she desired me to be her ambassadress, and con
vey the present to its destined recipient.

"And tell him if he'll take it I'll come and teach him
to read it right," she said; "and if he refuse it I'll g
upstairs and never tease him again."

I carried it, and repeated the message, anxiously
watched by my employer. Hareton would not open hi
fingers, so I laid it on his knee. He did not strike it of
either. I returned to my work. Catherine leaned he
head and arms on the table, till she heard the slight rustl
of the covering being removed; then she stole away and
quietly seated herself beside her cousin. He trembled
and his face glowed; all his rudeness and all his surl
harshness had deserted him. He could not summor

courage at first to utter a syllable in reply to her questioning look and her murmured petition,—

"Say you forgive me, Hareton, do. You can make me so happy by speaking that little word."

He muttered something inaudible.

"And you'll be my friend ? " added Catherine interrogatively.

"Nay, you'll be ashamed of me every day of your life," he answered, "and the more ashamed the more you know me ; and I cannot bide it."

"So you won't be my friend ? " she said, smiling as sweet as honey, and creeping close up.

I overheard no further distinguishable talk, but, on looking round again, I perceived two such radiant countenances bent over the page of the accepted book that I did not doubt the treaty had been ratified on both sides, and the enemies were thenceforth sworn allies.

The work they studied was full of costly pictures, and those and their position had charm enough to keep them unmoved till Joseph came home. He, poor man, was perfectly aghast at the spectacle of Catherine seated on the same bench with Hareton Earnshaw, leaning her hand on his shoulder, and confounded at his favourite's endurance of her proximity ; it affected him too deeply to allow an observation on the subject that night. His emotion was only revealed by the immense sighs he drew as he solemnly spread his large Bible on the table, and overlaid it with dirty bank-notes from his pocket-book, the produce of the day's transactions. At length he summoned Hareton from his seat.

"Tak' these in to t' maister, lad," he said, "and bide there. I's gang up to my own rahm. This hoile's neither mensful nor seemly for us ; we mun side out and seearch another."

"Come, Catherine," I said, "we must 'side out' too. I've done my ironing. Are you ready to go ? "

"It is not eight o'clock," she answered, rising unwillingly.—"Hareton, I'll leave this book upon the chimney-piece, and I'll bring some more to-morrow."

"Ony books that yah leave I shall tak' into th' hahse,"
said Joseph, "and it'll be mitch if yah find 'em ageän.
Soa yah may plase yerseln."

Cathy threatened that his library should pay for hers,
and smiling as she passed Hareton, went singing upstairs, lighter of heart, I venture to say, than ever she
had been under that roof before, except, perhaps, during
her earliest visits to Linton.

The intimacy thus commenced grew rapidly, though it
encountered temporary interruptions. Earnshaw was
not to be civilized with a wish, and my young lady was
no philosopher and no paragon of patience; but both
their minds tending to the same point—one loving and
desiring to esteem, and the other loving and desiring to
be esteemed—they contrived in the end to reach it.

You see, Mr. Lockwood, it was easy enough to win
Mrs. Heathcliff's heart. But now I'm glad you did not
try. The crown of all my wishes will be the union of
those two. I shall envy no one on their wedding-day.
There won't be a happier woman than myself in England.

CHAPTER XXXIII.

On the morrow of that Monday, Earnshaw being still
unable to follow his ordinary employments, and therefore remaining about the house, I speedily found it would
be impracticable to retain my charge beside me as here-
tofore. She got downstairs before me, and out into the
garden, where she had seen her cousin performing some
easy work; and when I went to bid them come to breakfast, I saw she had persuaded him to clear a large space
of ground from currant and gooseberry bushes, and they
were busy planning together an importation of plants
from the Grange.

I was terrified at the devastation which had been accomplished in a brief half-hour. The black currant trees
were the apple of Joseph's eye, and she had just fixed her
choice of a flower-bed in the midst of them.

" There ! That will be all shown to the master," I exclaimed, " the minute it is discovered. And what excuse have you to offer for taking such liberties with the garden ? We shall have a fine explosion on the head of it—see if we don't.—Mr. Hareton, I wonder you should have no more wit than to go and make that mess at her bidding ! "

" I'd forgotten they were Joseph's," answered Earnshaw, rather puzzled, " but I'll tell him I did it."

We always ate our meals with Mr. Heathcliff. I held the mistress's post in making tea and carving, so I was indispensable at table. Catherine usually sat by me, but to-day she stole nearer to Hareton, and I presently saw she would have no more discretion in her friendship than she had in her hostility.

" Now, mind you don't talk with and notice your cousin too much," were my whispered instructions as we entered the room. " It will certainly annoy Mr. Heathcliff, and he'll be mad at you both."

" I'm not going to," she answered.

The minute after, she had sidled to him, and was sticking primroses in his plate of porridge.

He dared not speak to her there—he dared hardly look ; and yet she went on teasing till he was twice on the point of being provoked to laugh. I frowned, and then she glanced toward the master, whose mind was occupied on other subjects than his company, as his countenance evinced ; and she grew serious for an instant, scrutinizing him with deep gravity. Afterwards she turned and recommenced her nonsense. At last Hareton uttered a smothered laugh. Mr. Heathcliff started ; his eye rapidly surveyed our faces. Catherine met it with her accustomed look of nervousness and yet defiance, which he abhorred.

" It is well you are out of my reach," he exclaimed. " What fiend possesses you to stare back at me continually with those infernal eyes ? Down with them ! and don't remind me of your existence again. I thought I had cured you of laughing."

"It was me," muttered Hareton.

"What do you say?" demanded the master.

Hareton looked at his plate, and did not repeat the confession. Mr. Heathcliff looked at him a bit, and then silently resumed his breakfast and his interrupted musing. We had nearly finished, and the two young people prudently shifted wider asunder, so I anticipated no further disturbance during that sitting, when Joseph appeared at the door, revealing by his quivering lip and furious eyes that the outrage committed on his precious shrubs was detected. He must have seen Cathy and her cousin about the spot before he examined it, for while his jaws worked like those of a cow chewing its cud, and rendered his speech difficult to understand, he began,—

"I mun hev my wage, and I mun goa. I *hed* aimed to dee wheare I'd sarved fur sixty year, and I thowt I'd lug my books up into t' garret, and all my bits o' stuff, and they sud hev t' kitchen to theirseln, for t' sake o' quietness. It wur hard to gie up my awn hearthstun, but I thowt I *could* do that. But nah; shoo's taan my garden fro' me, and by th' heart, maister, I cannot stand it. Yah may bend to th' yoak, and ye will; I noan used to't, and an old man doesn't sooin get used to new barthens. I'd rayther arn my bite an' my sup wi' a hammer in th' road."

"Now, now, idiot," interrupted Heathcliff, "cut it short! What's your grievance? I'll interfere in no quarrels between you and Nelly. She may thrust you into the coal-hole for anything I care."

"It's noan Nelly," answered Joseph. "I sudn't shift for Nelly, nasty ill nowt as shoo is. Thank God! *shoo* cannot stale t' sowl o' nob'dy! Shoo wer niver soa handsome but what a body mud look at her 'bout winking. It's yon flaysome, graceless quean that's witched our lad wi' her bold een and her forrard ways, till—— Nay, it fair brusts my heart! He's forgotten all I've done for him, and made on him, and goan and riven up a whole row o' t' grandest currant trees i' t' garden!" And here he lamented outright, unmanned by a sense of his bitter injuries and Earnshaw's ingratitude and dangerous condition.

"Is the fool drunk?" asked Mr. Heathcliff.—"Hareton, is it you he's finding fault with?"

"I've pulled up two or three bushes," replied the young man, "but I'm going to set 'em again."

"And why have you pulled them up?" said the master.

Catherine wisely put in her tongue.

"We wanted to plant some flowers there," she cried. "I'm the only person to blame, for I wished him to do it."

"And who the devil gave *you* leave to touch a stick about the place?" demanded her father-in-law, much surprised.—"And who ordered *you* to obey her?" he added, turning to Hareton.

The latter was speechless. His cousin replied,—

"You shouldn't grudge a few yards of earth for me to ornament, when you have taken all my land!"

"Your land, insolent slut! You never had any," said Heathcliff.

"And my money," she continued, returning his angry glare, and meantime biting a piece of crust, the remnant of her breakfast.

"Silence!" he exclaimed. "Get done, and begone!"

"And Hareton's land, and his money," pursued the reckless thing. "Hareton and I are friends now, and I shall tell him all about you."

The master seemed confounded a moment. He grew pale and rose up, eyeing her all the while with an expression of mortal hate.

"If you strike me, Hareton will strike you," she said, "so you may as well sit down."

"If Hareton does not turn you out of the room I'll strike him to hell," thundered Heathcliff. "Damnable witch! dare you pretend to rouse him against me? —Off with her! Do you hear? Fling her into the kitchen!—I'll kill her, Ellen Dean, if you let her come into my sight again!"

Hareton tried, under his breath, to persuade her to go.

"Drag her away!" he cried savagely. "Are you staying to talk?" And he approached to execute his own command.

"He'll not obey you, wicked man, any more," said Catherine, "and he'll soon detest you as much as I do."

"Wisht! wisht!" muttered the young man reproachfully. "I will not hear you speak so to him. Have done."

"But you won't let him strike me?" she cried.

"Come, then," he whispered earnestly.

It was too late. Heathcliff had caught hold of her.

"Now, *you* go!" he said to Earnshaw. "Accursed witch! this time she has provoked me when I could not bear it, and I'll make her repent it for ever!"

He had his hand in her hair. Hareton attempted to release her locks, entreating him not to hurt her that once. Heathcliff's black eyes flashed—he seemed ready to tear Catherine in pieces; and I was just worked up to risk coming to the rescue, when of a sudden his fingers relaxed; he shifted his grasp from her head to her arm, and gazed intently in her face. Then he drew his hand over her eyes, stood a moment to collect himself apparently, and turning anew to Catherine, said with assumed calmness, "You must learn to avoid putting me in a passion, or I shall really murder you some time! Go with Mrs. Dean, and keep with her, and confine your insolence to her ears. As to Hareton Earnshaw, if I see him listen to you I'll send him seeking his bread where he can get it. Your love will make him an outcast and a beggar.—Nelly, take her; and leave me, all of you!—leave me!"

I led my young lady out. She was too glad of her escape to resist. The other followed, and Mr. Heathcliff had the room to himself till dinner. I had counselled Catherine to dine upstairs, but as soon as he perceived her vacant seat he sent me to call her. He spoke to none of us, ate very little, and went out directly afterwards, intimating that he should not return before evening.

The two new friends established themselves in the house during his absence, when I heard Hareton sternly check his cousin on her offering a revelation of her father-in-law's conduct to his father. He said he wouldn't suffer a word to be uttered in his disparagement. If he were the devil, it didn't signify—he would stand by him; and he'd rather she would abuse himself, as she used to, than begin on Mr. Heathcliff. Catherine was waxing cross at this, but he found means to make her hold her tongue by asking how she would like *him* to speak ill of her father. Then she comprehended that Earnshaw took the master's reputation home to himself, and was attached by ties stronger than reason could break—chains forged by habit, which it would be cruel to attempt to loosen. She showed a good heart, thenceforth, in avoiding both complaints and expressions of antipathy concerning Heathcliff, and confessed to me her sorrow that she had endeavoured to raise a bad spirit between him and Hareton. Indeed, I don't believe she has ever breathed a syllable, in the latter's hearing, against her oppressor since.

When this slight disagreement was over, they were friends again, and as busy as possible in their several occupations of pupil and teacher. I came in to sit with them after I had done my work, and I felt so soothed and comforted to watch them that I did not notice how time got on. You know they both appeared in a measure my children. I had long been proud of one, and now I was sure the other would be a source of equal satisfaction. His honest, warm, and intelligent nature shook off rapidly the clouds of ignorance and degradation in which it had been bred, and Catherine's sincere commendations acted as a spur to his industry. His brightening mind brightened his features, and added spirit and nobility to their aspect. I could hardly fancy it the same individual I had beheld on the day I discovered my little lady at Wuthering Heights, after her expedition to the Crags. While I admired and they laboured, dusk drew on, and with it returned the master. He came upon us quite unexpectedly, entering by the front way, and had a full view of the whole three ere we could raise our heads to glance at him. Well, I reflected, there was never a pleasanter or more harmless sight, and it will be a burning shame to scold them. The red fire-light glowed on their two bonny heads, and revealed their faces animated with the eager interest of children; for though he was twenty-three and she eighteen, each had so much of novelty to feel and learn that neither experienced nor evinced the sentiments of sober, dis-enchanted maturity.

They lifted their eyes together, to encounter Mr. Heath-cliff. Perhaps you have never remarked that their eyes are precisely similar, and they are those of Catherine Earnshaw. The present Catherine has no other like-ness to her, except a breadth of forehead and a certain arch of the nostril that makes her appear rather haughty, whether she will or not. With Hareton the resemblance is carried further. It is singular at all times; *then* it was particularly striking, because his senses were alert, and his mental faculties wakened to unwonted activity. I suppose this resemblance disarmed Mr. Heathcliff. He walked to the hearth in evident agitation, but it quickly subsided as he looked at the young man—or, I should say, altered its character, for it was there yet. He took the book from his hand and glanced at the open page, then returned it without any observation, merely signing Catherine away. Her companion lingered very little behind her; and I was about to depart also, but he bade me sit still.

"It is a poor conclusion, is it not?" he observed, having brooded a while on the scene he had just wit-nessed—"an absurd termination to my violent exertions? I get levers and mattocks to demolish the two houses, and train myself to be capable of working like Hercules, and when everything is ready and in my power I find the will to lift a slate of either roof has vanished! My old enemies have not beaten me. Now would be the precise time to revenge myself on their representatives. I could do it, and none could hinder me. But where is the use ? I don't care for striking ; I can't take the trouble to raise my hand. That sounds as if I had been labouring the whole time only to exhibit a fine trait of magnanimity. It is far from being the case. I have lost the faculty of enjoying their destruction, and I am too idle to destroy for nothing.

"Nelly, there is a strange change approaching ; I'm in its shadow at present. I take so little interest in my daily life that I hardly remember to eat and drink. Those two who have left the room are the only objects which retain a distinct material appearance to me, and that appearance causes me pain, amounting to agony. About *her* I won't speak, and I don't desire to think, but I earnestly wish she were invisible. Her presence invokes only maddening sensations. *He* moves me differently; and yet if I could do it without seeming insane, I'd never see him again. You'll perhaps think me rather inclined to become so," he added, making an effort to smile, "if I try to describe the thousand forms of past associations and ideas he awakens or embodies. But you'll not talk of what I tell you ; and my mind is so eternally secluded in itself, it is tempting at last to turn it out to another.

"Five minutes ago Hareton seemed a personification of my youth, not a human being. I felt to him in such a variety of ways that it would have been impossible to have accosted him rationally. In the first place, his startling likeness to Catherine connected him fearfully with her. That, however, which you may suppose the most potent to arrest my imagination, is actually the least; for what is not connected with her to me ? and what does not recall her ? I cannot look down to this floor but her features are shaped in the flags. In every cloud, in every tree—filling the air at night, and caught by glimpses in every object by day—I am surrounded with her image. The most ordinary faces of men and women —my own features—mock me with a resemblance. The entire world is a dreadful collection of memoranda that she did exist, and that I have lost her. Well, Hareton's aspect was the ghost of my immortal love, of my wild endeavours to hold my right, my degradation, my pride, my happiness, and my anguish——

"But it is frenzy to repeat these thoughts to you: only it will let you know why, with a reluctance to be always alone, his society is no benefit, rather an aggravation of the constant torment I suffer; and it partly contributes to render me regardless how he and his cousin go on together. I can give them no attention any more."

"But what do you mean by a *change*, Mr. Heathcliff?" I said, alarmed at his manner, though he was neither in danger of losing his senses nor dying, according to my judgment. He was quite strong and healthy; and as to his reason, from childhood he had a delight in dwelling on dark things and entertaining odd fancies. He might have had a monomania on the subject of his departed idol, but on every other point his wits were as sound as mine.

"I shall not know that till it comes," he said, "I'm only half conscious of it now."

"You have no feeling of illness, have you?" I asked.

"No, Nelly, I have not," he answered.

"Then you are not afraid of death?" I pursued.

"Afraid? No!" he replied. "I have neither a fear, nor a presentiment, nor a hope of death. Why should I? With my hard constitution, and temperate mode of living, and unperilous occupations, I ought to, and probably *shall*, remain above ground till there is scarcely a black hair on my head. And yet I cannot continue in this condition. I have to remind myself to breathe, almost to remind my heart to beat. And it is like bending back a stiff spring; it is by compulsion that I do the slightest act not prompted by one thought, and by compulsion that I notice anything alive or dead which is not associated with one universal idea. I have a single wish, and my whole being and faculties are yearning to attain it. They have yearned towards it so long and so unwaveringly that I'm convinced it *will* be reached—and *soon*—because it has devoured my existence. I am swal-

owed up in the anticipation of its fulfilment. My con-
fessions have not relieved me, but they may account for
some otherwise unaccountable phases of humour which I
show.—O God! it is a long fight, I wish it were over!"

He began to pace the room, muttering terrible things
to himself, till I was inclined to believe, as he said Joseph
did, that conscience had turned his heart to an earthly
hell. I wondered greatly how it would end. Though he
seldom before had revealed his state of mind, even by
looks, it was his habitual mood, I had no doubt. He
asserted it himself; but not a soul, from his general
bearing, would have conjectured the fact. You did not
when you saw him, Mr. Lockwood; and at the period of
which I speak he was just the same as then, only fonder
of continued solitude, and perhaps still more laconic in
company.

CHAPTER XXXIV.

FOR some days after that evening Mr. Heathcliff shunned
meeting us at meals, yet he would not consent formally
to exclude Hareton and Cathy. He had an aversion
to yielding so completely to his feelings, choosing rather
to absent himself; and eating once in twenty-four hours
seemed sufficient sustenance for him.

One night, after the family were in bed, I heard him
go downstairs and out at the front door. I did not hear
him re-enter, and in the morning I found he was still
away. We were in April then. The weather was sweet
and warm, the grass as green as showers and sun could
make it, and the two dwarf apple-trees near the southern
wall in full bloom. After breakfast Catherine insisted
on my bringing a chair and sitting with my work under
the fir-trees at the end of the house; and she beguiled
Hareton, who had perfectly recovered from his accident,
to dig and arrange her little garden, which was shifted
to that corner by the influence of Joseph's complaint.
I was comfortably revelling in the spring fragrance
around, and the beautiful soft blue overhead, when my

young lady, who had run down near the gate to procure some primrose roots for a border, returned only half laden, and informed us that Mr. Heathcliff was coming in. "And he spoke to me," she added, with a perplexed countenance.

"What did he say?" asked Hareton.

"He told me to begone as fast as I could," she answered. "But he looked so different from his usual look that I stopped a moment to stare at him."

"How?" he inquired.

"Why, almost bright and cheerful. No, *almost* nothing—*very much* excited, and wild and glad!" she replied.

"Night-walking amuses him, then," I remarked, affecting a careless manner—in reality as surprised as she was, and anxious to ascertain the truth of her statement, for to see the master looking glad would not be an every-day spectacle. I framed an excuse to go in. Heathcliff stood at the open door. He was pale, and he trembled, yet certainly he had a strange, joyful glitter in his eyes that altered the aspect of his whole face.

"Will you have some breakfast?" I said. "You must be hungry rambling about all night." I wanted to discover where he had been, but I did not like to ask directly.

"No, I'm not hungry," he answered, averting his head and speaking rather contemptuously, as if he guessed I was trying to divine the occasion of his good-humour.

I felt perplexed. I didn't know whether it were not a proper opportunity to offer a bit of admonition.

"I don't think it right to wander out of doors," I observed, "instead of being in bed. It is not wise, at any rate, this moist season. I dare say you'll catch a bad cold or a fever. You have something the matter with you now."

"Nothing but what I can bear," he replied, "and with the greatest pleasure, provided you'll leave me alone. Get in, and don't annoy me."

I obeyed, and in passing I noticed he breathed as fast as a cat.

" Yes," I reflected to myself, " we shall have a fit of illness. I cannot conceive what he has been doing."

That noon he sat down to dinner with us, and received a heaped-up plate from my hands, as if he intended to make amends for previous fasting.

" I've neither cold nor fever, Nelly," he remarked, in allusion to my morning's speech, " and I'm ready to do justice to the food you give me."

He took his knife and fork, and was going to commence eating, when the inclination appeared to become suddenly extinct. He laid them on the table, looked eagerly towards the window, then rose and went out. We saw him walking to and fro in the garden while we concluded our meal, and Earnshaw said he'd go and ask why he would not dine ; he thought we had grieved him some way.

" Well, is he coming ? " cried Catherine, when her cousin returned.

" Nay," he answered ; " but he's not angry. He seemed rarely pleased indeed ; only I made him impatient by speaking to him twice, and then he bade me be off to you. He wondered how I could want the company of anybody else."

I set his plate to keep warm on the fender, and after an hour or two he re-entered, when the room was clear, in no degree calmer—the same unnatural (it was unnatural) appearance of joy under his black brows ; the same bloodless hue, and his teeth visible, now and then, in a kind of smile ; his frame shivering—not as one shivers with chill or weakness, but as a tight-stretched cord vibrates—a strong thrilling rather than trembling.

I will ask what is the matter, I thought ; or who should ? And I exclaimed,—

" Have you heard any good news, Mr. Heathcliff ? You look uncommonly animated."

" Where should good news come from to me ? " he said. " I'm animated with hunger, and seemingly I must not eat."

" Your dinner is here," I returned ; " why won't you get it ? "

" I don't want it now," he muttered hastily. " I'l
wait till supper. And, Nelly, once for all, let me be
you to warn Hareton and the other away from me.
wish to be troubled by nobody. I wish to have thi
place to myself."

" Is there some new reason for this banishment ? "
inquired. " Tell me why you are so queer, Mr. Heath
cliff. Where were you last night ? I'm not puttin
the question through idle curiosity, but——"

" You are putting the question through very idl
curiosity," he interrupted, with a laugh. " Yes, I'l
answer it. Last night I was on the threshold of hell
To-day I am within sight of my heaven. I have my eye
on it—hardly three feet to sever me. And now you'
better go. You'll neither see nor hear anything t
frighten you if you refrain from prying."

Having swept the hearth and wiped the table, I de
parted, more perplexed than ever.

He did not quit the house again that afternoon, and
no one intruded on his solitude, till, at eight o'clock
I deemed it proper, though unsummoned, to carry a
candle and his supper to him. He was leaning against
the ledge of an open lattice, but not looking out ; hi
face was turned to the interior gloom. The fire ha
smouldered to ashes ; the room was filled with the damp
mild air of the cloudy evening, and so still that not onl
the murmur of the beck down Gimmerton was distin
guishable, but its ripples and its gurgling over the pebbles
or through the large stones which it could not cover.
uttered an ejaculation of discontent at seeing the disma
grate, and commenced shutting the casements, one afte
another, till I came to his.

" Must I close this ? " I asked, in order to rouse him
for he would not stir.

The light flashed on his features as I spoke. O Mr
Lockwood, I cannot express what a terrible start I go
by the momentary view—those deep black eyes, tha
smile and ghastly paleness ! It appeared to me no
Mr. Heathcliff, but a goblin ; and in my terror I let the

candle bend towards the wall, and it left me in darkness.

"Yes, close it," he replied, in his familiar voice. "There, that is pure awkwardness! Why did you hold the candle horizontally? Be quick, and bring another."

I hurried out in a foolish state of dread, and said to Joseph,—

"The master wishes you to take him a light and rekindle the fire." For I dare not go in myself again just then.

Joseph rattled some fire into the shovel, and went; but he brought it back immediately, with the supper-tray in his other hand, explaining that Mr. Heathcliff was going to bed, and he wanted nothing to eat till morning. We heard him mount the stairs directly. He did not proceed to his ordinary chamber, but turned into that with the panelled bed. Its window, as I mentioned before, is wide enough for anybody to get through; and it struck me that he plotted another midnight excursion, of which he had rather we had no suspicion.

"Is he a ghoul or a vampire?" I mused. I had read of such hideous incarnate demons. And then I set myself to reflect how I had tended him in infancy, and watched him grow to youth, and followed him almost through his whole course, and what absurd nonsense it was to yield to that sense of horror. "But where did he come from, the little dark thing, harboured by a good man to his bane?" muttered Superstition, as I dozed into unconsciousness. And I began, half dreaming, to weary myself with imagining some fit parentage for him; and repeating my waking meditations, I tracked his existence over again, with grim variations, at last picturing his death and funeral, of which all I can remember is being exceedingly vexed at having the task of dictating an inscription for his monument, and consulting the sexton about it; and as he had no surname, and we could not tell his age, we were obliged to content ourselves with the single word, "Heathcliff." That

came true : we were. If you enter the kirkyard you'll
read on his headstone only that, and the date of his
death.

Dawn restored me to common-sense. I rose and went
into the garden as soon as I could see, to ascertain if
there were any footmarks under his window. There were
none. " He has stayed at home," I thought, " and he'll
be all right to-day." I prepared breakfast for the
household, as was my usual custom, but told Hareton
and Catherine to get theirs ere the master came down, for
he lay late. They preferred taking it out of doors, under
the trees, and I set a little table to accommodate them.

On my re-entrance I found Mr. Heathcliff below. He
and Joseph were conversing about some farming business. He gave clear, minute directions concerning the
matter discussed, but he spoke rapidly, and turned his
head continually aside, and had the same excited expression, even more exaggerated. When Joseph quitted
the room he took his seat in the place he generally chose,
and I put a basin of coffee before him. He drew it
nearer, and then rested his arms on the table and looked
at the opposite wall, as I supposed, surveying one particular portion, up and down, with glittering, restless
eyes, and with such eager interest that he stopped
breathing during half a minute together.

" Come now," I exclaimed, pushing some bread against
his hand, " eat and drink that while it is hot ; it has
been waiting near an hour."

He didn't notice me, and yet he smiled. I'd rather
have seen him gnash his teeth than smile so.

" Mr. Heathcliff ! master !" I cried, " don't, for God's
sake, stare as if you saw an unearthly vision."

" Don't, for God's sake, shout so loud," he replied.
" Turn round and tell me—are we by ourselves ? "

" Of course," was my answer—" of course we are."

Still I involuntarily obeyed him, as if I was not quite
sure. With a sweep of his hand he cleared a vacant
space in front among the breakfast things, and leant
forward to gaze more at his ease.

Now I perceived he was not looking at the wall, for when I regarded him alone it seemed exactly that he gazed at something within two yards' distance. And whatever it was, it communicated apparently both pleasure and pain in exquisite extremes—at least the anguished yet raptured expression of his countenance suggested that idea. The fancied object was not fixed either : his eyes pursued it with unwearied diligence, and, even in speaking to me, were never weaned away. I vainly reminded him of his protracted abstinence from food. If he stirred to touch anything in compliance with my entreaties, if he stretched his hand out to get a piece of bread, his fingers clenched before they reached it, and remained on the table, forgetful of their aim.

I sat, a model of patience, trying to attract his absorbed attention from its engrossing speculation, till he grew irritable, and got up, asking why I would not allow him to have his own time in taking his meals, and saying that on the next occasion I needn't wait—I might set the things down and go. Having uttered these words he left the house, slowly sauntered down the garden path, and disappeared through the gate.

The hours crept anxiously by ; another evening came. I did not retire to rest till late, and when I did I could not sleep. He returned after midnight, and instead of going to bed, shut himself into the room beneath. I listened and tossed about, and finally dressed and descended. It was too irksome to lie there harassing my brain with a hundred idle misgivings.

I distinguished Mr. Heathcliff's step restlessly measuring the floor, and he frequently broke the silence by a deep inspiration resembling a groan. He muttered detached words also. The only one I could catch was the name of Catherine, coupled with some wild term of endearment or suffering, and spoken as one would speak to a person present—low and earnest, and wrung from the depth of his soul. I had not courage to walk straight into the apartment, but I desired to divert him from his reverie, and therefore fell foul of the kitchen fire, stirred it, and began to scrape the cinders. It drew him forth sooner than I expected. He opened the door immediately, and said,—

"Nelly, come here. Is it morning? Come in with your light."

"It is striking four," I answered. "You want a candle to take upstairs. You might have lit one at this fire."

"No, I don't wish to go upstairs," he said. "Come in and kindle *me* a fire, and do anything there is to do about the room."

"I must blow the coals red first before I can carry any," I replied, getting a chair and the bellows.

He roamed to and fro, meantime, in a state approaching distraction, his heavy sighs succeeding each other so thick as to leave no space for common breathing between.

"When day breaks I'll send for Green," he said. "I wish to make some legal inquiries of him while I can bestow a thought on those matters, and while I can act calmly. I have not written my will yet, and how to leave my property I cannot determine. I wish I could annihilate it from the face of the earth."

"I would not talk so, Mr. Heathcliff," I interposed. "Let your will be a while; you'll be spared to repent of your many injustices yet. I never expected that your nerves would be disordered. They are at present marvellously so, however, and almost entirely through your own fault. The way you've passed these three last days might knock up a Titan. Do take some food and some repose. You need only look at yourself in a glass to see how you require both. Your cheeks are hollow, and your eyes bloodshot, like a person starving with hunger and going blind with loss of sleep."

"It is not my fault that I cannot eat or rest," he replied. "I assure you it is through no settled designs. I'll do both as soon as I possibly can. But you might as well bid a man struggling in the water rest within arm's length of the shore! I must reach it first, and then I'll rest. Well, never mind Mr. Green. As to repenting of my injustices, I've done no injustice, and I repent of nothing. I'm too happy; and yet I'm not happy enough. My soul's bliss kills my body, but does not satisfy itself."

"Happy, master?" I cried. "Strange happiness! If you would hear me without being angry, I might offer some advice that would make you happier."

"What is that?" he asked. "Give it."

"You are aware, Mr. Heathcliff," I said, "that from the time you were thirteen years old you have lived a selfish, unchristian life, and probably hardly had a Bible in your hands during all that period. You must have forgotten the contents of the book, and you may not have space to search it now. Could it be hurtful to send for some one (some minister of any denomination—it does not matter which) to explain it, and show you how very far you have erred from its precepts, and how unfit you will be for its heaven, unless a change takes place before you die?"

"I'm rather obliged than angry, Nelly," he said, "for you remind me of the manner in which I desire to be buried. It is to be carried to the churchyard in the evening. You and Hareton may, if you please, accompany me; and mind particularly to notice that the sexton obeys my directions concerning the two coffins. No minister need come, nor need anything be said over me. I tell you I have nearly attained *my* heaven, and that of others is altogether unvalued and uncoveted by me."

"And supposing you persevered in your obstinate fast, and died by that means, and they refused to bury you in the precincts of the kirk?" I said, shocked at his godless indifference. "How would you like it?"

"They won't do that," he replied. "If they did, you must have me removed secretly; and if you neglect it you shall prove, practically, that the dead are not annihilated."

As soon as he heard the other members of the family stirring he retired to his den, and I breathed freer. But in the afternoon, while Joseph and Hareton were at their work, he came into the kitchen again, and with a wild look bade me come and sit in the house ; he wanted somebody with him. I declined, telling him plainly that his strange talk and manner frightened me, and I had neither the nerve nor the will to be his companion alone.

"I believe you think me a fiend," he said, with his dismal laugh—"something too horrible to live under a decent roof." Then turning to Catherine, who was there, and who drew behind me at his approach, he added, half sneeringly, "Will *you* come, chuck ? I'll not hurt you. No ! To you I've made myself worse than the devil. Well, there is *one* who won't shrink from my company. By God, she's relentless ! Oh, damn it ! It's unutterably too much for flesh and blood to bear—even mine."

He solicited the society of no one more. At dusk he went into his chamber. Through the whole night, and far into the morning, we heard him groaning and murmuring to himself. Hareton was anxious to enter, but I bade him fetch Mr. Kenneth, and he should go in and see him. When he came, and I requested admittance and tried to open the door, I found it locked, and Heathcliff bade us be damned. He was better, and would be left alone ; so the doctor went away.

The following evening was very wet—indeed it poured down till day-dawn ; and as I took my morning walk round the house I observed the master's window swinging open, and the rain driving straight in. He cannot be in bed, I thought ; those showers would drench him through. He must either be up or out. But I'll make no more ado ; I'll go boldly and look."

Having succeeded in obtaining entrance with another key, I ran to unclose the panels, for the chamber was vacant. Quickly pushing them aside, I peeped in. Mr. Heathcliff was there, laid on his back. His eyes met mine so keen and fierce, I started ; and then he seemed to smile. I could not think him dead ; but his face and throat were washed with rain, the bedclothes dripped, and he was perfectly still. The lattice, flapping to and fro, had grazed one hand that rested on the sill. No blood trickled from the broken skin, and when I put my fingers to it I could doubt no more—he was dead and stark!

I hasped the window; I combed his black long hair from his forehead; I tried to close his eyes—to extinguish, if possible, that frightful, life-like gaze of exultation before any one else beheld it. They would not shut—they seemed to sneer at my attempts; and his parted lips and sharp white teeth sneered too. Taken with another fit of cowardice, I cried out for Joseph. Joseph shuffled up and made a noise, but resolutely refused to meddle with him.

"Th' divil's harried off his soul," he cried, "and he may hev his carcass into t' bargain for aught I care! Ech! what a wicked un he looks girning at death!" and the old sinner grinned in mockery. I thought he intended to cut a caper round the bed; but suddenly composing himself, he fell on his knees, and raised his hands, and returned thanks that the lawful master and the ancient stock were restored to their rights.

I felt stunned by the awful event, and my memory unavoidably recurred to former times with a sort of oppressive sadness. But poor Hareton, the most wronged, was the only one who really suffered much. He sat by the corpse all night, weeping in bitter earnest. He pressed its hand, and kissed the sarcastic, savage face that every one else shrank from contemplating, and bemoaned him with that strong grief which springs naturally from a generous heart, though it be tough as tempered steel.

Mr. Kenneth was perplexed to pronounce of what disorder the master died. I concealed the fact of his having swallowed nothing for four days, fearing it might lead to trouble; and then I am persuaded he did not abstain on purpose—it was the consequence of his strange illness, not the cause.

We buried him, to the scandal of the whole neighbourhood, as he wished. Earnshaw and I, the sexton, and six men to carry the coffin, comprehended the whole attendance. The six men departed when they had let it down into the grave. We stayed to see it covered. Hareton, with a streaming face, dug green sods and laid them over the brown mould himself. At present it is as smooth and verdant as its companion mounds, and I hope its tenant sleeps as soundly. But the country folks, if you ask them, would swear on the Bible that he *walks*. There are those who speak to having met him near the church, and on the moor, and even within this house. Idle tales, you'll say, and so say I. Yet that old man by the kitchen fire affirms he has seen two on 'em, looking out of his chamber window, on every rainy night since his death. And an odd thing happened to me about a month ago. I was going to the Grange one evening—a dark evening, threatening thunder; and just at the turn of the Heights I encountered a little boy with a sheep and two lambs before him. He was crying terribly, and I supposed the lambs were skittish and would not be guided.

"What is the matter, my little man?" I asked.

"There's Heathcliff and a woman yonder, under t' nab," he blubbered, "un I darnut pass 'em."

I saw nothing; but neither the sheep nor he would go on, so I bade him take the road lower down. He probably raised the phantoms from thinking, as he traversed the moors alone, on the nonsense he had heard his parents and companions repeat. Yet, still I don't like being out in the dark now, and I don't like being left by myself in this grim house. I cannot help it. I shall be glad when they leave it and shift to the Grange.

"They are going to the Grange, then?" I said.

"Yes," answered Mrs. Dean, "as soon as they are married, and that will be on New Year's day."

"And who will live here then?"

"Why, Joseph will take care of the house, and perhaps a lad to keep him company. They will live in the kitchen, and the rest will be shut up."

"For the use of such ghosts as choose to inhabit it," I observed.

"No, Mr. Lockwood," said Nelly, shaking her head. "I believe the dead are at peace, but it is not right to speak of them with levity."

At that moment the garden gate swung to; the ramblers were returning.

"*They* are afraid of nothing," I grumbled, watching their approach through the window. "Together they would brave Satan and all his legions."

As they stepped on to the door-stones, and halted to take a last look at the moon—or, more correctly, at each other by her light—I felt irresistibly impelled to escape them again; and pressing a remembrance into the hand of Mrs. Dean, and disregarding her expostulations at my rudeness, I vanished through the kitchen as they opened the house-door, and so should have confirmed Joseph in his opinion of his fellow-servant's gay indiscretions, had he not fortunately recognized me for a respectable character by the sweet ring of a sovereign at his feet.

My walk home was lengthened by a diversion in the direction of the kirk. When beneath its walls I perceived decay had made progress, even in seven months. Many a window showed black gaps deprived of glass, and slates jutted off here and there beyond the right line of the roof, to be gradually worked off in coming autumn storms.

I sought and soon discovered the three headstones on the slope next the moor—the middle one gray, and half buried in heath; Edgar Linton's only harmonized by the turf and moss creeping up its foot; Heathcliff's still bare.

I lingered round them under that benign sky, watched the moths fluttering among the heath and harebells, listened to the soft wind breathing through the grass, and wondered how any one could ever imagine unquiet slumbers for the sleepers in that quiet earth.